PERFECT
UNYIELDING BOOK THREE
RAGE

NEW YORK TIMES BESTSELLING AUTHOR

NASHODA ROSE

Perfect Rage
Published by Nashoda Rose
Copyright © 2016 by Nashoda Rose
Toronto, Canada

ISBN: 978-1-987953-10-7

Copyright © 2016 Cover design by Louisa Maggio at LM Creations
Content Edited by Kristin Anders, The Romantic Editor
Editing by Hot Tree Editing
Formatted by Champagne Formats
Proofreading by Allusion Graphics, LLC/Publishing & Book Formatting

*Any editing issues are my own. I am Canadian and on occasion I may use Canadian spelling rather than U.S.

The characters and events portrayed in this book are fictitious. Any similarity to real persons, living or dead, is coincidental and not intended by the author.

All rights reserved. This book may not be reproduced, scanned, or distributed in any printed or electronic form without the permission of the author, except in the case of brief quotations embodied in critical articles and reviews.

Except for the original material written by the author, all songs, brands, and artists mentioned in the novel *Perfect Rage* are the property of the respective owners and copyright holders. Any brands mentioned do not endorse or sponsor this book in any way.

Perfect Rage is the story of Connor and Alina.

Must be read in order:
Perfect Chaos (Unyielding, #1) Deck and Georgie
Perfect Ruin (Unyielding, #2) Kai and London
Perfect Rage (Unyielding, #3) Connor and Alina

*This book contains offensive language and sexual content. 18+

CHAPTER ONE

2005

Catalina (Alina)

"THEY DON'T LIKE civilians around, especially journalists. Don't take it personally," Jaz whispered as we followed the lieutenant who had said no more than three words to us since we arrived on base. Two of which were 'no photographs'.

He'd taken us directly to base commander, General Maunder, who reiterated the no photos rule, and that we, under no circumstance, were allowed to walk around base unsupervised. He also told us we'd leave for the orphanage at 0600. Then he ordered the lieutenant to take us to meet Corporal O'Neill.

The strict formality did nothing to help my nerves that had caused a perpetual churning of my stomach. I was in a war-torn country on a military base where I was obviously not welcome and would be traveling across perilous roads to an orphanage where I'd spend the next month.

Yeah, I was nervous as hell.

Jaz nudged my elbow and slowed. "It'll be fine."

I nodded. "Yeah, I know." But I didn't know. Jaz did because he'd been doing this for twenty or more years. I'd never been out of Colombia.

We passed row after row of enormous canvas tents when finally the lieutenant stopped abruptly at a clearing where six shirtless, muscled military guys jostled one another for a ball.

"O'Neill will be free in a minute. Wait here, please," the lieutenant ordered, then spun on his heel and walked to a guy who stood watching the game. He said something to him, nodded in our direction, and then disappeared into a nearby tent.

"Get your camera, but discreetly," Jaz said. "I can do a sideline story."

"The commander told us no photos."

"You want to be good at this, you need to take risks and get the shots no one else does."

Jaz had reported all over the world in dangerous environments, whether it was from natural disaster or war. I was like a shiny new car who had never been driven off the lot and gotten her tires dirty. But the lot hadn't exactly been safe and I'd been exposed to the elements. Those elements being a Colombian drug lord named Carlos Moreno.

I was here to escape the unwanted attention of Carlos and the only reason I obtained this position was because my brother worked for the magazine, and the photographer broke his leg the week before they were supposed to leave.

"I'm here at an army base in Afghanistan. That's enough risk and I really don't want one of these guys angry at me." Besides, I wasn't here to take photographs of hot military guys playing football or as they'd call it soccer. Still, I couldn't help but look at the guy who currently had control of the ball.

He grinned as he volleyed it back and forth between his feet while making his way toward the makeshift goal. The grin was a little mischievous, a little cute and a lot cocky. His deep blue eyes were filled with amusement and I heard his raspy chuckle when one guy slid into the dirt attempting to kick the ball away from him, but Blue Eyes saw him coming and heeled the ball backward at the last second.

My eyes trailed over his hard chest to the tattoo down his left side, then to his flexed abdomen. Definitely an eight-pack and even though I couldn't see his thighs because he wore cargo pants, it was obvious they were muscled, too.

But he wasn't the only one. All the guys playing were in incredible shape.

"Deck, you bastard," Blue Eyes barked, as a guy who I assumed was Deck elbowed him in the ribs and stole the ball. He then dodged a seriously built guy who attempted to block him. "Gate. Fuck. Take him out."

I smiled when Blue Eyes' grin was replaced by a fierce scowl as he ran after Deck who was close to the goal with no one on him.

Obviously, this guy was competitive and didn't like to lose because any playfulness had turned to resolve as he darted left to avoid a guy trying to block him from reaching Deck.

"Riot!" a guy yelled. His back was covered in a tattoo of a bird, like a hawk or something.

Riot. The call sign suited Blue Eyes as he undeniably appeared like he'd be fun, but also dangerous with that aggressive determination.

Deck hitched his leg back to kick the ball into goal at the same time as Riot reached him. He body checked Deck to the left, then kicked the ball hard out of the path of the goal.

Out of the path meant toward the sidelines—where we were standing.

It happened in slow motion and my reaction time was non-existent as the ball flew through the air right at me.

"Ah, fuck," Riot shouted just before the ball hit me in the forehead.

I staggered back from the impact and Jaz grabbed my arm at the same time as I put my hand to my head.

"Holy shit, you okay, Alina?" Jaz asked.

The loud smack vibrated in my head and there was a burning throb in the middle of my forehead. Hard, air-filled plastic hitting the skull hurt, but it was more shocking than anything. "Ah, yeah. Fine."

"Shit. Sorry. Didn't see you there, ma'am." It was Riot and he stood in front of me, sweat dripping down his chest and his eyes no longer twinkling, but genuinely concerned. "You okay? Do you need to sit down?"

I stared at him, a little dazed, but I was uncertain if it was from the ball hitting me in the head or from the hot guy standing inches away from me. I went with a combo.

I breathed in and his scent wafted into me. It was all man, no cologne, just a natural earthy smell with a hint of mint, as if he'd just used one of those breath strips.

And he was tall. Like really tall and I was five foot five so I wasn't tiny, but he still towered over me. With his broad shoulders and bulging arms, I felt like a pixie standing next to him.

"Ah, yeah... umm, no, I mean, I don't need to sit. I'm good," I finally sputtered. I didn't normally sputter, but my nerves had already been sparking and now they were out-of-control fireworks.

I froze, eyes widening when Riot's fingers gently caressed the spot where the ball hit me. It was so soft I barely felt it. Except I did and goose bumps rose and my belly flipped.

"It's red, but I don't think it will bruise," Riot said, his gaze drifting from my forehead to land on my lips then slowly back to meet my eyes. "Corporal O'Neill." He held out his hand and I took it, noticing how it completely engulfed mine. His palms were rough and his handshake firm. Not painful, but with purpose.

"Yo, O'Neill!"

He turned and I looked past him to see the guy Deck across the yard with his gear in hand and his shirt back on. "Bird landed. See you back in the world," Deck called. "One month."

Riot, or rather Corporal O'Neill, did a fist pump in the air.

Deck jogged off with the seriously scary built guy they called Gate.

O'Neill's attention shifted to Jaz who had yet to say anything and I knew why when I looked at him. He was grinning ear to ear as his gaze moved from O'Neill to me and back again.

"Jaz Klein." He offered his hand and they shook. "Journalist for the *Miami Messenger Magazine*. The girl you smacked with your ball is Alina, my brilliant photographer. I'm writing a story—"

"On the orphanage," O'Neill finished and his eyes shot back to me, but there was a scowl now and it was a little scary because his square jaw clenched and his lips pursed.

"Yeah," Jaz said. "Are you one of the guys giving us a ride?"

He didn't answer him; instead, his intense eyes were on me and I shifted uncomfortably. "The magazine sends *you* to an unstable country to take photos? Not fuckin' smart. And I don't have time to babysit civilians."

Jaz cleared his throat. "I understand your concern, Corporal O'Neill, but the public wants to read more than just about the war over here. And I plan to give it to them." I hadn't realized I was holding my breath until O'Neill's eyes moved from me to Jaz. "I've been to hundreds of *unstable* places and am very aware of the risk."

O'Neill paused while looking him up and down. Jaz was in his forties, appropriately dressed, wearing black cargo pants with a snug, long-sleeved shirt, black combat boots and his head was buzz cut like the military guys, so he fit in.

O'Neill had about an inch of dirty-blond hair and two days scruff that gave him a rugged look.

"Yeah. Maybe." O'Neill's attention shifted back to me again and I stiffened. "But I wasn't referring to you."

Whoa. What? I looked down at myself. I had on dark green fitted pants with laced boots and a white blouse that I thought was appropriate considering the unbearably dry heat.

"I'll speak to my staff sergeant and advise him that you're both to be airlifted out of here at the first opportunity. The story on the orphanage needs to be told, but not now. PR was crazy allowing this. Come back in a few years when shit settles. Or when you find another *brilliant* photographer." Then he added, "One that's out of high school."

Oh, my God. Did he just say that? He could only be a couple of years older than me.

I was too shocked to say anything and Jaz was having a coughing fit with his hand over his mouth, so I knew damn well the guy was laughing. *Laughing.*

"Jaz." I kicked his ankle and he cleared his throat and said, "Umm... yeah, listen, don't worry about her. She can handle herself."

"It's my call and I say she can't." Corporal O'Neill's eyes lingered on mine for a second then he nodded. "Ma'am. Sir." Then he walked away.

What the hell just happened? He was going to tell his sergeant to send us home? Could he do that? This story was not only my escape from Carlos Moreno, but my catapult into my dream job as a photographer.

And there was no way this guy was ruining my chances. I wasn't being sent home with my tail between my legs.

I ran after him.

"Alina!" Jaz called out to me, but I ignored him.

I caught up to O'Neill who had managed to cover a large amount of ground with his long, lean legs and snagged his arm. "Wait," I said, my fingers curling around his forearm. But they didn't even come close to encompassing the span.

He stopped, his gaze landing on my hand and I saw a flash of heat flare in the depths before they darkened and there was that fierce scowl again that sent my heart racing. I suddenly wondered if I should've just let Jaz deal with this. But it was me he had an issue with.

I released his arm. "I need this job. It's really important."

He replied, "You won't need it if you're dead."

"We're going to an orphanage."

"That we have to drive to. You know about roadside bombs, right? Suicide bombers? You do know what's going on in this country?" God, he was being an ass. "You hear about the stories of reporters being held for ransom or even worse, terrorists torturing them for months before videoing their head being blown off? They're all true. This isn't a place for a young girl who probably hasn't witnessed death, let alone heard a gun go off. Go home. Finish school and take photos of families with their dog." He turned and started walking away again.

Jesus. What right did he have telling me how to live my life? I was good at what I did and I wanted to take photographs that told a story. "I know how to handle a gun and I've seen men die," I blurted.

He stopped, broad back stiffening and then swung around and headed for me. *Shit.* I backed up a couple steps because he was really intimidating with that severe scowl and overly confident swagger.

I swallowed. "My father taught me to shoot when I was ten."

He snorted. "A squirt gun doesn't count."

"Funny." What a dick.

He leaned in closer. So close that his warm breath swept across my face. "Do I make you nervous? Because you sure as hell look it. Pulse throbbing in the curve of your neck, quick inhales, fingers curled in the sides of your pants and your teeth chewing on that plush bottom lip. How nervous do you think you'll be if the Taliban gets a hold of you?"

I hastily released my lip and his eyes flicked to my mouth.

Bastard. But he read me perfectly. I was nervous. He made me nervous and I'd grown up around dangerous, powerful men, my father being one of them. He flew cocaine from Colombia to Miami for Carlos Moreno ever since I could remember.

I'd never personally met Carlos until three years ago, when I was sixteen. I'd been with my mother and father in the market when a Jeep slowed beside us. It was Carlos and his right-hand man, Diego. My father told me to go home, but Carlos already had his eyes on me and asked for an introduction.

The man was old enough to be my father and yet he stared at me with the corners of his lips curved up and his gaze lingering on my breasts. There was a gleam in his eyes that made my stomach lurch and my pulse race with fear.

My father was so nervous he stumbled over his words and kept looking from me to Carlos, his face pale. It was my mother who moved in front of me to block Carlos's view of me, but it was too late. I had his unwanted attention.

But he never did anything about it for three years, then one night Carlos's man, Diego, showed up unannounced at the house and he and my father had a huge argument. It was then my father contacted my brother, Juan, who lived in the States.

Last time I'd seen my brother, I was ten years old. He'd bought me my first camera, his goodbye present. He'd told me once he was settled and had enough money I would live with him in the United States. I soon realized why he left when he did—to escape Carlos Moreno's grasp.

I straightened my shoulders as I faced off with Corporal O'Neill. "Then make sure the Taliban doesn't get ahold of me," I retorted. "And you can't disobey orders." I really wasn't sure about all the rules, but I was pretty sure he couldn't just refuse for the simple fact that he thought I was too young and obviously disliked me.

He grunted, shaking his head. Crossing his arms, a hint of a smile emerged. "I wasn't ordered. I volunteered. Now I'm unvolunteering."

"That's not even a word."

He produced a full-on smirk. "Sure it is. We're in my world now and I'm sure I have lots of words you're not old enough to understand."

Asshole. But I bit my tongue because if the magazine fired me, my United States visa ended and I'd have to return to Colombia. "Why don't you like me?"

His smirk fell away. "Listen, it's not that I don't like you. I don't know you well enough to judge whether I like you or not. But this isn't the place for you. I'd expected to escort two experienced men who knew what the fuck they're getting into."

I hated to admit that he had a point. I probably shouldn't be here, but the reality was home wasn't safe either.

I lifted my chin. "Yeah, I'm young and inexperienced, but I know the risk. And it's my decision whether to take it or not. Your duty is to drive me there."

That was when my belly flipped and my breath caught in my throat because he stepped closer, the heat off his body seeping into me.

"Oh, I know my duty, *ma'am*." He lowered his voice and I guessed it was because a couple guys walked past and eyed us. "It's not happening. Get over it."

I grit my teeth then took a deep calming breath. "Jaz already spoke with your commander when we arrived on base. He's met me and he doesn't have a problem. And your PR department approved this." I rarely lost my cool and was always polite, but I was exhausted and he'd pissed me off. "So you're the one who will have to 'get over it'."

He swore beneath his breath and he definitely looked pissed with his lowered brows and narrowed eyes.

He was quiet a minute then he shrugged and said, "Okay, ma'am."

Huh? That was it? 'Okay, ma'am.' Umm, what just happened?

He didn't wait to see if I followed him as he strode across the yard where they'd been playing football. He stopped briefly to snag his shirt off the back of a folding chair and tugged it over his head.

He must have noticed I wasn't behind him because he looked back at me and scowled. "You waiting for hand-holding because that's not going to happen."

I looked around for Jaz, but he was nowhere in sight. Shit. I slowly walked toward him. "Where's Jaz?"

"Probably in the mess grabbing chow. We'll do the same, then I'll show you where you can crash for the night."

"Hey, O'Neill." I glanced to the right and saw two guys dressed in full gear. "What's with the ice cream? You going to lick that?"

Ice cream? Lick that? My mouth gaped, but O'Neill either didn't notice or didn't care as he walked across the yard. His strides ate up the ground and I was forced to jog to keep up with him.

The other guy yelled, "What's her flavor?"

"C and C," O'Neill replied without turning.

C and C? Her flavor? What was he talking about?

"No shit!" the guy shouted.

I kept up with O'Neill as he led the way to what he referred to as the mess. By the time we stopped outside a tent, I was resigned to the fact that I found O'Neill attractive. Way attractive.

I knew that the second my eyes landed on him. Any girl, whether she liked men or not, would appreciate a man like O'Neill. Tall with a lean, toned body that he obviously looked after. His brilliant blue eyes made me want to drown in them and his manly scent soaked into every cell and caused them to swell with heat. But it was his grin that ensnared me, and it bothered me that I wanted to see it again.

From the way things were going, that wasn't going to happen anytime soon. "What's C and C mean?" I knew there was a lot of military jargon and Jaz, who'd been reporting for twenty years or more with the magazine, had filled me in on some, but C and C hadn't been one of them.

He turned to me and there was that twinkle in his eyes just before a slow-forming grin emerged. "Cookies and cream."

"Cookies and cream?" I pursed my lips together wondering what that meant until I pieced it with the licking comment and realized that he was referring to me as a flavor of ice cream. "Oh, my God. I'm ice cream."

"It's a compliment."

His grin was still there and I was pissed that I found him so damn attractive and at the same time so damn irritating. "You're comparing me to a flavor of ice cream? How is that a compliment?"

He chuckled. The sound was raspy and deep and to my further irritation, goose bumps popped and my belly leapt off a cliff. "It's a great flavor. One of my favorites, actually. I'm a huge ice-cream fan, tried every flavor there is. Used to take my sister to the parlor down the street all the time. She never had anything but vanilla." He lifted the tent flap and said, "After you, Alina…" He paused, brows lifting as he waited for me to fill him in on my last name.

"Diaz," I offered.

"Alina Diaz," he drawled. His tongue slid slowly over each syllable, and it was the most intimate panty-melting two words a man had ever said to me. And from his cocky smirk and wink, he damn well knew it.

Jesus. I ducked under his arm and hurried inside, trying to put some distance between us. I saw Jaz sitting at a long table with a bunch of other men and he waved me over. I didn't bother to see if O'Neill came in after me as I darted for Jaz.

CHAPTER TWO

Question 1: Would you rather be a vampire or werewolf?

The Mess

O'NEILL DID COME in after me. He also stayed annoyingly glued to my side as we helped ourselves to the hot meal. He even told some guy to move over so he could sit beside me at the table. And to my utter horror, his thigh continuously brushed mine when he leaned over to talk to Jaz. Jaz was enjoying himself immensely chatting to all the guys and completely at ease as he shoveled in meatloaf.

"O'Neill." It was the guy I was introduced to as Gunner, who sat on the other side of Jaz. "Aren't you taking the bird with Deck and Vic Gate? Thought you were trying for the JTF2 with them?"

"JTF2?" Jaz asked, looking from one to the other. "What's that?

Never heard of them."

"Canadian," Gunner explained. "Joint Task Force 2, an elite special operations force." He leaned forward to address O'Neill. "You're still going, right?"

O'Neill nodded. "Doesn't start for six weeks. Headed in a few. Have shit to do here first."

I was guessing the 'shit' referred to accompanying Jaz and me to the orphanage.

Jaz and Gunner talked about the JTF2 while I concentrated on eating and not choking on my food every time O'Neill's leg, arm, or hand touched me. He was causal about it, therefore I was uncertain if he did it intentionally or not, so I didn't call him out on it.

"Tell me about yourself, Alina Diaz," O'Neill said. This time, his thigh knocked mine on purpose and my heart skipped a beat.

Why was I reacting to him this way? I'd met good-looking guys before, the guy I'd dated last year being one of them, but the butterflies had been baby ones, nothing like what O'Neill did to me.

O'Neill had this casual confidence that was really attractive. He was also intense and yet playful.

And the jerk thought I was an innocent schoolgirl when I was probably the same age as him.

I decided my best course of action was to pretend I was unaffected by him. "I'm a photographer."

He laughed, shaking his head. "Yeah, I got that. How about something with a bit more meat?"

I was naturally guarded having grown up in a household surrounded by illegal activity, so I was hesitant about how much I told anyone. "How about you go first?"

He shrugged. "Okay. I love to do anything that gets my adrenaline pumping. I've been bungee jumping, heli boarding, and scuba diving with sharks. But what gets my heart racing more than those things"—*oh, my God, please don't say it*—"is a motorcycle beneath me. Feeling the vibration, hearing its deep roar and the wind against my skin as I fly across open road.... Gives me goose bumps and a sweet-ass high. That's fuckin' heaven."

Oh. Huh. I hadn't expected that. I'd expected the daredevil stunts, but not how open he was about how it made him feel.

He angled toward me and whispered into my ear. "So what gets your heart pumping, Alina?"

Shivers trickled across the back of my neck and I dropped my fork on the table. It made a loud clatter and I jumped.

God, no chance was I telling him my heart pounded because of him.

He intently watched me with those gorgeous blue eyes then picked up my fork and passed it to me. "Babe, you seriously need to stop chewing that lip," he muttered.

I instantly let it go. "Nervous habit," I said.

"So I make you nervous, Alina Diaz? Why is that?" He actually looked interested to hear my answer. There was no cocky smirk, rather a curious expression, brows lifted and smooth lips resting lightly together.

"Well, you have a really angry scowl."

He laughed. "Yeah. Been told that. Sorry, I was pissed." I was thinking that was an understatement. His laughter died and he shuffled the last of his meatloaf around on his plate. "Look at this from my standpoint. I've been here two years. Seen shit happen. Had a few close calls myself and lost some good buddies." I imagined a lot of these guys had and I respected every single one of them for being here. "I see this beautiful, sexy girl who I meet by kicking a stupid ball into her head, so I'm already pissed at myself, and then I find out she's the one I'm driving over dangerous terrain and taking to the orphanage. Don't like it much."

He thought I was beautiful? Sexy? I'd never been called sexy in my life. I had wide hips and a narrow waist, smallish breasts and kind of plain features. Nothing that stood out which was a good thing, in my opinion. I liked being the one behind the lens rather than in front of it.

But it was nice that someone actually said I was sexy, especially a hot guy who could, and probably did, get any girl he wanted with his looks.

"But you're not mad now," I said. Actually, he'd been pretty relaxed since we came to eat. What had changed?

"Nope. Life is too short to hang onto shit." He shoveled in the last bit of meatloaf then stood and put his leg over the bench while picking up his plate. "You want more?"

I snorted because he'd already had a huge amount of food on his plate and he was going for seconds. "You can fit in more?"

He grinned. "Hot meals are a rarity here. You shovel as much as you can in until forced to undo the top button of your pants."

I smiled because that was what it was like on Navidad, Christmas day.

He winked.

I watched him stroll away, stopping to chat with a few buddies. He had an easygoing casual way about him, quick to laugh and his smile genuine. But I'd seen the other side, too, the dangerous edge to him.

"How's the head?" Jaz asked.

I'd forgotten about my forehead, but it was only a minor sting. "Fine. How does it look?"

He leaned closer and squinted. "Not bad. A faint pink spot. Nothing that will deter a certain someone's interest in you."

"That's good," I replied, not really listening to the second half of that sentence because I was watching O'Neill. If he were trying for a Special Forces unit, then he was obviously determined and fearless. I'd seen movies about the training those guys endured and it was grueling. They were the best of the best and if you couldn't be the best, then you didn't make it.

He'd make it. I barely knew him, but what I did know was that he was competitive, confident, and resolute. And from watching him talk to the guys, he had a lot of friends, which meant he was probably a team player.

As if he knew my gaze was on him, he looked up from whomever he was talking with and our eyes locked. My belly dropped and heat flared not just in my cheeks but everywhere. It was like he was caressing my body with the tips of his fingers, scattering goose bumps, making my breath hitch.

Then his grin faded and his brows lowered. He said something to the guy he'd been talking to without taking his eyes off me. I realized I was chewing on my lip again and released it.

Shit, I liked him. I really liked this guy and there was nothing I could do to stop it.

"Oh, man," Jaz muttered. "They're a disaster waiting to happen."

Gunner chuckled. "Yep. A ticking time bomb." I only partially listened because O'Neill's gaze had flicked to my mouth then along the curve of my neck then back up again. "Explosion imminent."

"You said it." Jaz gently kicked me under the table. "We leave tomorrow."

And I'd more than likely never see O'Neill again.

Gunner said something, but I went back to eating my meatloaf and tried to erase the image of O'Neill's beautiful intense eyes on me.

But I was a photographer. Images didn't erase, they embedded, and Corporal O'Neill's had become permanent.

0600 Hours

Okay, freaked out was too subtle a word to describe how I felt sitting in the back of the Humvee. The possibility of being blown up at any second played havoc with my mind.

Was this what they felt every time they left base? They certainly didn't look scared. Actually, they appeared pretty relaxed considering, but still alert.

Jaz sat beside me, Gunner across in full gear and a Corporal Trent beside him. O'Neill drove and Corporal Drummond was in the passenger seat. There were two more vehicles behind us. I'd discovered the truck was loaded with 600 pounds of blankets, toys, clothing, and school supplies for the orphanage.

Mr. Completely Calm Jaz had his legs stretched out, ankles crossed as he chatted with the few men in the squad about being in Honduras after the devastating Hurricane Mitch in 1998.

I'd heard the story already on the plane and was thinking about last night. When O'Neill returned to the table with another plate of meatloaf, he'd insisted on playing twenty questions, said he did it with every new recruit in his unit and since I was hitching a ride with him in the morning, that constituted being in his unit.

It was a ridiculous reason, but I agreed to it as long as he reciprocated. He readily agreed which made me a little uneasy because what guy wanted to answer silly questions about himself.

Apparently, O'Neill.

I discovered he was really patient because I thought about each question before I answered while he shot off his answers like gunfire. He laughed at some of my responses, and I laughed at some of his questions because they were off the wall and random. Like, how was I supposed to know that a polar bear dip meant jumping into freezing cold water and not swimming with a polar bear?

He stayed clear of anything sexual, which I hadn't expected, because there was no denying there was something sexual between us.

The most basic question he'd asked was what my favorite color was, to which I'd told him powder blue. Then I asked what his was and he said blue, too. He said it reminded him of the ocean and how powerful it could be and yet calm and peaceful at the same time. Then he started on about the color orange. He hated orange.

But it was more than hate. He abhorred it and I was glad I didn't have orange hair; otherwise, he'd have never agreed to take us to the orphanage. He went on to tell me he refused to eat carrots and oranges, and orange candy was out of the question.

I laughed until my stomach cramped because he took his hatred of orange really seriously and it was ridiculous. But it was sort of cute, too.

Question nineteen was what is the best sound in the world and I answered without hesitation, a child's laughter. His expression changed from light and playful to surprise and then his brows furrowed.

He remained silent for a minute and then said, "Yeah. Mine, too."

That was it. The game ended on question nineteen and he abruptly stood and told me he'd see me at 0600 and Gunner would show me where I was staying and would get me in the morning. He reiterated I was not allowed to go anywhere without supervision. Then he'd left. I hadn't seen him until this morning and he'd barely nodded in my direction before he said we were 'moving out'.

The drive was slow and steady, and we had to stop at several checkpoints where Jaz and I had our passes checked. It took an hour to reach the orphanage just outside of Kabul. When we stopped, it was the first time I think my heart beat normally.

Jaz patted my hand, smiling. "You did good."

The doors opened and we all piled out. The first thing I heard was yelling kids, but it was with happiness as they bombarded us. Well, not exactly us—O'Neill. There were about twenty-five kids who had seen us arrive and they obviously knew O'Neill, but they called him Riot as they crowded around him jumping up and down, the ones closest to him, hugging him.

I quickly pulled my camera out of my bag and moved closer, but not so he'd notice me and I started taking shots. It was why I loved taking photographs, moments like this. There was a story behind every frame. How did the children know who he was? Why were they so excited to see him? I was seeing a side to O'Neill that I really liked and I was disappointed he was leaving.

O'Neill grinned as he ruffled kids' hair and chatted with them, but I was too far away to hear what he said. My chest swelled as I watched from behind the lens. He was really good with them, so patient and sincere.

It said a lot about him. I respected O'Neill for what he did for his country, all these men and women, but seeing him with the kids, it became much more.

I lowered the camera when he glanced over at me, a huge grin on his face. My heart skipped a beat and I returned the smile. 'Laughter,' he mouthed.

Yeah, the laughter of kids who had very little was the best laughter of all.

There was a lot of commotion as the supplies were unloaded. Jaz and I helped and there were several people with the agency who ran the orphanage who came and also assisted.

The place was overcrowded and run down, with kids wearing shoes too big and ragged dirty clothes. Their ages ranged from five or six, right up to older teens, and there were definitely more boys than girls.

Jaz and I chatted with Sarah, a British woman who had been there for several months and she offered to show us around when Gunner yelled, "Stay safe. Pick-up thirty days."

"Thanks, Gunner," I called and Jaz waved.

He nodded then hopped in one of the Humvees, so did Drummond and Trent. But no one got in the Humvee that O'Neill had been driving.

That was when I heard booted steps come up behind me. I turned to come face-to-face with O'Neill's chest. I peered past his shoulder and saw the kids were off playing with some of the donated toys.

Jaz cleared his throat and said, "Sarah, how about you show me where I'm crashing."

Sarah smiled. "Sure. Corporal O'Neill knows his way around. He can show Alina where she's staying." They walked away and we were left alone.

I was a little confused as to what was happening and even more so when the tires crunched behind us as the vehicles moved out. "Umm, they're leaving. Don't you have to go?"

"No. Going to stay a bit."

"You are?" My heart sped and my breathing increased. "But how can you? I mean aren't you on duty or something?"

"Nope. On leave as of yesterday, but I was coming here to bring supplies before I went home." And that was why he'd volunteered to bring me and Jaz because he was coming here anyway. "Now, I'm staying longer."

"You're staying?" He was staying here with me? Well, not *with* me, but it kind of felt like it all the same.

"Need to be home for training in a month. I'm free until then."

"You're free until then," I repeated quietly, wondering why he'd choose to stay here when he could go home, but the answer was in the photos I took. O'Neill cared about these kids.

He reached toward me to tuck a strand of hair behind my ear and my body quivered. It was intimate and sweet, and yet he was scowling. "Not leaving you here alone. Don't care what Jaz says about you being able to handle it."

My eyes widened. What? "When did you decide that, O'Neill?"

"Connor." Oh, I liked his name—a lot. "Since question nineteen."

I frowned. Nineteen? "You mean the twenty questions game?"

Then he grinned. "Nineteen. Never asked you number twenty." Because he'd left the table. "Wrote them in my journal so I wouldn't forget."

"You did? Why?"

"Nineteen pieces of you. Be nice to remember those pieces years from now."

"Silly pieces," I said, laughing.

He smirked. "Yeah. I can't believe you'd prefer being a werewolf over a vampire." He shook his head. "Disappointing."

Laughing, I smacked his arm. "I don't want to bite people."

"No. You just want to tear their heads off." He moved to the Humvee, opened the back door and disappeared inside. He came out with two bags and threw them over his shoulder. "I want more pieces, Alina." Before I could reply, he said, "Come on. I'll show you where you'll stay."

"Do you do this with all your cookies-and-cream girls. The questions?"

He laughed. "Don't let it go to your head. But there's never been a cookies-and-cream girl."

He'd said it was his favorite flavor, so I did let it go to my head a little because he was staying. With me. Because he didn't want to leave me here, and he wanted more pieces.

This was so not a good idea liking this guy. We both knew where it was going. But the issue was how it would end.

Because there was an end.

Thirty days was the end.

"Not asking anything of you, Alina." He approached me, cupped the back of my neck and half smiled. "It's what I do, protect people I like. And I kind of like you, so I plan to keep you safe until I put your ass back on a plane out of here."

Wow. As if seeing him with the kids wasn't enough to solidify that I liked him. "Okay," I said, smiling. "Thank you, Connor. And I kind of like you, too."

He snorted. "Kind of? Shit, I thought I was doing better than that," he teased.

He was. Way better. And that was what scared me.

CHAPTER THREE

I LOWERED THE LENS, letting the weight of the camera dangle from my neck as I watched him. We'd pretty much spent five straight days together and it was natural and easy being around him. There wasn't one day that he didn't laugh or make me laugh. He was also dedicated to making the kids laugh and have fun.

He tossed the blanket in the air and it parachuted then settled on the floor. He walked around and pulled the corners out so it lay flat then grabbed the black duffel bag and threw it on the blanket before dropping to his butt and unpacking lunch.

I never expected Connor. Never expected to fall for him so fast. He was protective, teasing and sweet, and yeah, there was the arrogance and bossiness, but I liked how he was self-assured because he made me feel safe. I'd never really felt safe before.

He glanced up at me and grinned. He was stretched out on his side. Perched up on his elbow with his ankles crossed. I smiled back, my belly whooshing and my heart racing.

"Shutterbug, let's eat."

He started calling me that on day two when he saw I was never without my camera. "You know this is really silly. We're having a picnic in your sleeping quarters." I walked over, pulled my camera strap over my head, and set it on the blanket as I sat.

"Nothing wrong with silly. And my room is the only place I can have you all to myself. Our first date."

My brows lifted. "So this is a date now? You failed to mention that. I think your words were, 'Let's grab some chow in my room'." But I was totally into him calling it a date.

He laughed. "Babe, what did you think I meant?" He handed me a sandwich wrap then a bag of chips.

I held up the small potato chip bag. "Where did you get this?"

"My private stash." He opened his chip bag and the air released. It crinkled as he reached inside, pulled out a chip and then tossed it in his mouth.

"Didn't your mother teach you to eat dessert last?"

"Fuck yeah, she tried." He chucked another chip in his mouth and I heard it crunch as he chomped down on it. "But I don't live by the rules at home. Have enough here. Mom gave up teaching me anything a long time ago. Now she just gives me a disappointed look that makes me feel like shit."

"What's her name?" I opened my chips, took one out and put it in my mouth.

"Karen. Dad is Frank and I have a little sister, Georgie." Then he told me how he was worried his sister was being bullied at school and I knew from the way his tone dropped that he was upset he wasn't there to protect her.

I was betting once in his circle, there was nothing he wouldn't do to protect you.

He put down his chips, picked up the bottled water and chugged back a big gulp before holding it out to me. Our hands brushed as I reached for it and tingles erupted.

In five days, there'd been nothing except accidental touches and I couldn't help but want more. A hell of a lot more. God, I wanted him to kiss me. Touch me. Anything. He was driving me insane and I had a feeling he knew it.

Luckily, I'd been fairly busy getting photos of the kids in their classrooms, or in the yard or doing chores. The place needed desperate attention and had too many children with too few volunteers. Countless times I found myself having to lower the camera because my eyes filled with tears as I watched the kids.

Jaz was busy doing interviews with agency workers and the kids who spoke English. We had plenty of time and Jaz wanted to get a feel for what it was like living here day in and day out.

Connor spent a good amount of the time interacting with the kids, playing football or helping with repairs. But every morning he had breakfast with me and Jaz, and most days, lunch and dinner. But today, he insisted on us eating alone.

He bit into his wrap and a few grains of rice fell onto the blanket. He nodded, chewing then swallowed before he said, "Are you going home after this?"

Home. I hadn't told him anything about home. He knew I grew up in Colombia, but I kept my father's illegal activity and any involvement with Carlos Moreno a secret. I had a strong feeling that with Connor's protective nature he'd be unhappy to hear that I was running from the attention of a powerful drug lord.

"I'm not sure yet," I answered honestly. "Jaz and I have to return to Miami and then we'll see." I was hoping the magazine liked my work enough to hire me and extend my visa.

He didn't say anything for a few seconds and then, "Stick with Jaz. He's a good guy. Knows what he's doing. He'll look out for you."

Jaz was experienced and I really liked him, kind of like a father figure the way he was with me, but a cool, laid-back father.

We talked for an hour about where I saw myself going with my photography. Then I asked about his passion for motorcycles, which I discovered stemmed from when he was a kid and raced dirt bikes.

Then we just talked. Inconsequential stuff like music, movies, and books, to which I found out he loved to read and write. I guess that was why he kept a journal.

I reached for my camera, unsnapped the lens cover and adjusted the focus before lying back beside him and holding it above us.

I pressed the button and took several pictures, but it was impossible to tell what exactly I was shooting and I was sure they were awful, but I wanted something of this moment to take with me.

Connor moved. It was lithe and agile as he rolled up on his side, his hand cupping my chin and tilting my head toward him.

I froze, breath catching in my throat.

"Keep shooting, baby," he murmured in a low, sexy voice that made me quiver.

I kept shooting. "Connor?" I whispered.

His knee settled between my legs before he shifted so he hovered half over me. He kissed the edge of my jaw, then the curve of my neck, then the spot just below my ear. I continued to press the shutter having no idea how many pictures I took of us because all I was thinking about were his lips on me.

"Alina," he drawled.

Connor took my camera, gently snapped on the lens cover and set it on the blanket beside us. Then he wrapped his fingers around my wrists and eased my arms above my head, locking them down with one hand.

His brows lifted and he grinned, dimples accentuating. "I've wanted to kiss you since I hit you with the soccer ball."

"You did?"

"Yeah. But then I also wanted to spank your ass and put you back on a plane." He lowered himself agonizingly slow.

I inhaled and exhaled hard and fast, chest rising and falling irregularly as his weight sank into mine and I sighed at the feel of him.

I licked my lips and his eyes darted to my tongue then back to my eyes. "Fuck, Alina."

A wave of heat settled over me as he whispered my name, his lips a breath away from mine. Oh, my God, I wanted him to kiss me. I'd never felt such an uncontrollable need in my life, a need so strong, I'd do anything to make certain he finished what he started.

Anything.

His playful grin vanished, and desire smoldered in his eyes. Our lips were so close I smelled the salt from the chips and I wanted to taste it on my tongue.

"Damn it, kiss me," I said, yanking on my wrists to get free and pull his head down to mine.

I expected a chuckle, but his brows dipped and he murmured, "I'll give you any-fuckin'-thing you want, Alina."

His mouth slammed down on mine and his weight dropped.

Our mouths entwined in a flurry of need. After five days of denying, our boundaries ruptured with a single kiss.

Staining.

That was what kind of kiss it was—staining.

His mouth imprinted as his lips roamed with purpose. A demand. A control. And I succumbed. I fell into the erotic web of Connor. And I knew from the moment he made his move and kissed me that without a doubt, I'd fallen for him.

Five days. I'd fallen for him in five days.

But whatever this was. It was temporary. We both knew that.

"Baby," he murmured against my mouth. "Get out of your head."

"Huh?"

He half smiled. "Just be here with me now."

He was right, but it was easier said than done. I understood that was how Connor lived, in the now and not worried too much about tomorrow, but I thought things through. I contemplated. I worried.

He sprinkled kisses along my chin, down my neck then along my collarbone. I moaned, arching into him, fingernails digging into my palms. "Connor."

"I didn't plan this." He slid his hand down my side to my waist then back up again, bringing the material with him so it bunched beneath my underarms. Palm on my skin, thumb stroking back and forth over my ribs, his hand moved under my bra. "Can't plan something like this."

I wrapped my legs around his waist. He groaned as his cock pressed up against my pelvis and then his mouth was on mine again.

His hand slipped in my bra, finger flicking over my erect nipple. I gasped, body tensing as a wave of intense pleasure soared through me. God, his hands were gentle yet touched me with certainty. Confident and skilled, just like his mouth.

"Let me go," I murmured.

He instantly broke away, sitting up, eyes wide and concerned. "Babe? Are you not good with this?"

I reached for him, fingers curling in the bottom edge of his T-shirt. "Let my wrists go. I want to touch you."

Relief crossed his face. "Jesus. I thought you weren't into it."

It was cute, Connor being apprehensive, and I was betting that didn't happen very often. "I'm into you." I slowly shimmied his shirt up and it untucked from the waist of his cargo pants. My knuckles brushed up against his hard abdomen and he sucked in air. "I'm way into you." I smiled, liking that I caused that reaction. I lifted farther and farther until he finished yanking it over his head.

"God, how do you get a body like this," I exclaimed as I ran my hands down his chest, muscles bulging beneath my touch.

He half grinned and said, "Need to run faster than bullets, shutterbug."

I hated to think of any bullets being shot at him.

I caressed his skin, my fingers tracing the tattoo on his shoulder, to his chest and down his left side. Intricate lines of black etched into his skin, carving across his body and accentuating his exquisiteness.

When my hands reached the belt of his cargo pants, his hands landed on mine, curling around them and dragging them away.

"Alina. I didn't bring you to my room so I could fuck you. I like spending time with you. I just wanted privacy for us to talk and"—he smirked—"to kiss you if I was lucky enough."

I lifted my brows. "I know." And I did, because Connor was pretty straight up and I was sure he could've charmed me into his bed on day two.

His mouth pursed and he scowled. "You know the scenario here, right?"

I did. I wasn't okay with it, but I accepted it. My hands eased back to his pants and his hands followed, but this time he didn't stop me as I undid his belt. I pushed the button through the slit in his pants. "Yeah, I do. You have protection?"

I figured he did. I wasn't stupid. Connor was a player and a player without condoms was no longer a player but a bystander. And I suspected Connor would never be a bystander in any part of his life. On duty or not I was pretty sure he kept condoms on him.

"Bag," he said.

But he didn't move as he hovered over me, his eyes intense and heated. There was something else, too, that I couldn't decipher. Almost as if he were the one hesitating and unsure about doing this.

I put my hands on his chest and shoved. "I suggest you hurry up and get one."

Then that hesitation vanished as he grinned with a low chuckle. I melted. That sound. That look. It was like it erased all the bad I'd seen growing up and replaced it with a cocoon of protective warmth.

"You have a bossy side. Interesting," he said, popping to his feet. His belt dangled, the clasp bouncing off his rock-hard thigh when he stood. Then he bent, picked up my camera, unsnapped the lens cover and put it to his eye.

"What are you doing?"

"Capturing you," he said and then I heard the shutter go.

I laughed and he clicked again. "Stop." I held out my palm and tilted my head to the side. "I'm the photographer so I never have to be the one in front of the camera."

He lowered the camera and placed it back on the blanket. "I want one of those."

"Huh?"

"Send me one of those." I didn't say anything. "I'll give you my email."

It was just an email, but I inwardly smiled because I liked him giving me that. I was betting he didn't give it out freely.

Temporary, Alina.

He walked over to his duffel, shuffled around and was back. My insides whirled as he stood standing over me, a little gold package between his fingers. He stared at me with lust blazing and my toes curled with anticipation.

I sat up, ripped off my shirt and tossed it aside. Then I undid my pants and shimmied them down my legs and pulled them off my feet.

When I looked up at him, he hadn't moved. But his eyes had and they trailed a smoldering path down my body, stopping on my panties.

I had a thing for panties. Some girls collected shoes. I collected panties. I liked how they made me feel, even though I was the only one who knew I was wearing them. Besides, money was always tight, and shoes were a hell of a lot more expensive than nice panties.

I had all kinds, colors and styles, but traveling meant I only had enough room for my favorites and today I was wearing a cobalt blue thong with thin black lace straps. I had what some might call childbearing hips and what I referred to as a protective *fall* layer. If I fell, it would hurt a hell of a lot more without that layer, so I considered it a necessity.

"Jesus." He dropped to his knees between my legs. His fingers traced from my right hip along the edge of my panties to the center where he paused before he stroked downward with a light brush of his fingers.

I sucked in air, arching, eyes closing. He applied pressure and I moaned as my sex clenched with need. I bent my knees, thighs opening to him and he took full advantage, his finger dipping into my panties.

"So fuckin' wet."

His other hand slid up my abdomen, over my ribs to my breasts where he cupped me, thumb grazing my nipple, back and forth. But he didn't linger as his hand moved back down again. Then he dragged my panties down and off.

He held them up. "Love these. But I have to taste you, baby." He shifted to his stomach, his mouth so close to my sex that his heated breath wafted across my clit.

"Your smell is so damn addictive, Alina. A drug."

He lowered his head and with a slow agonizing drag of his tongue, he licked me.

Then he did things to me I never dreamed a man could do with his tongue. Skilled was an understatement. This man knew exactly what he was doing.

And when his groans vibrated against me, the sensation was so erotic that it made me groan, too.

"Connor." My fingers dug into his scalp, but he either didn't notice or didn't care because he continued tasting me, his tongue flicking over my clit back and forth until I lifted my hips, thighs trembling. "Oh. God. Connor."

"That's it, baby," he murmured against me. Circular motions, faster and faster.

"Connor!" I screamed.

My body stiffened, hips off the ground, eyes closed as wave after wave shot through me. "Oh, God. Oh, my God."

The orgasm was nothing I'd ever experienced before. Long and hard, pulsing over and over again until I collapsed in a pool of sated bliss.

He moved up my body as I lay completely spent and then his mouth was on mine and I tasted myself on his lips. It was slow and sweet, my lips still throbbing from his earlier kiss.

Connor was attentive, sweet and demanding and there was no question he knew how to kiss a woman.

His mouth lifted from mine and he put the condom package up to it. He placed the edge between my teeth and I ripped it open. Then he lifted and I saw he already had his pants off. When did he take his pants off?

I gawked at his thick, hard cock that jutted out from his body. God, it was beautiful. I never thought a cock could be beautiful, not that I'd seen many, actually only one, but he kept the area trimmed and it gave me a good view of his cock and his balls.

Jesus. I never wanted a man so desperately inside me as I did now. I'd had sex a few times with a guy I'd dated last year. But the sex had been groping and awkward, both of us fumbling.

Connor did not fumble or grope. He owned.

I took the condom from him and wrapped my opposite hand around his cock.

His eyes closed. "Alina," he murmured. "You're killing me."

I smiled, loving that I did that to him. Slowly, I rolled the condom over the length of him. I didn't know which gave me more pleasure, looking at his cock or the expression on his face, head tilted back, neck muscles strained, eyes closed and features tight as if he were in pain.

I saw when he lost it. The moment he wasn't waiting any longer.

His jaw got tight, eyes opened and he glared, but not with anger; it was with fierce desire. He grabbed my thigh and hitched it up on his hip. I raised the other one to match then he slid his cock up and down, my wetness clinging to the length of him.

"Can't do this any other way, Alina. Need you hard and fast."

I nodded, breathless. "Okay."

"Next time we'll go slow. I want that, too."

I chewed my lip. I liked the sound of there being a next time. "Okay." I slid my palms over his shoulders, down his back and urged him closer. "I want to come again." Because that was the best feeling in the world and I wanted him inside me when it happened.

He grinned. "Oh, baby. There's no question you're coming again."

Then he pushed inside me and I gasped at his thickness.

"So fuckin' tight."

He tilted his hips, pushed all the way in, and groaned. The sound was raw and primal. His eyes blazed before his mouth crashed into mine.

Awakening.

It was an awakening of my body. I didn't know if he felt it, too, probably not, but for me it awakened something inside me. Like it lived and breathed with all these new emotions.

It was a free fall as he thrust inside me. Not knowing where I'd land. If I'd survive. But nothing mattered except the beauty in the fall.

There was no hesitation in Connor; he had sex like he lived... without rules. I was on my back, stomach, knees, then in his lap as he continued to fuck me, hands bunched in my hair, on my breasts, hips, everywhere.

Now I was on top of him, rocking my hips while he suckled my nipples, his teeth nipping then tongue soothing. "Connor," I moaned.

He grabbed me by the hips then flipped me over so he was on top again. "Fuck, Alina. Fuck. Can't wait any longer. You close, baby?"

I nodded. "Yeah."

He moved, deep and slow. But that didn't last and before long he was pumping wildly into me, one hand above my head to give him balance while the other reached between us and circled my clit, quick and matching the rhythm of his thrusts.

"Fuuucckk," he growled.

"Oh, God. Oh, God!" I screamed as I came at the same time, my body jerking and contracting as wave after wave tore through me.

"Jesus," he whispered next to my ear. He dropped his head to kiss my shoulder. "Jesus."

I stroked my palms down his back and his cock twitched inside me. "Yeah," I whispered.

He lifted his head and his eyes met mine, searching. For what I didn't know, but his brows lowered and it looked as if something was bothering him.

"What's wrong?" I asked, my hand moving up his back to cup his neck. But I had a feeling what might be bothering him, because what just happened was special. It was more than I thought either of us expected.

He rolled to the side, took off the condom, tied a knot in it and tossed it aside, then he reached for me. His arm curved over my shoulder and he brought me into him. "It isn't enough time."

I tried to lift my head, but he pressed me back down so my cheek rested on his chest.

"Need to hold you a minute, shutterbug."

I kept quiet, listening to his heartbeat as I curled into him, his hand slowly caressing my back.

We lay like that a while, catching our breath, settled in the silence.

He stopped caressing and I tilted my head to look up at him. He was already looking at me.

"I've been with a lot of chicks, Alina. I'm not proud of it, but I don't regret it either. It means I also know when something is fuckin' special. And that was something fuckin' special. Not sure what to do with that."

Before I could respond, his mouth was on mine and he kissed me again. It was gentle and sweet and it was something more. *We* were

something more.
    And I wasn't sure what to do with it either.

CHAPTER FOUR

Question 2: What was your favorite thing to do as a teenager?

Day 28

Connor

"TWIRL," I SAID while holding the little girl Fariba's hand and raising my arm so she could spin under it. She smiled, her eyes wide and laughing as I danced with her, the music echoing in the night air.

I called Deck this morning and left him a message. I asked if he'd check in on Georgie and my parents as I'd decided to stay longer at the orphanage, but would be back in time to go to JTF2 training. I didn't mention Alina. Didn't actually know what to say because this was all new territory for me. Plus it sucked talking on voice mail.

I read over my journal last night while she was showering. Besides the nineteen questions and her answers, I wrote other things about her, little things like how she spilled her coffee the other morning when it was too hot. The next morning, I tested her coffee first.

Had ever since. Don't know why, but fuck, I liked doing that. I liked every single second we spent together.

Our paths had intersected when I least expected and soon we would be separating on completely different roads. Maybe that was how it was supposed to be and for the last few days, I'd been trying to convince myself of that.

I was doing a shit job.

Because Alina meant something.

The song ended and I bowed to the little girl and she curtsied before running off to her friends with a bounce in her step. It wasn't much, but it was all I could give them, the laughter. It was what kept me going when images of what I'd seen haunted me. Laughter kept the lightness. It fed you life.

My eyes caught a glimpse of white coming out of the building and I turned. Then my breath caught in my throat and I froze.

She stood in the doorway, her hair loose and gently falling over her shoulders, her white linen pants bristling around her legs in the gentle breeze and her face illuminated by the full moon. She was smiling, her eyes on the kids dancing to the music trickling from the shitty radio.

Carved. Etched. Engraved. Fuck, it was everything. Her standing there was an image I'd never forget. Didn't need a fuckin' photo to remind me.

Her eyes shifted across the yard and she waved to Jaz who was dancing with a group of kids. He winked at her and then her gaze drifted to me and locked.

My chest swelled. It fuckin' swelled, never had that with a chick before. No, Alina wasn't some chick. She was the woman I'd fallen in love with.

PERFECT RAGE

She headed toward me, graceful and a little shy as she tucked strands of hair behind her ear. Most of the time she wore it tied back, but tonight, it hung in soft waves down her back and over her shoulders. Long layers framed her face, the strands that always escaped her ponytail.

The music slowed and Evanescence's "My Immortal" played, her haunting voice riding on the gentle breeze. My heart beat faster as she drew near, her smile now a hesitant half smile. Eyes searching, probably wondering what the fuck I was thinking.

Because we both knew our time was almost up.

She lowered her eyes when she stopped a foot away from me. I moved into her, arm sliding around her waist, and I slowly drew her up against me.

"Alina," I murmured then cupped her chin and tilted my head, lowering until my mouth found hers.

The plush velvet surface of her lips molded to mine, following my direction. Her body sagged, palms gliding up my chest to my shoulders before wrapping around my neck.

I'd never had sweet. Never had this undeniable swell in my chest or the fear of losing something.

I'd fucked around a lot, and that was why I knew this was different.

That she was something special.

I drew back and released her chin. Running my hand over her shoulder to the back of her neck, I weaved my fingers into her thick, long strands.

"I love this," I murmured.

Her brow twitched with question. "What?"

"This. You in my arms. You're so damn beautiful."

Heat rose on her cheeks and it was cute. Alina was confident and sweet, definitely sassy when she wanted to be, but she also had a vulnerability that made her soft. I already knew she had an amazing heart and compassionate soul, as I'd seen her with the kids. She'd even taken to helping some of the kids with learning English.

She was natural and genuine, and I knew how rare that was. And she'd told me about her numbers the other day. It was ridiculous and completely adorable and made me fall for her even more.

One. One. Five.

She'd said it took her one second to know she was attracted to me. I'd grinned at that because that rocked. One hour before I made her laugh until she had tears. That was during our nineteen questions when I went on about hating the color orange. And the number five was five days before she fell for me. That was our bedroom picnic.

I'd asked her when she knew she was in love with me. She told me she'd let me know.

She hadn't. Not yet. But I'd bet my life it was number twenty-eight, for today, because I sure as hell loved her.

Fuck yeah, I loved her. "Dance with me?" I asked.

I didn't wait for her response, but swayed with the music, her body pressed up against mine. We moved in perfect rhythm together just like we did in everything. I uncurled her from my arms to twirl her then pulled her back in again.

Jesus. What was I going to do?

I was leaving to join one of the toughest military units in the world. She was going to Miami and then who knew where the magazine would send her next. And if they didn't keep her on, she'd return to Colombia.

Fuck, I couldn't let her go. It was completely selfish, but I couldn't imagine her with anyone else. Just the thought of her with another guy drove me crazy. But I couldn't expect her to give up her life for me because that was what she'd have to do. She'd be alone for months at a time while I was off on a mission having no idea where I was or if I'd come back alive.

"Connor?" She angled her head to look at me.

"Yeah, baby?"

"Let's not worry about it tonight."

And right then I knew I couldn't do it. I was willing to be a selfish prick and ask her to give up everything for me.

"Can't do that." She frowned and I caressed her cheek with the back of my knuckles. "Not until you tell me you won't go. You'll stay with me."

Her eyes widened and she stopped moving to the music. "Connor? What are you saying?"

"I know what we said, that this was temporary, but fuck, I can't do it. Every day I'm holding on tighter. It doesn't make sense, me leaving for training, but we can make it work. I can fly with you to Miami. We can see if the magazine can give you a reference and maybe you could work in Toronto. I'll be gone a while, but I'll introduce you to my sister and parents, my friends. I can't let you go, Alina. When I'm gone, I want to know you're waiting for me. It's so fuckin' selfish, but I can't help it." My heart raced as I spoke. I hadn't planned saying this; I just knew it was right. It felt right saying it. "Alina, I love you." She inhaled, her lips parting. "I know it's too soon, but I live in the now. I have to because there might not be a tomorrow and that makes this even more selfish of me. But fuck, just please say you'll stay with me."

I expected questions or hesitation, or telling me it was fuckin' crazy, but Alina simply smiled, her eyes filled with tears and she said, "Okay."

Okay. That was it. And it was the best fuckin' word I'd ever heard pass anyone's lips. A simple okay with her in my arms, breathless and beautiful, and now she was fuckin' mine.

"Twenty-eight," I said.

She scrunched her nose. "Huh?"

"Your numbers. I want to hear you say it."

She laughed. "Connor, it's so silly."

"I love the silly parts of you, Alina. Tell me."

She sighed. "Okay. Twenty-eight. It took twenty-eight days for you to man up and tell me you loved me."

I chuckled. "Babe. No."

She laughed again. "And it took twenty-eight days before I told him I loved him back."

My brows lifted as I waited and she made me wait a good thirty seconds. "Well?"

Her smile faded and her eyes locked with mine. Then her hand reached up and cupped my cheek. "I love you, Connor O'Neill."

"Fuckin' right you do." I hitched her up and she curled her legs around my waist, her arms curving around my neck. Then I strode across the yard to the building.

Two kids ran ahead of us and opened the door. I caught Jaz's huge grin and grinned back. Then I winked at the kids as I took my girl inside.

My girl.

Alina was fuckin' mine.

CHAPTER FIVE

Alina

THE NEXT DAY I headed out to the shed behind the main building to grab canned beans for the cook. I was helping in the kitchen for a few hours because one of the volunteers was sick. Jaz was busy writing and Connor had headed into a neighboring town with another guy to pick up a few essentials like he'd done for the last three Wednesdays.

He left me in bed this morning completely sated after he'd woken me to kisses between my legs, which soon had me moaning and arching for release. When I came, he simply crawled up beside me, lightly kissed me and said, 'Love you, shutterbug' then he was gone.

That was two hours ago and I'd been thinking about him sinking inside me ever since. My cell vibrated in my pocket and I frowned. No one ever called me as my cell was for emergencies only. Besides, the only people who would were the magazine or my brother. My parents couldn't afford to call me here.

I pressed the answer button. "Hello?"

"Hello, Catalina."

Fear didn't creep, it slammed into me. My stomach coiled and I swallowed several times as bile rose.

No. No. No. It couldn't be.

"Carlos."

"How are you? Or, perhaps, the more accurate question, where are you?"

My mind sparked off like faulty wiring as I tried to think of what to tell him. Did I tell him? Did I lie? If I lied and he found out, he'd hurt my family. I knew how it worked. That was why I'd disappeared.

God, why now?

"I've been very patient. It's time for you to come home now, Catalina."

I jerked, hand tightening around the phone. "I… I can't."

There was a mild chuckle that caused the hairs on the back of my neck to dart to attention. "Oh, but you can. And you will." Then he added in a grated rough order, "Right now."

Full-blown panic set in. He was too confident for not knowing where I was and that terrified me more than anything.

I knew the power he wielded. I knew the lengths he'd go to get what he wanted. My father was scared of him and his man Diego. There was gossip in high school as to what was done to men who failed Carlos. Men who tried to leave his 'business'. That was why my brother left when he did.

He continued, his words slow and precise, "It wouldn't be right to have your father's funeral without his daughter present."

My knees gave out at the same time as I choked back a strangled cry. "No. Oh, God, no. Please." I sat on the ground, tears streaming down my cheeks.

"Unfortunately, there was…" he paused then said, "an accident. Diego offers his condolences."

There was no explanation needed. Carlos wasn't stupid. He'd never admit to killing anyone, especially over the phone. According to my father, many of the authorities were in his pocket, but a few who refused to be bribed were trying to take him down.

Oh, God, why? Why would Diego kill him? My dad had worked for him for years and was loyal. He'd been loyal to him.

"Come home now, Catalina. We have much to discuss."

Run. Run. Run. Pounded though my head. Run to Connor. Run with him. I could go to Toronto and Carlos wouldn't know. He didn't know where I was. I could disappear. My brother was safe in Miami, but my mother… oh, God.

"Stop your sobbing. I don't have time to listen to your sniffling over a man who lost me a great deal of money. I don't like losing money, Catalina. But since I'm a generous man, I'll allow you to cover the loss."

Me? "Carlos, I don't have the money."

He laughed. "Of course you don't. I'm willing to make an exception and accept you as payment for the money your father lost." My heart slammed into my chest. No. I wouldn't. Never. "I know what you're thinking, but your brother is here beside me and I think he'd prefer if you came home."

I heard a fierce grunt in the background then, "Alina, no. Don't you dar—" There was another grunt then nothing.

Juan. He had Juan? That was how he found me. He had Juan.

I tipped over, clutching my stomach, the phone pressed tight to my ear as his words repeated over and over in my head. "Please. Carlos. Don't hurt him. I'm begging you."

"Come home, Catalina. I'll give you two days." The phone went dead and it slipped from my grasp into the dirt. I covered my face with my hands and rocked back and forth sobbing. My dad was dead. My brother… Juan had left home to escape this. He had been trying to get me out, too.

I could run. Leave. Go to Canada with Connor.

But, I'd never be able to live with myself if I was responsible for my brother's death.

And it wouldn't stop there. My mother would be next. Maybe the guy I dated last year. The girl I talked to at the market.

Oh, God. No.

Carlos's reach extended far and he had friends everywhere because he made certain he did. His wealth meant he was able to line the pockets of those in high places to look the other way at his indiscretions.

If Carlos wanted something, he took it. If he decided to end an entire family, he ended it.

I was here with Connor, living a fantasy. I should've known this couldn't last. My life was never meant to be a happily ever after. I grew up knowing that. I'd accepted it.

Until him.

Until Connor.

There was a wave of warmth thinking about him, yet at the same time, tidal waves of dread slammed into me.

I had to leave him.

It was like my insides were being ripped apart and all the hope and joy slowly bled out of me.

I had to leave and Connor couldn't know why. If he knew, he'd never allow me to go back. He'd tie me up if he had to. Connor protected his team. Protected his friends. He'd do anything in his power to protect those he cared about.

And that included me.

Carlos would kill him just like he was going to kill my brother. Like he had my father.

I had to leave. Now. Right now. Before Connor returned. I couldn't let him see me or he'd know something was wrong.

Jaz. I had to find Jaz. He'd find a way to get me back to base and on a flight. I'd tell him… God, I had to lie.

I was treading water and with each ragged breath, I sank further and further into the darkness of despair.

There was no choice. I had to go home. And I had to make sure Connor would never come after me.

I had to hurt him. I had to hurt him so badly that he'd hate me.

I'd leave him a note in his journal. But just thinking about the words I'd have to write, broke me. It was complete devastation.

Oh, God, Connor. I'm sorry. I'm so sorry.

But risking my brother's life wasn't an option, and telling Connor wasn't an option.

In my world, it's not if you love something set it free. It's if you love something, don't let Carlos Moreno know.

Carlos Moreno could never know I love Connor O'Neill.

To Corporal Connor O'Neill,

We were always meant to be temporary. You're a good man and I wish you all the best. But I'm not in love with you. I'm sorry I lied.

By the time you read this, I'll have gone. I'm returning home to my fiancé.

Catalina

"You ready?" Jaz asked, standing in the doorway of the small, bare room I'd been sharing with Connor.

I nodded, looking up from the tear-stained page filled with hurtful lies. I tucked it inside his journal and placed it in the middle of his cot. He didn't know my handwriting, so it was doubtful he'd notice how shaky it was. Even if he did, Connor would be so pissed off that I was pretty sure the paper would end up in shreds before he even read the last line that was a horrible lie.

"Alina, are you sure you want to leave without seeing him?" Jaz had his bag over his shoulder and was ready to go. When I told him I had to leave, there was no hesitation that he'd leave with me. We only had another day here and we had what we needed for the magazine.

"Yeah." I reached for my bag, hand shaking and I was barely able to keep myself from falling into a sobbing puddle on the floor. I'd told Jaz the truth about my father dying, but for obvious reasons, none of the details. I also had to tell him the lies in the note. I don't know if he believed me or not, but he did believe that it was an emergency probably from the state I was in. He'd immediately organized for us to be picked up and taken back to the air base.

"Okay. Well, our ride is here. You know we can wait—"

I shook my head. "No. I can't Jaz. I know I'm being a coward, but trust me, it's better this way."

He slowly nodded. "You might be right. He's not a guy who will take this well."

No, but that was the point.

I glanced one last time at his journal, the corner of my note sticking out at the top edge.

He'd hate me. Connor's morals were about loyalty, integrity, and honesty. I just crushed all of those traits in three simple sentences.

He'd forget me. One day he'd forget, but he'd never forgive and I had to live with that.

I wouldn't forget him. Not ever. Because I was leaving all of *me* with him. He just didn't know it.

CHAPTER SIX

Question 3: One word to describe you that starts with a "p"?

Present Day

Connor

NOTHING WAS CERTAIN except detonation.
Detonation of my mind. A complex web of unsettled darkness that threatened to spark and explode at any moment.

That was my fuckin' certainty.

Uncontrollable.

Uncontained.

The drug Vault had me on for years made me into a hard, cruel killer without a past. Without memories. And that made me dangerous as fuck.

Now the drug had stopped, but it was worse, because the memories filtered back in and with them surfaced a deep inner rage.

I was too dangerous to be near her and yet I sat on my bike across the street from the bar, Avalanche, the engine idling with a rumble beneath me.

So fuckin' close. Too close for her own good.

A car door slammed and I lifted my head.

I stiffened. Fingers dug into my thighs as I watched Deck, my ex-JTF2 team leader and ex-best friend walk around the front of his car then open the passenger door.

The streetlight hanging above swayed in the breeze and the light shimmered over him, but I couldn't see his face. It was tilted down as he helped some chick out of his car.

But it wasn't some chick; it was my fuckin' sister.

He put his arm protectively around her shoulders and she leaned into him, arm around his waist as they walked toward the entrance of the bar.

Sweet, innocent Georgie-girl. There were purple streaks in her hair and it was unkempt and carefree. She wore a mid-thigh, tight black skirt, V-neck top that was a rainbow of purples, and red stiletto heels. There was an assuredness to her step that she'd lacked as a kid. I was betting she no longer had a color-coded closet. She definitely wasn't concerned about her hair being impeccable.

All grown up and completely fuckin' different.

Emotions sparked as I watched them. Not good emotions. Anger. Rage.

Before they disappeared inside, Deck stopped, turned into her, and slid both hands down her sides to settle on her hips. Then he lowered his head and kissed her.

They drew apart. I couldn't see Deck's face as his back was to me, but I saw how he was with her. How he held her, how he protected her with his body facing the street, how he kissed her then gently moved to cup the back of her neck as he leaned in and whispered something in her ear.

She laughed and the sound rode the warm breeze and drifted into me. I tried to let it in. Let it sink into my cold, fucked-up soul, but it bounced off me and dissipated into the air.

My past was gone.

My sister.

My parents.

They were dead to me now.

Didn't need them. Didn't care about them. The only thing I felt was rage.

That was a lie. I did care about one thing. I didn't want to care. Tried like hell not to, but she refused to be killed off.

Her. My girl. My Alina.

She was the reason I spent three straight days and nights riding my bike from Miami to Toronto while catching short naps on the side of the road.

I never slept longer than a few hours at a time. If I did, I woke with adrenaline pumping through my veins. Volatile adrenaline that was unstable and made me unpredictable. I had the urge to hurt something. To destroy. It grabbed onto me so tight that I couldn't breathe.

The only way to stop it was get on my bike and ride. Fast. Hard. The threat of dying always a millisecond away.

I should be dead. But fate was getting its kicks out of playing with me.

Yeah, well, I knew how to play, too, just not the same way I used to. Now, I didn't play nice.

A raindrop hit the tinted shield of my helmet and glided down the plastic. I wiped it away with my gloved hand leaving a streak.

What the hell was I doing?

Everything about being here was stupid. If Deck or any of my old buddies saw me, I was uncertain what they'd do, but I was guessing it wouldn't be a friendly handshake.

And Alina. What would she do? The last time I'd seen her was six weeks ago when I'd dragged her through a house filled with dead bodies. Bodies I'd killed in order to get to her. Then I left her tied up in the sewer while I went to kill her worthless drug lord husband, Carlos Moreno.

I hadn't said one word to her. Not one.

She'd been crying. I left her sobbing in the fuckin' sewer, but the crying wasn't because I was leaving her there or that she was scared or afraid for her life.

No, Alina wouldn't cry for herself. She cried for others. And that day she'd cried for me. She fuckin' cried for me. Begged me to talk to her. To say something. But I didn't. Not with the fragmented memories and uncontrollable rage ripping through my body.

And that rage was focused on the bastard who stole Alina from me and destroyed us. Who kept me locked up in a cell for years torturing me with videos of her. Who stole my life. My memories. My ability to feel or care about anyone by forcing a drug into me.

Another drop of rain hit the back of my glove.

Fuck this.

I looked away from the bar, put my hands on the handlebars, revved the engine, then kicked it into gear, lifted my feet, and pulled away.

It was ten minutes before I pulled a U-turn and headed back. The light sprinkles of raindrops had turned into a steady drizzle and the pavement glimmered under the streetlights with slick wetness.

All I heard was the deep roar of my engine and the pellets of rain hitting my helmet and leather jacket. Rhythmic, like several drums banging the exact same beat over and over again. I was used to it. The pounding. But most of the time when the pounding in my head hit, it was painful.

No, it was agonizing.

PERFECT RAGE

This was calm. I was calm and I knew why: I was headed back to the bar.

My grip on the handlebars tightened. No, I was headed back to her. She was now my addiction. My craving. My need.

I pulled into the alley behind the bar and parked. Getting off my bike, I lifted my helmet and hooked it on the handlebar.

I took off my gloves, opened my satchel, shoved them inside and pulled out my lock pick tools. Walking to the door, I crouched and inserted the two metal pieces. It took some effort to pick the lock, but I'd always had a knack for it.

I remembered being outside my sister's grade three classroom at midnight picking the lock. I'd already broke through the main doors of the school, which took a little more work than a flimsy classroom door. Flashbacks of me breaking into her school to steal the hamster Fiddlehead surrounded me. Georgie said the kids were teasing the rodent and the teacher ignored it. So, I was breaking Fiddlehead out of purgatory and bringing him home.

My fuckin' memories were better off forgotten, but they refused to leave me the hell alone, and continued to haunt me.

If they'd remained buried, I wouldn't be here right now. I'd probably still be in Colombia where I'd spent several weeks dying in some fuckin' filthy motel room after taking Moreno down. Where I'd prayed for death as I retched my guts out. Where I'd fought the nightmares that turned out to be memories. All the time not knowing what was real and what wasn't.

I'd destroyed the room. Fist through the television, then the drywall.

Unable to face looking at myself in the bathroom mirror, it ended up shattered on the floor.

Demons. Shadows. I fought them all until I couldn't anymore.

Finally, I collapsed on the floor, my body shaking so bad it took me hours to pull myself into bed where I lay for who the fuck knows how long.

I knew I was dying from the drug withdrawal. Felt it since I escaped the basement where Deck and the other assholes had kept me prisoner, attempting to gradually wean me off the drug. That was when I remembered Catalina.

No, Alina. She'd always been my Alina.

But they weren't all good memories. They were of Alina and me in Colombia with Moreno. I'd been on Vault's drug and had no fuckin' idea who she was.

I'd done things to her… watched her cry. Watched her beg.

And I'd fucked her. I'd goddamn fucked her. I was cruel and cold and hadn't given a shit if her husband killed her for fucking me.

And when I remembered and went after Moreno for what he'd done to both of us, I hadn't planned on leaving Colombia alive. Whether Moreno and his men killed me or the drug withdrawal did. All I knew when I went there was there was no chance I was leaving this fuckin' earth until Alina was free of that sick bastard.

Nothing else mattered.

Once she was safe and Moreno was dead, I didn't have to fight anymore. I wanted to die. I didn't want to remember.

The fucked-up thing was Deck and his buddies had been there to take down Moreno, too. So, I used him to get Alina out of the sewer and out of the country. Away from the cartel because they'd never let her go even if her husband was dead. You didn't walk away from that shit alive.

I knew Deck would get her out. He never failed. He didn't know how to fail.

And now, I was back in Toronto where I grew up, walking into a bar where I probably knew half the people, ones I had no intention of ever seeing again.

The lock clicked.

I stood and pocketed my tools in the front pocket of my rain-soaked cargo pants.

I opened the door, not all the way so as not to let the moonlight filter in, just enough to slip inside. It clicked closed behind me.

It opened into a hallway where there were two doors on opposite sides, one a ladies' washroom, the other the men's. I walked down the hall then into the bar, staying in the shadows as I weaved through the empty tables.

No one even glanced at me. Un-fuckin-believable. I was in a bar with military… no, elite military guys, and not one of them gave a shit that some guy just crashed their party. Maybe they were cocky enough to believe they could easily take me out if they needed to.

I huffed. Fuck, yeah, they were cocky enough to believe that. We were the elite. The best at what we did and I'd been one of the cockiest on my team. I still was, but it was no longer because I knew I was good at what I did, but because I didn't give a fuck if I lived or died.

I scanned the darkened bar, eyes landing on Deck who stood on stage, his voice echoing over the microphone as he made some speech about Georgie.

His words hit me—hard. It was like he swung a sledgehammer into my abdomen.

He fuckin' loved her. My sister. My sweet innocent sister who was no longer sweet and innocent. He brought her into our dark world, a place I never wanted for her.

I snorted.

A few heads turned my way, none I recognized; although, I could have known them, just one of those missing puzzle pieces I had yet to find.

No one made a move toward me though as their attention turned back to the stage.

I easily fit in with the crowd in appearance, but I was nothing like them. Not anymore.

I was a ticking time bomb with no timer. I had no idea when I'd explode, but if I did explode, these guys, friends or not, would try to take me down, and it wouldn't be friendly.

The tables were empty at the back of the bar as everyone hovered around the stage. I found a spot I could easily scan the entire place and still remain partially hidden.

I casually leaned against the brick wall. The granules pressed into the back of my shoulders as I watched under the hood of my eyes. But there was nothing casual about me, not anymore.

Arms crossed, head tilted away from the dim light, I waited like a cougar in the shadows for his unsuspecting prey.

The crowd erupted into deafening cheers and I tensed, lifting my head to catch my little sister leap up on stage and into Deck's arms.

The tats on my arms expanded over my bulging muscles as anger played at the corners of my mind.

I lowered my gaze from them, shaking my head back and forth. It felt like it was yesterday when I'd told Deck to stay away from Georgie. Told him not to date her, kiss her and sure as hell not fuck her.

He'd obviously done all of the above.

A lock of my unruly dirty-blond strands hung in front of my eyes as I kept my chin tilted down, eyes on my black leather motorcycle boots while I concentrated on breathing in and out, attempting to keep the anger contained.

The swinging door behind the bar pushed open and my body tightened. I knew it was her. My prey. The reason I'd come back to Toronto and stood in a bar filled with family and old friends, risking everything because I was unable to stop myself from seeing her.

The door hesitated on its hinges before it swung shut again, and for a second the light from the hallway behind her illuminated like a halo and I saw her face clearly.

Alina.

The veil I suffocated under lifted and I breathed in a lungful of air. Memories of her laughter filtered into me and the rage eased as I watched her movements. The graceful way her hips swayed with each shift of her body. The steadiness of her hands while she poured amber liquid into two frosted glasses.

But it was her eyes I craved.

Needed.

The bartender lifted the bar flap for her and she turned her head and half smiled at him. Her lips moved and even though I couldn't hear, I knew she thanked him. She'd always been polite.

My eyes narrowed as the guy grinned and winked at her. I inhaled a long drawn-in breath to calm the overwhelming need to stride across the bar and pull her away from him. It was illogical. I knew that and yet it felt as if another predator was about to steal away what was mine.

Patience. Stillness. Control.

It existed in me before the drug, during the drug, but no more. Instead, I was unpredictable and the fragile control would easily snap whether I wanted it to or not.

And that was the kicker of all this. The pretense that I had some sort of control, but the reality was I didn't.

I lived in a dark, delicate shell that perched on the ledge of a cliff ready to fall into the depths of the raging waves below. That was where I'd drown over and over again being tossed around like a fuckin' pebble, not knowing which way was up, which way to swim and escape the tumultuous sea of rage.

I gritted my teeth, eyes shifting from her to the floor as my head throbbed. The pain had begun. I teetered on the edge of the cliff.

The band kicked into gear and the crowd cheered and clapped, not paying any attention to me, not that it mattered. I'd take the chance anyway in order to be near her again.

She was worth the risk. Besides, I no longer had the ability to give a shit about the risks I took. It was like the capability to feel that emotion had been erased.

She picked up empty beer bottles from tables and placed them on a tray she carried. I was pissed as hell when I discovered she worked here. Last night, I'd watched her walk out of here at two in the morning to hop in a cab. Yeah, the bartender came out and stood with her, but I didn't like it. It wasn't safe doing shit like that.

I'd been watching her for three days now. Took me a bit to find her, but once I found Deck, it didn't take long. There was always a trail. You just had to find the first breadcrumb and Deck had been mine. He had no reason to hide her, so it hadn't been difficult. But as soon as he knew I was here, there'd be a reason.

She moved closer.

Ten feet.

Nine.

Eight.

She was so close I tasted her on the tip of my tongue.

I uncrossed my arms and pushed away from the wall. Every nerve shot off in sparks the second she passed me to clear off the table five feet away.

She bent, her hand reaching for an empty beer bottle.

I saw it. The moment she sensed me behind her.

Scent. It was primal. It was what made the deer run before the coyotes were within eyesight.

Her hand slipped from the bottle and it toppled over, the remnants, spilling out onto the table then dripping onto the floor.

She ignored it as she straightened, her entire body stiff as she froze.

"Alina," I drawled.

Her breath hitched and I loved that fuckin' sound. Not for the reason it was now, but from when I'd touched her. When I'd made her tremble and arch and scream beneath me.

She slowly turned.

Her eyes widened as they locked on me and she staggered back a few steps until her spine hit the wall. The tray filled with empty beer bottles wobbled unsteadily in her hands and I moved quick, stepping in front of her and taking the tray then setting it down on a table to my left.

Then I turned back to her.

She was nervous. Couldn't blame her.

She no longer knew who I was. Fuck, I didn't know who I was anymore. Living in blackness splattered with the tainted blood of what I'd done.

"Connor," she whispered in that husky sweet voice.

I stepped closer.

She tensed, hands out as if to warn me to keep back, but when I was close enough, her palms rested on my chest.

I leaned forward and put one hand on the wall above her head.

Caged in. Trapped.

She was an average height, but I still towered over her.

"You don't belong here," I said. Not sure why that was the first thing out of my mouth, but I no longer had a filter and I hated seeing her working here. She didn't belong in a bar serving drunk assholes who stared at her ass.

Alina was a brilliant photographer and that was what she should be doing. This wasn't her.

Shutterbug. My fuckin' shutterbug.

Jesus, what the fuck was wrong with me? She wasn't mine. Couldn't ever be again and yet, everything inside me said she was.

Her eyes got bigger and her bottom lip trembled. "You… here."

I expected this reaction. The fear. Not knowing if I was that cold, cruel man in Colombia or something else entirely.

People feared me now. Even walking into a convenience store people stayed out of my way and if they couldn't, their discomfort was obvious by stiff spines, eyes unable to meet mine and quickened breaths. It didn't bother me anymore. But fuck, it bothered me seeing the fear in her because I put it there.

"Yeah."

The pulse in her throat throbbed and her hands resting on my chest twitched. "I don't understand. Deck said…" She stopped, her face paling. "Are you here to kill me?"

It was the wrong fuckin' thing to say to a man hanging on by a thread.

The delicate film of calmness tore and I clenched my jaw, furious that she'd think I was there to kill her. But the reality was I didn't know what I'd do. I fuckin' didn't know and yet here I stood, risking her life by being close to her.

Her hands on my chest pushed, but not enough to attract attention or make me move. I met her terrified eyes and my words tumbled out in an angered, graveled tone. "If I'd wanted to kill you, you'd be lying beside that piece-of-crap husband of yours in a pool of blood instead of leaving you in the fuckin' sewer." Harsh, but all I had left was truth and I wasn't filtering it for anyone, even her.

"Why… Connor… why didn't you talk to me? Why didn't you say anything? You left me in the sewer and I didn't know what was happening. I didn't know who—"

I huffed. "Say what, Alina? What the fuck was I supposed to say? That I remembered us. That I hated you all over again for leaving me with nothing except a goddamn note. That I hated myself for fucking you in Colombia as a cold, cruel bastard who treated you like a piece of meat. Or should I have told you I was dying and wanted to fuckin' die?"

"I don't know," she whispered, lowering her eyes from mine. "I don't know. But something. Anything. All I knew was what I saw. Carlos's men dead all over the house and you covered in blood. I had no idea what was happening, who you were, which man you were."

"I couldn't," I said, shaking my head.

That day my focus was on what had to be done. That was all I could think about. If I'd lost focus, I'd have lost control and would've spiraled into a black hole. "Why the hell did you come to me? Why did you let me fuck you, Alina? Why? Fuck, why damn it?" It was killing me. The memory haunted me for weeks knowing I'd fucked Alina as a killing machine who didn't give two shits about her.

She was quiet.

"Why, damn it?" I repeated harshly. Christ, just the thought of what could've happened drove me insane. "I could've killed you."

She shook her head and the few strands that had come loose from her ponytail brushed her cheeks. "No. You wouldn't have."

"You don't fuckin' know that. I called you a bitch. I fucked you with tears in your eyes." I lowered my voice and growled, "I put bruises on your arms."

"It wasn't the real you," she whispered, her voice ragged.

"You sure as hell got that right. It wasn't me, so why the hell would you risk coming to me with Moreno five-hundred yards away?"

Her breath hitched as she choked back a sob. "Connor… I had to. I had to try to get you to remember." She lowered her head and sniffled. "I'd have done anything to help you."

"Jesus." It tore me apart knowing what I'd done. I'd loved this woman. I'd loved her so much I'd have done anything for her and I'd poisoned the beauty of what we were. Now, I had to live with how I'd treated her in Colombia.

"You were supposed to stay safe. Carlos was never supposed to find out about you," she said.

"Fuckin' safe? You think I wanted fuckin' safe, Alina?" My voice rose. Jesus, I had to keep my shit together before I had this entire bar on me. "I wanted you. I didn't give a fuck how complicated it was to keep you." The tightness in my chest made it hard to breathe. I was losing my control. "That's not how it works. That's not how I work and you left me with a note telling me we were nothing. That what we shared was bullshit. Fuckin' bullshit."

This wasn't how it was supposed to go down. Unfortunately for her, my head was messed up and I was pissed as all hell. I knew why she'd left me that note, and I didn't blame her. Not once I learned the truth.

"You fucked me in Moreno's goddamn pool house. Jesus. Fuckin' Christ." I shoved away from her then punched the brick wall beside her. "He would've killed you if he'd found out." I think that pissed me off more because she *knew* Carlos would've killed her. "You knew I wouldn't have given a shit what he did to you. Jesus, so damn stupid." I lowered my voice, but my fingers tightened on her hip. "Look at me." She didn't. "Look. At. Me."

Her chin rose, and tears trailed down her cheeks.

Fuck. Alina had been a little sassy, a lot sweet, and strong, and it pissed me off knowing I put those tears there—again.

What the hell was I doing here? I should've left this alone, left her alone. I was losing my shit. I had to get away from her, get on my bike and ride. Just fuckin' ride.

"It was still you." Her soft whisper cut through the tension in my body and then her hands reached for me, fingers curling into my T-shirt. "It was you." She choked on a sob. "It was still you and I needed you to remember so you could escape them."

Somewhere inside me I knew that. That flicker of light that kept being snuffed out by the anger. "Yeah," I dragged out. "Yeah."

God, I was so damn tired of the constant battle in my head, the memories of what I'd done. They were clips from a horror movie where I was the villain, the monster.

I wanted to forget again. Just fuckin' leave everything and forget.

"Alina," I whispered as I leaned into her, bending so my forehead rested in the crook of her neck. Her heart beat erratically and her body trembled against me. "I hurt you. What I did to you… damn it, baby, I don't know who the fuck I am anymore."

"Connor," she said. "You'll always be Connor."

My spine stiffened and my body thrummed with sparks of warning. I knew eyes were on me; I was trained to know when I was being watched.

I had to get out of here before I had ex-military buddies all over me and my sister finding out I was fifty feet away and very much alive.

Being here was fuckin' stupid. Irrational.

I had to get the fuck out and ride. Ride until I was too far away to turn back. Escape.

But death was my only escape.

I stepped back from her and my shirt stretched as she held onto it a second before finally letting go. The material dropped back in place.

There was no point in hiding from whoever had recognized me and I didn't really care. I was leaving anyway. I turned my head and met Kai's eyes drilling into me.

Kai was the unknown.

I didn't know him, although I'd fought him in the Toronto Vault house. And he was good, knew how to handle a knife better than me. I knew his bitch mother who he'd killed. Kai turned on her and Vault, and from what I'd seen, he was now with Deck.

I knew how Deck would react if he saw me. He'd be on me, but he'd be calm about it. He'd never kill me, but he'd try to take me down.

Kai, I wasn't so sure about.

I positioned myself in front of Alina like a wall and Kai wrapped his arm around the girl beside him. My eyes flicked to her and my gut twisted. It was like being slammed with a baseball bat in the abdomen as I met the familiar eyes.

One of my nightmares. Her. On the ground bleeding while I held a gun in my hand. My breath locked and I shook my head trying to erase the image. I wouldn't fuckin' do that. I'd never shoot a woman.

But I had.

I knew with everything inside me, I had. And it had been Kai's woman, London. I'd shot her and taken her into Vault's web.

I'd hurt Alina, too, but in a much different way.

Alina touched my arm, fingers sliding down my tatted skin to my wrist. "Let me bandage your hand."

I jerked away, knowing I had blood dripping off my knuckles from punching the wall. I did a quick scan of the bar to see if anyone else had noticed me but all eyes were on the band.

Then I briefly met Kai's eyes again before saying over my shoulder to Alina. "Find another job. I don't want you working here."

I moved and headed for the back door.

I didn't say anything else to her. I didn't look back at her or Kai. I didn't check to see if Kai had his knife out and was going to throw it across the bar into my back.

I simply walked down the hall that led to the fire exit, shoved my hip into the metal bar on the door and went out into the back alley.

Then I dug my hand into the front pocket of my black cargo pants and pulled out my keys. I strode to my bike, pulled on my helmet, threw a leg over, started it up.

The engine rumbled beneath me.

Freedom.

I gambled with death every time I got on my bike and I craved it then more than ever.

I snapped the tinted shield closed.

The back door of the bar opened and Alina stood with her hand covering her mouth, tears streaming down her cheeks.

I revved the engine then took off.

CHAPTER SEVEN

Alina

RACKING SOBS TORE through me as I watched Connor ride off. Fist to my mouth, teeth biting down, I tried to contain the utter devastation of what just happened.

My stomach twisted and my body shook as I stared into the darkness of the alley. I heard the rumble of his bike, but soon it faded and then… nothing.

Emotions were like a tornado whirling with no clear destination or end, but precise in its destruction.

Shock.

Pain.

And fear, not for me, but for him.

Oh, God, Connor. What has he done to you?

But I knew what he'd done. The mind games were Carlos's favorite because that was how he broke you. Except he'd been unable to break Connor.

He couldn't break him through games or torture, so he did much worse. He killed who he'd been with the drug.

Because of me... Connor was like this because of me. My photographs. The pictures I'd taken of Connor and me in Afghanistan, Moreno had found them.

The drug made him into a cold, harsh, emotionless man I didn't recognize, but this was worse. Because Connor now had to come to terms with what he'd done and his values were strong. They were what defined Connor. Protect those he loved. Protect his country. Protect children. Help others and live in the now. With his memories returning, he had realized he'd crushed every moral and value he had as a man while under the influence of the drug.

Oh, God, Connor.

I couldn't breathe.

I couldn't breathe.

I stumbled back into the brick wall, arms wrapped around my abdomen as I inhaled abrupt breaths.

I wasn't this person. This weak, vulnerable girl who felt as if she were breaking apart into thousands of delicate, flimsy pieces. But seeing Connor... the hurt on his face layered with rage, it destroyed me all over again.

The door opened and I tensed, not wanting anyone to see me like this. I was good at hiding the pain, but this... this... the emotions grabbed hold and took control.

Kai emerged then London, who immediately approached me and placed her hand lightly on my arm. "Breathe. Slow and deep."

I closed my eyes, inhaling the cool, night air into my lungs and choking back the sobs. Where was my armor, my strength? It was as if Connor punched his fist right through it and tore it from my body and left me raw and bleeding.

PERFECT RAGE

But he was the one raw and bleeding. Hurt. On edge. I saw the unsettled darkness in his eyes. No, I felt it.

London's hand rubbed up and down soothingly. "Shhh, it's okay. No one will hurt you."

I wasn't upset about the possibility of Connor hurting me. I was upset because he hurt. He would never forgive himself.

"Kai and I will take you home."

I shook my head. "I just need a minute."

"Yeah, we're in the back alley," Kai said into his cell. "He was here... need eyes on her house tonight." He lowered his phone, put it in his back pocket and looked at me. "What did Connor want?"

I wiped the tears from my face with the back of my sleeve and sniffed. "I... I...." I didn't know what to say. To tell me I shouldn't have risked being with him in Colombia? To ask me why I slept with him? To tell me he didn't know who he was anymore? "Nothing."

"He shows up in a bar filled with people he wants to think he's dead? Why? He wants something. And he wants that something from you."

Despite living among dangerous men my entire life, Kai was scarier, and I think it was because he had confidence without a weapon in his hand. Most of the men I'd been around were confident, but that was because they held a gun; without one, they were just pathetic assholes.

Besides, many of them pissed themselves when they fucked up and stood in front of Carlos. I couldn't imagine Kai trembling in fear even if some kingpin like Carlos had a gun to his head and a knife to his throat.

Neither would Connor.

"Kai," London said softly. "Not now."

His brows lifted slightly, but he didn't say anything.

The door swung open.

"Ernie," Kai said. "Close the door. We don't need Deck and Georgie hearing about this. Not tonight."

Ernie's eyes shifted to me, taking in my tears, then they went back to Kai before he nodded and closed the door behind him.

As soon as it clicked, Ernie said, "Matt saw it go down." His words were directed at Kai, but then he turned his attention to me and his voice softened. "You okay?"

No. "Yeah. It's fine. I'm fine."

Ernie was in his forties and he was Kai's man. He was a good guy. I knew that the second Deck introduced me to him on our way to Toronto from Colombia. His smile was genuine. No cruelty hid beneath the surface like Carlos or his right-hand man Diego. I'd liked him immediately.

But right now, there was no smile. "You don't look fine," Ernie said.

I remained quiet because if I spoke, the tears would start again and I'd be a quivering mess, but thankfully Kai spoke for me. "She needs to go home."

Deck had set me up in a quaint three-bedroom house, a block away from the beach. It had a perennial garden out front and a wide porch with an overhanging willow tree that desperately needed trimming. A friend of Deck's lived downstairs in the basement apartment. I had yet to meet him as Deck said the guy had flown home to Ireland for a couple months, but he was expected back any day now.

The door opened again and Matt appeared. "What's going on?"

Matt owned the bar Avalanche and I'd learned fast that he was really protective of his staff. He didn't let anything slide and his customers knew that. You messed with his staff, you were banned. Clear cut and simple. No second chances.

I felt safe working here and Matt made it that way.

"Alina?" Matt asked.

"We're handling it," Kai said.

Matt ignored Kai and moved closer to me. "Alina?"

"I'm okay, really, Matt."

PERFECT RAGE

His eyes narrowed. "I have rules at Avalanche. A guy making one of my girls cry is not okay. I deal with it and you come to work feeling safe knowing any guy gives you a hard time, won't set foot in here again. But if I don't know who put those tears on your face, I can't make sure you feel safe working here. You get what I'm saying?" His eyes remained locked on me until I nodded and then he shifted to the right to look at Kai. "I want answers."

Kai's brows lifted. "Just because Deck and I are now working together doesn't mean I'm cool with his friends."

Matt half smiled. "Good. We're on the same page. Makes things easier."

Kai chuckled. Then the grin slipped away as he said to Ernie, "Vic needs to stick around. Tell him whatever you want to make sure that happens, but Deck doesn't get wind of this tonight. I'll take her home and secure her house."

Ernie nodded. "I'll be right behind you."

Kai nodded. "Good."

"Be nice to know what the hell you guys are talking about?" Matt said.

"A situation. Ernie, give him what he needs. Babe." Kai held his hand out to London who took it, but she also put her arm around me.

Ernie opened the door and slipped inside. Matt hesitated looking at me. "Take a few days off. Come back to work when you can."

"I'll be here tomorrow." I liked working. It gave me a purpose and made me feel like I was living.

He hesitated before nodding and followed Ernie inside.

We walked to Kai's car parked in a Green P parking lot a block away from the bar. It was an impressive silver car with black leather seats and tinted windows. Classy, like he was, so they suited one another.

I sat in the back, staring out the window as Kai weaved in and out of the Friday night city traffic while London fiddled with the radio until she found a station playing jazz. She kept the volume low and I guessed she was fiddling because she was uncertain what to say to me.

Kai pulled up to the house and before I could unclip my seatbelt he ordered, "Key." He held out his hand to me. "Need to check the place."

"Umm, okay." Arguing with Kai didn't seem like a good idea, so I put my house key in his palm.

"Stay here." Then he opened his door, got out and walked up to my house. I didn't have the front porch light on and all I saw was a shadow then nothing as the massive willow tree blocked the view to the front door.

London shifted in her seat to half turn toward me. "You can stay with us if you want."

"Thank you, but I'm okay." And I was. I would be. Who wasn't okay was Connor and I was worried.

"Are you sure? Because—"

"I'm good."

"Okay." London was silent a minute while chewing on her lower lip. Then she said, "The drug... I've done a lot of research on it, but Alina, I don't know the long-term effects after withdrawal."

Because Connor had been Vault's only test subject.

Carlos had wanted me to know what he'd done to Connor. It was his way to torture me. Never physically. That wasn't his style. I knew London's father had developed the drug for Vault, heard his name mentioned a few times. What I hadn't known about until Deck told me was the compound with the kids. Kai and his sister, Chess, had grown up in a place like that. Cruel. Harsh. Training kids to be emotionless killers.

She continued, "My father warned us that abrupt withdrawal caused severe seizures... then death. Connor survived it." She paused, her grip on the back of her seat tightening. "But I don't know the damage it's done, Alina." She took a deep breath. "He looked pretty unstable tonight."

She was right. Connor was unstable.

Kai opened my car door. "House clear. Tomorrow I'll talk to Deck and we'll decide what to do."

What to do? "What do you—"

Kai interrupted, "Tomorrow an alarm will be installed. Eyes are on the house tonight."

I knew which eyes—Ernie's. "Umm, okay," I said because there was no choice in this. What made me nervous was the 'decide what to do'. They wouldn't hurt Connor, would they?

"Call if you need anything," London said.

I half smiled at London. "Thank you."

She smiled back.

I slid out, shut the door, thanked Kai then opened the busted green picket gate into the front yard. I walked along the uneven stone path, the overgrown wildflowers on either side of me swaying in the breeze and making a fluttering sound.

I stepped up onto the porch that desperately needed repainting then opened the door.

Kai drove away and I caught a glimpse of Ernie in his car across the street. I stepped inside and shut the door.

Only then did I slide to the floor and fall apart.

CHAPTER EIGHT

Question 4: Favorite color?

Alina

IT WAS FOUR in the morning and I stood on the porch under the low branch of the willow tree. I curled my hands around the wood railing, staring at nothing, just staring.

I couldn't sleep because every time I closed my eyes, I saw Connor.

So instead of fighting it, I distracted myself by cleaning the bathroom top to bottom, then when that was done, I scrubbed the tiled backsplash in the kitchen, then the floors, then the inside of the fridge.

It was cathartic and mind-numbing and yet when I was done, Connor still lingered.

God, it was there… in his eyes. The anguish. The anger. I searched and searched for the flicker of something, anything, of the man I once knew.

The man who made me laugh. The man who danced with me under the stars with the music trickling from the radio. The man who taught a six-year-old orphan girl with shoes three sizes too big to dance.

That man was gone.

The drug had stopped, his memory returned and he was free from Carlos and Vault, but Connor was now a prisoner of his memories.

I sensed his volatility and that scared me. *He* scared me.

But love wasn't a choice. And I loved him. I fell in love with him in Afghanistan and I loved him years later when Carlos brought him to Colombia as a cold-hearted and cruel killer. And I loved him now.

A dog howled in the distance and then another joined in. I closed my eyes, listening to the sounds while I breathed in the cool night air.

The porch boards creaked behind me. I spun, but not fast enough and a hand clamped over my mouth. I was yanked backward to land against a hard chest then dragged into the darkness of the far corner of the porch where the light failed to illuminate and a tree concealed us from the street.

My scream came out muffled and barely audible.

"Shhh," he murmured against my ear.

Connor?

His warm breath wafted over the side of my neck and goose bumps popped along my skin. But it wasn't from fear, well, maybe a little, but it was more an awareness. Like my body awakened to his touch.

"They put a man on you."

Ernie. He'd seen Ernie. Connor managed to get by an ex-navy SEAL. It shouldn't surprise me. He excelled at being invisible. But the question was had Ernie seen him?

"He's good. Took two hours before I had the chance." And he'd always been patient. "Are you going to stay quiet if I remove my hand?"

I did my best to nod, but his grip on me was constricting and I only managed a slight dip of my chin. His hand slid from my mouth to the curve of my neck where his fingers enclosed, not harsh, but firm.

His rough whisper rumbled, "Can't leave yet. Tried to. Bike found its way back here." His body stiffened. "I don't know what the hell I'm doing."

Oh, God. I squeezed my eyes shut as tears pooled. I was uncertain what he'd do to me right now. He was on edge, but I couldn't stop the overwhelming need to curl into his arms and take his pain away.

His body stiffened and his forearm across my breasts squeezed. I whimpered under the pressure, but didn't struggle.

"I'm sorry. Fuck, I'm so sorry about your family, shutterbug."

My breath locked and a tear teetered then fell. Wetness trailed down my cheek. I hadn't heard him call me that in eleven years and it was as if I were back there with him, falling in love all over again.

His fingers splayed on my neck gently applied more pressure. It wasn't restricting, but it was controlling and I knew he'd easily cut off air if he wanted to. But I trusted that Connor would never willingly hurt me.

It was the graze of his lips on the edge of my jaw that sent my heart rocketing and my belly into a perpetual whoosh. Confusion and desire clashed as my body and mind fought against one another.

"You should've chosen me," he murmured.

I had chosen him. Everything I'd done was me choosing him. But that wasn't what he was talking about.

"You should've chosen me," he repeated then nibbled on the lobe of my ear, his teeth grazing the sensitive skin. "Why? Why didn't you kill me instead?"

Oh, God, Connor.

He was referring to one of Carlos's games. The day I was forced to make a choice. Shoot Connor or one of his men.

Connor protected. It was who he was and they'd taken that from him. He remembered what he'd done while he was on the drug and it was killing him.

He'd never forgive himself.

It was why he said I chose wrong and should've killed him.

But no matter who they made him into, I couldn't. And Carlos knew that.

The pulse in my neck throbbed beneath his fingertips and tingles erupted. My body recognized him and always would.

He groaned, arm holding me locked to his chest, sliding down my front then fingers skimming my bare skin between my waistband and my top. Sparks ignited as his thumb stroked back and forth just above my hip. His hand on my throat released and moved to cup my chin.

It was unyielding and harsh as he forced my head to tilt to the side and up, where our eyes met. Everything in me stilled for a split second before my heart shot off into a wild frenzy and shivers rushed through me.

"Connor," I breathed.

He towered over me from behind, head bent, lips a breath away. Only in my fairy tale did Connor appear like this. Holding me. Looking down at me, the moonlight illuminating the side of his face. I wanted to catch this moment with my camera so I'd never lose it.

But I'd never take a photograph again. Never.

My heart had been permanently damaged when I was forced to leave him. Nothing could've stopped the pain and I hadn't fought it; instead, I'd embraced it.

Craved it.

I'd needed to feel the pain of losing him over and over again. It was my reminder of him. It kept him alive within me.

Our time had been a mere breath in the wind, but I'd left with a lifetime of love. I'd walked away thinking he would spend his life doing what he loved. I'd survive Carlos and what I had to because Connor was safe.

But he wasn't safe.

It blew up in my face the day I walked into Carlos's living room and saw the photographs I'd taken of Connor and me strewn all over the glass coffee table.

Then my world fell apart.

My heart broke.

My insides splintered.

Disjointed. That was when it happened. Every part of me disconnected and the light went out. Darkness. Complete darkness.

Connor's grip on me tightened and I looked up into his tumultuous blue eyes.

His brows furrowed, fingers bruising on my chin. "You were fuckin' mine," he said in a harsh, grated tone.

Then his mouth slammed down on mine. Our teeth hit as he claimed my lips with a sweet desperation.

And I surrendered. There was no other way. We'd never had a choice in us.

We were.

We are.

And neither of us could change that. Our link to one another was unbreakable by time, by cruelty, by drugs, or even by death.

His kiss was starved, unforgiving and cruel like what we'd both been dealt in life. But it was real. It was him and within the bruising kiss, it was beauty.

"Fuck." His lips vibrated against mine before he pulled back abruptly, but it was only to bring me closer as he swung me around to face him. It was fast and hard, and knocked the air from my lungs when I landed against his chest. I managed a short inhale before his mouth crashed onto mine again.

Unbending.

Ravenous.

And I wanted more. God, I wanted more of him. It would never be enough. With him the hunger would never be satisfied. No matter who

PERFECT RAGE

we'd been, our bodies knew where we belonged.

He pulled back. "Go inside. I'll meet you there."

I nodded then he leapt over the porch railing and disappeared in the shadows. I walked to the front door, opened the screen and it made a loud squeak. I went inside, wondering if this was right.

We were too damaged to be together.

Too broken to find our way back to what we used to be.

But when he appeared in my back hallway, strode toward me then picked me up in his arms and carried me to my bedroom, I didn't argue.

I didn't stop him. I didn't ask how he knew where my bedroom was. I didn't care.

I wanted this.

He set me on my feet then moved into me. The backs of my legs hit the mattress and I tipped backward then bounced on the bed.

He shifted to the side and I heard a clunk as he put something on the nightstand. The mattress sagged under his weight as one knee pressed into it beside my thigh then the other followed as he straddled me.

His hand slipped beneath my white camisole and I sucked in air. He caressed up my abdomen to my ribs, his fingers gently stroking beneath one breast. Then the other.

My insides quaked and burned. I wanted him to touch my breasts so goddamn bad.

His thumb brushed over my erect nipple. Once.

Twice.

Three times.

I whimpered and arched into him. "Please," I begged.

I didn't want gentle and slow anymore. I wanted uncontrolled and raw—unrestrained and powerful.

That was what we were. A desire that conquered.

He broke our kiss and hovered above me, his chest heaving in and out while he looked at me. I slid my hand up his arm to his shoulder then around to the back of his neck where I weaved my fingers into his hair.

His hair.

He'd had short-cropped hair when we first met, then in Colombia it was a little longer, but now the dirty-blond strands were unruly subtle waves and hung a couple of inches below his ears.

Playful like he was. Or had been. There was nothing playful in him anymore.

"Kiss me, Connor," I said while tugging on his hair and attempting to bring his mouth back to mine, but he resisted.

He blinked several times then squinted and shook his head, dislodging my hand from his hair. His temples throbbed and his lips pursed. A low growl emerged and he ground out, "Fuuucck."

My heart pounded as the agonizing sound ripped from his throat. "Connor?"

His thighs clamped mine as his body tightened, the muscles in his neck strained as he stared up at the ceiling.

"Connor? What's wrong?" My stomach twisted and terror gripped me. What was happening? God, he looked as if he were in agony. "Connor? Please, you're scaring me."

Had I missed something? Was he hurt? My eyes and hands ran down his shirt looking for blood, anything that might explain what was wrong.

His eyes flashed open.

My breath hitched. The surfaces of his eyes were glassy and wet with a haunting darkness lingering behind the pain.

"Please, tell me what's wrong?" I begged in a choked whisper as my hands moved up his abdomen to his chest.

He held my eyes for a few seconds before he lowered his head to rest it in the crook of my neck. His breathing heavy, palms flat on the mattress, elbows bent on either side of me at my shoulders holding some of his weight.

"Connor?" I whispered.

He didn't answer or move for a minute.

When he finally lifted his head, he said, "Alina."

Then his mouth found mine again. But this time, it was a gentle caress, tasting, savoring.

He nipped my lower lip then kissed the spot with a light playfulness. Then his kiss deepened, our mouths melded.

Whatever had caused that pained look had faded and I felt the give in his body as he relaxed, his hand now cupping the back of my neck, fingers bunched in my hair.

My belly was in a unending free fall, thighs trembling and between my legs quivering with the sweet squeezes. "I need you. I've always needed you."

He broke from our kiss and pushed up, so his arms were straight. Then he stole my breath away when I saw the tiniest twitch at the corner of his mouth and his eyes sparked.

There.

Right there was the piece of Connor my heart ached for.

It had been hidden behind a shield of... rage. Memories. Agony. All of them tied together.

But within a flash it was gone again.

His hand tightened in my hair as he said, "I'm leaving. After tonight I won't be back. I can't, baby. What I did, who I am now... ." He paused, eyes darkening. "Nothing of this night passes your lips."

"But we can get help. We can—"

His grip in my hair tightened as he scowled. "No. You'll say nothing and I'm not staying. Do you understand me?"

I nodded. "Yes." I'd do anything he asked of me and I'd take once over nothing. I'd always take once because I knew that life could throw a curve at any time. I knew what it was like to lose.

And I wasn't losing this moment he was giving me.

"Connor?"

His scowl lingered and I wanted it gone. "Yeah?"

I ran my hand down his back and felt the scars, scars that hadn't been there when we first met. My stomach twisted at the thought of what he'd been through.

"I left you that day, but I left me too. I left *me* with you." He remained quiet so I continued, "When I dreamed, those dreams of you kept me sane when all I wanted to do was to go insane missing you."

"Dreams that turned into nightmares," he said between clenched teeth. "I fucked you and I hadn't been nice about it."

He had. "It was still you," I said quietly.

"Yeah," he murmured.

"And it's you now," I said then added in a whisper, "I missed you. I missed you every single day we weren't together."

He hesitated then something gave as his expression and the lines around his mouth eased. He didn't respond. Instead, he kissed me. It was brief and hard, but it was enough to tell me that he'd missed me too.

He sat up. "Shirt."

He gripped the bottom edge of my camisole and I half lifted as he pulled it over my head then tossed it aside. He crossed his arms and yanked his black T-shirt over his head and I was left staring at his naked muscled chest. My eyes trailed over his beautiful tattoos over his left pectoral, to his shoulder and down his bicep to his elbow. He'd told me it took ten sessions for the artist to complete the intricate tattoo. What I hadn't seen was a new one under his left arm and down his ribs. I was unable to see all of it, but I caught a glimpse of what looked like numbers within a web of complex lines.

My eyes hit his hard abdomen then traveled back up again. Connor was breathtaking. Always had been. He just did it for me.

The type of guy who you see across the room and know there is something between you. An energy. A connection.

My eyes cut to his cargo pants that sat perfectly on his hips, cock straining against the material.

Connor was here. He was here and he remembered.

I trailed my fingertips down the center of his chest to the cusp of his pants. My eyes lifted to his and his nostrils flared and eyes burned as he watched me. I popped the button through the slit and his chest expanded as his breath caught.

My body was an inferno as the anticipation built, ready to explode the moment he finally sank inside me again.

He was on his knees, hands resting on his thighs, but they weren't resting; they were strained and tight.

I dragged down his zipper, my fingers brushing against his hard bulge. He stiffened. Eyes widening for a second, he exhaled as the zipper reached the end. Only then did my eyes leave his and go to his cock, rock hard and pushing against the black cotton material.

I grazed my knuckles over the hard bulge. Up. Then down again. Barely touching, but enough to feel it jerk.

I swallowed. Almost afraid to end the anticipation and yet unable to control my need any longer and by the sound of his ragged breathing, neither was he.

I slipped my hand in his boxer briefs and he sucked in air then groaned as my fingers enclosed around his heated cock.

"Fuck!" Connor roared and it was loud. Really loud.

A door slammed.

I froze.

Connor stiffened.

It sounded like the side door, the basement apartment. "I think it's—"

His eyes landed on me and he shook his head once.

I shut up. I was going to tell him about the guy who lived downstairs who was expected back any day, but I was worried that it was Ernie.

He lifted, grabbed my wrist, yanked my hand from his pants,

tossed me to the side and climbed to his feet. He reached over to the nightstand, eyes never leaving the door as he snagged the gun off the surface.

A gun? When had he put a gun there? What scared me was why he had one.

I hated guns. I knew how to shoot and had grown up around them and I never had an issue until that day Carlos forced me to choose. Ever since, I felt sick whenever I saw one or heard the loud bang. But worse than both of those was the smell in the air after a gun fired. I'd never forget that smell.

I sat up as he strode to the door, opened it then disappeared.

He was gone for maybe three minutes, but it felt like forever and I was nervous. He obviously didn't want anyone to know he was here and I was uncertain the lengths he'd go to make sure that happened.

I didn't hear him come back down the hallway. He suddenly appeared in the doorway, gun at his side.

I scooted up the bed as he stalked across the room toward me. He set the gun back on the nightstand then his hands went to the waist of his pants and he lowered them.

I wanted to ask if everything was okay, but I didn't because he was taking off his pants and he wouldn't be doing that if everything wasn't okay.

My lips parted and breath hitched as I watched him bend, step out of them then move to his boxer briefs. With this, he was quicker as he shoved them down his muscular thighs and stepped out of them.

There was no insecurity with Connor. No inhibition as he stood in front of me naked. He'd never been shy about his body and I loved that about him, even if at the time he'd been annoyingly cocky about it.

But there was no playful cockiness about him now. Intense. Dangerous.

But he was real. And real would always… always… be better than imagined and I'd imagined him a lot.

Every day we were apart, I'd imagined the smell of him with each inhale. The taste of him, the touch, the sound. God, the sound of his voice was enough to send me over the brink and into the abyss of Connor.

My imagination, my dreams, and yeah, the nightmares, couldn't compare to this, even if he was different, even if I was scared of him.

The mattress dipped as he leaned a knee on it, the other following. I tried to sit up so I could move into him and taste his lips, but he placed his palm on my ribcage and pushed me back down.

"No. Wait for me."

I'd wait for him. I'd wait forever. And I had a feeling when he left tonight, it would be forever.

His hands paused on the ribbon of my white pajama pants and he scowled. I noticed the immediate change in him as his body tensed, mouth got tight and his chest rose and fell erratically.

Like before, he squeezed his eyes closed, bowed his head then shook it. His hand left me and went to his temple where he bunched his hair in his grip and groaned.

I laid my hand on his chest, feeling his heart beat erratically beneath my touch. "Connor," I said, but he didn't respond. "Look at me." He flinched and he was so tense that his legs clamped around me hurt. "Let me help."

"You can't," he said in a strained voice.

"But—"

"Don't you get it?" he barked. "It's too fuckin' late."

I sucked in air at his harsh, cruel tone that reminded me of the Connor in Colombia.

His eyes flashed open and within the depths was pure rage. And what was worse, I didn't think he even saw me. It was as if he stared right through me.

My eyes widened when his arm drew back, hand curled into a fist. *Oh, God.*

I didn't move, but closed my eyes, waiting for the pain. For the crunch of bone when his fist plowed into my face.

I heard a loud thud behind my head at the same time as he shouted, "Fuck. No!"

I slowly opened my eyes. Flecks of drywall were on the pillow beside me and Connor's arm was lowered, as was his head, so I couldn't see his eyes.

It terrified me seeing him like this, a man who had so easily grinned and teased. Who lived in the present. Who had passionately loved his family and friends. Protected them. This was harder to see than when he'd been on the drug.

He collapsed to the side of me, tatted forearm draped over his eyes. His chest rose and fell in harsh ragged breaths as if he'd run a marathon. A bead of sweat dripped down his cheek to the edge of his jaw.

I shuffled onto my side, leaning over him and caught it with the pad of my finger.

"Connor?"

He didn't say anything.

"Connor," I begged. I rested my hand on his abdomen. "What's happening?"

He moved fast, arm moving off his face and then his hand latched onto my wrist and pulled it away from his abdomen.

"Talk to me," I said quietly.

He scowled and flung my arm away. Sitting up, he swung his legs over the side of the bed. He bent, elbows resting on his knees, head cradled in his hands.

"I don't want to fuckin' talk, Alina."

"Okay. Then come back to me."

His spine stiffened, but he remained where he was as he growled, "I almost hit you."

I shifted onto my knees, came up behind him then gently lowered my hands onto his shoulders. I hesitated a second to see if he'd throw me off, but he didn't, so I peppered a trail of kisses across his neck.

"You didn't," I murmured. "You won't." Although, I wasn't completely certain of that. "Give us this, Connor."

He didn't move.

"You won't hurt me."

He hands dropped to his thighs and he lifted his head and when he did, it was slow and methodical. He turned to face me. "Damn it, you don't know that!" he growled. "You don't know me at all. And you didn't fuckin' know me in Colombia. You fucked a stranger. I was a stranger."

"No. Connor, no. Even when you didn't know who you were, I did. I knew. And I know you'd never hit me," I said softly. "Please. Come back to me."

I didn't know how long I waited before he finally sighed, closing his eyes, the lines on his face easing.

He edged back on the bed, moved over top of me. Grabbing the underside of my thighs, he slid his hand down to my calves then yanked so I lay flat on my back.

His hands went to my pajama pants again and he slowly untied the bow. His fingers curled around the waistband and he peeled them off.

It was silly at a time like this, but I secretly thanked God I was wearing a nice pair of panties, although they were not my favorite color. Since I'd had to leave everything behind in Colombia, when we reached Toronto, Deck's man, the scary Victor Gate who I'd first seen playing football at the base a million years ago, took me to the shopping mall.

It was obvious he wasn't happy about it as he waited outside the stores with a fierce scowl. I even noticed customers avoid walking into the stores when they noticed him lingering.

Essentials to me were nice panties and bras and Vic was not impressed it took me so long to pick out the panties and bras. After half an hour he'd marched in, grabbed a shitload of thong panties from a bin, piled them in my arms, shoved me toward the counter and said to the sales lady, "Ring them up." Then he tossed down the plastic. Deck's company credit card.

I didn't argue even if some of them were the wrong size.

I tried to pay Deck back with my tips from Avalanche over the last few weeks, but he'd refused and arguing with Deck was pretty much the same as arguing with any of these men. Battles were picked carefully and that was not one I'd win.

The dark purple thong I wore now had a lavender frill along the top edge and pink bow on the front. But it also had elephants printed on them.

Connor's fingers hooked the edge of the material and I watched his eyes blaze as he took them in.

Nothing was more erotic than having this man appreciate my panties. It was so simple in the course of what was happening right now, yet I needed something as simple and normal as him loving me in lace with a cute pink bow, lavender frill, although I wasn't sure about the elephants.

And to make it even better, when his eyes finished taking them in, they lifted to mine and there was a subtle twitch of amusement playing at the corners of his mouth.

I melted. God, I melted.

"Elephants, baby?"

I smiled. "Yeah." I kept it to myself that these particular panties were in the 'Vic arm sweep' and I hadn't picked them out. But they were sexy and cute, so I liked them.

He closed his eyes and took a deep inhale. When he opened them again, he said, "Missed this," he murmured, his voice all husky. "Missed it so fuckin' much." His finger slid back and forth under the edge of the material.

Goose bumps rose across my heated skin. "Me too." God, me too.

He tensed for a second then relaxed again before he leaned over the side of the bed, snagged his pants and reached in the side pocket. I heard the crinkle of foil and a tear. He then slid on a condom.

When he glanced at me again, his mouth was tight and brows low. "The gun," he said. I frowned, glancing at it sitting on the nightstand then back at him. "Use it, if you need to."

"Huh?" What was he talking about?

His hand moved fast as he cupped my chin. "Don't always know what I'm doing. You've seen that twice now." His eyes hardened. "I lose it… this time, you choose me. Don't fuckin' hesitate."

Oh. My. God. "Connor? Are you insane?" I balked, horrified, my stomach twisting as I realized what he was saying. He wanted me to use it on him. I wouldn't even touch a gun anymore.

His fingers tightened on my jaw. "I just punched the wall behind your head, seeing something other than you, not knowing what the fuck I was doing. Missed you by inches. Next time it might be your face."

"You wouldn't—"

He abruptly cut me off. "You don't know fuckin' shit what's going on inside my head, Alina."

I swallowed, throat tight. He was right. I may have thought I knew who this man was on top of me, but the reality was I didn't. But I hadn't known him in Colombia either and he'd been a much more dangerous man than he was now.

His grip hardened. His eyes hardened. And his voice hardened. "Swear it or I leave right now."

My heart slammed into my chest. I didn't want him to leave.

He moved to get off the bed when I grabbed his wrist. "No. Please… I will. If I need to." It wasn't exactly a lie.

He stared at me as if taking his time judging on whether this was still a good idea or not. He could easily go for the gun and outmaneuver me. He was elite ex-military and a trained killer, but I suspected Connor wouldn't, no matter what was screwing with his head. He'd react before he lost it and get as far from the gun as he could.

I glanced at the gun then tilted my head and peered back at him. His face was stoic and unflinching then he nodded.

He gripped his cock in his fist before sliding it down my wet sex.

"Connor," I breathed. My body tingled and ached for him so bad.

"Say my name again," he said.

"Connor," I replied then reached for him.

He drew back. "Don't touch me."

I paused, not liking that but nodded. "Okay."

He pressed the head of his cock at my entrance then with a slow glide, he tilted his hips and pushed inside of me.

I gasped, eyes closed, head back, body arched.

"You clenched around my cock and barely breathing… so fuckin' good." His words growled into my ear.

I pushed my hips up.

"Stay still," he ordered. He kissed along my jaw, down my neck then across my collarbone to my shoulder where he nibbled then licked.

"Connor, please." I wanted him to move. Needed to feel his cock slide in and out of me. Hard. Soft. Whatever he wanted as long as he moved.

"Wait. Need you to wait, baby. I can't… ." He stopped and inhaled a ragged breath. "I can't forget this."

"You won't." But I'd give him whatever he wanted. We'd do this anyway he wanted.

He was on his knees, weight lifted, but still deep inside me. He trailed one finger down between my breasts, over my abdomen then between us as he coated the pad of his finger with my wetness. Then he pressed on my clit.

I sucked in air. A volley of heat shooting through me.

"Love you like this." He started slow and controlled, circling the spot that nurtured deep inner waves of desire. "Under my control. Powerless to deny me."

My hands fisted in the pillow on either side of me. "Oh, God. Yes."

His finger played, tantalized, explored then when I was close, he stopped. I was panting and ready to scream with frustration. He must have sensed it because he leaned over me, mouth next to my ear.

"You'll wait for me."

I frantically nodded. "Okay." I'd said okay numerous times now. But there were no other words. He stole them with his touch. He smothered them with his kisses. All I had left was 'okay' because I'd do anything he asked right now.

Then his finger circled my throbbing sex again and I quivered beneath his touch, legs shaking, body aching.

"Please, Connor. I need you to move."

His body left me and that meant so did his cock and I felt empty. God, so empty.

His hand wrapped around his thick length.

Our eyes locked and the corner of his lips curved upward.

I couldn't take my gaze off him, as he placed the finger coated with my wetness into his mouth and sucked. "Missed tasting you."

I wanted Connor to sink inside me without control. I wanted his hands on me. I wanted his mouth. I wanted everything.

He guided his cock's tip into me again.

"Fuck, so tight." With one hand on my hip, he gripped me before he shoved his hips forward and his cock sank deep again.

I moaned, closing my eyes.

He moved slowly at first then he plunged harder. Faster. Our naked bodies smacking together. "Fuckin' beautiful."

The bedframe creaked with his thrusts.

"Oh, God," I panted.

"Jesus," he murmured.

Our eyes locked and I disappeared into him. Into his eyes. Into his body.

His muscles bulged as he moved, hand gliding up my body to my breast.

I arched, belly dropping when his fingers tweaked my nipple. He groaned as he bowed his head, mouth taking hold of the sensitive flesh and suckling. His teeth scraped, his heated wet tongue swirled and I closed my eyes, tilting my head back.

His mouth left my breast and he sprinkled kisses up my collarbone to my neck then my chin until finally he reached my mouth. "I need to kiss you when I make you come."

"Okay," I whispered in a ragged voice.

"Okay," he repeated and then he smiled. It was brief and subtle and it lasted only a second before it was gone. He raised his hips then thrust hard into me again at the same time as his mouth crushed mine in a wild frenzy.

I took a chance he'd be okay with me touching him and slid my hand down his arm until my fingers found his then I linked them together on the pillow above my head.

Connor kissed me while he fucked me.

While he took every part of me.

My body stiffened and legs quivered as I teetered on the edge. "Connor… God…!" I clamped my thighs around him as I came—hard.

My body shuddered in huge waves over and over again.

"Fuck!" he growled then followed with his own orgasm, his last two thrusts harsh before his body stiffened and a low groan erupted.

Then everything stopped.

No movement except our chests heaving in and out, his cock still inside me.

Slowly, he lifted.

My eyes hit his and disappointment blanketed me when I was met with a fierce scowl. His brows dropped over his narrowed magnificent blue eyes.

Then he said, "I forgot. Jesus, I forgot you. How could I ever forget you? I fucked you and I didn't know who you were." He bowed his head and kissed me again, slow and lingering and I ignored what he told me about touching him and slid my hand up his arm, over his shoulder to his back then up to his neck where my fingers weaved into his hair.

"You knew," I said softly. "Somewhere inside, you knew."

He didn't say anything, but I felt the tension in his body. He didn't believe me.

Then he lifted, climbed out of bed and stood.

I sat upright, heart still pounding from the sex, but also from what I knew was going to happen now.

I couldn't stop it.

Nothing would shield the hurt.

And there was nothing I could say that would change the outcome.

I watched him dress with his back to me then he walked to the bedside table, picked up his gun and shoved it in the waist of his cargo pants.

Look at me, Connor. Please, don't leave without looking at me.

He didn't.

Not once.

He strode to the door then hesitated with his hand on the doorframe. I held my breath hoping he'd turn, praying he'd come back to me. Say something.

Connor strode out and disappeared.

CHAPTER NINE

Connor

AFTER I LEFT her, I rode the highway until the sun rose and burned away the wet pavement. I was soaked, pants plastered to my legs, leather jacket ruined, hand glued to the throttle as I revved the engine faster, harder. Pushing the limits and trying to ease the rage.

I was impulsive, too impulsive.

I walked into the bar because I had to see her right then. I showed up at her house with Kai's man watching because I had to be with her tonight. My control was nonexistent when it came to Alina.

After hours of riding, I finally turned off the highway, took a few side streets and then pulled over on the shoulder. I parked near the boardwalk at the beach where a few joggers passed. I took off my helmet and gloves before getting off.

PERFECT RAGE

Some chick jogging past glanced at me, slowed her pace and bravely smiled. I didn't.

I pocketed my keys then walked across the beach. The sand clung to my wet boots and the bottom of my pants as I made my way to the water. The beach was deserted, probably because it was cool and too early.

The subtle sound of the waves rhythmically easing up on shore was soothing. I'd always found water calming even in JTF2 training when we had grueling drills in the water. It was where I excelled. It was where I'd kicked Deck's ass.

I stared across the lake.

It was wrong, so fuckin' wrong me coming home, being close to her, bringing her into my darkness. She deserved freedom from all that shit and I was bringing it back into her life.

But I couldn't stay away. How the hell could I stay away?

I sat on the sand, bent my knees, arms hanging over them as I listened to the waves. I was so fuckin' tired.

I rarely slept and when I did, it was with my nightmares. I fell back on the sand and closed my eyes.

Then I stopped fighting.

I lay facedown on a steel table in a dark, musty basement with the scent of piss and death. And I knew death. I'd witnessed horrific conditions, seen footage of what happened to prisoners. As one of the elite military of JTF2, we were prepared for capture, trained to endure pain.

Time no longer made sense as they kept me awake for days, weeks.... Fuck I didn't know how long I'd been here. Everything was a blur, my mind a black hole filled with nightmares.

I had no idea who these people were or where I was. The last thing I remember was riding in the Humvee with my team when all went to hell.

Chaos. A blast took out the vehicle in front and I couldn't see shit. I went to radio Deck who was ahead, but I didn't get the chance.

Another blast hit the back of us then nothing.

I woke up with steel clamps snapped around my wrists and ankles. My dog tags gone and minor burns covered my arm and right side.

I didn't fight the shackles because it was pointless. They were unbreakable, but then so was I. And they'd eventually find that out.

Whatever they wanted from me, they wouldn't get, although they had yet to ask me any questions. I suspected they were trying to break me first, make me beg.

I'd die before I gave into these bastards and death was a good possibility. If I was here as ransom, ransoms weren't paid. The only way I was getting out of here was a Special Ops extraction and Deck and the JTF2 team were the ones to do it. That was if they knew I was alive.

I gritted my teeth as the familiar sound of chains being rolled through the pulley echoed in the cell. There was one bright light above me like a spotlight and it gave off intense heat onto my naked bleeding back.

I knew torture tactics. Shit, I'd seen them and whoever these people were, they had a handbook on them. I embraced fear. Lived my life as an adrenaline junky, liked the rush, the anticipation of doing something that could kill you.

There was no adrenaline rush for what was to come in this underground hell; instead, I felt calm. Fear ate your sanity. It took your control and I was also a control junky. Fuck, it wasn't always a great quality, but I wasn't perfect.

The chains grew taut and my muscles strained as they stretched, legs kept locked to the end of the table. I closed my eyes, cheek resting against the hard, smooth surface of the table then concentrated on my breathing.

The clinking of chains stopped with a bang as they were locked in place. Burning pain tore through my limbs and despite trying to relax, my body trembled under the pressure of being stretched past its limits.

"You going to say something one of these fuckin' days?" I asked.

PERFECT RAGE

The words were difficult to get out with my dry throat and I coughed several times which jerked the chains and hurt like a fucker.

There was a shuffle of feet and low, indistinguishable whispers behind me. A door opened and closed.

Fuck.

I'd be here a while, probably until I passed out and then they'd find a way to keep me awake. And they seemed to know when I was about to pass out so I knew they had a camera in the cell.

Fuck them.

Fuck all of them.

I was a crap singer, at least my sister told me I was, which made this all the sweeter if they were listening.

My throat killed and it hurt like hell, but I sang anyway.

I fuckin' sang the Canadian national anthem twelve times before some guy came and gagged me.

CHAPTER TEN

Question 5: How do you take your coffee?

Alina

I WOKE TO KNOCKING and then a girl's muffled call. "Alina?"
It was London.
I moaned, flopping onto my back, arm over my eyes to block the morning sun and wishing I'd closed the window and the drapes last night.
Last night.
Then it all flooded back.
Connor.
Inside me.
His mouth on mine.
Punching the wall.

PERFECT RAGE

The anguish on his face.

I darted upright and looked at the empty spot beside me where Connor had been hours before.

He was gone, but then I'd seen him leave.

And I didn't know if I'd ever see him again.

I closed my eyes as an intense ache hit my chest. No, it was more than an ache; it was emptiness which was far worse. Pain meant I felt. This... this was nothing, just a cold, dark hole left inside me. He took it with him.

He told me he couldn't stay. I knew that before I slept with him. It didn't make it hurt any less.

"*Pet*, you need to cool it with the knocking." I frowned at the accented, unfamiliar male voice. Who was that?

The door slamming last night. It had been the guy living downstairs.

I strained to hear London's reply, but it was muffled.

"Flew in late last night..." His voice lowered and I couldn't hear what else he said.

But I heard London retort. "You did *not* just ask me that?"

He laughed then, "Guess that's a no."

"It's a hell no."

Then he said, "Spare key is under the blue gnome with the red overalls."

Oh, my God, the guy knew where a key was to the house? Well, my part of the house.

I threw my legs over the side of the bed, my feet hitting the smooth hardwood, then grabbed my pants from the oversized lounge chair in the corner of the room and tugged them on. I snagged a light pullover and put it on as I ran down the hall, down the stairs and yanked open the front door.

London stood looking a little flustered as she held her cell in her hand. Shit, I'd turned my ringer off at work and never thought to turn it back on with everything that happened.

"I tried calling first," she said.

"Sorry, I had the ringer off."

My eyes shifted to the guy leaning against the porch railing watching us. Wow. He was so not like Deck or any of the other guys.

He was covered in tattoos and I mean covered. Arms. Neck. Throat. And he had a trimmed, neat beard with dark brown hair chin-length in the front and cropped short in the back. He had an attractive face, defined and masculine with eyes that drooped in the outer corners giving him a doleful look, but it contradicted the twinkle in the hazel depths.

He also smelled like coffee and cigarettes with a hint of aftershave.

Deck knew this guy? And he thought he was cool living downstairs? He didn't seem like he'd fit in with Deck and his commando guys. And he definitely didn't fit as a friend of Kai's.

My eyes shifted down his cut body to his legs in snug, worn jeans that had a rip in the left knee and then back up again.

When my eyes met his, he grinned at me, having obviously noticed my perusal. "Deaglan," he offered. "Your roomie. You must be Catalina? Deck said you moved in upstairs." He stepped forward, holding out his hand.

"Please, call me Alina." I hated anyone calling me Catalina ever since Carlos.

I politely shook his hand, despite being a little peeved that he was giving out a spare key to my part of the house. I didn't mind because it was London, but that wasn't the point.

He had callouses on his palm, and his handshake was firm. I expected it to be though; he had an air of confidence about him, but not surprising with the way he held himself. "You have a key?"

His brows lifted. A slow smirk emerged and he had deep dimples. "Sure, pet. Why wouldn't I?"

"Because I live here. And I wouldn't say roommates exactly," I corrected.

He shrugged. "Same house. But whatever you want to call it, good with me. Not particular who I live with unless you're wanting me to fix the shelves for those freaky little statues. You see those things?" I had, but I didn't respond and he obviously didn't expect me to because he went on. "Mamó Kane collected them."

"Mamó?" I asked.

"Grandmother. She was my dad's mother. Her house." He shook his head. "Fuckin' sweetest woman you ever met. A man can't meet that woman and not love her. She had this garden on the side of the house," he nodded to the right, "grew carrots and shit, she'd be out there before the crack of dawn digging in the dirt. Miss seeing her there." He lifted his brows and asked, "You still have all her knickknacks up? I can load them in a box. Never got around to doing that after she passed."

"I'm sorry for your loss. And the statues are fine." I didn't take the guy for a rambler and it wasn't a nervous ramble. It was more as if he wanted to talk about his grandmother. It was kind of sweet how he talked about her garden.

London frowned, asking, "Wait a sec. Kane?"

"Yeah. Killian's grandmother," he said.

"Killian?" I asked.

London replied, "The band that played last night. Killian is the drummer. Everyone calls him Kite though," London said.

Oh, right. The drummer who had a brow piercing and tattoos... My eyes darted to Deaglan's as did London's, who then asked, "So you're—?"

"Cousins," he replied. "Our dad's are brothers. Met Deck a long time ago through Killian. Was taking the wrong road in life and he straightened me out. Now do odd jobs for him. Run in the same circles."

"Baby, are you coming back to bed," a female voice called.

Deaglan winked at me then grinned at London. "Last chance."

Last chance?

"You're a dick," London said.

He shrugged. "I'm a twenty-eight-year-old guy. What do you expect?"

He strolled toward the side railing then put both hands on it and hopped over the side and disappeared, but we heard him. "Babe, fuck, get that sexy uniform back on. You need to vacate. Told you, I have shit to do today. Thought you were working another flight?"

Whoa. Vacate? Get dressed? I turned to London and both of us stood with gaping mouths.

London said, "Not sure how Deck is friends with that guy, even if he is related to Kite."

Yeah, I wasn't sure either. "Did you want to come in for a coffee?" I asked.

"Sure. I came by to see if you wanted to go to the Center with me. Chess is meeting me there."

"Umm, okay. I'd like that," I said.

Chess was Kai's sister and I met her a few times. She came across as incredibly strong-willed, but friendly and warm. I'd liked her immediately, especially when I'd heard about the place for the kids.

It was a project Tristan Mason, Chess's man who owned Mason Developments, was building for the kids rescued from the compound. It was called the Treasured Children's Center and was a project that gained lots of attention considering the size of it and the media coverage over getting the kids immigrated into Canada.

My paperwork was still being processed, but in the meantime, thanks to Deck, I had a temporary visa to stay and work here.

"Do you think Ernie wants coffee?" I asked, glancing out to the street where his car had been last night. I didn't really want to talk to Ernie after Connor managed to sneak by him, but I did feel bad he'd been out there all night.

"Ernie left and is with Kai and the guys."

"Oh." I held the screen door open and London stepped inside. I followed, letting the screen door clang closed behind me. I didn't bother shutting the solid door.

We walked past the wooden staircase, down the narrow hall with the printed floral wallpaper to the small but quaint olive-green kitchen. The fridge was old with an oversized metal handle and made a constant loud humming sound. The yellow ceramic tiled backsplash clashed with the green walls and screamed 1950s, as did the crown molding above the cupboards. But I loved the crown molding and it was in every room throughout the house.

I pictured Deaglan's grandmother, pottering around the house with a warm smile. Then I pictured this tall, tatted-up guy trailing after her as she rambled on about what she needed fixing.

It was cute and sweet.

"Kai would go insane in a house like this," London said as she peered around the kitchen. "We live in a warehouse, open concept, modern, simple and definitely no knickknacks." She picked up a little dog statue from the shelf above the kitchen table. "I should get one of these and put it on the coffee table. See how long it takes him to notice. Then when he does, I'll tell him it's practice for the real thing."

"Are you getting a dog?"

"Kai with a dog?" She laughed. "No chance. I'd love one, but I love Kai more. And I love him happy, so I can live without a dog. But I like to tease him."

I faced the counter, my hand on the tap. My chest tightened and it hurt because I wanted that. I could've had that with Connor. Instead, life had other plans for us.

I pushed up on the tap and the water sputtered and pipes grumbled, shaking the cupboard beneath the sink, before it flowed. I put the carafe under the water and filled it.

"I start classes in a few days, so I wanted to see the Center before my schedule gets insane. Chess says it's nearly finished."

"Classes?" I walked over to the coffeemaker, lifted the back lid and poured the water in.

"Yeah, I'm going for my doctorate."

"Wow." That was impressive, but then her father had been a well-known scientist. "Do you have a focus?"

"Yeah, kicking cancers butt." She sat at the small rectangle kitchen table that had a marbled beige laminate top and stainless-steel legs. It was also peeling in the corners and you could see the cork underneath.

The chairs were old too, wood, wobbly and worn on the seats. But I loved them. I loved everything about this house. It had personality with memories imbedded in every room. And now finding out that a sweet lady had lived here… it was a piece of nice.

I put a new filter paper in the basket then scooped dark roasted granules into it. The intense scent wafted into me and I closed my eyes, as I pictured Connor taking that first sip of my coffee every morning.

He did it to make sure it wasn't too hot.

"Alina? You okay?"

I pressed the ON button. "Yeah. I'm fine." But I didn't turn to face her. Instead, I stared out the kitchen window into the backyard. The grass was overgrown and the cabana at the back near the fence needed painting.

I frowned when I saw Deaglan appear and stride toward the cabana. He wasn't wearing a shirt, which meant I could see he had even more tattoos except for one spot, his right shoulder and chest was bare of any ink.

He crouched at one of the pillars then took a metal tool from his back pocket and began scraping the lose flecks of white paint off. That was his 'I have shit to do'?

London talked about her classes while the coffee percolated and dripped into the glass carafe. Then she mentioned how Kai and Deck were merging their businesses to which she laughed and then said, "They disagree on everything, so I expect there will be a few… kinks and I'm betting the name of the company will be at the top of the list."

I half smiled. I knew what she was trying to do, talk about everything except Connor showing up at the bar and it was thoughtful, but I wanted to know more about the drug because it was obvious Connor had serious side effects. Not that I could help him right now, but I wanted to know.

"Being on the drug for so long..." I paused and London's chair scraped on the hardwood as she shifted. "What will it do to him?"

I tried to look nonchalant, but my heart pounded and my breath quickened. I reached up, opened the cupboard with the tarnished brass knobs and pulled out two green mugs that matched the walls.

"Alina, I wish I knew, but I don't. He was the only one Vault tested it on." I nodded. Carlos took delight in informing me that Connor was the first test subject for the drug. "He needs to see a doctor and have blood tests done. If you know where he is, then you should tell Kai or Deck."

She was right; he should see a doctor, but I didn't know where he was and even if I did, I wouldn't tell anyone because he asked me not to. "I don't."

She paused then said, "Okay."

I walked over and set a mug in front of her then went to the fridge and took out the milk and placed it on the table. Turning, I grabbed the carafe now filled with dark liquid and poured coffee into her mug then mine. "Sugar?"

She shook her head.

I put the carafe back then pulled out the chair across from her and sat. After pouring a dab of milk in my coffee, I lifted the mug and took a sip.

Seeing Connor again had reawakened everything.

God, I wanted him sitting here beside me right now. I wanted him to reach across and pick up my mug and take a sip. I wanted his fingers to brush against mine as he did it.

"You don't have to tell me, if you don't want to, but why did Connor come see you at the bar? I don't get it. Of all places… it just seems odd why he'd risk showing up there."

I was quiet a long time before I said, "He wanted to talk. And I don't know why. I don't think he knows why," I admitted.

"Do you think he'll stay here? I know Deck would do anything to help him. Any of those guys would. And Georgie. His parents. You."

Connor didn't want help and it's probably why he refused to see any of them.

Who I was uncertain about was Kai because he had never been a friend of Connor's. "Kai was part of Vault."

It was a statement but she replied anyway. "Yes."

I'd never met Kai before they'd rescued me, but I'd heard Carlos mention his name on a few occasions while on the phone. I lifted my chin to meet her eyes. "He won't hurt Connor, right? If he decides to come back?"

London shook her head. "No. But he knows what Vault is capable of doing to a person, Alina, and Connor is a risk." She sighed. "Kai doesn't think he can come back from what they did to him. It's not so much the torture, but the memories returning. Connor did things that went against the type of man he was. That can break a man." She met my eyes. "Kai didn't do anything last night because of Deck and Georgie, but it doesn't mean he thinks it was the right thing to do."

I slowly turned my mug between my hands on the table as my heart pounded. "What do you mean?"

"Just that Connor isn't safe to be around. I think you know that."

I did know that, but Connor hadn't been safe to be around in Colombia either.

Pushing back my chair, I rose. "Umm, I'll go get changed."

London half smiled. "Yeah, sure, take your time." Her tone lightened as she smiled. "I'll text Chess and tell her you're coming with me and that we're leaving soon."

I went upstairs and changed with uneasiness laying like a chunk of cement in the pit of my stomach.

I was scared that the anger lingering in Connor's eyes would consume him. That he'd disappear and the pain would stay with him forever.

And I was scared that Kai was right.

CHAPTER ELEVEN

"**D**AMN IT, BACON. Noooo," Chess yelled as she landed on her ass, feet up in the air.

The little boy, Danny, whose nickname was Trick, held his belly laughing until the pig barreled into his calves and took him out too.

The pig raced for the gate at breakneck speed, which was fast considering the oversized potbellied pig had stubby legs and a definite potbelly. He tore across the dirt path then ducked under the horse pasture fence and he did it squealing the entire way.

London hooted with laughter until she saw an unamused Chess get up, who threw London a glare.

London sobered until Danny stood, dusted himself off then headed out the gate calling over his shoulder, "I'll get him."

Chess moaned and plopped down on her butt in the dirt.

London laughed again. I smiled.

Danny was determined to teach Bacon how to go through a tunnel. Bacon was determined to hang out with his pal, Rocket, the three-legged goat. According to the nine-year-old, after the tunnel was mastered, he would teach Bacon to go up and over an A frame, jump, and weave through bending poles.

Chess said Danny was addicted to the animal channel. He'd seen the agility competitions with the dogs and was determined for Bacon to be an agility pig.

It was cute and funny, but it also hurt because Connor should be here. He'd love to help Danny teach Bacon and he'd be good at it.

And that was heartbreaking to think that he may never do that again.

Chess called over to us, "No wonder he's bonded with Tristan. They're both stubborn as hell." Her eyes were on the spindly boy running through the long grass after Bacon.

London rested her hip against the plank fence, one hand on her abdomen. "He keeps looking to you for approval. The boy adores you," she called to Chess.

My chest ached at the sobering reality of where Danny had been and what he'd been through. With his smile and excitement, the flush in his cheeks, a stranger wouldn't know that his life began in the streets at age six and then ended up in Carlos' compound.

I swallowed several times and took deep breaths. Jesus, it made me sick to think about those kids being trained for Vault. That Kai and Chess's mother had started it with her own children and Carlos was part of that. I never knew. Not that I could've done anything, but I'd have tried. I'd have died trying and maybe that was why Carlos had kept that from me. Killing me was never an option for him. I was his obsession, had been since he saw me in the market that day.

I heard snorting and half smiled when Danny walked through the gate, head high with Bacon in his arms. "Chess, look. He let me carry him," he said.

"Sure did," Chess replied and climbed to her feet.

Then Chess and Danny spent the next hour coaxing Bacon with raisins to trot over the pole on the ground while London and I watched.

"Babe." Kai strode up looking very business-like in black suit pants and a white and light blue pinstriped shirt, sleeves rolled up once, top two buttons undone.

I hadn't heard him approach and it was unnerving how quiet these guys moved. Connor moved like that, too.

London turned and smiled. "Hey, hon, what are you doing here? I thought you were with Deck for the day."

Kai stopped at the fence, brows raised as his eyes shifted from London to Bacon, who was currently trotting happily through the tunnel, his tiny curled tail wiggling as he emerged and snorted on the ground for his raisins.

Danny jumped up and down clapping, his russet eyes gleaming then he fell to his knees and hugged Bacon.

"A pig?" Kai questioned.

London leaned over the waist-high picket fence and looped her arms around his neck. His hand went to the back of her neck, disappearing in her hair. "Can we get one?"

Kai's brows rose. "Are we talking about a pig or a kid?"

I couldn't imagine Kai having a pet pig and if London was referring to wanting a child, well, I couldn't imagine that either. Kai with a baby in his arms or changing diapers did not fit.

She shrugged. "I'm good with either or both." He grunted and she stood on her tiptoes, her mouth going to his ear.

Whatever she whispered in his ear, he liked because he drew her in for a kiss. I looked away, but heard him say, "Always, braveheart." Then his attention turned to me. "Deck wants to talk to you about Connor."

I tensed, stomach dropping. "I don't really have anything to tell him." Well, there was nothing I would tell him.

Kai gently unhooked London's arms from his neck and stepped

back to open the gate. "Not an option, Alina. Deck is concerned and wants Connor found, which means we need everything."

Connor didn't want to be found.

Chess strode over, hands on her hips. "Hey. What's going on?"

"Chess." Kai nodded to his sister.

She gave an exasperated sigh then rolled her eyes and walked over and kissed his cheek. "Kissing your sister hello isn't so hard, is it, Kai?"

Kai ignored her and was all business as he said to me, "Deck and the guys are meeting us at your place." Then he turned to London, eyes softening. "You good?"

She nodded. "Yeah." She glanced at me then back at Kai. "But maybe it would be helpful if I came with."

"This is business and Deck specifically asked none of the girls be present." He grinned. "I think he knew you'd say that, babe. And as much as I enjoy pissing him off, this isn't the time." He nodded to me. "We're putting in the alarm today."

An alarm to keep Connor out.

Not that it was needed. Connor said he was leaving.

My problem was going to be lying to people who had given me a new start, a chance at something nice.

When we arrived at my place, there was a silver SUV out front and a black motorcycle pulled up behind it.

My heart slammed into my ribcage and the cement that had been sitting in my stomach, dropped out.

Connor? His bike had been black, right?

Kai hadn't even put the car into park before I had my door open and headed for the bike. But as soon as I was twenty feet away, I knew it wasn't him even from behind.

Connor was taller, his body more defined. He also had this way he held himself when he sat. Even when he was on the drug, he was recognizable. He was assertive as if nothing could touch him. If there was something to hitch his leg up on, then he did, so he looked casual and unconcerned, but completely in control.

The man sitting on the bike had the same confidence, but there was nothing else that reminded me of Connor. And when he pulled off the helmet, I saw it was Deck.

He lifted his leg over the back of the bike and stood. The doors of the SUV opened and Tyler, Josh, and Vic hopped out.

But it was Deck who had all my attention, his eyes intense as he asked, "Was he here last night? And I don't mean at the bar."

Shit. He didn't dick around. And why did he ask me that? Had Ernie seen Connor leaving?

Kai put his hand on the small of my back and guided me toward the house. "Wait until we're inside, asshole. Your unstable friend more than likely has a sniper rifle on us right now."

Deck snorted.

My eyes widened for three reasons, the possibility that Connor was still around, that he had a sniper rifle, and that Kai thought we'd be targets.

"If he is, you'd never see him," Deck said from behind me. "Fuckin' ghost. And now he's a pissed-off ghost with nightmares for memories."

Kai held the door open for me. "Then maybe you should've listened to me months ago and ended this shit when we had him."

"We don't *end* any of our men," Deck retorted.

"I should've finished this last night," Kai muttered, shaking his head.

I stopped on the top step of the porch and looked at Kai. Finished? Finished what?

Deck glared at Kai then his eyes cut to me. "No one is finishing anything, Alina. We have a deal. Kai isn't allowed to touch Connor. He's trying to piss me off."

I found it hard to believe that Kai wasn't allowed to do anything. And if it was true, then there had to be one hell of a good deal.

Kai shrugged but there was a mild play at the corners of his mouth as he held the screen door open for Deck and me. "Deal is a rather strong interpretation. It was more of a suggestion."

"A suggestion that if you don't follow, puts you in a body bag."

Kai laughed. "I think you've already forgotten how easily I broke into your penthouse and held a knife to your throat."

Deck glanced over his shoulder at Tyler and chin-lifted to the right side of the house.

"Sure thing, boss." Tyler veered off toward the basement apartment.

I bit my lip uncertain what was going on between Deck and Kai. They were working together, but London was right; it looked like the kinks would take a while to smooth out. If that were even possible.

I was cautious who I trusted because the reality was, in the world I'd been exposed to, money was more important than loyalty. And loyalty was due to fear of getting cut into pieces and fed to the sharks.

Connor wasn't the only one who'd changed.

Deck led us into the living room then walked to the bay window and closed the curtains. Kai's brows lifted and he smirked. Deck ignored him.

Did Deck think Connor was outside watching? That he'd really put a bullet in one of us?

"No, I don't think he'd kill us," Deck said as if reading my thoughts. "He might Kai."

Kai stood off to the side, in the archway and out of view of the window. Even with the curtains closed, he took precaution.

Vic came in the house and stopped in the foyer. Deck nodded to him and Vic in return disappeared. I heard him jog up the stairs. Josh followed. These guys didn't have to say anything and they knew what the other wanted. Being in the military, they had to read one another's signals.

"What's going on?" I asked.

"We've decided you can remain at the house, but with precautions." Huh? They'd considered me moving? "If Connor wants to find someone, he will, and we aren't here to piss him off. We want to help him. But if we suspect Connor is a risk to you, you'll be relocated. For now, we'll install an alarm as long as Deaglan gives the okay." I guessed from my earlier conversation with Deaglan that he now owned the house since his grandmother passed. What I didn't get was why he rented out the upstairs while he stayed in the basement. "The alarm won't stop him if he comes here. But it will slow him down and give us warning," Deck said.

Tyler said, "Vic is checking the windows and doors that will need wiring."

I thanked God I'd covered the hole in the drywall above my bed with a picture because if Vic saw that, he'd be questioning it.

Deck stood with his legs braced, arms crossed and looking like an immovable tree trunk. Even worse was his eyes were on me. And they weren't friendly eyes. They were narrowed and dark. Intimidating as hell. "Are you going to answer my question now?"

The answer was no, but I wasn't saying that aloud. I hadn't decided yet what I'd say. I owed Deck my life for getting me out of Colombia, but I did Connor, too, and I'd protect Connor no matter what.

So, I remained quiet.

Deck continued, "He was at Avalanche."

"Briefly."

"Why?"

I knew this was coming. I'd been thinking about what to say all the way here in the car. Connor was Deck's best friend, well, had been, and he'd want to know everything Connor had spoken to me about, even if it wasn't significant.

He continued, "From what Kai told me went down at the bar, I think you know Connor is unpredictable." I did know that. "Since he's here, his memory is returning or has returned and it will be fragile at best." He paused. "I've known Connor since we were kids, Alina. Know him better than just about anybody and the shit he's done for Vault won't sit well with him. Goes against everything he is. That means we don't know what he'll do."

Kai moved to sit on the paisley pink couch, his arm resting on the back and his feet up on the coffee table, ankles crossed. "A man doesn't come home and walk into a bar filled with friends he wants to believe he's dead. Not without a purpose."

Even I didn't know his reason for doing that. But I suspected Connor didn't need a reason. As Deck said, he was unpredictable and his rationale for doing anything right now was skewed.

"And if you'd told me last night, instead of keeping it from me, maybe we'd know his purpose," Deck directed at Kai.

Kai sighed. "Been through this. Not doing it again."

"Then I hope you listened because I'm not merging companies with an asshole who keeps shit from me."

"You know about it now," Kai casually returned, unconcerned that Deck was seriously pissed off.

They were both Alpha men and Kai was Vault, meaning he'd worked alone much like Connor had done while on the drug. Deck was all about working with a team.

Kai scowled, but not at Deck. He was eyeing a shelf beside the TV with an array of porcelain animal figurines. London was right; he'd never live in a place like this and he definitely wouldn't be good with kids hanging off him. He turned to me and nodded to the shelf. "You good with seeing that shit around?"

He really didn't like the knickknacks. "Yeah. It's kind of nice. London was admiring them this morning. She mentioned setting up a cabinet or something in your place to put a few in."

Kai's brows dropped and his gaze darted to the porcelain figurines then back to me. "That won't be happening." He shook his head. "No fuckin' way."

The screen door squeaked open then slammed shut and Tyler and Deaglan walked in. Deaglan had white paint chips all over his jeans and in his messy strands of hair. He grinned when he saw Deck, walked over and slapped him on the back while shaking his hand. "Good to see you."

"Deaglan," Deck returned. "All okay at home?"

He shrugged. "Few quirks. Brother is causing shit. I had to straighten him out."

Deck huffed. "Still trouble?"

Deaglan chuckled. "An understatement. The little shit. He's going to get his ass kicked out of school."

Deck nodded to me. "You meet Alina?"

"This morning." Deaglan winked at me then he looked at Kai. "You must be Kai?"

Kai's eyes were sharp and alert as he accessed Deaglan and when he was done, he half smiled. "Yeah."

"Met your girl London this morning," Deaglan said. "I don't think she liked me much."

Kai's brows lifted. "What makes you say that? She does a lot of charity work helping the homeless. You fit the profile."

Deaglan laughed. "And Deck said I wouldn't like you." Kai grinned. Wow, what an unlikely friendship that would be. "I asked her if she wanted to join me and Jen, the flight attendant." His brows knit together. "Or Jan, fuck, it was a J something."

Tyler laughed.

Deck shook his head.

I thought Kai would throw Deaglan out the bay window. Instead, Kai laughed too. "Surprised you don't have a black eye."

I was surprised that Kai wasn't giving him the black eye. The way Kai was with London, he was super protective, but I was also getting that he trusted her implicitly and that was why Deaglan's comment had no effect. Kai was completely confident in his relationship with London.

"You good with us putting in an alarm?" Deck was talking to Deaglan again.

"Sure. Killian and I haven't decided if we're selling yet." His eyes hit me then went back to Deck. "Is there an issue? Need my help?"

"Don't know yet if we have an issue," Deck said. "Connor showed at Avalanche last night."

Deaglan's brows lifted. "No shit?"

Deck nodded then turned to me. "He came to see Alina. She was about to tell us what he wanted."

I stiffened. Mind racing as to what I should or shouldn't say. I liked Deck. I wasn't fond of Kai, but that was more because he scared me. Tyler was cute and funny, Josh quiet, and Vic... well, Vic was the scariest of them all, but he had gone panty shopping with me and hadn't killed me even if he looked like he'd wanted to.

"He didn't really want anything important," I said.

Deck's brows lifted. Yeah, that answer wasn't going to cut it with these guys.

I was saved from saying anything else when Vic and Josh strode into the room. "Three windows need wiring upstairs," Vic said. "Alarm on three doors downstairs, eight windows, new deadbolts front and side doors." Then Vic's eyes cut to me. "Use the air conditioner. Windows stay shut from now on."

Deck said to Deaglan, "Do you need to call Kite? We'll cover the costs."

He shrugged. "No, he left me to deal with the house. And if it's upgrades, I'll pay out of the money she left us. Kite sure as hell doesn't need the money and I don't care about it so if we can use it to upgrade the house, all the better."

Josh said something to Vic and they walked out, Vic with his cell in his hand typing something. Then the screen door opened and shut.

"You're not on a job?" Deck asked Deaglan.

"Nope. Just tidied one up before heading to Ireland. I'm free."

"Good, may need you. I'll be in touch with the details."

"Sure thing," Deaglan said while taking out his phone. "I have to finish scraping that piece of shit cabana before dark."

"Be faster to tear it down and build a new one," Tyler said.

Deaglan huffed. "Reckon it would. But that was her tea spot, kind of attached to it now. Before she died, every fuckin' afternoon unless the weather was bad, she sat there." He headed for the door while typing on his phone then hesitated and looked over his shoulder at me. "You get scared, pet, my door is always open."

Deaglan may not have the look of one of Deck's commando guys, but he definitely had the arrogance of one. "Thanks. I'll be fine." And all of this was overkill. Deaglan went back to typing on his phone and left. I turned to Deck. "I don't think all this is really necessary," I said.

"Yeah. It is. He'll be back." That was Kai. "And from his fist smashing in to the brick wall above your head at the bar, I'd say you need a fuck of a lot more than an alarm. But Deck seems to think Connor will be more receptive to getting help if we don't piss him off too much."

Goose bumps rose on my arms at the thought of Connor coming back. They were making certain he stayed out of my house when all I wanted to do was let him in. Although, maybe the alarm wasn't to keep him out, but rather a warning for them so they could find him.

Deck's piercing eyes narrowed in on me. "Where's his head at, Alina? What did he say to you in the bar?"

All eyes focused on me and I felt like I was facing a firing squad of hot men. I swallowed, not wanting to answer, but knowing he'd push until he had something, so I gave a partial truth. "He came to say goodbye to me."

Kai chuckled while shaking his head. "Yeah, that's bullshit. He had that chance when he left you tied up in a fuckin' sewer." My eyes shot to Kai. "The man I saw wasn't coming to say goodbye. He may think that. May have told you that. But the only way that guy is saying goodbye to you is if he's fuckin' dead. And my guess is that's the only reason why he left you in the sewer and told us to get you out in the first place. He thought he was going to die from the drug withdrawal."

My eyes widened, heart pounded and my body quivered. I lowered onto the arm of the couch before my legs gave out.

Deck had his arms crossed, legs shoulder-width apart as he stared at his feet as if contemplating.

After a minute, he lifted his head. "We search every known place he used to go to in the area. If he's remembering shit, he may return to one of them. Tyler, I want a printout of all hotel guests within a twenty-mile radius. Those who have paid cash and have no checkout time. He'll be using another name. Not sure how he's getting money, but I assume Vault had him set up with an account with access to cash." Kai nodded to confirm this. "Okay, that means he can easily get what he needs. I want silence on this. No authorities unless he becomes a threat. All I want to do is talk to him for now." His eyes landed on me. "Alina, I get you want to protect him. There's history between you. But you know Connor is my best friend. *Is*, Alina. Don't give a fuck if it's been eleven years and he's not the man he was. We don't leave a man behind. You get what I'm saying?"

"Yes." I did. Connor used to talk about the bond all the guys shared. They'd throw themselves on top of a grenade in order to save each other's lives.

But my loyalty to Connor was strong, too. And I was the only one who really knew him as the cold, hard man with no memory.

Despite wanting to help Deck, I'd do what Connor wanted because he needed that from me.

"You're not going to tell me anything, are you?" Deck continued. I shook my head.

Kai's cell rang and he got up and left the room before he said, "Baby? You good?"

Deck came toward me and I didn't like that I was sitting as he towered over me. But then he crouched and put his hand on my knee.

His eyes softened as he said, "I like that you're protecting him." I opened my mouth to deny it, but he half smiled and continued before I had a chance. "We trained together. I know his moves, even if he's been MIA for years. I also know he's remembering shit. Don't know what damage that's doing to him, but I think you do.

"I'm going to trust you to know when it's important to tell me what I need to know to keep you and everyone else safe." He stood as Vic and two other guys came in with a bunch of electronic devices and rolls of wire in their hands. Deck continued, "The silent alarm will notify us, not the police. We don't want to hurt him, Alina. We want to get him help and we're going to do that if we can." I wanted to help him, too, but Connor didn't want help. "Either Tyler or Vic will take you to and from work until we decide otherwise."

"I can take a...." My voice trailed off when I met his unyielding stare. "Yeah, okay."

Deck nodded then squeezed my shoulder before he strode out of the living room where I heard him talking quietly to Vic.

The house became a whirlwind of hot military men moving about as they installed the alarm. Well, Kai didn't; he'd left after the phone call.

"You got it?"

I jerked and glanced up at the alarm guy, I think Vic said his name was Jim or John or something. "Umm, sorry. Can you show me again?"

"No problem." He smiled, turned to the alarm, and started going over how it worked again.

I picked my numbers for the code and then we practiced a couple times.

When Jim/John was satisfied I knew what I was doing, he told Deck and everyone cleaned up and left. Well, all except Tyler who was driving me to Avalanche.

I left him watching TV and went upstairs and showered.

That's where I sat on the tiled floor, the warm water pouring down on me, and I let myself fall apart—again.

CHAPTER TWELVE

Question 6: What kind of pet or pets have you had?

PAST

Connor

THEY SHOVED ME against the filthy cement wall then cuffed my hands to a metal ring above my head. I was able to turn around, take a step in either direction, but that was it.

I knew what was next. They hosed me down once a week, threw a bucket of some kind of disinfectant on me that burned my nostrils and stung my eyes. If they didn't hose it off fast enough, my skin felt as if it were on fire.

This was the only cell I'd been in that had a football size window and the only time I breathed in fresh air in this fuckin' shithole.

PERFECT RAGE

Over the last few weeks, they fed me half decently, but I couldn't figure out why. They never questioned me and I never told them shit. Never would.

Something was different. Like they were making sure I lived.

I noticed a collapsible table with a monitor sitting on it over by the door. I'd never seen it before and it was pretty obvious it was set up for me. At least we were finally getting somewhere after months of this shit.

Was a ransom being paid? Fuck, I hoped not. I'd rather die than give these bastards what they wanted. Deck knew that. Vic, too. All of us felt the same way.

It was hours later when a guy came in. His face wasn't covered, which was never a good sign for me getting out of here alive. He had olive skin and thick dark hair that covered his wide forehead. I wanted someone to fuckin' say something so I could at least try and decipher their accent. I'd originally assumed we were in Afghanistan, where the roadside bombs took out the Humvees, but now I knew there was no chance we were because there was distinct moisture in the air and I'd heard the rain on more than one occasion.

"You assholes going to show me movies?" I asked, voice scratchy. "Because I'm a huge Jason Statham fan. Or, fuck, how about a superhero movie. That would be cool."

He ignored me, just like the million other times. No one said shit and that drove me crazy. Not knowing why I was here or what they wanted. Well, maybe that was ending today.

He pressed the button at the bottom of the screen and it flickered a multitude of colors for a second before an image appeared.

My heart stopped.

My insides froze. It was like shards of ice stabbing me as my life tilted on its axis.

No. Fuck, no.

Alina?

My Alina. No. It was impossible.

My mind was a whirlpool of confusion and I was unable to grasp what the hell was going on. Why the fuck was Alina on the video screen? I hadn't seen her in almost two years. Not since the note.

The fuckin' note. A note I'd destroyed along with the pages in my journal that contained her answers to the questions and little details about her. I'd erased her. And I fuckin' hated her.

She was dead to me. I hadn't told Deck about her. I'd told no one because Alina Diaz was a lying, cheating bitch and no longer existed.

Until this moment.

My stomach dropped out and my heart stopped before it started again in a stampede of beats.

"What the fuck? What the fuck is this?" I yelled.

I yanked violently on the cuffs, my body swinging back and forth banging into the wall as I tried to get free. Blood trailed down my arms, my sides, and finally soaked into my pants.

"What the fuck is this? Where is she?"

Why? Jesus, why would they have her, too?

Seeing her on screen raised all the buried emotions I felt for her and they rushed back into me like a wall of bricks.

The guy leaned in front of the screen and pressed a button. Then the video played.

I froze. Staring at the screen as my mind tried to catch up with what I was seeing. The date. The date of the video was in the corner of the screen.

No.

Fuck no.

It was a week after she'd left me. A week. The video was almost two years old.

Cold dread washed over me as I watched.

Alina was on her knees sobbing uncontrollably. Her face pale, hair a mess and covering half her face with strands stuck to her wet, tear-

PERFECT RAGE

streaked cheeks. Blood splattered her clothes as she rocked back and forth, a man's head cradled in her lap.

She softly stroked his hair as she cried.

After a minute, she glanced up at whoever was in front of her but out of camera shot.

"Why? Why?" she choked out.

"You need to know what will happen if you ever disobey me," a man's voice replied.

She shook her head back and forth. "I came back. I came back."

Fuck. Fuck. Fuck.

No, Alina.

But the pieces were coming together in my fucked-up head. The note. Why she'd left me.

Who was the asshole behind the camera? She was obviously forced to go back to him.

The man in the video laughed and it was like tires squealing. "Yes. You did. But unwillingly. And you refused my offer."

She collapsed on top of the dead man, her body violently shaking. "Oh, God, Juan. Juan."

Fuck, it was her brother. The dead body she cradled in her lap was her brother. She'd left me to go to this man because he'd had her brother.

The man off camera said, "You ever try and leave me, there will be severe consequences, Catalina."

My blood boiled and I curled my fingers into my palms.

She lifted her head. Her lower lip trembled and her voice quivered as she said the words. "I won't. I swear. I won't. Please leave my mother alone."

No fuckin' way. This couldn't be happening.

Then all hell broke loose and I lost it.

"Alina! Jesus," I shouted.

The ring I was cuffed to clinked against the cement as I flailed back and forth. I knew better than to fight. It only gave them pleasure and made shit worse for me. There was no escape or winning here. I won by being calm. By zoning out.

But zoning out failed me as the video played then stopped and started from the beginning again. I tore at the chains that locked me to the wall.

Her sobs broke through my rage and I stopped. Breathing harsh and ragged as my eyes darted to the screen again.

Crushed. It was like my insides were in a garbage disposal, spinning around and around, the blades chopping me up into tiny mashed-up segments.

Whoever these people were, they'd had her since she left me. I'd gone and done my training with JTF2, done missions and all that time I'd hated her while she was the prisoner of a psycho.

Why? What the hell was going on?

I swallowed the bile as it threatened to rise. Everything inside me was a war of emotions as the video on the screen blared in my head.

"You bastards." I had no other words as the pain ripped through me. Not the physical pain, I could handle that. This was worse. So much worse.

I snarled. "What the fuck do you want?"

The screen went black.

"Where is she?" I shouted, looking around the room for the guy, but he was gone.

I hadn't heard him leave because I'd been too focused on the video.

What did Alina have to do with me being here? How did they even know about Alina and me? Why did they care?

The screen lit back to life and her sobs started over again.

And again.

And again.

Even when I couldn't watch it anymore, I heard her.

PERFECT RAGE

I fuckin' heard her.

Hers cries echoed. Her words. The constant barrage of hatred, pain and despair tearing through me over and over again.

No. She was mine. I was supposed to protect her.

CHAPTER THIRTEEN

Present

Alina

I HADN'T SEEN OR heard from Connor since he'd shown up and we'd had sex. It had been a month and I felt every single second he'd been gone.

My heart skipped a beat every time I heard a motorcycle. I jumped when someone came up behind me and I constantly searched for him in the shadows of the bar. When I couldn't sleep, I stood on the porch, hoping he'd come.

He didn't.

Work was my savior. I took extra shifts when I could and the bar was usually busy, especially Wednesday to Saturday when Matt had bands playing.

PERFECT RAGE

I visited the Center with London once a week, and discovered how much I enjoyed interacting with the animals. I loved how honest they were and if they didn't like you, you knew it.

I considered adopting a cat, an older one who needed a home. Something permanent. Something to love and care for and who'd love me back.

The goat, Rocket, was almost as cute as Bacon, but way more mischievous. He was impossible to contain because he'd get on his belly and wiggle under the fences. Even with only three legs he was agile.

If he was in a stall, he'd fiddle with the latch until it opened; for safety reasons, locking him in wasn't an option. So, Rocket roamed free on the property, but he never went far as he'd formed a strong attachment with Bacon.

He wasn't a problem until he jumped on the hood of Kai's car.

London and I were in the barn when it happened. We heard a car door shut and then, "What the ever living fuck?"

Then there was a loud bleat and a rhythmic pitter-patter like tap shoes on metal.

When we came outside, Kai stood in front of his car in a stylish, dark blue pin-striped suit staring at Rocket who was staring at him while standing on the hood of his car.

"Get off," Kai growled, but he made no move toward the goat.

Rocket stomped his hoof and since he only had one front leg, it meant he reared up, then he bleated. I winced because if you spoke goat, that was definitely a 'make me'.

Kai didn't say anything for a minute as they stared at one another then he grunted.

Then he chuckled.

He chuckled.

And that worried me because no man would chuckle and be that calm when his car was being trampled on by a goat. This was Kai though and he liked to throw people off as to what he was really thinking.

London leaned into me. "I think he's impressed by Rocket's bravery."

"I'm not so sure. There's a goat on the hood of his car." A really expensive, beautiful car.

London nodded. "And he does love that car."

Over the last month, I'd slowly warmed up to Kai and the reason was because I saw how he was with London. And that man didn't love his car. I'm sure he liked it, but he didn't care about it. All he loved and cared about was London.

The goat bleated again.

It was like Rocket laughed at him.

London laughed, too. I wasn't so sure that was a good idea.

Kai walked toward us. "Babe. You can forget getting a pet."

London asked, "What about a cat?"

I winced when hooves clonked. Rocket had leapt onto the roof.

Kai looked over his shoulder. "I swear he's doing that on purpose. One dent and you know what happens to that goat."

London smiled. We both knew Kai would never hurt the goat. She stood on her toes and kissed him. It was sweet because no matter how pissed he was, Kai still wrapped his arm around her, brought her into him and kissed her back.

And, yeah, my chest ached seeing it because I missed having that. Each day that passed, the hope that Connor would return faded, but the hurt didn't. It hurt just as much as the first day, maybe more because with each day I missed him more and I worried more.

"How were classes? You feeling better today?" he asked, leaving the subject of the goat in order to find out how her day was.

"Feel great today. Classes are hard, but good. I didn't realize how much I missed being in the lab. I'm going back later tonight to do some research."

"I'll go with you," Kai stated. She opened her mouth, but Kai continued, "You're sexy as hell wearing a lab coat and I want to watch you work." Then he looked at me. "You doing okay?"

"Yeah. Fine thanks."

He nodded. Rocket then bleated a piercing sound and stomped as if he were pissed none of us were paying attention to him.

Kai tensed and the laidback calm vanished. "You need to deal with that fuckin' goat, braveheart." He gestured with his chin to Rocket. "He head-butts any part of that car, he's meeting my knife."

"The vet took him off the meds. He's a little more rambunctious than usual." London smiled at him. But Kai was done with the niceties.

"Don't give a shit if the vet gave him a brand new fuckin' leg and a new heart. Get him off the car."

"I'll get the chips." I dipped back into the barn. Rocket was stubborn, but he had a weakness— potato chips—and we found that out because he stole an entire bag out of Danny's hand three weeks ago. So now we kept chips in the feed room, a padlocked feed room.

I heard Kai say, "Babe. Told you, I don't want one. Give you anything, but no pets in the house." I couldn't hear London's reply but I heard Kai's. "I'm not sharing you with anything. Are you sure you're feeling okay? Did you make an appointment?"

When I came back with the chips, I lured Rocket off the roof then London and I took Kai on a tour of the finished house for the kids. It was more of a mansion than a house. It was Tristan and Chess's design to make sure the place was like any other house and didn't look like a cold, sterile facility.

Afterward, Kai dropped me at Avalanche for my shift as London had gone straight from the Center to university. The escort with Vic or Tyler to and from work had stopped a couple days ago since there'd been no sign of Connor. Deck told me all leads had turned up empty and while they were going to keep looking, other jobs required their attention. London informed me that they were 'visiting' all known Vault associates to make certain everyone knew Kai was in charge of its new direction with Deck.

When I got home after my insanely busy shift, I had a quick shower and for the first time in a month, I fell asleep within minutes.

I woke to heated breath against my neck and a graveled whisper. "Baby."

My eyes flew open. "Connor?"

"Yeah," he said against my neck, his lips vibrating on my skin.

He spooned me from behind, one arm locked around my waist, his palm settled on my abdomen and his hard body pressed against me with only a sheet between us.

My heart pounded and stomach flipped. But it wasn't just a flip; it was a long drawn out one like I was riding up that first hill on a roller coaster, not knowing what to expect.

Anticipation. Fear. Excitement. All whirled around inside me like a tiny tornado. And I was holding on for dear life because I really wasn't sure why, after a month, Connor suddenly showed up in my bed.

In my bed.

In the house.

Oh, shit. I pushed at his arm as panic hit. "The alarm." Deck and the guys would come here. "There's a silent alarm that—"

Connor clamped me down with one leg thrown over mine and his chest half on top of me. "It's good."

What did he mean it's good? It's good that in five minutes Deck, or worse, scary Vic shows up, busts down the door, and storms into my bedroom? That so wasn't good.

My palms pushing on his chest had no effect, but I pushed anyway. "It's not good."

PERFECT RAGE

I'd make up something. Tell them I forgot to disarm the alarm when I went outside to sit on the porch.

Shit, Deaglan. It wouldn't be a few minutes before one of the guys got here. Deaglan was downstairs and would be upstairs in five seconds if the alarm went off. It could be going right now and I had no idea.

I wanted more than anything for Connor to get help, but I didn't want it to happen by them catching him here. And I was pretty sure that wouldn't go over well with Connor.

"You have to go."

Connor wasn't paying attention to me or if he was he didn't appear concerned that his ex-military buddies were going to find out he was here and in my bed.

Instead, he kissed below my ear and shivers danced across my skin. I really didn't want Deaglan to walk in, so despite the shivers and sweet clenches, I shoved as hard as I could on his chest while sliding out from under his caged arm.

"Stop," he ordered before my feet hit the floor. "I disarmed it. And your guard dog downstairs isn't home. He's with Kai." Deaglan was with Kai? "They've eased up on their surveillance."

He knew they'd been watching me? And if he did know, then he'd been watching me, too.

My eyes darted to him for the first time and even though it was still dark, the streetlights illuminated the room enough for me to see his face.

Calm. He appeared completely calm. "You turned off the alarm?"

"Saw it installed." He had? His brows lowered and eyes darkened to that stormy ocean blue. Now, not so calm. "Saw the guy teach you how to work it. Five fuckin' times."

I couldn't remember how many times. It was a month ago.

He snaked his arm around my chest and dragged me back under him, but this time there was no sheet separating us. He nipped my ear and his hand slipped under my camisole and caressed my abdomen.

It was slow.

Gentle.

And made me forget what we were talking about, especially when the tip of his baby finger slid along the edge of my panties under the seam.

"Didn't like him standing close to you."

"Huh?"

"Didn't like how he looked at you either." His leg slid up my calf to my knee then down again. The denim of his jeans rubbed my naked skin, then the heat of his bare foot followed.

He kissed the edge of my jaw, with another closer to my lips.

"He stood next to you with his eyes on your breasts. I didn't fuckin' like it." He drew a pattern across my abdomen. "Nearly pulled the trigger, wanted to pull the trigger."

That dragged me out of my haze and my eyes flew open and my belly flipped for a completely different reason. "Who? What are you talking about?" Pulled the trigger? Holy shit. Was he talking about the alarm guy John or Jim?

"You're still working at the bar."

It wasn't a question. But I was still back on the 'nearly pulled the trigger'. "Are you saying you nearly shot the alarm guy because he was staring at my breasts? Which isn't true." At least I didn't think so. I'd been paying attention on what to press so I didn't mess up and have Deck and Kai's team here because I pressed the wrong buttons. I couldn't imagine any of the guys, especially Vic, being pleased about being dragged out of bed in the middle of the night for a false alarm.

I sucked in my breath, fingers clamping on Connor's wrist to stop him from caressing my abdomen. "How did you know the numbers to shut off the alarm?"

"Babe, let go of my wrist," he growled.

I didn't because I couldn't focus when he was touching me. "How did you know the numbers?" I repeated.

His body tensed and his eyes narrowed. "Let go. Now!"

It was how he forced out the word 'now' that sent a wave of fear through me and I quickly pulled my hand away. He immediately relaxed, well, as relaxed as Connor could be anymore.

I thought of the scars on his wrists and realized why he didn't like it. God, what did Carlos do to him? There were parts of me that wished his memory hadn't returned. That he never had to remember what was done to him.

Even if that meant he wouldn't remember me.

He moved. It was quick and agile as his leg went to the other side of me and he straddled me. He locked my arms down on either side of my head with his hands on my wrists then he tilted forward.

I was a little afraid because he was scowling, but I took solace in the fact that his body was relaxed and his breathing was slow and steady.

I couldn't say the same for mine as my chest rose and fell in quick succession.

He released one wrist to cup my jaw, thumb lightly playing with my bottom lip. "Didn't need to see to know what numbers you'd pick, shutterbug."

I froze. Holy shit. Holy shit. The numbers. He remembered my numbers?

I didn't think he'd remember something so silly. But he had and my chest swelled. "You remember?"

"Yeah, baby." He tipped his head and kissed the hollow of my neck.

God, I loved that. When I picked the numbers for the alarm, I hadn't even thought about it. I just tapped them in when the guy told me to—11528.

He trickled kisses down between my breasts and I inhaled, closing my eyes, shivers, twinges, sparks, all of them erupting at once.

"Connor?"

"Yeah?"

"Can we go back to the 'nearly pulled the trigger'? It's freaking me out." That was putting it mildly.

His thumb stilled on my lip. "Didn't see him." Connor sighed, closing his eyes for a second, his head dropping. "Didn't see him beside you, babe. I saw Moreno." Oh, shit. "So, yeah, I nearly pulled the trigger. I can't stand the thought of what you went through, being forced to stay with him. I want to kill him again and again."

There was nothing for me to say to that. The alarm guy was lucky to be alive and Connor was, too, because if he had pulled the trigger, there were elite commando guys all over the place who would've hunted him down. I wasn't so sure if Deck would've kept his word and not harmed him.

He continued, "I got on my bike and rode. Wasn't planning on coming back."

That was why he disappeared. "Where did you go?"

"The track."

"The track?"

"Where I used to race dirt bikes. It's abandoned now. Spent a couple days there, until Vic showed up." I stiffened. "He didn't see me, but it was too close, so I left. I drove for a while and thought I could keep going."

"But you came back."

"Yeah." He cupped my cheek, eyes closed, head still tilted down. "It's the last place I should be, but I can't stay away." He stopped for a second. "Fuck, Alina. I need every single part of you."

"Connor, you have me," I said. Maybe it was the catch in my throat or my words, but he stilled then lifted his head and my heart stopped. It fucking stopped when his eyes met mine.

Because in the depths I saw devastation. Not just devastation, it was more powerful than that. It was the wreckage of a soul.

"I forgot you."

PERFECT RAGE

Oh, God.

He bent until his forehead rested against mine, his eyes closed. "I forgot you," he repeated in a ragged whisper. "I went years without you in me." He lifted and his eyes met mine. "I watched you sob. Watched you beg him not to make you do it as he held you in his arms, forcing you to hold the gun. I watched while you killed the man beside me. Watched you make a choice between me or him." He shook his head back and forth, a lock of hair falling in front of his eye. "When my memory came back..." I could barely hear him, words spoken almost as if to himself and not to me. "...I got pieces. Jagged, fucked-up pieces. Pieces I didn't want to see and had to." He paused then whispered, "It killed me that I forgot you."

"Connor, you forgot everything. Everyone. The drug did that."

He stared at me a minute, neither of us moving, only the sound of our breath and the slight rustle of the sheets as our chests rose and fell.

"I can't forget you again," he said. I opened my mouth to tell him he wouldn't, but his eyes narrowed. "I. Can't. Forget."

"You won't," I said.

"I came back, so I wouldn't forget."

Oh, Jesus. He was worried he'd forget again. I settled my hand on the back of his neck, curling my fingers into his hair. "You won't forget. I won't let you. Just stay with me. We can get you help."

His eyes darkened. "Don't ask me to do that, Alina."

"But your friends—"

He moved fast, hand grabbing my chin, fingers bruising. "No!"

I stopped breathing, but persisted. "Connor, why?"

"What the fuck do you think happens to a guy like me? The second I lose my shit, they pump me full of drugs and lock me up. I'm never being drugged or locked up again. Never." I understood that, but how was he supposed to get better? "I don't want to be near anyone except you." His voice hardened. "Don't mention it again. It's too late for fuckin' help. Got it?"

"Yeah." I said the word, but I didn't get why he didn't want to see his friends? His best friend and his sister who he'd adored? God, his parents.

But fear lingered inside me. That stormy look in his eyes. The rage lingering ready to erupt with the slightest push. The thought that he nearly killed a man because he thought it was Carlos. The thought that he may disappear again and at the same time, that he wouldn't.

His hand slid down the front of me, burning a path between my breasts, my abdomen, to the bottom edge of my camisole where his fingers curled and he tugged it up to my ribs. "You want me to fuck you tonight?"

Was I weak because the answer was yes? That it would always be yes? My body ached for him. My belly did flips and somersaults and nosedives. And what was happening between my legs was an explosive need.

But this was much more than desire.

It always had been.

"Yeah," I whispered. Maybe it was stupid, feeding this need between us, but I'd been starved for him and even if I could only be fed tiny morsels through sex, I'd take it.

I just didn't know for how long.

He stared at me for several seconds as if trying to read whether I was really okay with this. I didn't honestly know if I'd be okay with this tomorrow. But I was now and that was all I could think about.

"You're mine," he murmured beneath his breath as he lowered his head, lips a breath away. "Never his."

I inhaled sharply just before his mouth claimed mine.

I surrendered. There was no other way to describe it because he did that to me. I always surrendered to him.

But it was real. It was him and within the bruising kiss there was purity and beauty.

"Fuck, baby." His lips vibrated against mine.

I needed more. I had to have all of him. His hand cupped the back of my neck and fingers bunched in my hair.

"God, Connor."

He sat up on his knees, undid his jeans and tugged them off, taking his boxer briefs with them. Ripping his T-shirt off over his head, he tossed it aside.

My gaze trailed down his muscled chest to his cock. It was thick and hard and ready for me. It jerked under my stare and my eyes flew back to his eyes.

Connor watched me. A slow half grin formed and my heart stopped at the magnificence of it. I missed that look. The way it captivated me in its brilliance and warmed me inside. How it reached every part of me like I was lying naked in the sun, my skin damp after soaking in a cool refreshing lazy river. All of it was in his smile.

The grin I'd captured with my camera the day after our picnic in his bedroom. We lay on the hood of the Humvee, him tickling me as I attempted to take a picture of us. It was off center and candid, with half my face covered in my windblown hair, my head tilted back with laughter. His grin was broad and his magnetic blue eyes blazed with playfulness.

It was the first picture I'd seen on Carlos's coffee table. Lying on top of all the others. It was also the one Connor held up to the lighter, the orange flickering flame quickly eating up his grin.

Carlos. Vault. They burned away Connor's grin.

"It's over. Stop thinking," Connor murmured against my throat as he trailed kisses down to my collarbone.

"What Carlos did to you—"

His head jerked up. "Shut the fuck up," he growled.

My breath hitched and I stilled beneath him.

"You don't say his name—Ever." His eyes drove into me. "Say it."

"I don't say his name."

"Again," he ordered.

"Connor…" His eyes narrowed and I quickly said, "We don't talk about him ever. I will never say his name again."

He stared at me a second, his body thrumming with tension. Then he sprang from the bed, spun and stalked from the room.

Oh, God, what just happened?

I leapt out of bed and made it to the hallway just as he jogged down the stairs and disappeared around the corner toward the back of the house. I heard a door slam. But it wasn't the outside door. It was the door to the downstairs bathroom.

The pipes jerked and grumbled as the water turned on.

I walked down the hallway, down the stairs, then around the corner until I stood outside the bathroom.

The water rushing through the pipes was the shower.

I wasn't sure if what I was about to do was a good idea or not, but I did it anyway. I turned the doorknob.

It was unlocked. I walked inside, closed the door behind me so the heat wouldn't escape and leaned against it.

He wasn't in the shower. He had his hands curled around the edge of the countertop with his head bowed, hair hanging in front of his face, body tense.

"Get the fuck out," he said without looking at me.

I didn't move.

"Jesus. Get the hell out of here, Catalina." By the strained tone, he was having trouble keeping his anger contained.

He never called me Catalina except in Colombia. "No." My heart was going to leap through my chest at any second and my knees were going to give out, but I wasn't leaving. I gripped the door handle with both hands behind my back.

"So fuckin' stupid," he murmured.

I was uncertain if he was talking about me being here and refusing to leave, or something else. It didn't matter. I wasn't leaving unless he made me leave, which had a good possibility of happening.

But I never ran from fear. I think that was one of the reasons Carlos was drawn to me. It didn't mean I was always brave when faced with something that terrified me. I just didn't run.

Well, except once and it had been from Connor.

I released the door handle.

He didn't move.

Then I walked up behind him and placed my hands on his shoulders. He flinched but didn't move away or say anything. Then I moved into him and rested my cheek on his back, hands sliding down his arms to settle in the crook of his elbows.

His breathing was heavy. Heartbeat erratic. Body tense.

I remained quiet. I think he needed the silence. I wasn't sure why he turned on the shower, but hearing the rhythmic sound was calming.

We stood like that for several minutes, neither of us saying anything until his head lifted. I moved slightly to the side, to look past his shoulder. Our eyes met in the reflection of the mirror.

His stormy blue waves. Mine steady chocolate warmth.

It happened fast. He spun, grabbed my ass and lifted me off the floor. My arms hooked his neck and within a second, we were under the spray of the water, my back hitting hard against the tiled wall.

Then his mouth was on me.

He let my ass go and my feet slid to the ground. He peeled my arms off his neck and slammed them against the wall above my head, locking my wrists together with one hand.

We were soaked as the heated water pounded into us. My camisole stuck to my skin and I felt my erect nipples pressed against the material.

His lips broke from mine and a deep graveled sound emerged before he drew my nipple into his mouth through the shirt.

Nipping. Flicking.

"Take this damn shit off," he growled.

But he didn't wait for me to pull it off. His fingers grasped the collar of the camisole and then he yanked—hard. It cut into the back of my neck, but quickly gave under the pressure and ripped down the front.

He kept me locked up against the tiled wall with his hand as he parted the material with the other. Then his mouth was on my nipple again. His heated tongue swirling, tasting, teasing, his teeth dragging across the sensitive nipple.

"God. Connor," I murmured, eyes closing as my body quaked and trembled.

His hand went between us and I arched, moaning as his fingers glided through my wetness.

"So fuckin' wet for me, baby. Just me. Not him."

My eyes flew open and my breath hitched, but Connor was kissing my neck and I wasn't even sure he knew what he'd said.

'Not him'. He was talking about Carlos, the man who destroyed us. The man whose name Connor never wanted me to say again.

There was only one reply—the truth. "Only you," I whispered.

He groaned.

With his hard body pressing me into the wall, mouth on mine, hair bunched in his hand, he tilted my head to the side to position me where he wanted.

His cock pressed against my thigh. "Need inside you," he said against my lips. "Now."

"Condom," I said. I had been on birth control when I was with Carlos, although he never knew. It was my one piece of control. I'd never have a child with him. I'd never bring a beautiful child into his cruel world.

The risk for me and the girl who obtained the pills for me was huge. Carlos would've killed her, but she took the chance because Carlos had killed her family.

Connor jerked back and grabbed my chin. "I saw your pills. We need fuck all between us."

He did? When?

PERFECT RAGE

As if he knew what I was thinking, he said, "Came here while you were at the bar tonight."

Oh. Wow. Shit. He went through my stuff? "Why?"

He ignored me and tilted his hips while grabbing his cock.

I pressed my palms on his chest. "Connor. I don't know who you've slept with. You need to wear a condom even if I was taking the pills which I'm not." Getting myself a physical had been one of the first things I'd done when I arrived in Toronto. Deck organized for me to see a doctor he knew and they'd given me the pills because I'd told them I'd been on them. But I'd never started them since I hadn't planned on sleeping with anyone.

The pressure on my wrists increased.

Okay, I was nervous. He looked scary and Connor was strong, really strong and the reality was he could do anything he wanted to me, even if I said no.

There was little to trust in him any longer and I knew he needed that sliver of trust from someone. But not this.

"I haven't been with anyone else, shutterbug."

I sighed as soon as he called me that, knowing that whatever fucked with his head had eased.

"Your memory—"

"Damn it, Alina. I know. I fuckin' know. I know you were the only one."

He waited, the storm in his eyes now settled and the tension on his face eased. I slid my hand from his chest to his face and then traced his lower lip with the pad of my finger.

Suddenly he sagged and shook his head, pearls of water dripping off the tips of his hair. "I don't have any condoms on me," he said. "I saw your pills earlier and I didn't think."

"Oh."

Then he picked me up off the floor, used one hand to turn off the water and carried me upstairs where he tossed me soaking wet onto the bed.

I came up on my elbows as he lowered onto the bed then yanked my legs apart. "We'll make do." He shifted so his shoulders were between my thighs.

Then his head lowered and I sharply inhaled as he tasted me.

He did it slow. He did it hard. Gentle. Lazily.

And I watched him as I moaned and arched until I couldn't anymore.

"Connor," I cried.

"That's it, baby." He slipped two fingers inside me and I clinched around them. He pumped in and out.

"Oh, God. Oh, God." I closed my eyes, body tightening as fireworks ignited inside me and I came hard and fast.

My body sated and tingling, he trailed kisses across my skin until he found my lips and kissed me.

I sagged into the bed. Melting. Bending. Yielding to his mouth.

I had no thoughts of yesterday or tomorrow.

It was just us. It was now.

Until it ended.

Until he pulled back and said, "I swear I'll never forget you again, Alina."

Then he threw on his clothes and left.

CHAPTER FOURTEEN

Question 7: Would you ever polar bear dip?

PAST

Catalina

"**H**E WANTS TO see you," Diego said.

He was behind me as I stood on the terrace where I'd been taking close-up photos of flowers. My passion was people, but Carlos didn't allow me to take pictures of anyone.

I lowered my camera and let it hang from my neck as I faced my husband's shadow.

Diego was Carlos's right-hand man. Deadly. Cold. Cruel. I hated him.

No, hate was too gentle of a word. I abhorred him. Carlos loved to play mind games with his victims while Diego thrived on physical pain. Torture. He'd never touched me, but I'd heard the rumors and I'd seen the twinkle in his eyes when Carlos asked him to 'look after' someone.

I knew what 'look after' meant—kill. But first there were hours or days of torture. Carlos fed Diego's need to inflict pain by tossing him scraps every once in a while. The scraps were people.

He wasn't that tall, maybe five foot ten, but what he lacked in height, he had in width because he was thick. And it was all muscle. His nose was large and had a crook in it, probably from having it broken a number of times, and he had a square jaw and thick brows.

Diego didn't wait to see if I'd follow him because he knew I would. Any fight had been snuffed out years ago when one of Diego's scraps had been my brother.

We strode through the garden, up the steps and into the open living room that overlooked the garden. The white curtains on either side of the entrance lay still, just like the air.

Still and quiet. Quiet was never good with Carlos.

He sat on the couch, one knee bent over the other, a drink in his hand. The ice clinked against the sides of the glass as he gently swirled the liquid.

"Come in, darling." He raised his hand, his finger flicking to gesture me closer.

I stepped into the room and walked toward him. Diego stood off to the side, hand on his gun at his hip. I tensed. Why did he have his hand on his gun?

My heart pounded and warning hairs rose on the back of my neck. Something wasn't right. Carlos had an unmistakable gleam in his eyes accompanied by a tiny smirk at the corners of his mouth.

My stomach knotted and goose bumps rose.

When I was close enough, he held out his hand and I took it. His fingers closed around mine and he guided me closer. "I've been gone a week. What kind of welcome home is that from a wife?" He glanced over at Diego. "A proper greeting would be a wife on her knees sucking his cock."

Diego laughed. Carlos chuckled.

I feigned a smile because he'd want me to, then leaned in and kissed him. "I'm sorry, Carlos. I missed you," I lied. I always lied. He wanted me to say the words whether they were lies or not. In the beginning, I refused. I told him he could own my body as payment, but he'd never own me. He'd never have me willingly.

Then he killed my brother and threatened my mother's life. Then the threat was no longer a threat and he killed her, too, last year. I didn't know why. He just did. My only consolation was that it had been quick, not like Juan who'd been Diego's play toy first.

"I have a gift for you."

Carlos gave me gifts all the time. Jewelry mostly, but they weren't for me; they were a show of his power and money.

I straightened and he reached into his side pocket and pulled out a wad of glossy papers. Photos? I was surprised it wasn't a velvet box and even more surprised he was giving me something I actually might appreciate. He knew how much I loved photography. It was the only part of me I had left.

When I put my eye to the lens, I saw freedom. I saw possibility. And now I saw a different story from the one I lived. Photographs used to offer me a glimpse into other people's lives. Now they let me escape my own.

He uncrossed his leg then flicked his wrist and tossed the photos on the glass table. They scattered out across the smooth surface, several sliding too far and falling over the edge and landing on the white ceramic tiles.

It took a second before my mind caught up with what I was seeing. Then I broke.

I fell to my knees beside the table, eyes locked on the images of

Connor.

Connor.

Oh, my God. The photos I'd taken at the orphanage of Connor. Some of them were of me and Connor. A few were of just me that Connor had taken.

I reached out unconsciously, forgetting Carlos watched me and skimmed the surface of the images with the tips of my fingers.

It had been seven years since I left him with a note. Seven. No, I never really left him. My body did, but I was still inside him. I left myself there.

I slowly sifted through the overlapping photos, my heart slamming into my chest as tears teetered on the edge of my lids. One slipped and fell, landing on the image of Connor holding a kid on his shoulders, his strong hands holding his legs as he kicked the ball. The five-year-old was laughing, eyes bright and filled with happiness.

Another of Connor crouched with kids all around him. He was wearing his gear as it was the day we arrived and I'd captured the photo just as a boy threw his arms around Connor's neck, his eyes shining with wonder.

I jerked when Carlos tossed another photo onto the table.

When my eyes hit it, the tears finally fell in steady streams.

It was one of my favorites, Connor and me having our indoor picnic. Day five. The day I knew I'd fallen for him.

God, it was a lifetime ago. So surreal that sometimes I wondered if it had been real at all.

"Did you think I wouldn't find these, Catalina?"

I jerked at the sound of his voice and a slow building terror cocooned me in its grip. No. This couldn't be happening.

I shook my head. "Carlos. No. He's not important. Please, it was a long time ago and he meant nothing." My chest tightened with panic and I couldn't breathe.

His brows lifted. "Pictures don't lie, Catalina. You of all people know that. They tell a story. You always liked stories, although I'm not sure you'll like the next one."

I swallowed the bile threatening to rise. Oh, God. "He was nothing. We were nothing. We've never spoken again. Carlos, it was seven years ago." Why would he do this now? What did he have to gain from going after Connor?

He sighed, leaned back on the white couch, the leather crackling under his weight. "An elite military soldier. Did you not think it was important to tell me about him seven years ago? What if he came after you? Caused difficulties for me and my business? For Vault."

My heart pumped faster and my knees trembled. "He wouldn't. He didn't know where to find me. I ended it. I swear."

His fist slammed down on the coffee table and photos scattered. "I asked you. And you lied to me," he shouted.

Oh, God. When I returned to Colombia, he asked me if there was anyone I'd been seeing. I'd lied. I never told him about Connor because I knew what would happen. If he thought Connor was a threat, he'd kill him.

And now he knew about him.

Connor. Please, not Connor.

"A girl doesn't keep pictures hidden of a man she cares nothing about."

I'd put the SD card with the photos under the floorboards beneath my bed. How did he find it? When did he find it? "Carlos, please. It was so long ago and I've never spoken to him since." Carlos nodded to Diego, who silently slipped out the door.

"It's too late for please, my love." My stomach plummeted. "Far, far too late. You see, Catalina. I found the SD card the day you put it under your floorboards. Do you think I'm stupid? You live in this mansion because I don't make mistakes and I'm thorough with everything I do." *Oh, God. No. No. No.* "But what are useless photos when you can have the real thing." I choked back a sob as I tried to keep it together, but I failed as my world crumbled in front of me. "It took me a long time, a lot of resources and a lot of persuasion of Vault's board in order to risk taking him. He had friends, military friends, but you see, I had a vision for Vault. And today you will see the result of that vision."

"He's a good man, Carlos. Please. Don't hurt him." I was full-out sobbing now as fear gripped me. No, it was stronger than fear. It was terror.

"You might want to rephrase that to *was* a good man." He leaned forward, elbows on his knees. "I should thank you. With his training and background, he was a perfect test subject once the drug was ready and then... well, you will see how receptive he is to it. But today is the final test. Him seeing you again."

I couldn't form words. They drugged him? I didn't understand. Why would they drug him?

"I've taken great care to make sure Connor has been looked after over the years while we waited for my vision to grow. I even allowed him to watch you." Pure dread slammed into me. "Movies of you. How you begged for your brother's life. You're mother's life. But I don't believe he enjoyed seeing you, Catalina. He was rather... upset."

I covered my face with my hands as tears streamed down my cheeks. Any numbness I'd managed to encase myself in cracked. "Why? Why him?" I mumbled.

I heard the door open and there were two sets of footsteps. Two. My heart sank, knowing who was with Diego. Knowing that the man I loved and left that day seven years ago was here.

"Connor. Welcome." Carlos placed his drink on the table right on top of the photo of Connor sitting in the shade, knees bent, sweat dripping down his brow, a cocky smirk on his face as he looked at the camera. At me. Right after I took the picture, he'd leapt to his feet and tackled me to the ground then kissed me.

I slowly dragged my eyes from the photo and looked up. And then... I saw him and it was like no time had passed.

PERFECT RAGE

Time stood still like in a photograph.

We were the photograph.

Connor.

I never thought I'd see him again. Never breathe in his scent. Never thought I'd have the chance to see his cocky smirk and deep blue eyes filled with laughter.

Except there was no cocky smirk in the man standing twenty feet away. No laughter in his eyes. He was blank.

There was no reaction to seeing me at all.

I bit the insides of my cheeks so hard I tasted blood.

My mind spun with ways to get Carlos to let Connor go. But I knew the answer. There wasn't one.

"Connor, meet my wife, Catalina."

Meet me? My eyes darted to Carlos then back to Connor who gave a brief nod. It was like… it was like he had no idea who I was. But that was impossible.

"You have a job for me?" Connor said, his voice monotone.

Carlos chuckled. "Your loyalty to Vault is impressive."

My breath hitched. "Connor. No." I couldn't stop the words slipping from my throat. He worked for Vault? No, Connor would never do that. He'd never work for anyone like Carlos and whoever else was involved with Vault.

I scrambled to my feet and ran toward him. I couldn't stop myself. It was stupid, maybe, but I had to touch him again.

I stopped inches away then reached up and cupped his cheek. "Oh, God, Connor."

He moved fast, hand latching onto my wrist, his grip bruising as he twisted my arm until I winced. He then shoved me away so hard I fell to the floor.

Connor scowled. "Touch me again and I'll break your wrist."

My breath hitched. This wasn't Connor pretending. This wasn't Connor at all. I looked to Carlos. "What… what did you do to him?"

"I told you. My vision. And he is the first test subject, darling. He's turned out perfect. Elite military and everyone thinks he's dead. Of course, that was my doing." Carlos grinned then strode over to Connor. "I have a Vault business acquaintance arriving next week. He is interested in seeing the result of the drug. You'll remain here until then." He turned to Diego. "He'll stay in the pool house."

I staggered to my feet and ran to Carlos, placing my hands on his chest. "Please. I'll do anything. Anything. Please. Let him go."

He stroked the back of my head and smiled down at me. "I know you will, my love. But you don't have to worry. The drug won't kill him, at least I don't think so. There are a few quirks to be worked out but the scientist is working on it. This was our first test, to see if he'd remember you. It's remarkable. He has no idea who you are. Seems it's worked rather nicely."

Seeing Connor, seeing what they'd done to him, seeing the photos, I couldn't stop myself. I lost it and attacked him.

"You bastard," I screamed. I hauled off and punched him in the face. "You disgusting piece of crap." I tried to punch him again, but he blocked me with his arm. "Let him go. Let him go. You have me, damn it. Isn't that enough?" I was crazed, raking my fingernails into his skin wherever I could while kicking and flailing.

It lasted five seconds before someone dragged me off him then forced me to stand still with an arm locked around my throat and another my chest.

I hadn't noticed it before, but there was a metal garbage can beside the coffee table. Carlos picked it up and with a sweep of his arm he pushed all the photos off the table into the trash can then set it in the middle of the table.

"Connor. Do me a favor." Carlos reached in his pocket and took out a lighter.

Diego kept me locked to his chest, his arm crushing my breasts. Connor walked over to us and took the lighter.

"Grab the photos on the floor," Carlos ordered.

Connor did.

"Burn them."

Connor flicked the lighter and held the picture of us to the flame. There was no hesitation. No reaction to what he did. They were just pictures. But this was way more than that. This was Connor burning our past.

The flames ate away at the paper. At us. Then Connor threw it in the trash can with the rest and flames took hold, crackling as black smoke billowed.

Carlos held the SD card up for me to see then he tossed it in, too.

I sagged in Diego's arms, eyes closing as my heart burned with the memories.

It was three in the morning when I opened the balcony doors, slipped outside and peered over the edge. There was a bush beneath my window that would softened the landing and it was only two stories.

I had to see him. It had been four days since my meltdown and Carlos had kept me locked in my room, but today he let me out. I still wasn't taking the chance anyone would see me go to the pool house by walking through the house.

I climbed over the railing, the tips of my toes balancing on the tiny lip. I shuffled my hands down the thin pillars as I crouched and then slid my feet off the edge.

The weight of my body jerked on my arms as I dangled from the balcony. I peered over my shoulder to make sure none of the patrolling guards were around then let go.

I dropped into the bush, the tiny thistles scratching my skin. I was in my nightgown just in case I was caught then I could explain that I was unable to sleep and came outside to get some fresh air.

Crawling out of the bush, I crept under the veranda, avoiding the lights and staying in the shadows as I made my way toward the pool.

Footsteps.

I held my breath and pressed my back against the wall. The scent of cigar drifted into me and I knew who it was… Diego. He smoked cigars all the time. He also rarely slept.

He walked along the path on the opposite side of the veranda, stopped briefly and puffed on his cigar. The lit end glowed and heated then a small tornado of smoke lifted and dispersed into the air.

He glanced in the direction of the pool house then walked away, disappearing on the other side of the house.

I sagged against the wall. This was a bad idea. If Diego caught me, I don't know what he'd do or more accurately, what Carlos would do.

But I had to see Connor.

I waited a few more seconds to make certain Diego was far enough away and then raced across the patio stones around the pool to the pool house.

When I stood in front of the door, I raised my hand to knock, and paused. God, what if I failed? What if he told Carlos I came to see him? No. Connor would remember me. He'd—

The door flew open.

"Better have a fuck of a good reason why you're standing outside my door at three in the morning."

My eyes widened. "I ah… I have to talk to you."

"Why?"

"Please, can I come in?" I glanced over to the main house, praying Diego wasn't back.

"No."

Shit. "Please. Just for a minute."

His eyes ran the length of me before he stepped back, his arm holding the door open. I ducked under, feeling as if I were the rabbit stepping into the wolf's den.

The door clicked closed. I shivered, rubbing my arms up and down while biting my lower lip. Was this a bad idea? What if he told Carlos I was here? But the question was, did it matter anymore?

Connor was the last piece of my life that had been untouched by Carlos. I survived, knowing he was living his life, helping kids, his country, surrounded by people he loved. And, yeah, I prayed he'd found a woman to love. I wanted that for him. He deserved that.

But now that hope had been ripped from me and I was drowning in despair with nothing left to cling to. Connor had to remember. He had to get out of here and away from Carlos and Vault.

He moved past me and I turned to follow him with my eyes. I noticed the bed hadn't been slept in and his bag sat on the island in the small kitchen. It was unzipped with a few pieces of clothing spilling over the sides.

There was nothing of the man I knew standing in front of me. Physically, he was the same and his scent... his scent was what told everything inside me that it was him and not a twin brother I didn't know about. "What did they do to you?"

He opened the fridge and took out a bottle of water, cracked the seal, chugged half of it back then set it down next to his bag.

I wrung my hands together. "You really don't remember me?"

His expression remained the same, which meant expressionless. "Listen, bitch, if you're not here to suck my cock, then get the fuck out."

"What?" My heart tore into shreds as I stared at this man I hadn't seen in seven years, but loved every single day since. He'd never talk to me that way. Ever. He had to remember. He had to. "Connor," I whispered as I moved toward him.

He tensed, eyes narrowing as he watched me, but he didn't move. I stopped when I was an inch away and he had to tilt his head down in order to keep his eyes on me. "You loved me."

He snorted, brows knitting and lips tight. "You're delusional."

I placed my hands on his chest, closing my eyes as the touch of him erased the years of separation.

I shouldn't have. He told me not to touch him and I hadn't listened.

He grabbed my upper arms, grip bruising, fingers that would leave marks on my skin. "Told you not to fuckin' touch me." I winced, but refused to cry out in pain. "I tell you when you can touch me and where. And right now, you're pissing me off and I don't even want my cock sucked by you, bitch."

It didn't matter what he did to me. All I cared about was getting through to him. "Connor, you have to listen to me. They're giving you a drug. This isn't you." I was frantic now as he glared at me, his hands so tight I was sure he'd break my bones. "Toronto. Go to Toronto. Deck. Deck…" Shit, I didn't know his last name. Connor had always called him Deck. "Deck is your friend. He'll help you." I inhaled a long, ragged breath. Oh, God, that wasn't good enough. "Please. Just leave Colombia. Get away from Carlos. He's not a good man." Tears slipped down my cheeks from the pain, but more than that was the agony of seeing Connor like this.

He'd forgotten me.

He'd forgotten everything.

"You called me shutterbug," I cried, my voice breaking.

His eyes widened for a split second then he abruptly released me and stepped back, his hands going to his head. "Get out. Get the fuck out."

I saw it. It was there on the cusp, the sliver of something.

So, I didn't leave. I pushed. "Georgie. She's your sister. She's in Toronto. That's where you grew up. You went into the military with Deck." I rambled on faster. "And your favorite color is blue like me because it reminds you of the ocean and how powerful it can be and calm and peaceful at the same time. You love every flavor of ice cream and hate carrots because you hate the color orange. Like really hate it." He stalked toward me, eyes wild and tumultuous. I stepped back as I stammered on. He had to remember. People didn't forget these things. "You buried your sister's hamster in the backyard when she was ten." What was the name he told me? It was something odd, like a food or... "Fiddlehead. His name was Fiddlehead and you'd rescued him from the science lab."

My back hit the door and I reached behind me for the doorknob, my eyes on Connor as he continued to stride slowly toward me. I lifted my chin, breathing ragged.

His arm rose, hand curled into a fist.

Oh, God, he was going to hit me. I held my breath and turned my head, ready for the blow, but it never came. His fist smashed into the door beside my head.

"You talk too much." His fingers weaved in my hair and then he fisted his hand, jerking my head back. "Does he know you're here?"

"No," I whispered.

His other hand roughly ran down the front of me, over my breast to my ribs then my abdomen to between my legs. My nightgown bunched as he cupped me—hard.

I couldn't move. My body instantly recognized him and tweaks erupted between my legs. "Do you remember?" I whispered.

He scowled. "Bitch, there's nothing to remember. Shut the fuck up about it."

"Then why—"

He didn't let me finish. "Haven't fucked a chick in... don't know how long. Never think about it." He moved in closer so his chest was pressed against mine and I trembled. "Now I'm thinking about it. Open your legs for me."

I barreled down on the crook of his arm with my fist and dislodged his palm from between my legs. "I didn't come here to fuck you." I elbowed him in the chest, but he was immovable. I knew that. He'd used his weight to get what he wanted all the time and I'd fought him. But it was playful. This wasn't playful. "Carlos will kill you and me if he finds out."

Connor chuckled. "You came to me, remember. Doubt he'll kill me, and I don't give a fuck what he does to you."

My mouth gaped. This wasn't the man I fell in love with. This man was mean and cold and I didn't like him. But for a second... one second I saw the conflict on his face, like he was fighting something. Like maybe he'd remembered something.

"Unless you're spreading your legs, get out, bitch. And don't come back unless you want to be fucked." He abruptly let me go, turned then walked back into the kitchen.

I scrambled to get out the door, desperate to be strong, but falling into pieces at his cruel words. I knew it wasn't him speaking; it was what they'd done to him, but it still hurt.

I finally opened the door, darted out, shut it behind me then leaned against it.

I couldn't stop shaking. I crossed my arms and put my hands under them, attempting to control the vibrating.

God, Connor, what have they done to you?

This is my fault. My fault.

The pictures. The pictures. Carlos found the pictures.

My pictures had destroyed Connor.

I went back up to my room, took out my camera and smashed it into pieces.

CHAPTER FIFTEEN

Present Day

Alina

CONNOR HAD BEEN gone twelve days.

Twelve days.

He said he couldn't forget me, but he left—again. I didn't expect him to stay with me, but I expected something. Anything. Not just him disappearing again.

And it pissed me off. I was trying to understand. I knew he was tackling serious issues, and I felt selfish, but I couldn't help it. I was angry.

"Another round of shots," Georgie said to the waitress.

Georgie, Chess, London and I were having drinks at a high-class bar on King Street. London volunteered to be the DD, so she drank sparkling water.

Coming out tonight had been Chess's idea and I'd declined, because I wasn't comfortable hanging with Georgie, although I really liked her. She was fun and outgoing and she said things that made me laugh, but she was Connor's sister. And there was constant guilt for being unable to tell her I'd seen him and that made me angrier with Connor for putting me in this position.

Chess, I discovered, was a lot like her brother in that no wasn't an option. So, here I was having drinks at a bar and having my first ever girls' night out. Since I'd had no friends growing up because everyone was scared of my father's involvement with Carlos. And they were right to be.

We were celebrating Georgie opening a second location of her coffee shop and we did it drinking margaritas. I'd never been a drinker. In the beginning it was because I'd been focused on photography, and then because keeping all my senses was imperative while living with Carlos.

After three margaritas, I realized drinking had the bonus of numbing out the pain. Or at least dulled the stabbing ache in my chest. And I really liked hanging out with the girls. I'd never had this before and it felt... well, normal.

Chess said something about Bacon being able to do a wide plank teeter-totter and how Tristan had hired a teenager to come after school on Thursdays to help Danny with Bacon.

"And if Bacon and Danny are good enough, maybe they can do a demonstration at the Royal Winter Fair. That's a big thing supposedly."

"Yeah," Georgie said. "It's once a year at the Canadian National Exhibition. A horse show and agricultural fair." Georgie plucked her straw from her drink and placed it on the napkin. "Connor took me when I was six."

I coughed on my drink. Oh, God. I shifted uncomfortably in my seat and London, who sat beside me, reached under the table and squeezed my hand and I glanced up at her. She offered me a half smile. She had no idea Connor had been with me, but she saw us at the bar together that first night. She saw how devastated I'd been.

Georgie was still talking, but I'd missed some of it, "... Connor had the best smile, but the fiercest scowl and he used that scowl to get me spots right in the front rows so I could watch some of the small events. The bigger ones were in the coliseum that you needed tickets for."

My heart thumped and goose bumps rose.

"Shots," Georgie announced.

I looked up as she slid a small glass toward me. "Sex on the Beach." She held up her glass and I picked up mine, as did Chess, and London with her sparkling water, and we clanged glasses.

"To great coffee," Georgie said.

We chatted about the Center, Danny, the band Tear Asunder who were good friends with Deck and Georgie. Then Chess dragged me up to dance when Georgie and London moved the conversation to Deck and Kai merging their businesses, which was between fits of laughter.

I was a little tipsy, cheeks heated and feeling giddy as I danced with Chess. I loved dancing, and in my early teens I used to dance on the rooftop of our house with the radio blaring. I'd close my eyes and let the music take hold of me. Live it. Become it and everything else would slip away except the beat thrumming through my body.

As I moved to the music now, I let the feeling take over. This was what I wanted. To be able to dance when I wanted. To laugh. To feel alive. I'd missed years of feeling alive.

We weren't alone for long as a couple guys danced with us. The music was too loud for talking, but we weren't on the dance floor to talk.

Chess and I danced a couple more songs then refused the offer of a drink from the guys and headed back to the table.

I veered off to the washroom, which thankfully didn't have a line out the door, went into one of the stalls, had a pee then came out and walked to the sink to wash my hands.

"Alina."

I stopped, head snapping to my right. "Connor."

He leaned up against the counter, arms and ankles crossed appearing completely at ease as if he were meant to be here. As if it were no big deal him suddenly appearing out of nowhere.

Twelve days.

Twelve days he'd disappeared and now he stood in the girls' washroom at a bar like this was normal.

This wasn't normal.

I looked around, frowning. The washroom was empty. It hadn't been empty when I came in. There'd been a number of girls giggling in front of the mirror while freshening their makeup.

A girl emerged from a stall and squeaked when she saw Connor then quickly ran for the door. It took her a couple tries to escape because Connor had turned the deadbolt.

As soon as she realized, she unlocked the door and fled. Connor pushed off the counter, walked to the door, relocked it then he stalked toward me.

I had yet to move. I couldn't move.

He stopped beside me at the sink then leaned over, pressed his palm down on the soap dispenser and a thick stream of pink squirted into his palm.

"Hands, baby." He was perfectly calm as he patiently waited for me to do what he asked.

Maybe my inability to react properly had a little to do with the alcohol-induced haze. But mostly it had to do with shock.

I lifted my hands and he took them in his then caressed the soap into my skin. He did it slowly and gently, his fingers gliding between mine until my hands were covered with pink foam.

"What are you doing here?"

"Washing your hands," he replied.

With one hand still in mine, he turned on the taps, tested the water and then urged me forward to put my hands under the steady stream.

I resisted. "Here. What are you doing here?"

He moved behind me, pressing his hard body into me, arms on either side enclosing me in his embrace and giving me no choice but to put my hands under the water.

I closed my eyes, soaking in the feel of him, breathing in his scent, his touch as he carefully rinsed the soap from my hands.

"Hey! What's going on?" It sounded like a fist banging on the door.

"Fuck off," Connor growled.

I jerked from my haze and looked in the mirror at Connor's reflection.

"You can't be in here. Connor, you can't lock the door," I said. His hands entwined with mine under the water as he gently continued to wash the soap off, but it was already long gone. "Please. You need to go." The last thing I wanted was a scene and for something to happen to him. He'd had everything happen to him already.

"Open the door. I have to go pee, damn it," a girl yelled.

Shit. There was a bunch of voices and then nothing. I was betting the bouncers would be pounding on the door next and I didn't want to think how Connor would react to some guy forcing him to leave the bar.

Connor shut off the taps and moved away, but not to the door. He strode over to the paper towel dispenser, peeled off a few sheets then walked back and dried my hands before tossing the paper into the trash can.

He held out his hand. "Babe," he said.

As soon as I linked my fingers with his, he tugged. I stumbled into him, a combination of too much to drink, high heels and still a little shocked. He swept my hair back over my shoulder then rested his hands on my hips.

He kissed the top of my head. "So beautiful. Fuck, you took my breath away out there dancing."

My breath hitched and I tilted my chin up so I could meet his eyes. "You saw me dancing?"

"I did." He tensed and pulled back a bit so he could cup my chin. "But dancing with the guys I didn't like."

I was about to reply when I heard a commotion outside and I tensed, pulling out of his arms. "Connor. You should go. You can't be here."

He frowned. "You're coming with me."

I stiffened. "Excuse me?"

"You heard me."

I had, but I was shocked that he'd even think I'd just up and leave with him. "Umm, no. I'm not."

He reached for me. I stepped out of his reach, which earned me a fierce scowl, the kind that Georgie had been talking about. "You're not staying here with drunk assholes ogling you."

I was a little drunk, okay, maybe a lot, and maybe that was why I half laughed when I said, "Ogling?"

His brows dropped dangerously low. "Yeah, ogling."

And the last shot must have taken effect because I ignored his scowl and my pissed-off self re-emerged.

"Maybe I like being ogled?" I didn't. Diego had ogled me all the time and I'd hated it. But I really hadn't noticed guys *ogling* me. Again, that may have had something to do with the alcohol.

"You don't," he ground out.

I glared. "Fine, I don't."

He gave me a self-satisfied smirk. "Bike's out front." He grabbed my hand and headed for the door.

"No," I protested, yanking back. He kept going, which meant he propelled me forward and since I was on high heels and tipsy, I stumbled after him. "Connor, I'm not going with you. Chess and London and... Georgie is here, too."

He stopped fast while turning toward me and I banged into him. "I know exactly who the fuck you're with. I know how many margaritas you've had. How many shots. And that there were three guys edging closer to you on the dance floor. And one who danced with you too fuckin' close."

Oh, Jesus. He was here all night watching me? That means he must have been at my house when London picked me up.

I wished my head wasn't so fuzzy and I hadn't drunk that last shot. I tensed as it hit me. "You've been in Toronto? You never left?" His silence said it all. He had. "You've been watching me for twelve days and you never came to me. Never said anything?"

"I told you."

I was sobering up pretty damn fast as the adrenaline hit me. "Told me what?"

"That I can't forget you again."

I hadn't realized I'd been stepping back until my butt hit the counter. "So, I'm supposed to get out of that you're here watching me?" He remained quiet, so I went on, "You didn't think I'd be worried? That I'd want to know if you were okay? That I'd want to see you?"

His jaw twitched and he crossed his arms over his chest. "I'm standing here now."

Oh, my God. "Twelve days, Connor. Twelve days. And before that it was a month." My stomach churned and suddenly I didn't feel so good. Mental exhaustion, shock, anger, and alcohol did not mix.

"You haven't quit working at the bar," he said. "And you're not taking photos."

Did he really just say that? I was about to say that out loud when my attention was drawn to the door as a girl's squeaky voice said, "Yeah, it's locked. Some guy told me to fuck off."

Uh oh.

Connor's eyes shifted from me to the door and his entire body stiffened, arms uncurling, and hands forming into fists.

He stalked toward the door.

I ran after him, latching onto his arm. "Connor, stop. You can't start anything. Please. Let me go out first."

"Like hell you're going first," he replied and then placed his hands on my shoulders. "Stay behind me."

"But you—"

"I'll deal with it," he interrupted.

Okay, this was one of those times where arguing was pointless. So, I did the next best thing to try to keep him from doing something that might land him in jail. I grabbed his hand, linking my fingers with his.

Connor flipped the deadbolt and opened the door. There was a crowd of girls and one guy who stood in front of them all. He was bulky, a muscular bulky, with a trimmed beard and shaved head. He was dressed in black pants with a black T-shirt with the bar's logo in gold on the front.

His eyes ran the length of Connor, probably deciding if he could take him on, then shifted to me. "You okay, miss?"

I nodded. "Yeah. Sorry. It's my fault. I wasn't feeling well and just needed a minute—"

Connor's hand squeezed mine. I quickly glanced at him and his eyes were dark, mouth tight as he stared at the bouncer, his expression definitely threatening.

Connor had always been dangerous because he was trained to be, and with his muscled build, the tattoos on his arms, his scowl, he looked dangerous. But it had been more his attitude, the calm, controlled fearlessness.

But that was a long time ago. Now it was a raging, unpredictable fearlessness.

"You sure you're okay, miss?" The bouncer stepped into the bathroom.

"Yeah. I'm sure." I smiled, but it was shaky and I wasn't sure he bought it. "Thank you. Sorry about the door."

The bouncer obviously didn't believe me and with Connor's near explosive attitude, I kind of understood why. It was the guy's job to make sure the girls in the bar weren't harmed. I knew that firsthand. If we were at Matt's bar, they'd have already taken Connor out. Or tried to.

"You want to step outside, miss. I need to speak with the gentleman."

Shit. Shit. Shit.

Okay, I had to do something. If they so much as stepped into Connor's space, he'd explode. His body thrummed with anger and it was completely unreasonable, but I'd seen him lose it before. He told me himself he'd nearly pulled the trigger on the alarm guy because he wasn't seeing the alarm guy, he was seeing Carlos.

"Connor?" I quietly moved into him, my chest against his, one hand still in his and the other looping around the back of his neck. He was tall, really tall and since he was still looking at the bouncer, I had to stand on my tiptoes in order to kiss him, yet still my mouth couldn't reach his.

I applied pressure to his neck until he bent and my lips met his.

At first, his mouth remained unyielding beneath mine.

"Please, hon," I begged under his lips. "Kiss me."

Kissing him was like pushing up against a wall. Immovable. But then he suddenly gave.

His mouth melded to mine and his fingers weaved into my hair, bunching strands in his fist then pulling back to tilt my head farther so he could deepen the kiss.

There was a throat clearing and several voices behind us, but I kissed him until I felt his body give and relax. I slowly pulled back, my eyes searching his. Steady. Calm. "We have to go. Okay? Don't do anything. Please."

He hesitated before nodding. "Yeah."

"Okay."

He kept hold of my hand and still making certain his body protected me, he stalked toward the door and the bouncer.

It was fine. We'd go outside and he'd leave. He was okay.

And he was until the bouncer touched my arm on the way out the door. "You sure you want to go with him."

That was when all hell broke loose.

"Get your fuckin' hand off her." Connor shoved the bouncer in the chest so hard he staggered back into the wall.

"Connor. No." The bouncer pushed away from the wall, his cheeks red. Oh, shit. "Please. We're leaving. He's leaving."

"Damn right he is," the bouncer said.

"Alina? Hey. You okay?"

Shit. It was Chess and she was pushing toward me through the crowd of girls who had been waiting for the washroom.

She stopped when her eyes landed on Connor's hand clasped in mine. Then her mouth dropped open as she recognized whose hand I held.

I didn't have time to think about what to say to her because I had to get him out of here before there was a bigger scene and Georgie found out what was going on. It was not a good way to discover her brother was here.

"Go wait for me outside," Connor ordered without looking at me. His glare zeroed in on the bouncer who was five feet away. I was sure the bouncer was waiting for backup, which I had no doubt would be here any second.

Bouncers watched one another's backs. At least they did at Avalanche. So, I knew exactly what would happen. I also knew that as long as I stayed next to Connor, they'd avoid forcefully removing him. Instead, they'd try to talk him into leaving quietly.

"Connor, let's go." I tugged on his hand, which was like trying to unearth a tree. "We need to leave before your sister sees you."

That got his attention. He looked down at me, face stone cold then he headed for the door, taking me with him. The crowd of girls moved out of his way and as I looked back over my shoulder I saw the bouncer following us out.

Connor brushed right by Chess without even glancing at her, but I was uncertain if he'd even known who she was.

I managed to whisper to her on the way past, "Don't tell Georgie. Please. Let me talk to Deck first." I had no time to say anything more as we weaved through the bar to the front door.

His bike was literally right out front. Connor passed me the helmet and threw his leg over the seat. I glanced at the door.

Chess stood there frowning, so did the bouncer who chatted with another bouncer while his eyes remained on Connor.

The bike roared to life. "Babe," he said.

Pulling the helmet on, I did up the chinstrap, which took a few tries because my hands shook. Then I climbed on the back of his bike, pelvis snug to his ass and wrapped my arms around his waist.

"Good?" he asked.

"Yeah." But I wasn't good. I was confused and scared and I hated both those things.

The bike took off down the road and I didn't think about much except holding on. I did notice he kept it slow and took the corners easy and I wondered if that was because I'd been drinking.

It was only ten minutes before he turned down my street and stopped several houses away and I knew why—Deaglan.

I got off the bike, undid the chinstrap and pulled the helmet off, passing it to him. He threw his leg over then curved his arm around my shoulders bringing me up against him. "I need you to stay here a minute."

I stiffened, knowing exactly why he wanted me to stay here. "If Deaglan is there, we can talk to him. Tell him you're here then—"

His hold on me tightened. "Then what, Alina? You know where it goes from there." I did. Deaglan would call Deck and I was pretty sure Deck would be here within minutes. It would all come out soon enough though. Chess wasn't going to keep the secret for long.

"Then go. I'm capable of finding my way to the house." I was rarely snarky, never actually. But his coming and going, the hiding, the wondering if he was okay or if I'd ever see him again, all of it was pounding down on me.

He'd just dragged me out of the bar because he didn't like guys ogling me.

I pushed out of his embrace and turned to head to the house. I managed three steps before he snagged my arm. "Alina."

"What?" I shot back.

His brows lowered. "I need more time."

"Well, your time has run out because Chess saw you tonight. You know who Chess is, don't you? Kai's sister. I'm guessing she'll give you until morning because I asked her to and then Kai will know. Then Deck. And you know what happens after that?" I didn't give him a chance to answer. "You disappear."

"Shutterbug." He pulled me into his arms, hand on the small of my back, the other cupping my cheek.

Did he really have to do that? It wasn't fair and I already felt myself wavering. "Don't call me that."

"I won't disappear. I'm here. I've always been here." His voice softened and his thumb stroked back and forth on my cheek. "Baby, please. Let me do this my way."

I sighed, head bowing and his hand slipped away. I was not a fighter. Connor was. He was also tormented and alone and I was the only person he had let back into his life. "Fine. I'll go in alone and you do what you normally do and ghost your way in after. I'll leave the alarm off."

He hesitated, his eyes on the barely lit street.

"It's a residential street, Connor. I'm fine."

He finally nodded and I walked home, but there wasn't a moment I didn't feel his eyes on me. I smelled cigarette smoke on my porch and knew Deaglan was home. He rarely smoked, or so he claimed, but on the odd night he came outside and had one.

"London didn't drop you off?"

I dropped my key that I was about to put in the lock at the sound of Deaglan's voice. "Ah, no. I got a ride." I bent, picked up the key and inserted it in the lock. "Do you have company?" I asked, meaning a girl in his bed.

"Nope."

"Guess it's an off night then." I opened the door.

He leaned his arms on the railing of the porch. "Don't have off nights, pet. I have nights off. So, who gave you the ride?"

"A friend. I'll see you." I rushed inside and shut the door then disarmed the alarm.

I climbed the stairs and had just put my purse on the chair when Connor appeared in the doorway.

"Oh, my God. How did you get in so fast?"

His brows lifted, an arrogant smirk appearing on his lips. "Distraction, baby. Deaglan was talking to you, not paying attention to me. I came in through the back when I heard you punch in the alarm code." He came toward me. "Come here. You look like you're about to fall over."

"It's the heels." I yanked them off and the arches of my feet breathed a sigh of relief.

He snorted. "It's the margaritas."

Reaching me, Connor slipped his hand in mine and guided me into the bathroom. He picked me up and set me on the counter. He grabbed my toothbrush from the yellow ceramic jar, put toothpaste on it then passed it to me.

"Thanks," I mumbled before I shoved it in my mouth. While I

brushed, he stood in front of me, hands on my thighs and watched. I pulled the brush from my mouth. "Why are you watching me?"

He reached up and wiped his thumb over the toothpaste on the corner of my mouth. "I watch you all the time."

"All the time?"

He shrugged. "When I'm here. Yes."

"Can you see me in the house?"

"Yes. When the drapes aren't drawn."

"From where?" I tipped forward to look into my bedroom at the windows.

He gently shoved me back. "From another house."

I scrunched my nose. "You know they have a name for that. It's called stalking. And it's creepy."

There was a twitch upward at the corners of his mouth. "Do you think I'm creepy, Alina?"

I stuck the toothbrush in my mouth and brushed again as I thought about it. He watched me from another house. Was that creepy? It would be really creepy if it weren't Connor and knowing why he was doing it. He was also honest about doing it, although it was after the fact.

I pulled the brush from my mouth again. "No. I don't think you're creepy. But I'd prefer if you'd watch me from inside my house."

"It's safer this way. You done?" he asked.

I nodded and he put his hands on my hips and helped me down. He turned on the taps and I rinsed my mouth then the toothbrush before dropping it back in the jar.

He led me into my bedroom and undressed me. I tried to argue that I was capable, which I was, but Connor ignored me as he unzipped the back of my dress and then peeled it down my body until it pooled at my feet on the floor.

I stepped out as he turned me so he could undo the clasp on my bra. I shivered when his fingers brushed my bare skin and I was pretty sure he noticed because there was a subtle groan.

PERFECT RAGE

He gently slid it off my arms and then tossed it on the chair where he picked up my camisole. "Arms."

I held up my arms and the silky material fell into place.

I thought he'd kiss me then, but he didn't. He drew back the covers and I slid into the bed, but he made no move to join me.

"You're leaving." It was a statement.

"Yeah. Not a good night for me, shutterbug."

I was uncertain what exactly that meant, whether it was because of what happened at the bar or outside in the street or if his head was bothering him a lot. I pushed up in bed. "Maybe, if you stay with me for a bit, it will get better?" He walked to the door, so I added, "Please. Until I fall asleep."

His hand was on the door frame.

I saw the second he gave as his shoulders sagged. He turned and headed back to the bed then said, "Not long and the boots stay on."

I smiled. "I don't care about the boots on the bed, Connor." And I knew why he wanted them on. So he could leave fast. I was pretty sure he was thinking about what I said about Chess knowing and if she decided to tell Kai tonight, we could have company at any moment.

He sat on the bed, leaned against the headboard then lifted his legs and crossed his ankles. His black motorcycle boots clashed with the pale yellow flowered sheets and the crocheted blanket at the end of the bed. He also looked completely uncomfortable.

I shimmied over to him and snuggled into his side with my cheek resting on his chest, my palm over his heart. "I like it when you ogle me."

He grunted.

"Connor?"

"Yeah?"

"Can you tell me if you're going to leave for a while again?"

His hand settled on my head and he softly stroked my hair. I was almost asleep when he said, "Yeah, baby."

"Promise me."

"Yeah, I promise you."

It was a few hours later when I woke in the darkness.

Connor was still sitting up in bed with his arm around me, our hands linked while resting on his chest.

His head was back leaning on the headboard and his eyes were closed, breathing deeply. He was asleep.

CHAPTER SIXTEEN

Question 8: One superpower you'd want to have.

Alina

I BOLTED UPRIGHT AT the sound of glass shattering. It took me a second before I wrapped my foggy mind around what the hell was happening.

Another crash.

I threw the covers back and leapt out of bed wincing as my pounding head rejected the idea of moving too fast.

Margaritas and shots definitely did not sit well the next day.

A quick as my head would allow, I snapped on my bra and pale blue V-neck that lay over the lounge chair then dashed over to my dresser and yanked out my jeans. I pulled them on while I hopped on one foot toward the door.

Zipping up my jeans, I ran down the hall. When I reached the top of the stairs, the front door opened and Deaglan appeared. His eyes immediately landed on me. He shook his head and gestured with his hand to get back.

I didn't. Because if it wasn't a stranger making a racket in my kitchen, I knew who it was—Connor. He'd stayed with me last night.

I ran down the stairs and Deaglan grabbed my arm before I managed to dart by him and scramble into the kitchen. "No fuckin' way. Get behind me."

It was then I saw the gun in his right hand and fear clutched my chest. "Deaglan. It's Connor."

His eyes narrowed, lips pursed. "Connor?" He didn't wait for an answer because he knew I wouldn't make something like that up. "Fuck." He let me go and reached in his pocket and took out his cell.

I put my hand on his arm. "No. Please. Don't call him yet."

He paused, his finger resting on the illuminated screen. "You know I can't do that." I did. Deck was Deaglan's friend and he was asked to keep an eye on me.

"Then give me ten minutes. Please. He stayed here with me last night. He's been here before." His eyes widened with surprise then quickly narrowed. "And if he sees you with a gun… Deaglan, if he's confronted, it won't end well. I can calm him down."

He snorted. "No chance. Deck would kill me."

"Connor will kill you if you go in there with a gun."

Another crash but it wasn't glass. I didn't know what it was.

Deaglan looked at his phone and tapped on the screen "Sorry, pet. Nope. We call in Deck and you're going outsid—"

I took off for the kitchen.

"Fuck." He raced after me.

I ran faster. I made it around the corner into the kitchen just as he snagged my arm.

I panicked, eyes darting to him. "Deaglan, your hand. He'll freak if you're holding me."

He must have read my panic because he instantly let me go, at the same time as Connor noticed us, his eyes wild and red, shifting from me to Deaglan then back again.

I was thankful that Deaglan was behind me and Connor couldn't see the gun because I knew he'd react to it especially with me being close.

No one moved.

I stared at the disaster. All the cupboard doors were open, a couple hanging at odd angles as he'd obviously yanked on them too hard. Connor had ripped the cutlery tray out of the drawer and dumped the utensils on the counter. Forks, spoons, and knives were scattered everywhere, some having landed on the floor.

There were several plates on the floor, too, broken pieces everywhere and the figurine of a dog, a tan and white boxer that sat on the windowsill.

It wasn't mine, but I liked it and I was sure Grandma Kane had liked it since it had its own special spot.

Oh, my God. What was he doing?

"Connor?" I stepped forward, ignoring Deaglan's low growl not to move. "What's wrong?"

I nearly ran when his eyes darkened and hands curled into fists at his sides. Nearly. But I'd been with the machine Connor. I'd been with the overprotective sweet and cocky Connor and I'd been with this Connor. The man who was trying to come to terms with what he'd done while on the drug.

"The pictures," he shouted, voice threaded with anger. "What happened to them?"

"Oh, God." I covered my mouth with my hand. I stared at all the open drawers and cupboards. He'd been searching for the pictures. "They're gone."

I felt Deaglan's eyes on me and as long as he was there, it meant he wasn't calling Deck.

Connor dropped the drawer he held in his hand and it clattered to the floor. It was all over his face. The way his eyes half closed, how his brows knitted together, how his shoulders sagged.

He knew. That was what this was about. He'd remembered burning them and he didn't want to believe it was true, so he was looking for them. "I burned them."

I nodded.

He lowered his head then collapsed into the chair, his legs parted, elbows resting on them as he cradled his head. "You watched me," he muttered. Again I nodded, although he wasn't looking at me.

I remembered hearing the fire crackle as it ate away at our memories. The smoke billowing into the air and the scent drifting into me. Our memories turned to ash within minutes.

"Why the fuck would I do that?" His fingers curled into his hair. "Why?"

I heard Deaglan swear beneath his breath. Connor either didn't notice or didn't care anymore.

I moved into him so my thighs touched his knees. I wasn't sure whether I should touch him or not. "You didn't know."

He lifted his head then reached for me. His hands went to my hips then he pulled me into him. I parted my legs and moved up onto his lap and straddled his waist.

I glanced over my shoulder at Deaglan who watched us. He nodded to me before turning and leaving the room, but not before I saw him lift his phone and tap on the screen.

Shit. He was calling Deck.

"I fell asleep last night, baby. You in my arms.... Fuck, I fell asleep for too long and this shit messed with my head. I woke up and didn't think it was true. I thought if I found them.... Jesus, what the fuck did I do?" He ran his hands up and down my back. "I need you safe. That's all I can think about."

PERFECT RAGE

"He's dead, Connor. I'm safe. You're safe," I said.

He sighed. "Yeah."

I inhaled a deep breath then said, "Connor, this can't continue. Showing up at the bar last night was too much." He remained quiet. "You can't follow me and expect me to do whatever you say. I know you want to stay hidden, but I don't. I was hidden away for eleven years and I want to live a normal life. Or as normal as I can."

He tensed and drew back. "Drinking and dancing in front of a bunch of guys wanting to get in your pants is not living."

"Yeah, it is."

"No. It fuckin' isn't."

"I was dancing."

"I didn't like it." He stood, taking me with him then let me go as he crouched and picked up shards of glass. I went to help when he shot me a glare. "No, babe. I'll do it. You're in bare feet and there's glass on the floor. Sit."

My chest swelled and my belly flipped. Connor. That was so Connor. It was what he did. He protected others. He wouldn't ask me to get the broom or the vacuum; he'd make sure I was looked after first and foremost.

He did that with everyone. Except there was no longer everyone, because he wouldn't let anyone else in. There was only me and even I was something tentative.

"I never had friends, Connor. Not like you did and despite what you think—still do." I tucked my feet up onto the chair and wrapped my arms around my legs. "Kids were too scared to be my friend with my dad's involvement with...." Still crouched and picking up shards from the dog figurine, he stopped, eyes lifting to meet mine. "I have friends now and I don't want to lose them, but I want you, too.

"I fell for you, Connor. I fell in love with you a long time ago. I may not have known all of you, but I knew who you were, what type of person. And I loved who I was with you."

"You love a man who's dead. That's not me now, Alina."

"Maybe not. But whoever you've become, you're still the man I love. You're still him and remembering what you've done is killing you. But you know why it is? Because you still have the good parts. If you didn't care, none of the stuff you did while drugged would matter to you."

He lowered his head and stared at the broken fragments on the floor. "It drives me nuts seeing you around other guys. All I can think about is you being taken away from me again. All I see is him."

Maybe I understood that, but it was something he had to work through. I couldn't stop living. "I want to do stuff I missed doing. I like working in a bar and I like being around people."

His head jerked up and he tensed. "You don't belong in a fuckin' bar. You should be taking photographs."

I sighed. He didn't get it because all he saw was me being surrounded by people and he didn't like it. "That's not the point. I get to decide where I want to work. I get to decide if I want to dance or if I want to drink until I pass out. I decide, Connor. Me. Finally, I have a choice." I paused then said, "And you're my choice, too. I choose you. I want you and I'll give up things in order to have you, but not living."

He abruptly stood. "You want to feel alive, shutterbug? I'll show you alive." He picked me up and carried me across the room then set me on my feet. He linked his fingers with mine and headed down the hallway for the front door.

But Deaglan blocked the door and he had his phone to his ear. He said, "Get here." Then he slowly lowered the phone, his eyes locked on Connor.

But Connor was looking at me. He nodded to my black flats on the matt. "Baby, shoes."

Right. Shoes. I let go of his hand and slipped into them then he put his hand in mine again.

"Move," Connor said to Deaglan.

PERFECT RAGE

Deaglan's hand went to his waist and my heart skipped a beat. "No," I said, stepping in front of Connor, which he seriously didn't like as he abruptly shoved me behind him. I squeezed his hand. "He's just protecting me, Connor."

"I don't give a shit what he thinks he's doing. And if he were any good at protecting you, he'd have known I was here last night."

Deaglan glared, but he didn't take out his gun. "Deck's on his way."

"Good for him. Now out of my way."

"She stays here." Deaglan nodded to me.

Connor laughed. "How about this? We ask her. She wants to stay then I walk out alone. But she wants to go with me, you let us pass without a fight." He smirked. "You know as well as I do where you'll end up if there's a fight though."

I did. On the floor with a gun in his face. I didn't know Deaglan's combat experience, but I knew Connor's and from Deaglan's slow nod, he did, too.

I hated being put in this position. I was beginning to like Deaglan and he was trying to protect me, but if Connor left without me... I didn't know what he'd do.

"I'm sorry. I have to," I said to Deaglan. "He needs me."

Connor squeezed my hand and I looked up at him and he half smiled.

"You need to talk to Deck, Alina." Deaglan stepped to the right of the door, letting us pass.

"I know," I said.

Connor remained quiet, but his eyes never left Deaglan as he unlocked the deadbolt and opened the door. Then he kicked open the screen with the toe of his boot and held it open for me to pass through first.

"Say the word," Deaglan asked before I walked out.

I smiled. Okay, I really liked him. Despite his playboy status, he was a good guy because he was laying it down for me. He'd fight Connor if I didn't want to go with him, even knowing he'd lose. "Thanks. Tell Deck, I'm good, okay? That he can trust me."

He nodded while Connor urged me out the door with his hand on the small of my back.

I jogged to keep up with him as we walked down the street to an old abandoned house that had the windows boarded up. It was where he'd dropped me off last night. I'd seen the for sale sign out front since I moved here.

Oh, God, this was where he watched my house.

He steered me down the driveway to the right side of the house where I saw a blue tarp draped over something. He let my hand go and yanked it off.

His bike. He'd left it on the street. "I didn't hear you start your bike last night."

"Rolled it here while you were walking to your house."

"Oh."

He unhooked his helmet from the handlebar and turned to me, sliding it on my head then gently tucking in strands of hair. I shivered at the soft touch of the pads of his fingers. He did the chinstrap up, then tightened it. I felt like I had a bowling ball on my head. It was also too big so when I tipped my head forward, it dropped in front of my eyes.

"I'll buy you one." Staring at me a second, a slow grin appeared. "Fuck, you're hot, baby."

"You saw me in it last night." But my heart pitter-pattered. Not so much that he thought I looked hot, although that was amazing, it was that he grinned.

I melted at his grin. It was how I got into trouble with him in the first place. His grin could win over any girl. It was magnetic, with the way his blue eyes sparked and his brows lifted slightly while dimples danced on his cheeks.

"Yeah, but last night was a clusterfuck and my head was on getting you out of there." He threw his leg over his bike, started the engine, shifted his weight to straighten it and then kicked up the stand.

Connor liked to go fast. At least he told me he did on the dirt bikes he used to race, so I was a little nervous.

"I'll look after you," he said, reading my thoughts. "Couldn't look after you for eleven years. Now I can." He nodded to his bike. "This bike is the only place I feel alive unless I'm with you." He smirked. "Get your sweet, sexy ass on the bike. I want to be between your legs."

Heat settled in deep. He was teasing and he smirked.

He took my hand as I stepped closer. "Living is one big spin of the wheel, baby. Might as well enjoy the ride until it stops."

I stared at him a second and he caressed the side of my face. He'd whispered those exact words to me once upon a time. I repeated the same response as I had then. "I get dizzy on rides."

Connor's brows lifted as did the corner of his lip. "That's the point of the ride."

As the wash of his words drifted over me, I closed my eyes. They were words he'd said before all this hurt and pain.

He reached out and snapped the visor down on my helmet. "Get your ass on the bike before I change my mind and take you on a different ride."

I was okay with that ride, too, but I was thinking it was better to get out of here before Deck and the others showed up.

But that was coming to a head. Deck would be all over this and Connor was good, but I don't think he'd be able to watch me any longer without Deck knowing about it.

Things were changing fast. I just didn't know which way they'd go.

Connor leaving or Connor confronting his demons.

I slid on the back of the bike, pressed my body up against his while settling my hands on his abdomen then he tapped my hands once and we took off.

NASHODA ROSE

CHAPTER SEVENTEEN

WE RODE FOR hours on deserted roads, my body snug to his, the vibration of the engine beneath me, the wind catching the loose strands of my hair and tickling my cheeks.

He was right. This was living. The open air with the sun rising and nothing but the road in front of you.

No destination. No tomorrow.

It was freedom. Something both of us had lost for a long time.

He pulled onto a dirt road and the back tire skidded but he easily straightened it out. He drove slowly along the gravel before turning down a path into the trees. There were two well-worn tire tracks in the hard-packed dirt.

The tree line ended and there was an open space. And a dirt track, *the* dirt bike track. This was where he used to hang out. He'd told me about racing here as a kid, then when he was older, helping the younger kids.

He'd brought Georgie here, too.

He stopped the bike and I got off, my legs a little shaky after the long ride. He slid off as well while I took off my helmet and set it on the seat. Without saying anything, he put his hand in mine and walked toward the winding, hilly track.

It appeared unused. There were weeds growing on the track and the grass surrounding was overgrown. It was secluded being surrounded by trees and far enough away from the main road. A perfect spot for teenagers to hang out and roar around on a Saturday afternoon.

I imagined a young Connor standing on the sidelines laughing with his friends. Connor would've been the fearless one. The kid who tore around the track ahead of everyone else.

I'd trade anything to capture a picture of that.

He let go of my hand and I stopped while he bent, picked up a stone and tossed it off the dirt path. "Wiped out right here," he said, nodding to the steep mound that sharply curved to the right. "Bike was fucked. I wasn't much better. Couldn't ride for weeks and I remember thinking it was hell not being able to get on my bike."

He sat, legs bent, arms hanging over them. "Babe, sit."

I sat beside him and he continued, "When I came here for two days, I did nothing except remember. And I hated myself. Hated everything. It fuckin' rained for several hours straight. Seemed rather fitting."

He picked up a handful of dirt and let it slip through his fingers. "The track was always a nightmare when it was wet. Barely able to see where the hell you were going because there was so much mud splattered on your visor. But fuck, it was fun. Heart pounding, adrenaline pumping, and one huge rush. No rules out here, just riding because we loved it. We loved the risk. The danger. The edge as the bike thrummed beneath you." He sighed, shaking his head, before lying back and throwing his arm over his eyes. "I'm on edge, Alina. Constantly. But it's different, not like before. It's like my finger is on the trigger and if I make the wrong move, the gun will go off and it'll all end. Don't know what the end is." He sighed. "I don't trust myself. Do you know what

PERFECT RAGE

that's like? Unable to trust yourself?"

With the gentle breeze, the tree branches swayed in the distance and a few ducks squawked as they flew overhead. I lay back beside him and said, "Maybe it's not about trusting yourself, Connor, but first trusting those around you? The people who know you and love you."

He didn't respond, but maybe that was a good sign and he was thinking about it. He needed his friends. His family.

He shuffled onto his side, up on his elbow so he faced me. My hands rested on my upper abdomen and he gently lifted my shirt with one finger so there was three inches of skin showing. "Tell me something, babe. Something normal. Just talk. I want to hear your voice."

I lay on the grass and stared up at the clouds that half covered the sun. Normal. I was trying to find normal and I wanted Connor to find it with me.

"I'm thinking about adopting a cat. One a little older who needs a home. I've never had a cat, never had a pet, and I really like the barn cats at the Center." If he'd been following me, he knew about Tristan and Chess's Treasured Children's Center.

"Question six. You've never had a pet." He said it more to himself than to me.

His fingers traced over my skin, slow and rhythmic as if he were drawing something. And when I tilted my head to look at him, he was focused on what he was doing, so I continued.

"The cats come running whenever I walk into the barn. There's this little grey guy called Jiggy, because he does this little jig with his back legs before he takes off running. It's like he gets revved up." He leaned closer and my breath hitched as he gently kissed my belly button. Then he went back to drawing.

"I thought I'd go to the cat rescue on Saturday, see if there's one that wants to come home with me."

"They'll all want to come home with you, baby," he said while his focus remained on my abdomen.

Then I blurted, "Will you come with me?" It was a long shot. I mean I hadn't intended on asking him, and I had no idea if he even liked cats, but I wanted him with me and it was doing something normal together.

His finger glided along the edge of my jeans from one hip to the other. "To adopt a cat?"

I nodded.

"Anyone else going?"

"No."

"It's important to you?"

I nodded. "Yeah."

It was a good ten seconds before he said, "Okay, baby."

"Okay?" He'd come with me? I hadn't expected him to say yes. A smidge of hope rose that maybe there was a chance for us.

"No orange."

"Huh?"

"No orange cats."

I bit my lip, trying to control my laughter. Oh, my God, he really hated orange. I didn't care what color cat I brought home, so it didn't matter to me. "But I kind of had my heart set on an orange one," I teased. "The oranger the better."

He snorted, rolling his eyes. "Oranger?"

I shrugged. "Yeah. And maybe we could call him Orangey."

His was on top of me before I had the chance to get away, his hands digging into my sides, weight pinning me down as he tickled me.

I screamed. "Stop. Connor, stop." I wiggled and squirmed beneath him, half laughing, half screaming.

"No fuckin' orange cats."

"Oh, my God. Connor. Stop," I yelled while giggling.

"Alina," he growled. The sound was fierce, but the undertone was playful.

I was going to pee my pants if he didn't stop. "Okay. Okay. No orange cats."

The tickling stopped and I was breathing hard while he stared down at me grinning.

Grinning.

His hard cock pressed into my pelvis and there was unmistakable desire flaring in the depths of his eyes.

I slowly ran my tongue over my lips and his gaze followed. Curling my fingers into his shirt, I urged him closer, but he resisted.

Shit, the grin was gone and his brows furrowed.

"What's wrong?"

"Don't give up on me, Alina. You've been through hell, too, and I don't deserve you. Fuck, I destroyed your kitchen this morning. I can't stand seeing you with other guys. I dragged you from a bar. I fuck you and disappear. I'm a complete, messed-up asshole." He closed his eyes, sighing. "I'm lost, baby. I'm so fuckin' lost and you're the only one to keep me from disintegrating." He lowered his head, lips a breath away from me as he murmured, "I can't ever lose you again."

"I'm here, Connor," I whispered. "I'm right here."

His lips met mine and he kissed me. It was a combination of desperation with gentle warmth. And he controlled everything about it.

Connor took his time slowly undressing me.

Then took his time tasting me until my screams echoed in the air and I quivered against his mouth. That was when he put on a condom, flipped me so I was on top of him and I lowered onto his hard, throbbing cock.

I rode him fast like the bikes on the track. And it wasn't long before both of us were trembling in one another's arms as we came together.

Connor

"You should be taking photos, not serving drunk assholes." I hated this. I hated dropping her off at a bar knowing she'd have guys looking at her all night. It was ludicrous thinking, but I couldn't help it.

I never used to be the jealous type. I was too full of myself for that shit, but this wasn't exactly jealousy. This was about keeping her safe. I had this constant pit in my gut that someone was going to take her away from me again.

But what was worse, dropping her off two blocks away from Avalanche because I knew Deck and his men would be looking for us after what happened this morning.

I didn't like Alina having to walk to the bar by herself. I should be with her, damn it.

She passed me the helmet and I strapped it on the back as she said, "I don't want to take pictures anymore. And I like my job."

That was complete bullshit.

A passion like that didn't die. It was ingrained in you, a part of you. Alina had looked at the world through a lens and saw shit that others didn't. She saw beauty when there wasn't any. She fuckin' made beauty when there wasn't any. She captured life in her photographs.

I tagged her hand and pulled her into me. "You loved taking photographs, baby."

"You loved helping kids."

Fuck. "It's different."

"No. It's not," she replied. "You're avoiding your friends and family and helping kids who need you."

"Need me?" I snorted. "You think I can help kids like this? Jesus Christ, don't you get it? I'm damaged. I can never be around kids again. I'll never have kids, Alina. I don't want them. I'm not going to get that happily ever after and if you think that's where this is headed, you're wrong. It's not. Not even fuckin' close." She pushed off me, her eyes hard and narrowed. "What? You don't like hearing the truth? Well, that's the truth. And going to pick out some cat isn't going to change what this is."

"What this is? What is it then, Connor? Tell me because I just spent a morning with you and it sure as hell felt like something."

"It is something, damn it," I retorted. "It will always be something. But you need to get your head out of the clouds. I'm not who I used to be. Never will be."

She crossed her arms and glared. "Did I ask you to be?" she yelled. "Did I ever ask you to be anyone else than who you are now?"

"I fuckin' see it."

"No, Connor, that's all you. You think everyone, including me, won't accept you for who you are now. But it's you who can't accept it." I glanced away, hands curling around the handlebars. "You say you're lost? That's because you want to stay lost. You don't want to be found." Then she said, "I'm not the same person either, Connor. I've changed, too."

I straightened my bike, and started the engine. The rage pulsed, my head pounded. She was angry and Alina rarely got angry or raised her voice.

I did this to her.

Fuck, why the hell couldn't I just disappear, leave her the hell alone, so she could get her happily ever after? "Make sure someone puts you in the cab later," I said.

"Fuck you, Connor." She spun on her heel and walked down the sidewalk. "You want to see me, then get un-lost."

"That's not a word, Alina," I yelled.

"You're in my world now, so I'm making it one." She used my own words back at me from when we first met.

I sat on my bike staring at her walk away, engine vibrating beneath me, her words ripping through me.

It was the fuckin' cat. Telling her I'd go with her to pick out a cat. Spending the afternoon between her legs. Licking her pussy, tasting her, sucking on her clit as she screamed and tightened around me.

It was all of it.

And yeah, it was fuckin' something. But it sure as hell wasn't us going to pick out a cat together. It wasn't me dropping my girl off at work and telling her to have a good shift. It wasn't getting up in the morning and slipping between her thighs then having coffee while we sat in bed snuggling.

It was me breaking into her house and destroying her kitchen. It was me punching the wall above her head. It was me fucking off when the rage was too much.

That was what our something was now.

I put my feet up and took off down the street with the rippling tension shifting through me.

Christ, what the fuck did she want from me? This was it. This was me.

Volatile. Irrational. Impulsive.

And yeah, I was lost, but despite everything I just spewed, I wanted to go with her to pick out a fuckin' cat.

And if she wanted orange, I'd live with orange.

CHAPTER EIGHTEEN

Question 9: Swim or laze on the beach?

PAST

Catalina

"TAKE OFF YOUR clothes and lean over the couch."

I stood inside the door, hand clinging to the knob because my legs were shaking so badly. And it was for the simple fact I'd be able to escape before I made it all the way across the room.

No. Escape wasn't an option. I had to do this. It was my last chance to help him remember.

The pool house was one large room with a couch, a king-size bed and kitchen. Connor sat at the island on a swivel barstool, staring back toward me. There were bullets laying on the counter and parts of a gun.

"Are you going to stand there or do what I tell you, bitch?"

My heart felt as if it were beating in quicksand, sinking under a thick sludge with his callousness.

Because Connor would never speak to me so coldly.

"Or would you rather suck my cock first?" He held the barrel of the gun in his hand, a cloth in the other.

"I… ah… ." Jesus, I had to pull my shit together before he kicked me out and my last chance slipped from my grasp. Carlos had his meeting with the Vault associate and Connor was leaving tomorrow. It had been a week since the last time I stood in the pool house facing him, but this time, I was here to do more than talk.

But he scared me.

I couldn't read him and I wasn't entirely confident that he wouldn't kill me, or at the very least hurt me.

"On the bed," I said, straightening my shoulders and meeting his eyes.

His back stiffened and his hand stilled. He then tossed the gun on the counter and it made a loud clatter. "I didn't offer that option." His stool scraped on the ceramic tiles as he shoved it back.

I swear my heart was either going to stop or burst right through my chest. *I could do this. For him, I could do this.*

He stalked toward me. And it was a stalk. A predator approaching its prey. The question was how he intended to take me down.

I was stupid prey, too, because I should have had the instinct in me to run. But my instinct was skewed because everything in me said to stay still. I knew the outcome. He was going to break me into pieces then devour each one.

Regardless of his cruel words, my mind still saw the man he had been. His memories were gone, but mine were intact and being near him ignited my feelings for him.

And as he approached, his long lean legs confident with each step, my belly flipped and I felt the little tweaks between my thighs.

I inhaled deeply, released the door handle and raised my chin as he came toe to toe with me.

Neither of us moved.

I stared into his deep blue eyes, turbulent ice-cold waves. There wasn't a hint of playfulness with that cute smirk that used to make my heart flutter.

He half smiled, but it was stern and gave me chills. His hand curled around the back of my neck and it took everything I had not to close my eyes and sag against him. To throw my arms around him and sob. To have his arms fold me into his protective strength and take me away from here.

But this wasn't about me. It was about him.

His thumb stroked back and forth along my hairline. "Do you always fuck your husband's business acquaintances?"

I shook my head. "No."

"Then why me?"

He wouldn't accept the truth so I went with another truth. "My husband hasn't touched me in three years." I'd become his trophy, untouched and sitting on a shelf only to be admired. Sometimes I wondered why he kept me alive, but I was an obsession, a possession. Everything was a game, even me and Connor. We were one big game to him, for him to toy with our emotions, our lives.

The lines around his mouth eased. He stepped toward the couch, taking me with him with his hand still on my neck. "You don't have a choice where I fuck you."

I stopped. Time to be brave. "You want to fuck me, Connor. Then we do it on the bed and you wear this." I uncurled my hand and held out the shiny gold square package.

I'd stolen the condom from Diego's room. He had them scattered all over his dresser and I knew this because he didn't bother shutting his door even when he fucked girls.

His brows drew together as he stared down at the condom then he swiped it from my hand and stuck it in his front pocket of his black cargo pants.

He gestured to my blouse with a chin-lift. "Take it off."

Shit, well at least he took the condom. I was on birth control, but I didn't know who Connor had slept with over the years.

I licked my lips, took another deep breath to try to settle my nerves, and then undid the top button of my shirt. My fingers trembled so badly that it took me a while because I couldn't get the stupid things undone. What made it worse was Connor's eyes were on me.

"Christ," I swore under my breath as I fiddled with the third one and I couldn't push it through the little slit.

"Fuck. Let me." He shoved my hands aside then quickly undid the tiny white buttons. I was surprised he didn't just tear my blouse off, but it made sense he didn't. If I were caught going back to my room with a ripped shirt, questions would be asked.

I watched his hands. Hands that had held mine. Hands that caressed my hair while we'd danced under the stars. That cupped my jaw before he kissed me.

A choked sob escaped my throat.

Connor's fingers paused on the last button and his head lifted and our eyes locked. "Second thoughts?"

"I... I... no," I choked out. "No," I repeated stronger, more to convince myself than him.

"Stupid girl," he drawled.

He parted my shirt sliding it off my shoulders, the tips of his fingers lightly brushing my skin.

Goose bumps.

Tingles.

Quivers.

I stared at Connor, his hands gliding from my shoulders to my wrists while his eyes remained locked on me. Tweaks erupted between my legs and my chest swelled.

Connor. This was Connor. The man I gave myself to. Who I gave my everything. And when I left him seven years ago, I left my everything with him.

His fingers trailed a gentle path up my skin to my breasts. Across one nipple, pausing for a second to lightly pinch. Then he moved to the other.

My body reacted and I closed my eyes, "Connor," I whispered. "Please, remember."

I winced when his fingers suddenly squeezed my nipple hard. My eyes flew open and I was greeted by a fierce scowl. His hand shot to the back of my head, fingers cruelly bunched in my hair as he yanked my head back. "Did he send you?"

I swallowed. Heart aching as it slowly sank deeper in the thick sludge.

I put my hand on top of his trying to ease the pressure on my scalp. "You're hurting me."

"Answer me."

"No. He doesn't know. I told you that."

"You're terrified of me and yet you're here risking your life to be fucked. You know as well as I that if Moreno didn't send you, then he will kill you if he finds out. And if he doesn't, you'll wish you were dead. So,"—he yanked on my hair—"tell me the fuckin' truth."

The truth. The truth was a mess of forgotten moments. His forgotten moments. And maybe he was right and I was stupid for not running.

"I'm not scared." I gritted my teeth and straightened my spine, despite the fact that it caused more pain on my scalp.

"Keep telling yourself that, bitch."

We stared at one another, neither of us moving.

Then he threw back his head and laughed. It was far from the laugh that made my insides heat, and tingles to spread like wildfire across my skin.

No, this was severe and the lightness absent from his eyes.

"You're like a quivering rabbit hanging from a wolf's mouth." My chest rose and fell erratically as he forced me backward until the backs of my legs hit the edge of the mattress. "The truth," he growled, stepping so close I had no choice but to fall back onto the bed. At least he was giving into my bed demand or it was the simple fact the bed had been closer than the couch.

I managed to get up on my elbows, before he followed. Thighs on either side of me as he crawled on top of me. "What the hell do you want?"

"I want you to kiss me," I mumbled.

It was the truth. I did. Desperately. But I wanted him to kiss me as Connor, not this man who straddled my trembling body.

He ran his hand up my bare calf, underneath my skirt, to my inner thigh. "You sure about that? I'm not going to be gentle."

I suspected he wouldn't be.

I nodded. "I'm sure."

His hand was now between my legs and with one yank, he ripped my panties off. I curled my hands into the sheets on either side of me as I stared at him, refusing to look away as his fingers slipped between my lips.

He scowled, eyes narrowed and lips pursed. "You wet from fear, Catalina?"

Maybe. No, definitely, but also desire. Because I recognized Connor's touch, the feel of his weight on top of me, his voice, his smell. It was him and my body knew it. There was no question I was scared of what he was capable of, but I was also desperate to have him again.

What I hated was him calling me Catalina. He'd never called me that.

He kept his eyes locked on me as one finger slipped inside me. I closed my eyes and tilted my head back moaning.

"Fuck," he growled.

Then his mouth was on mine. Crushing. Bruising. Forcing my lips apart so his tongue could invade. And it was invasive and I didn't like it.

Oh, God, I didn't like it.

He shoved another finger inside me.

I lied stiff, unmoving. Hands scrunched into the sheet at my sides, tears pooled in my eyes as he cruelly kissed me.

Connor. It was the loss of him all over again. The agony. The hurt. The pain dragging me under until I had nothing left. But this was far worse than the months after I left him. Because now he was lost, too. Connor was gone.

A tear escaped.

This was a stranger. What made me think that it would be different? That once he kissed me, he'd remember?

His weight lifted slightly and I heard the package rip and then his zipper. I stared at the ceiling, trying not to cry.

This wasn't his fault.

I'd offered myself to him.

I gasped, tensing at the sudden intrusion. I hadn't pictured it this way. God, he was right. I was stupid. I thought…. God, it didn't matter what I thought. He had no idea who I was. Vault and Carlos had killed everything we'd had and that was more devastating than anything he could ever do to me now.

"Legs," he ordered, one hand grabbed my thigh and hitched it around his waist.

I bent my other one and he sank deeper.

His breathing was harsh and ragged as his cock throbbed inside me. "Look at me."

I briefly closed my eyes before meeting his cool blue eyes.

His brows flicked low and he shook his head then muttered, "What the fuck?"

I had no idea what was wrong, but there was confusion on his face as his gaze shifted from my eyes to my nose then to my lips.

His cock jerked inside me and his eyes darted back to mine.

It wasn't harsh. It was gentle as his eyes searched mine.

Hope. Fear. Pain. Desire.

It was all those things crushed together and pinballing around in my head. I was afraid to say anything. Afraid to move. Did he remember? Why was he staring at me like that? God, please say something.

He squeezed his eyes shut and a low groan escaped. His fingers holding my hip flinched and then he kissed me again.

It was harsh and rough, but there was something more. There was desperation. There was passion. There was a hint of Connor and I grabbed hold of that and relaxed beneath him.

Then I let go of the sheets and found myself holding him. Fingers weaving through his unruly hair. The other hand slipping beneath his shirt and stroking up his back.

I tensed when my fingers hit the raised lines. The scars. I knew what they were from and I knew they hadn't been there before.

"Oh, Connor," I murmured against his mouth. "I'm so sorry."

He broke our kiss and stared down at me, eyes hard. "Shut up."

But I ignored his harsh words and closed my eyes, clinging to the slice of Connor I'd found. "Stop telling me to shut up and fuck me."

He stilled for a second. Then I heard something completely unexpected. He chuckled and my eyes flew open at the familiar sound. Amusement sparked in his eyes as he stared down at me.

My heart fought the quicksand, beating fast to reach the surface.

Connor.

As fast as it came, it ended as he sat up, grabbed both my wrists and pressed them on the mattress above my head.

Then he fucked me.

Slow. Hard.

Hovering over me. Hips rotating and hitting my clit as he did it.

I closed my eyes, ignoring the pain in my wrists as he put all his weight on them while he continued to thrust.

"Fuck." He pumped harder.

In and out. The loud slap of our bodies over and over again.

The intense building in my belly was there, but it wasn't enough.

Connor slowed and I opened my eyes. "Touch yourself," he ordered. He let go of one of my wrists.

I lowered my arm and slid my palm between us. He lifted slightly, his eyes following my hand.

But I didn't touch my clit. I reached for his balls. He sucked in his breath as I cupped them, rolling them in my palm.

"Jesus," he growled.

He closed his eyes, head tilting back, neck muscles strained. His cock jerked inside me and I knew he wasn't going to last much longer.

I let him go then ran my fingers through my wetness before I circled my clit. The second I touched myself, my thighs clamped harder around him. "Oh, God," I breathed.

I didn't know if he was looking at me or my hand as I had my eyes closed while I played with myself. The building desire heated my core and I was going to burst into a zillion sparks.

"Oh, God, Connor. Oh, God." I stopped breathing.

He pulled almost all the way out then thrust hard inside me again. Once. Twice. On the third time, I fell. The zillion sparks exploded and it was a free fall into a pool of heated bliss.

Connor kept thrusting and my orgasm went on and on until he groaned a low agonizing sound as he came, too.

He collapsed on top of me, mouth against the side of my neck. I couldn't help it as I gently stroked his hair then kissed his shoulder. "I missed you," I whispered.

I'd said it more to myself than to him, but he must have heard me because he stiffened.

Shit.

Suddenly, he was off the bed with his back to me, but I heard the rubber of the condom and his zipper.

He turned. That was when my fear became real. Well, it was real before but I could handle it. This was altogether something different.

I scooted back on my hands, using my feet to push until I fell off the other side of the bed.

His face was the definition of fury. Unadulterated fury. Brows low. Eyes narrowed and hard. Jaw clenched and temples throbbing.

He strode to me, grabbed my arm and yanked me to my feet.

"What are you doing to me? Who the fuck are you?" His voice was a low graveled sound as he forced out each word.

He backed me into the wall so hard the shelf next to me rattled and the book resting on it fell with a smack to the floor. His other hand grabbed my chin, fingers digging into my jaw. "Who the fuck are you?" he ground out.

"Catalina." I whimpered as his fingers tightened.

"No. No." He was right in my face and if it wasn't for the wall and him holding me, I would've fallen my legs shook so badly. "You're fuckin' lying to me."

"Alina. You called me Alina," I quickly added.

"Alina," he said under his breath, brows lowering as if he was concentrating. "Alina," he repeated.

"Yes," I whispered then slowly reached up and eased his hand off my jaw. His eyes remained on me while I lowered his hand then linked our fingers together while resting on his chest.

He closed his eyes and for a moment, the lines around his mouth eased.

It was so beautiful I wanted to weep. Because in those messed-up, forgotten moments, hope was found.

He pressed his body up against mine, our hands crushed between us, our heartbeats pounding. He kept his eyes closed as he bent, so his mouth was a breath away from mine, but he didn't kiss me; instead, his forehead rested on mine and he inhaled long and deep.

PERFECT RAGE

Then he said, "Get out. We're done." He shoved away from me, turned, and took long strides across the room to the island. He picked up parts of his gun and clicked them in place. Then his fingers reached for the bullets and he placed them in the chambers.

He glanced at me and shouted, "Now!"

I quickly grabbed my blouse off the floor and yanked it on as I ran for the door.

I attempted to do up the buttons on my blouse, but my hands were shaking too badly, so I yanked it together and tied it like a halter-top.

Putting my hand on the doorknob, I hesitated. Shivers rose on the back of my neck and I swore his eyes were on me, but I didn't dare look back because I couldn't witness that coldness again.

I didn't want to know if he was pointing his gun at me. And I sure as hell didn't want to know if the man I loved was going to shoot me in the back.

I threw open the door and for the first time in my life, I ran with fear ripping through me.

CHAPTER NINETEEN

Present Day

Alina

THE DOOR CLICKED closed behind me and I was halfway across the bar before I noticed the unusual silence. Avalanche was still closed but the music was usually blasting and staff bustled and chatted while getting ready to open. No blasting. No bustling. No chatter.

I looked up and stopped.

Kai, Deck, and Vic were at the bar. Matt stood behind it and the only one sitting and looking relaxed was Kai. His brows lifted when I caught his eye and he offered a somewhat reassuring half smile. At least he wasn't pissed. Well, I couldn't be sure of that either. It was Kai, the master of concealing his true emotions.

Deck, on the other hand, had his arms crossed, stance shoulder-width apart and a seriously pissed off look. No concealment there as he boldly displayed his displeasure, but there was also what I thought was relief. "Are you okay?" he asked.

"Yeah, I'm fine."

Vic always looked pissed so I couldn't read whether he really was or not. I was beginning to wonder what Vic's issue was. I'd never witnessed him smile even when I'd first seen him playing football.

Something happened to that guy, but I had my own issues to worry about.

I straightened my shoulders and headed toward them, my shoes clicking on the floor and the air feeling a lot like it was heavy, thick smog. I glanced at Matt who flipped up the bar flap and approached me.

"You good?" He put his hand on the small of my back then positioned himself in front so he blocked the guys from me. "You don't want to talk to them right now, tell me."

God, he was a good guy. I was surrounded by people who really cared about one another. I never had that except with my brother. I'd never been close to my parents, mostly because they worked all the time. But the guys were close, even Kai, but I think that was because of London. She tied him to everyone and he'd do anything for her.

"I have to," I replied. Connor's time had run out and he was either going to disappear or he'd have to confront Deck. There was no other option because Deck would find him if he continued to watch me.

Matt nodded. "You need me, I'll be in the office. Staff are in the kitchen."

"We won't be long," Deck said. "Give us ten minutes."

"Sure," Matt said, then gave me one last glance before he went in the back.

Vic pulled out a barstool for me and I sat beside Kai, across from Deck, with Vic on my left. I felt like a mouse surrounded by lions and I kind of was because there was no question they'd easily devour me if they wanted to.

I clasped my hands in my lap to try to stop the trembling. Jesus, I was a wimp. I knew they'd never hurt me and it wasn't so much that as the pressure. I wasn't part of their tight-knit group. I was the outsider who was responsible for their friend being dragged into Vault and becoming a test subject that destroyed his life. And now I was the one who kept it a secret that Connor had been coming to see me.

"Alina," Deck said, his voice calm, but stern. "I told you before that I'd trust you to tell me when shit was no longer safe. From Deaglan's recap of this morning, the state of your kitchen and from Chess's summary of what went down at the bar last night, shit is no longer safe."

I chewed on my lower lip, my heart pounding and nervous tingles trickling through me. "He hasn't hurt me."

"Didn't say that," Deck said. "But shit no longer safe means doing something before it escalates to you or anyone else getting hurt. We are there."

Yeah. He was probably right.

I had no choice. Connor knew I'd be confronted by Deck today. It worried me that Connor had driven away and that he may never come back, especially since our last conversation was an argument.

"He's been watching me. For a while now."

"Since when?" This was Deck in a very scary deep voice.

"Ah, well, since he came to the bar that night of your engagement."

"I fuckin' knew it," Kai said. "There was no chance he was leaving town without her."

I continued, "He came to the house after the bar."

Kai's eyes widened with surprise and he sat up a little straighter. "He got past Ernie?"

Vic huffed. "Man, you have no clue who we're dealing with. The fuckin' guy aced JTF2 training. He doesn't want to be seen, you don't see him."

I shifted uncomfortably on my stool. "And, ummm," How did I say this? "He's been with me a couple times since." Kai smirked and shook his head. Deck cursed and Vic said nothing. "I'm sorry I didn't tell you, but he asked me not to. He doesn't want to be around people."

"But he'll show up at a packed bar to cause shit in order to get to you," Deck said.

True. "He said he doesn't trust himself."

Kai snorted. "No shit. He's a ticking time bomb. Irrational. Explosive. Unfuckin'stable with highly-trained military skills. He's dangerous as hell." Kai turned on Deck. "I fuckin' told you. A man doesn't come back from that shit."

"You did," Vic said.

"I grew up in hell, but I didn't have solid morals charred to ash. I killed bastards without giving a shit. It was who I was and all I knew. Connor risked his life for his country. He protected what he loved and cared about. Vault annihilated that." Kai chin-lifted to Deck. "If you suddenly woke up and found out you killed people for some scumbag for the last four years, don't you think that would put you over the edge? Guilt and self-hate can and will eat away at a man's soul." Kai leaned back on his stool, elbow resting on the bar top. "I was conditioned not to feel since I was a kid. No guilt. No self-hate."

"Alina," Deck said, "we need to know where Connor's at mentally. And the only way to get that is for you to tell us everything right from the beginning. You told us about the orphanage and the note you left, but did you see him while he was on the drug? Do you know what your husband did to him before Vault gave him the drug?"

I'd never told anyone about seeing Connor in Colombia. There'd been no reason to. Carlos was dead and Connor was free.

But it was time.

So, I told them everything and not once did they interrupt. They politely listened to the games Carlos played. The years Moreno kept him imprisoned, the videos of me, the scars on Connor's wrists and back. Then I told them about him being on the drug and coming to Colombia. About the pictures being burned and how I tried to get Connor to remember who he was by being with him.

"He's fighting his memories," Deck said. "They clash with who he is. A guy tortured for seven years, mind controlled, drugged and then he wakes up and finds out the woman he loves has been forced to be with the man he's been killing for." I flinched. "That he didn't protect her from that. It's enough to kill a man. Especially a man like Connor."

And it was killing him. How could he get over that? How could any of us help him?

"And now where's his head at?" Vic asked.

I gave them the rest. Even the incident with the alarm guy who he'd almost shot when he thought it was Moreno. I think that was when Deck got pissed because I probably should've said something then, but I couldn't betray Connor.

I finished off with going to the dirt track today and how he dropped me at the bar.

There was silence when I finished and I waited uncomfortably for one of them to say something.

My normal was being blown apart and I was pretty sure going to adopt a cat was on the list of impossibilities.

"Vic will stay at the house with you," Deck said with a pensive expression.

Okay. I kind of expected more than that because last time they said they'd move me if things escalated. "I don't know if he'll come. I told him to go fuck himself."

Vic's lips twitched. Kai laughed.

"He'll come," Deck said assuredly. "I'll make sure he does."

I had no idea what that meant, but the conversation was over as the guys got up to leave.

That's when the bar door opened and Connor walked in.

CHAPTER TWENTY

Connor

I QUICKLY SCANNED AVALANCHE, taking note of my escape routes if I needed them. Alina was standing between Deck and Vic, her eyes wide and shocked at seeing me.

After I'd dropped her off at the bar, I rode for a while, but it still bothered me leaving her. If I knew Deck, he'd have been searching for us all fuckin' day. But one place she always showed up was work and there was a good possibility he'd be waiting at Avalanche to interrogate Alina.

I didn't want to be here, but there was no chance I was allowing Alina to be bombarded with questions about me. Probably, the smart thing was to leave town, but her words haunted me because she told me not to bother seeing her again unless I got 'un-lost'.

I was sure I could work around that somehow, but not when she said, 'Fuck you, Connor.'

So now I was walking into a bar to tell Deck to back off my girl. If he had something to ask, he could damn well ask me and then leave me the fuck alone.

"Alina. Come here," I said, keeping my eyes on Deck.

If anyone made a move, it would be him because I was certain he'd given orders for no one to touch me except him. That was how Deck worked, always the one to take the risk. Of course it had been a while since he'd been my team leader but as soon as I walked in the door, he stepped forward, a couple feet in front of Vic and Kai. That was my clear indication as to who was taking lead on this.

Alina rose from the stool she'd been sitting on and stepped toward me. Deck's arm shot out and blocked her path.

"Don't move," Deck ordered.

The air was thick and the only sound was clanging dishes in the kitchen. Rage throbbed as my eyes cut from Alina to Deck. "Let her go."

"Not happening." Deck nodded to Vic who moved closer to Alina, not touching, but if she came toward me, he was in reach to haul her back. "Put the gun on the table."

There was no chance he was able to see my gun in the back of my jeans, but he damn well knew I'd carry one. And he should also know I'd not relinquish it. Fuck that. "You do not use her to get to me. Leave her out of this. You want to talk to me. Talk. This is your one and only chance." My eyes snapped to Kai who pulled out a stool and sat. The guy barely glanced at me as if unconcerned that I was here. He was ex-Vault and I'd met his cold, heartless mother who had been a queen in the deception of emotions.

"Connor. They're worried about you and were just asking me a few questions," Alina said. Vic's hand reached out and curled around her wrist then he whispered something to her. She stiffened and pursed her lips together, but didn't say anything.

PERFECT RAGE

The urge to kill him played with my mind. It was Vic, I repeated in my head. He wouldn't hurt her. I tried to focus on the good memories of Vic when we were buddies. *Gate.* Victor Gate was safe and he'd never hurt her. Slowly, the rage eased and I had my control back.

The territorial feeling around her was unwarranted. I knew that logically, but logic wasn't always easy to see when men surrounded my girl. It was instinct to protect her even from men who used to be my friends and had rescued Alina out of Colombia.

Except Kai, he'd never been a friend and never would be.

"What do you want with me?" I directed my question at Deck.

"I want you to get help."

"I don't want help," I retorted.

"You don't even know what I'm asking."

"Don't give a fuck. Help involves strangers I don't trust. It's not happening." I kept my feet braced in case he made a move. "Stop searching for me. And stop using Alina to get to me."

I glanced at Alina. She looked fragile standing with Deck and Vic, but I knew better than anyone that she wasn't. I still had the urge to drag her from between them and put her on my bike and leave, to drive away and not come back. I was sure I wouldn't get close enough to her. I was good, but two ex-JTF2 and one ex-Vault, there was no chance I'd escape with her.

"Can't do that," he replied. "You want to see Alina, then you see a doctor. Otherwise, you won't get near her again," Deck said while crossing his arms and meeting my stare as if daring me to do something.

"Is that a threat?" I ground out, fury boiling.

He'd always been an arrogant bastard, but we were friends because there was no bullshit with him. Honest and direct and every word out of his mouth he'd follow through with, and he could back up his words.

Deck shrugged. "No. It's just how things will go from here on in."

I was good, but not good enough if Deck had a man on her, and not just the prick Deaglan casually watching. There'd be one of them living with her and I was betting it would be Vic. He was making it clear that I had two choices: get help or fuck off.

The idea of leaving Alina was like a wool blanket slowly being pulled up over my head getting tighter and tighter. Did I have a choice?

"Connor," Alina's voice was soft and barely audible, "please."

Even from across the room, I saw the tears in her eyes. Damn it, why couldn't Deck just let it go? Because I'd fucked up. I'd dragged her out of a bar and destroyed her kitchen.

There was only one outcome here and from Alina's tears, she knew it, too. Leave. Because I wasn't seeing a doctor and being drugged and locked up again.

"You have anything else to say to me?" I asked Deck.

His eyes narrowed. I wondered if he was debating whether to take me down or let me walk out of here. I was confident he'd let me walk away, but then again, Deck had a damn good poker face.

I wouldn't kill him if he came at me. There were sane parts of me left and Deck standing in front of me brought back memories of the laughter we shared, the closeness, and the willingness to do whatever it took to protect one another. I hadn't felt that the last time I'd seen him, but my emotions were constantly changing, except those for Alina. They stayed solid and helped calm me.

"I have a hell of a lot to say, Connor, but I don't think you'll listen right now, so I'll save my breath." He was right. "I can tell you've already made your decision."

Right again. Alina swayed and Vic's hand on her arm tightened as he held her steady.

Our eyes met and I said softly, "I have to leave, baby."

She tried to pull from Vic and everything inside me tightened when he refused to let her go. The urge to grab her away from him pulsed through me and if I didn't get out of the room fast, someone was going to end up hurt.

She bit her lip and tears streamed down her cheeks. Fuck, I hated this and it was stupid of me to come back in the first place. I was better off starting over someplace without a past haunting me. "This was always supposed to be temporary." I repeated her words from the note she'd left me so long ago. It was cruel, but necessary. Easier for her to forget me if I left this way.

"Connor," she cried. "Don't do this."

Her ragged words bore a hole into my heart, and for a second I considered the consequences if I stayed. No. There were too many unknowns.

Would I be locked up? And if I wasn't, then would I go too far one day and hurt her. We'd been toying with that every time I was close to her.

The risk was not mine, it was hers.

Deck stepped toward me. "Connor, just see a doctor. Then we can decide how to proceed." I slowly shook my head in warning when he was five feet from me. He stopped. "You can't run from this. I know you care about Alina and your sister and parents—"

"I'm not running. I'm surviving. This is how I survive." I directed my eyes to Alina, but kept Deck in my peripheral vision. "Need you to be safe, Alina. That's all I want for you."

"Bullshit," she yelled and I stiffened at the fury in her voice. "You're an asshole. You won't even try. Why? Why did you come back and blow my world apart and give me hope only to tear it apart again. You're a selfish bastard, Connor. Go. Leave. Run. You're getting good at that."

"Alina..."

She shoved at Vic's hand gripping her arm. "Damn it, let me go. I'm going to be sick." He instantly let her go. She shoved past him and ran down the hallway and into the washroom.

I didn't think, I reacted and started after her. "Alina! Fuck." Deck stepped in my path and I was about to reach for my gun when a knife flew past my head and embedded in the door behind me.

I jerked my eyes to Kai who watched me, his brows lifted as if daring me to make another move.

My head throbbed and I knew I was going to lose it any minute. Fuck, I had to get out of here. "Keep her safe," I said to Deck.

He sighed. "Jesus, Connor. Let me in. Don't force my hand."

What the fuck did he mean by that? "What? Are you going to take me down? Chain me up again? Have some doctor pump me full of sedatives."

"No. All I'm asking is for you to have blood taken. We start there."

I moved my hand to my hip, close to my gun as I backed toward the door, because from his comment I wasn't sure Deck wouldn't try to stop me. "Don't hassle Alina again."

"And what are you going to do about it anyway?" he said. I jerked, mouth pursed. "You'll be gone. Off someplace pretending you're dead."

"I am dead," I shouted as the control broke and the rage pumped through my veins. "I'm fuckin' dead, damn it. There's nothing left of me except raw, jagged pieces of a man I hate."

"Bullshit!" Deck shouted back at me. "That's complete bullshit. You're here because you're alive and give a shit about Alina. You watch her because you care. And you hate who you are because you refuse to let in who you were."

I went for him.

My fist connected with his jaw and the sound of my knuckles hitting his bone echoed. He staggered back two steps from the impact but didn't go down. I had my gun out fired off a shot at the floor near Vic who came toward me. "Back off, Gate."

Deck held up his hand and Vic stopped and Kai lowered the knife.

Then I heard her. Alina. She stood with one hand settled on the wall her weight leaning into it as if it were what kept her standing. But it was the look in her eyes that made leaving so much easier.

Fear. Devastation. Hurt.

Jesus. She didn't deserve this.

I backed to the door then flung it open, my gun pointed at Deck.

"It's over," I said, more to myself than them.

Because holding a gun on Deck, on Vic, seeing Alina's pain, it was over. And until that moment, I never realized there'd been hope. But not now.

I'd gone too far and there was no drug to blame. No, this was just me threatening to kill my best friend while the girl I loved watched.

CHAPTER TWENTY-ONE

Question 10: What would you give up for your best friend?

Alina

I SAT ON THE porch with a half-full mug of steaming coffee in hand, the loveseat swing creaking back and forth as it swayed. After Connor confronted Deck at the bar, I hadn't seen him in five days, and my stomach had been unsettled ever since. I had a constant fluttering. I'd thrown up three times and I was unable to sleep.

His words continued to haunt me. 'It's over'.

Losing him again was too much and I hated that I cared. I should've known it would come to this. But giving up on him was never an option for me even though I'd been angry and said those things at the bar. I know if our places were switched, he'd never give up on me.

Just like Deck wouldn't give up on Connor.

PERFECT RAGE

He was confident that Connor would be back, so Vic became my shadow and lived at the house with me. When I went to work, either Deck or Vic remained at Avalanche, making certain Connor didn't try something. I wasn't sure what they expected him to do and when I asked Deck the previous day, he told me he thought Connor might try to take me with him.

He also told me Connor needed to be pushed. I didn't like the sound of that, but Deck promised that they wouldn't force him. Connor had to get to a point where he was willing to at least take a step toward getting some kind of help.

Deck thought I was the key. From Connor's obsessive need to watch me and keep me safe, he was confident Connor wouldn't leave town. Or if he did, he'd be back.

I still didn't get it. Even if Connor did come back, what were they going to do if they weren't going to force him to get help? What would push Connor into getting help?

The screen door squeaked open then banged closed behind Vic. He stared out onto the street for a few seconds then gave a brief nod before turning to me. "We need to move inside."

My breath hitched as my eyes darted to the street. Did he see Connor? Was he out there watching? "Is he here?"

"No."

"Then why—"

He cut me off. "I don't have time for this. Move it!" Vic ordered.

I scrambled to my feet and he grabbed my elbow using his body as a shield while he ushered me into the house, down the hall and into the kitchen.

That was when several gunshots sounded off like firecrackers from the street.

I screamed and Vic's arms wrapped around me as he pushed me to the far back wall. He was stiff and it was more like being surrounded by a piece of steel than a man. "You're safe. No one is trying to hurt you."

What? How did he know that?

It lasted about two seconds then silence followed, except the sound of my heart thumping in my head.

He pulled back, but still kept one arm around me while he took his phone out of his back pocket, tapped a few times and then put it to his ear.

"Yeah, all good." He paused. "See you in two." He hung up then urged me to sit, poured me a glass of orange juice and set it in front of me, but I couldn't drink anything.

Why was he so calm? I was shaking and freaked, having no idea what the hell just happened, while Vic opted to pour me a glass of orange juice rather than chasing after whoever had just shot at the house. Vic would chase after them, wouldn't he?

But he stayed with me and it only took minutes before the commandos arrived, Deck, Tyler, and Ernie. I didn't know where Josh was.

Tyler walked straight to me and gave me a hug. God, he was sweet. But then he said, "Sorry to do that to you, sugar."

My eyes widened and everything in me stilled. "Excuse me?"

Tyler's eyes shot to Vic. "You didn't tell her yet?"

I shot out of the chair. "Tell me what?"

Vic said nothing because Deck cleared his throat and Vic, Ernie, and Tyler abruptly left the kitchen.

"Deck, what's going on?"

Sirens blared.

"I'm pushing him."

Oh, God.

"I'm threatening the one thing he needs to keep safe, Alina. You. I need him to break and this is the only way I can think of to do that. The longer he continues to do what he's doing, the harder it will be to bring him back."

"You shot at the house?" Deck confirmed with a nod. "You want him to break." I didn't know what else to say. I was shocked. They did this on purpose. That was how Vic knew to get me inside when he did. Why he said 'no one is trying to hurt you.' "But that means you think he's watching me."

"Don't think. I know he has been. He never left. But there's no point us going after him. We need to give him a reason to come to us. To talk about getting help. That's the first step."

"What makes you think he'll change his mind?"

Deck's brows lifted. "Alina, we have a man obsessed with keeping you safe and your house was just shot up. Do you think he's going to let that happen? Shrug it off? Not a fuckin' chance."

"If he even hears about it."

"And why I've informed a few friends with the police. If he's not watching the house, he'll hear."

I wasn't so sure this was such a smart idea to push Connor. This might put him over the edge.

The police 'friends' of Deck's arrived. I kept it together, despite wanting to yell and scream and lose it on all of them because I was worried that this plan was going to backfire and Connor would do something reckless.

I moved out to the foyer and sat on the stairs and two officers came in and spoke with Deck.

One officer glanced at me while Deck spoke and then I heard Deck say, "You got what you need, Rick." It wasn't a question and Deck was obviously telling him it was time to clear out.

Ernie popped his head in the front door. "Incoming."

"Do you realize the amount of paperwork I have now, Deck? Jesus, you make my job difficult," the officer, Rick, muttered.

Deck half smiled. "I owe you."

"Fuckin' right you do. And I'll be collecting."

"Sir. Sir. You can't go in there," I heard someone outside yell.

I didn't have time to process as the screen door was nearly ripped off its hinges and Connor stormed in. His dark eyes landed immediately on me. Then it was like slowly letting out the air in a balloon as the explosive tension drained from his body in relief.

He had yet to look at another person in the room. Deck stared at him, the police officer who'd been telling him he couldn't 'go in there' was behind him, Vic was in the living room talking to Ernie and Officer Rick had his hand close to his hip where his gun sat.

Connor stalked toward me.

Officer Rick stiffened, "Who are—"

Deck was quick to interrupt, "He's the one."

I had no idea if Rick responded or what, because Connor had reached me and he was all I could focus on.

He stepped on the first stair, bent and took my hand and pulled me to my feet. Then we were moving down the hallway toward the kitchen. I looked back at Deck and his eyes followed us.

This was exactly what he planned, Connor showing up.

Shit, Connor was going to kill him when he learned the truth.

He led me into the bathroom that was next to the kitchen, shut the door and locked it. I was pretty sure a flimsy bathroom lock wasn't going to stop any one of those men out there if they wanted in.

Connor's hand slipped from mine and ran through his hair. His hair was wet and tangled and had left wet splotches on his grey T-shirt. He smelled like soap as if he'd just come out of the shower.

He stared at the floor as he walked to the end of the bathroom then back again. It was only three strides and he did it several times. His face was hidden because he kept it low, but the tension in his body was very obvious. The balloon had refilled and was about to burst.

I stood with my back against the door. Waiting. This was what Connor needed. Me to wait. Me to be patient. Me to be calm. Because it was everything he wasn't anymore.

But he was here. The question was would he stay?

"Jesus Christ, Alina." He stopped pacing and looked at me. His hands curled into fists at his sides and his breathing was ragged. "You're okay?"

I nodded. "Yeah, but—"

"Fuck," he muttered, cutting me off. "Fuck."

Then his face softened and the anger dissipated as he moved into me, his hands cupping my face, thumbs stroking back and forth on my cheeks. "I was at the hotel," he murmured. "I was in the shower while you were being shot at."

Even if I had a response, which I didn't, he didn't give me a chance as he kissed me. I tasted mint as his mouth moved over mine, gentle and warm, but just as consuming. He cradled my head between his hands, mouths and tongues melding together. He said my name a few times against my lips before he deepened it. I sagged into him, arms moving to loop around his neck, fingers in his hair, drawing him closer.

Connor broke the kiss then rested his forehead against mine. "I heard the police scanner say your address and gunshots. Fuck, I thought you were dead, baby. I thought you were dead and it scared the shit out of me." He had a police scanner? That's why Deck had the police involved. He knew Connor's moves. His hand stroked my hair. "I can't lose you. You're all I have left that's keeping me sane."

"You won't lose me," I whispered. "I'm okay. I was never in any danger."

At that he pushed back, brows knitted. "Someone put bullets in a fuckin' house you were in. It sure as hell was dangerous."

Oh, boy. He was getting revved up again and that probably was a bad combination with Deck waiting to talk to him and finding out this was Deck's plan to get him here. "Connor?" He was leaning on the counter, hands gripping the edge, head hanging. "You're here."

He snorted as his eyes met mine. "Of course I'm fuckin' here, Alina. You were shot at."

I continued, "You said it was over. I thought you left."

He straightened and came toward me, his hand cupping the back of my neck. "You. Were. Shot. At." He leaned in and briefly kissed me then said, "We'll leave. I'll get you away from here."

Whoa. That was impossible for a number of reasons, one of them being a bunch of commandos in the house. "Connor, no."

"We'll get on my bike and leave right now. Start over somewhere else."

Go? Start over? I had friends now. A job. I loved this house, not to mention that it was a horrible idea.

I wasn't running. I didn't run. "I can't leave, Connor. I like it here." Then I added, "I have a job and I like your friends and they're my friends now, too."

"Fuck." He strode to the opposite side of the washroom, faced the wall and pounded both fists into it, although not hard enough to break the plaster. "Fuck."

I swallowed, throat tight as I waited for him to decide what to do next. It felt like hours before he finally turned around. God, his eyes swirled with so many emotions, I didn't know how he was feeling.

He approached me, stopping inches away. "Fine." He cupped my chin, his grip tight, but not painful. "We stay in town, but not here. I won't have you being shot at." He let me go and reached for the doorknob. "I need to deal with Deck. He's not keeping me away from you any longer."

"Connor," I blurted before he had a chance to leave. It was better this came from me than Deck, although either way, Connor was going to freak being set up. "They weren't shooting at me."

His eyes darted to mine. "How do you know that? Does Deck know who the fuck it was?"

"Well, that's not it exactly."

His brows dropped. "Not it exactly?"

"I didn't know this was their plan. They just told me. I guess they were afraid if I knew about it, I might find a way to tell you." The pulse in his throat throbbed and his jaw tightened. Yeah, he was pissed.

"Deck shot the house."

He was quiet, but the air was heavy as he contemplated. "They shot up the house to draw me out. They scared you with fuckin' bullets just to get to me."

He was mad. Really mad. I hadn't seen him this mad as the lines around his lips accentuated, his eyes dangerously dark, and his body tight.

He pulled me away from the door, yanked it open and stalked out. Oh, shit. This was not good.

I followed until I saw Deck waiting in the kitchen.

Connor didn't waste time as he approached him. My eyes widened when I saw his right hand curl into a fist. He stopped in front of Deck, the tension pulsating off him.

I held my breath. I had no idea who would win in a fight between them, but Deck was definitely the calmer one. Too calm.

They stared at one another for a second and then Connor's arm drew back. I gasped at the same time as he plowed his fist into Deck's cheek.

Deck had been prepared for it and barely moved.

"Connor!" I managed one step toward him, before something grabbed my arm and tugged me back. I glanced at the fingers curled around my arm to then meet Vic's eyes. "He'll hurt him."

"Doubt it," Vic calmly replied. "They need to hash this out and you need to stay clear of it."

My head snapped back to Deck and Connor who now had him by the shirt up against the wall. "Fight me, asshole."

"Not fighting you, Connor."

"Fuck." Connor shoved him in the chest then let him go. He ran his hand through his hair and took a few steps away and smashed his fist into the side of the fridge.

Deck rubbed his jaw.

I wanted so badly to go to Connor, but I was scared, too. He was furious and I was freaking out. Not a good combination. As if sensing my apprehension, Vic leaned into me and said, "Deck can look after himself and Connor doesn't have his gun."

I glanced at the back of his jeans and there was no bulge beneath his T-shirt. He'd been in a hurry.

Connor's hands clenched at his sides, but he made no move to hit Deck again. "You used my girl to get to me. You fuckin' scared her to get to me."

Tyler and Ernie appeared beside me and Vic.

"Guess he knows now?" Tyler said.

I nodded.

"What the fuck? We don't work that way." Connor paced back and forth the width of the kitchen. "Jesus Christ. How could you do that to her?"

Deck appeared rather relaxed for just having been punched by his best friend. "You know why. Don't need to explain shit to you. This has to end. What you're doing with Alina. To me. Your family and friends. It stops today."

Connor stopped pacing and faced him. "Jesus Christ, why can't you leave me the fuck alone?"

"You know why," Deck answered calmly. "We don't leave a man behind—Ever."

Tears swam. This was why I trusted these men. Why I easily trusted Connor when we met. There was nothing stronger than their loyalty to one another and it was what men like this did. They stood by one another and fought for one another. And they weren't the type of men to sit back and do nothing.

Connor didn't comment.

Deck continued, "Every man gets home to his family, O'Neill. You're not there yet. You hearing me?"

"Yeah, I'm fuckin' hearing you."

"Let's give them some space," Vic suggested. Tyler and Ernie headed down the hall and Vic waited for me. I stole one last glance at Connor, turned and left.

CHAPTER TWENTY-TWO

Connor

DECK SET THIS up to get me here.

Fuck, I wanted to do a lot more than punch him. The hell I went through when I heard the police scanner go off while I'd been in the shower. I swear my heart burst through my ribs and I nearly ran out of my hotel room naked in order to get here. My head detonated with shards of fear at the thought of Alina lying on the floor, blood pooling around her.

I'd been fighting for five days with what I should do. I'd left the bar convinced it was over, but I hadn't left. I lied to myself because I damn well knew I'd never leave her. But Deck was true to his word. I'd never get near her.

Everything changed while driving here, picturing her bleeding out on the floor, eyes dead and lifeless.

Nothing else mattered except her. I'd do anything to keep her. Anything. As long as she didn't die.

Losing her wasn't a possibility. I couldn't go through that again. The fear escalated when I tuned onto her street and saw the flashing lights and cop car. I had some relief that there was no ambulance, but then it occurred to me it could've already come and taken her away.

I didn't think twice about storming into the house. Didn't think about the cops, Ernie, Vic, Tyler, or Deck. No one was keeping me from her.

And then I saw her sitting on the stairs and the relief was so overwhelming that I wanted to drop to my knees and cry.

Deck moved past me saying, "Let's take this outside."

I had the urge to punch him again and tell him to go fuck himself because I was still reeling at what he'd done. Not to me, but to Alina. She'd been trembling. They hadn't told her what they were doing and scared her. That shit was not cool.

I followed him out onto the porch.

As soon as the screen door shut, he got right to it. No bullshit Deck. "I didn't like doing that to Alina. But that's on you."

I crossed my arms to keep from punching him again and leaned against the railing. The anger throbbed, but it was more the fear for Alina. It didn't matter that I'd held her moments ago and I knew she was fine. I still pictured her dead on the floor.

Deck continued, "Vic says your girl hasn't slept in five days. Matt sent her home early from the bar the other night despite her insistence to work. She's been through hell, too, and doesn't deserve this."

"Jesus, don't you think I know that? She deserves someone who has their shit together, not a raging lunatic."

Deck huffed. "You're not a raging lunatic. Raging, yes. Lunatic, not yet. And I said she doesn't deserve *this*. She deserves you because you're a good guy. You've just forgotten that part."

"Do you know what I've done? Do you have any fuckin' idea?"

"Yes. You threatened you sister's life with a note. You killed for Vault. You shot London and took her into Vault. And you hurt Alina in Colombia. And none of it was your fault," Deck continued. "But this, what's happening now, that's all on you."

"Don't you think I know that," I yelled, hitting the railing with my fist.

Deck stepped toward me. "Moreno is dead. Vault is disassembled and being re-built into something good. The drug is destroyed and you and Alina are free. We all are. But even from his grave, he has a hold on you. We were trained to withstand torture. We know what that shit can do to a man's mind. And, yeah, I get you hate yourself right now, but I'm telling you again, Connor, you have two options on where this can go from here. Don't need to spell them out to you. It's a blazing billboard right in front of you."

It made me sick to think that my sister knew what I'd done. My parents knowing… God, that would shatter them. They'd been proud of me, for what I did for my country. Now, they'd find out I helped a man who used kids for his drug business and made them into killers.

I couldn't do that to them.

Deck stopped in front of me. "I see what you're thinking, buddy. Don't go there. None of this is your fault. It's time to fix this. Make it right."

I snorted. "Fix? I'm unfixable, Deck. I'm not feeling sorry for myself, that's just reality."

"What then? You sure as hell can't leave. So, you stay around and what… watch her? And what happens when she finally gets over you and wants to date, maybe start a family. What then? You going to kill or threaten any guy who comes near her?"

My eyes hit his, fury rising at the mere thought of Alina dating other guys. "Didn't I hit you hard enough the first time, asshole?" I retorted because it took everything not to slam my fist into his face again and again until… until what? I killed my best friend?

Fuck.

My chest felt as if it had a thousand pound weight on it and I was suffocating. Everything he said was true, but hearing it out loud was like a kick to the gut.

Deck had been my team leader, my rock. The man I trusted with my life more than any other and there were parts of me that wanted to let him in and stop fighting.

He got right in my face. "You know the story, Connor. How I beat my father to death. I blamed myself for my mom's death, for not protecting her. That was my job and I failed her."

"You were a kid," I muttered.

"And you were drugged."

Silence. I dropped my head forward and my shoulders sagged. I felt that every single day. Like I failed Alina and I still was.

"Head's a little fucked up," I finally said.

"A little?" Deck replied.

I snorted. Asshole. "A lot."

He nodded. "And her?"

"Can't fuckin' breathe without her."

"Know the feeling," Deck murmured.

I snapped my head up to glare at him. "How long have you been fucking my sister? She better have been of age or I'll kill you."

Deck's jaw tightened. "Jesus. What the hell? I'd never do that and you bloody well know it."

I did. It was a cruel comment. Deck was the most honorable guy I knew and he'd have tried to keep his word to me and stayed away from Georgie. "Yeah."

"Ten years," he said. "And I shouldn't have wasted those ten years not having her, but I did because I knew you were not cool with me bringing her into our type of life. Now I know it was stupid of me to make that promise to stay away from her. I wasted years not having her in my arms and I failed to protect her, too."

Fire burned in my stomach at his words and the fucked-up part was I didn't know why. He was right. At any moment, life could throw a hook and drag you under, but if you had that one person to hold onto, the fight to the surface was easier. That person was your reason to breathe.

I inhaled a deep breath. "Is Georgie happy?"

Deck hesitated. "She is now. But not completely. Don't think she'll ever be until she has her brother back. I'd like to tell her that's a possibility."

I lowered my head. "Does she know I'm here?"

"I'll never lie to her, Connor. So, yeah, she knows you were at Avalanche. I also told her we were looking for you, but she doesn't know you're here now. Not yet. But she will because I won't keep it from her and I won't stop her if you stick around and she wants to see you." Then he said, "Not cutting off my air."

"Yeah." I got that because my air was cut off thinking I'd lost Alina tonight.

The porch creaked as Deck shifted his weight. "You know, Alina protected you even though she didn't need to. I'd never hurt you, Connor."

"You chained me to a wall, sedated me, and handcuffed me to a pipe."

Deck nodded. "All necessary."

"Dick moves."

"You tried to kill us. I think it was appropriate for the situation. And I was trying to protect you from hurting yourself." His brows lowered and he said in a more serious tone, "We need to straighten out that head of yours, buddy."

"Jesus Christ, don't you think I know that?" I shouted.

I walked to the opposite end of the porch and stared at the boarded-up house through the trees. The window in the attic didn't have plywood over it because I'd removed it in order to watch her house. "I can't be with her and I can't stay away. I watch her so I won't forget her again. Every time I leave, my chest tightens and I feel like I'm drowning. You know what that is? Fear. I never used to feel fear. There was no room for it. You of all people know that, not in our line of work. But now I'm terrified I'll forget her again. That I'll lose her.

"Do you know what it's like to be afraid to fall asleep because of nightmares, but they aren't nightmares. They are real things I've done and I have to wake up again and live with that. But far worse is the constant fear of waking up with no memories at all. Forgetting her.

"I live with this rage pulsing and I don't know when it's going to detonate." I shook my head back and forth, kicking at a tiny rut in one of the planks. "She wants normal. I can't give it to her. I can't talk about what happened to her. I can't sleep or my nightmares invade and you saw the result in the kitchen. But I can't leave either."

I heard him approach and my body tensed, but I remained where I was, staring at that fuckin' attic window.

"You can't have it both ways, Connor. Staying and leaving. Because that's what you're doing. Half here and half gone."

Limbo. I was in limbo.

Deck stood beside me and faced the abandoned house. "Shit," he muttered. I glanced at him and he was staring at the attic window.

"You're slipping," I said, smirking.

"Thought Vic checked that place out."

"He did. I'm not slipping."

Deck chuckled. Fuck, it was years since I heard him chuckle. Such a rarity, I'd always been the one laughing and grinning. Maybe why we got along so well, we balanced each other out.

We had. Not any more.

"I'm not giving up on you, Connor," Deck said.

Deck's men returned home, whether they were dead or alive, they got back to their families and he wasn't giving up until that happened. And since I wasn't leaving Alina, I had to change what I was doing.

We stood in silence for a good two minutes before I said, "I see shit. PTSD. Or maybe the after effects of the drug. I don't know."

"Good possibility," Deck said. "That drug had some potent shit in it and it could be damaging and you don't even know it. You have to see a doctor."

Every muscle in my body tensed. "Fuck that. Do you know what they'll do to me? The second I lose it talking about the shit I went through, they'll pump me full of drugs and lock me up. I can't survive that. I won't. My mind can't take that shit. I was locked up for seven years. Seven, Deck. It will kill the last thread of sanity I have left."

Deck was silent. "Okay. We get blood taken. We start there. Nothing else."

"I'm not going to a hospital."

Deck said, "We have a doctor on company payroll."

"Unyielding Riot," I said, shaking my head. "Who the hell picked that name?"

Deck snorted. "So, you'll have blood work done?"

I ran my hand through my hair nodding. "I can't lose her. And I can't keep hurting her either. So, yeah." I moved away and opened the screen door and looked over at him still standing at the railing. "What you did was a dick move and if you pull that fucked-up shit again and scare my girl, it won't just be a bruised jaw."

"Understood."

"I'm staying here and Gate leaves. Only way it's going to be."

Deck stiffened. "How do I know you won't fuck off with her the second we leave."

I shrugged. "You don't. But Alina already told me she won't leave, otherwise we'd have been on my bike long before we had this conversation."

"If there is another situation like the kitchen shit, we're renegotiating the terms."

I didn't say anything and moved back inside the house to find Alina.

She was in the backyard with the guys sitting in the cabana. I stopped halfway there and swallowed the urge to drag her away from them.

I pursed my lips together. Shit, if I was going to do this, this overprotectiveness had to cool down. I didn't know how to do that yet, but the first step was not pulling out my gun, which I'd stupidly left at the hotel, or throw punches.

"Babe," I said and she looked up. Her eyes traveled the length of me, no doubt checking for injuries then her shoulders sagged and she smiled. She slipped from the cabana and walked toward me.

All the emotions that had been pulsing through me over the last ten minutes faded and it was like a warm wash of heated calm.

I slipped my hand beneath her hair, settled it on the back of her neck and tugged her into me. Her palms landed on my chest and she looked up at me with a hesitant smile. She didn't have to say anything. I knew why she was hesitant.

"I'll try to get un-lost." Her smile broadened and if I could breathe in a smile that was what I was doing because it filled me up with its lightness. "But, baby, I don't know if I can. And you have to swear to me you'll try, too. It kills me that you gave up photography." She opened her mouth to protest but I quickly cut her off. "We find our way back together, Alina."

"Okay," she whispered and reached up and cupped my cheek repeating, "Okay."

I tilted my head and kissed her, soft, gentle, brief like a snapshot. I peered over at the cabana and Tyler and Vic watched. I nodded once and they returned the gesture. Slipping my hand into Alina's, we went inside.

CHAPTER TWENTY-THREE

Question 11: Favorite flavor of ice cream?

Alina

CONNOR LED ME through the house, up the stairs and into the bedroom. With the heel of his boot, he shut the door then he walked me over to the oversized lounge chair and sat. He pulled me into his lap, and I curled into him.

"My head is pounding, shutterbug. I need a minute." He locked his arms around me, and to anyone looking in on us, they'd see lovers embracing, but there was so much tension in him. The crease between his brows accentuated as he rested his head on the back of the chair and closed his eyes.

"Okay, " I whispered, resting my cheek on his chest, hearing his heart thump erratically. He needed the silence. Usually he went in the shower or left on his bike, but instead, he held me in his arms. This was him fighting against what he was used to doing. He was trusting himself not to hurt me.

We sat for a long time in silence. Slowly, the tension in his arms eased, his heart slowed and the lines in his face faded.

I had no idea what Deck and him talked about, but Connor stayed.

He was going to try.

And maybe we'd have our second chance.

His hand stroked up my back to my neck where his fingers gently caressed beneath my hair. Goose bumps rose and I sighed, tilting my head to look at him. His brilliant blue eyes were open and calm as our gazes met.

I had so many questions, but it wasn't the time, so I gave him a subtle smile, my fingers curling into his shirt. "I like this." He remained quiet but he was listening so I continued, "You holding me until it passes. I like that a lot."

"Me too, baby," he murmured before he bent and kissed me.

It was slow, but there was nothing soft about it as his lips claimed mine. His hand on the back of my neck pulled me closer and I sank further into him. There was so much within that kiss as we held one another. It was his promise to me he'd stay this time. And it was our promise to keep fighting for one another.

He broke the kiss and rested his forehead against mine. "Love you so damn much, Alina." My heart nearly burst through my chest. "I don't want to hurt you. Tell me I won't hurt you."

"You won't hurt me, Connor. I trust you." The trust in himself was lacking but I had enough for both of us. Maybe it was what we went through that made it so strong. Maybe I knew he wouldn't because even when he was drugged, Connor had never hurt me. It didn't matter though, until he learned to trust himself again, I'd be there for him.

"I promised Deck I'd have blood taken. I don't know if it will help, but as long as I don't have to go to a hospital or some doctor's office, it can't hurt." A subtle grin appeared. "Except for that big-ass needle piercing my vein and draining my blood."

I smiled. "But you're okay with piercing people with your fangs and draining their blood?" Question number one, vampire or werewolf, he'd said vampire because they sucked on women's necks. And, of course, were strong as hell, he liked that fact, too.

He chuckled and my chest swelled at the sound. "I love that you remember, baby. But, shit, yeah. Vampires rule." Then he trickled kisses along my brow to my ear where his warm heated breath wafted across my skin. His tongue licked the side of my neck and then his teeth gently nipped.

I sucked in air then moaned as he licked the spot before he kissed it. "Connor?"

"Yeah?" He continued to kiss my neck, across my throat to the hollow where he swirled his tongue.

Oh, God, he had me wet with a few simple kisses.

My hands drifted across his chest to his pants where I slid the button through the slit. "I want to taste you. Then I want to ride you." I dragged the zipper down, where his cock was already hard inside his boxer briefs.

"Fuck," he said in a gruff, ragged tone.

I shifted off his lap to my knees, hands on his thighs as I slowly widened them and shuffled closer. My eyes trailed over the large bulge in his pants then my hand followed the path slipping inside his pants. My fingers curled around his heated cock and he groaned. I freed it from the confines then held the base firm in my grip before lowering my head.

He sucked in his breath when I licked the tip, the salty sweetness clinging to my tongue. His fingers weaved into my hair then he roughly fisted the strands.

"Jesus," he murmured as I drew him into my mouth.

I took as much as I could, relaxing my throat as his cock hit my gag reflex. I swirled my tongue and sucked, my hand squeezing the base harder.

"Alina." He raised his hips, shoving his cock further down my throat and I gagged for a second. "Sorry. Shit. Harder, baby. Harder."

I sucked harder.

"Faster."

I moved up and down, sucking, my hand moving up when my mouth did. God, I loved this. Not just his cock in my mouth, but what I did to him.

"Oh, fuck, baby. You need to stop. I'm going to come and I want to have my cock inside you when I do." He grabbed me by the shoulders and pulled me up. "Pants off. Now."

I smiled then licked my lips and he groaned, his eyes flicking to my tongue. His eyes blazed with desire, but there was also a hint of frustration as his brows furrowed.

"Now," he ordered and his hands moved to my grey yoga pants.

I stepped back from him so he was out of reach, making him scowl. "Babe."

I wiggled my hips as I dragged them down inch-by-inch, loving how his eyes were intense and heated as he watched.

Then I did the same with my panties, taking my time.

His control broke as his leapt from the chair.

I squealed as he grabbed me, shoved me against the dresser and put his hands on my ass, lifting so I sat on the edge of the smooth, hard surface.

He had a condom out of his pocket and unpackaged within seconds, then he rolled it on, all using one hand. He yanked me forward, so his cock pressed at my entrance and I settled my thighs on his hips.

"I never want to feel that scared again. Losing you isn't an option, Alina."

He thrust inside me and I gasped, head thrown back, eyes closing.

There was nothing calm and gentle about it as the dresser banged against the wall and whatever I had on it crashed to the floor at our feet.

It was an uncontrolled, fierce, wild need. It was as if he had to be certain I felt every part of him. As if he had to convince himself that this was real and at the same time, convince me that he wasn't going to leave me this time.

This was our chance at a second beginning.

This was us finding our way back to one another.

And it was a step toward being un-lost.

Connor slept.

It was still early afternoon, but he was exhausted and had been dozing for an hour. There were black circles under his eyes from the constant worry and lack of sleep.

So, I let him sleep.

I snuck out of bed, grabbed my shirt and yanked it over my head, then headed for the door to go downstairs for something to eat when my stomach lurched.

I ran for the adjoining bathroom, fell to my knees, and threw up in the toilet. God, I hated this. The constant uncertainty with Connor was taking its toll on me.

Flushing, I stood then grabbed my toothbrush, piled tons of minty toothpaste on it and stuck it in my mouth.

The door opened and Connor stood there with a concerned frown. "What's wrong?"

I spit the toothpaste into the sink. "Nothing. My stomach is upset."

He approached. "Why?"

I swished water then spit again before turning off the taps. "It's just from all this."

"All this?"

I dropped my toothbrush in the cup. "Yeah, all this. Everything that's happened recently. One day you're here. The next you're gone. Constantly worrying about you. I feel like a yo-yo being pulled in and out constantly. I haven't slept in five days, barely ate and when I do, I throw up. It's just catching up to me."

He sighed and moved into me, his finger tucking strands of hair behind my ear. "I'm sorry, baby. I never want you to feel that way. Fuck, I shouldn't—"

I shoved him in the chest, but all it did was shift his weight slightly. "Don't you dare say it! You don't get to say you shouldn't have left or come back, or anything like that anymore."

His hand slipped beneath my hair as he cupped my neck. "I wasn't going to say that."

"Oh."

"I was going to say I shouldn't have fucked you if you weren't feeling well."

Oh. "Well, I was okay then."

"Babe, I don't want you worried about me." He put his hand on my forehead then my cheek. "You sure you're okay?"

"Yeah, I'm fine now and really hungry."

He chuckled, his eyes flashing with amusement. "I can do something about that."

Sliding his hand in mine, he led me into the bedroom where he yanked on his pants then he took my hand again and we went downstairs to the kitchen.

Once he sat me on the counter, he made me the most delicious Greek omelet I'd ever tasted.

CHAPTER TWENTY-FOUR

MY PHONE VIBRATED on the nightstand and my eyes flashed open. It took a second to get my bearings and what was holding me so tight, but then I realized it was Connor's leg over my thighs and his arm snug around my waist.

He was in bed with me. He must have come in early this morning because he refused to sleep with me and stayed in another room.

It had been a week since the gunshots and Connor was still here. Vic was gone and everything had settled, except for my stomach.

"You going to get that, babe?"

"Ah, yeah." I blindly reached for my phone and held it up.

Chess's name flashed. I pressed the large green circle. "Hi, Chess."

"Alina. Hey."

We chatted a minute. I asked about Danny and Bacon and she told me he was planning a demonstration for Treasured Children's Center's grand opening.

Connor nuzzled my neck and goose bumps soared. Then his hand slid between my legs and teased me. "Sorry, what?" I had no clue what Chess just said.

I flipped over and scowled at him. Secretly, I was glad he was being playful and cute in the morning.

"I was asking if you could help out with the center," Chess said.

"Oh, sure. Yeah, of course. Anything you need." I was thrilled that Chess asked me for help. I wanted to be a part of the project and going once a week never felt enough.

"You're a photographer, right?"

I stiffened and Connor's hand that had been lightly circling my sex stilled. "Well, I was a long time ago."

"Great. Would you be able to take some photos of the place before the opening? Maybe come by this week and meet me. We can take photos of the animals and—"

I interjected, "I don't take photos anymore."

"Oh." She paused then, "If it's a camera you need—"

I didn't hear the rest because Connor took the phone from me. "We'll call you back." Then he hung up and tossed the phone to the foot of the bed.

"Connor, you can't do that." I wasn't even sure if Chess knew Connor was staying here with me. She could be freaking out.

"I just did."

Sitting up, I tried to go for the phone, but he grabbed my waist and threw me back to lie on my back while he hovered over me.

"Connor! I have to call her back."

"We need to talk about this."

"About what?"

"I hate that you don't take photos anymore and don't bullshit me about why you don't want to. I was there. I remember."

"It's not so simple," I murmured.

"Simple isn't something we've ever done, baby."

"Damn it, you wouldn't have been tortured and drugged if he

hadn't found the photos."

His brows dropped dangerously low and his mouth tightened. "We don't know that. But if that were true, then I'd be living a life without you, never knowing the truth. Still hating how you left me." He sighed. "Being with you now is worth everything."

Tears fell and he gently wiped them away with his thumb.

It made me sick to my stomach thinking about holding a camera again and my stomach was already in rough shape. The passion for photography had died and finding that story within the lens didn't exist in me anymore.

"Will any kids be there?" he asked.

"At the Center?"

"Yeah."

"No. They don't move there until after the opening. Danny will be with Chess. I'm sure she'll want photos of him with Bacon."

His brows lifted. "Bacon? Tell me that's not a pig."

I smiled. "Yeah. Danny named him. A potbellied pig."

"Then we do this together."

"Huh?"

"I'll go with you."

My breath locked and my eyes snapped to his. "You will?"

"I don't like it. But I want to be there for you." He cupped my chin, his thumb caressing back and forth over my lower lip. "Alina, you've never given up on me. I gave you every reason to and you're still here. So, yeah, I'll go."

Then he kissed me and it was another hour before I got around to calling Chess back and telling her I'd do it.

CHAPTER TWENTY-FIVE

Question 12: What type of bird would you want to be?

Alina

"**B**ABE, LOOK AT me."

We stood beside his bike at the Center and I had the helmet clutched between my hands, staring at the top of it. Connor pried it out of my grip, set it on the seat of the bike and took my hands in his.

"Today, you make new stories," he said. "Today, we make new memories." He put his finger under my chin and guided my head up so our eyes met. "It wasn't your fault. I've never blamed you. And I've never regretted us meeting. Not once." He leaned in and kissed me. "And I'm freaking out, too." My brows lifted because he didn't look like he was freaking out. Actually, there was no tension in his face at all. "The girl, Chess... I hit her, Alina. In France, after I'd brought London into Vault."

Oh, I hadn't known that. "That wasn't you."

"Still, the triggers are unpredictable as you know from the holes in your walls, shutterbug. Meeting her again. Being around a kid. Fuck, anything can set me off, but I have you and, babe, you calm me. It's like you're my reminder of what's real and I have to hold onto that."

Connor stayed—mostly. He took off on his bike a few times, punched the wall several times, and he refused to sleep with me through the night. I'd also woken in the early morning hours to him pacing downstairs, or hearing the shower in the downstairs bathroom going.

But his bike now sat in my driveway, his clothes were in my closet and he'd checked out of the hotel. He also drove me to work and picked me up, but he was never happy about it. He'd made it clear numerous times how much he hated me working at the bar.

And he'd bought me a camera. I was a little surprised because we'd never talked about money, but he obviously had some because it was a really expensive camera. And it sat in the box on my kitchen table for two days. There was a flash of giddiness when I first saw it like a kid with a brand new toy, eager to rip open the box and play with it.

But the overwhelming sick feelings of guilt and hate took hold and I couldn't. So, I'd left it there. Connor never pushed me and it remained as a centerpiece on the kitchen table until this morning.

Connor was really trying and he'd even gone to meet Deck and the doctor yesterday to have blood taken. Afterwards, we did something normal; we held hands and walked along the beach. There was a wooden boardwalk, but Connor didn't like that there were lots of other people walking, jogging, or biking along it, so we took off our shoes and walked along the sandy beach.

And now we were at the Center where I was going to take photos for the first time since the day I'd destroyed my camera at Moreno's.

Connor slid his hand down my arm then linked his fingers in mine.

"It's my turn to be strong enough for both of us, baby." He half smiled and my heart lifted. "I'll protect you from the demons."

"Aren't vampires and demons on the same side?"

His half grin turned into a full-out grin and my heart melted. "Not this vampire. This vampire is a rebel and in love with a fuckin' werewolf."

I laughed and some of the nervousness alleviated.

Make new stories.

Make new memories.

If Connor could try, I certainly could.

"Alina!"

I looked toward the barn at Danny who waved frantically. Chess stood beside Rocket who had his head stuck in a pink bucket, probably munching on his breakfast. She waved, smiling.

Connor unstrapped the camera case from the back of his bike then slipped it on my shoulder. "Ready?"

"Yeah."

We then walked toward our demons to face them together.

Demons weren't the issue though, Bacon was. He was apparently having a bad day and Rocket wasn't any help with his bleating from inside the barn where he was temporarily delegated, but the clatter of him playing with the latch meant his escape was imminent.

Connor meeting Chess and Danny went over well because neither of them made a big deal of it, although there was tension in Connor's body when he shook both their hands. His brows furrowed and lips pursed and it looked as if he was fighting one of his headaches, but he didn't leave.

For me it was all nerves with my hands trembling and my stomach churning as I set the camera on the ground and crouched to unpack it.

The photos scattered all over the glass coffee table flashed before my eyes and my screams and sobs echoed. Then seeing Connor's emotionless face and that crushing feeling of suddenly hating my passion with everything inside me.

Connor crouched beside me.

My hands frozen on the camera case, he gently pushed them aside then took the camera out and removed the lens cap. Before I knew what he was doing, he leaned into me, lifted the camera so it faced us then pressed the shutter taking a picture of us. Like we'd done so long ago.

He lowered the camera and kissed me. "Not going to happen again, baby. I won't let it." Then he handed it to me and rose.

Pictures of us. What had destroyed Connor and yet he was here.

I swallowed, glanced at him and he nodded encouragingly. If he could do this, so could I. I raised the camera and peered through the lens.

And then it was gone. All the fear vanished as the beauty in what I loved emerged again.

Two hours later, Rocket still screamed his displeasure from the barn and Chess was out in the horse pasture with three Clydesdale horses that Emily, the wife of the lead singer from the Tear Asunder band, had rescued from slaughter.

I stepped off the fence rail after taking a few shots of the pasture and turned to find Connor who had gone to check out the house. But he hadn't gone to check out the house. He was with Danny by the barn.

He sat on his haunches while he drew something in the sand using a stick. Danny had a fierce concentrated look, eyes focused, lips pursed, head bowed. I had no idea what Connor was drawing and it didn't matter. He said he could never be around kids again and yet there he was chatting with Danny.

He trusted himself not to hurt him.

I raised my camera, focused in and took a few close-ups. There was tension in Connor's shoulders and he scowled, but he was hanging out with a kid.

I approached and when I was close enough, I heard the strain in his voice. Despite his struggle, he did it. God, I loved him even more, if that were possible.

He was trying. Whether it was due to the gunshots or what he and Deck talked about, or a combination, whatever it was, Connor was fighting for himself and that meant us, too.

I glanced at the lines in the sand. Connor was drawing an agility course for Bacon in the gravel and explaining where the best place to put each obstacle according to Bacon's strengths and weaknesses.

It was sweet, thoughtful, and it was a piece of Connor that had been snatched away.

Until now.

Connor stood when he noticed me behind him, although I suspected he knew the minute I'd started toward him. His eyes rarely left me, always conscious of where I was.

"Thanks, Connor," Danny said, his eyes beaming with excitement.

Connor reached out to Danny, his hand inches away from ruffling his hair, but he drew back, fingers curling into fists at his side. "Show Bacon that you respect him and understand his wants and needs and he'll give you everything he has."

"I will. I will." Danny nodded enthusiastically.

Connor turned to me. "Babe, did you get what you need?"

"Yeah."

Chess joined us and Danny showed her the course and was rambling on about what Connor had told him using the stick to point to the map in the sand.

Connor drew me up against him and took a deep breath, some of the tension easing from his body. I suspected he'd been worried he'd have a flashback the entire time he'd been hanging with Danny.

"Let's go," I suggested. I turned to Chess and Danny to say goodbye when there was a loud bang in the barn and then hooves on the cement floor.

Chess and I looked at one another. "Rocket incoming."

Within seconds, Rocket was out of the barn and pushing between us, head-butting whoever was in his way. Connor took the brunt of it because he was in the way of my camera bag. Apparently, Rocket thought it tasted better than his potato chips.

Connor stroked his neck and Rocket settled, leaning into his leg and loving the attention. The sound of tires crunching on gravel had Rocket bleating and running toward the car and Chess swearing.

"I told him noon. He's early." The person who was early was Tristan and he was out of his classy black car and standing in front of it within seconds.

"No." Tristan blocked Rocket's path to the hood of his car. "I pay for your food and vet bills. You want to eat, you stay off my car."

"Dad," Danny yelled and ran to Tristan.

Chess sharply inhaled, her hand covering her mouth and tears filling her eyes. "He just started calling us Mom and Dad. I don't think I'll ever get used to it."

Tristan strode toward us, Danny now riding on his back and Rocket hopped along beside them, nipping at Tristan's suit pant leg. What made this day so special was them. How they didn't make a big deal at seeing Connor with me. Tristan and Chess were victims of Vault and knew what Connor had done for the organization, not specifically, but the type of jobs.

But they treated him like any other person, warmly with no pre-judgments.

Tristan Mason was just as tall and built as Connor, but more clean-cut. Due to Mason Developments, he was high profile and had endless media attention. But that was how they managed so much funding for the Treasured Children's Center.

"Connor," Tristan said, smiling. He lowered Danny off his back then held out his hand.

Connor shook it, but he was tense. He looked away and briefly closed his eyes. Shit. I was getting to know the signs of his headaches that put him on edge. Even a scent could cause him to react. But it didn't matter what it was. The important thing was to move away from it as that usually eased the headache before he lost it.

"We better go. I'll email you the photos," I said to Chess. "Nice to see you, Tristan."

"And you, Alina. Connor."

Chess smiled. "Later, guys."

Danny said goodbye, too, but he was tugging on Tristan's hand to show him Connor's drawing of the obstacle course.

Connor nodded once to everyone, locked his arm over my shoulders and we walked to his bike. He took my camera case and secured it on the back of the bike then placed my helmet on my head and did up the chinstrap. He threw his leg over the seat and started the bike before I got on behind him.

"I need to go for a ride, shutterbug. You up for that?" he asked. "Or I can drop you off at home."

"Yeah. I'm good with that. But can we go fast this time?" I was pretty sure Connor kept his speed slower whenever I was on his bike with him.

It took a second before he smirked. "Yeah, babe, we can go fast."

I shifted in closer to him, my pelvis snug to his ass and said next to his ear, "Because you're kind of a pussy on the bike."

Connor revved the engine. "Pussy?"

I bit my lip. "Yeah."

"There is no pussy here except yours. And I plan on tasting it and showing how damn *fast* I can make you come."

My belly flipped. I was hoping it was going to be a short ride. Actually, I was now hoping we'd go straight home. I was about to suggest that when he skidded out the driveway.

CHAPTER TWENTY-SIX

Question 13: Potato chips or chocolate?

I STIRRED THE TOMATO sauce in the pan while the pasta boiled. I had the night off from the bar and was making dinner for Connor. He'd left an hour ago to take a run down by the water. He'd started running last week instead of disappearing for hours on his bike. He still disappeared on his bike, but it wasn't every day anymore.

"Smells great, pet." Deaglan strolled into the kitchen with light green paint splattered on his T-shirt and jeans. "Do I get fed for painting your porch?"

I raised my brows. "Suddenly it's my porch, is it?"

He chuckled as he leaned his butt on the counter beside the stove. "Sure. Anything for a home-cooked meal."

"Yeah, well, you've never tried my cooking."

Deaglan had been scarce for the last week, but yesterday, he'd started fixing the porch. He'd sanded the railing and had moved on to painting it.

"I'm going back to Ireland soon," he said. "Not sure if or when I'll be back."

"Is everything okay?"

He crossed his ankles. "My little brother is causing shit again and the boarding school finally kicked his ass out. I need to do something about it."

"Oh." I stirred the sauce as I picked up a handful of mushrooms and red peppers and sprinkled them in the sauce. "He's a lot younger than you I guess?"

"Seventeen. Cocky. A kickass football player and a genius. Makes for a kid with an attitude." He cleared his throat. "Listen, I just came by to make sure you're good here, with Connor. Deck is cool with me leaving, but I wanted to check with you."

The floorboards creaked in the hallway and I stopped stirring to look and see Connor. His expression was tight and his eyes shifted from me to Deaglan.

He was soaked from his run and sweat dripped down his brow. But even sweaty, sexiness oozed. The tattoos on his arms gleamed with dampness making the ink pop and his muscles to accentuate.

"How was your run?" I rested the wooden spoon on the edge of the pan and walked to him. I placed my hands on his chest and stood on my tiptoes to kiss him, but I couldn't reach his lips until he tilted. The kiss was brief, but still possessive.

"Fine," he replied. He raised his head to look at Deaglan and I was uneasy as to how he was going to react to him being in the kitchen with me. "Deaglan." He nodded to him and I breathed a sigh of relief. The tension slowly eased from Connor and I smiled to myself. This was good. A month ago, he'd have been throwing punches and losing his shit.

"Connor. I was just telling your girl that I'm leaving as soon as I finish the porch. I need to head back home, and I'm not sure if I'll be back." Deaglan reached for the spoon and stirred the bubbling sauce.

"I heard." Connor's hand rested on my lower back. "And yeah, she's good with me here."

Deaglan smirked. "Hey, had to ask her. Your track record isn't that great." *Oh, my God, Deaglan. Shut up.* "Plus, I'd like to sell the place soon, so keeping the kitchen cupboards intact would be cool."

I moaned, clonking my forehead onto Connor's chest. Deaglan had no filter and was going to get his ass kicked, just like his little brother.

But Connor's reaction was unexpected as his chest vibrated with a half chuckle. "They'll be intact and if you need to leave ASAP, I can finish the porch."

Whoa. What? He would?

Deaglan nodded. "Shit. That would be cool."

Normal. That was what this conversation was, filling me with hope that Connor was adjusting.

Deck had come by the other day and they talked for ten minutes outside and there were no bruised jaws or shouting, which was a good sign.

Deaglan set the spoon down and pushed away from the counter. "I'll book a flight then."

"I'd like to talk to you before you leave for Ireland," Connor said.

"Yeah. Sure. Anytime." He winked at me. "Later, pet." Then he left.

I looked up at Connor. "What do you want to talk to him about?"

"Do you like the house?"

"Yeah, it's great. It even has a picket fence and wildflower garden. I love that."

The corners of his lips curved up. "A house by the water. Quiet neighborhood. Picket fence and you like it here." Was he saying what I think he was saying? "Babe, I can't promise I'm always going to be here in the morning or hold you when you go to sleep. Fuck, I want to and I'm trying, but even if I need to leave, I swear I'll always come back. We're permanent. We've never been any other way. And I want you to have a place that's permanent."

My heart skipped a beat. They were words I didn't want to hear and at the same time I did. We were permanent, and yet every single day there was a chance he'd leave. I knew that. But he'd come back and he wanted a place that was ours. Where he could always come back to.

But the reality was a house wasn't in the budget. "I don't have that kind of money, Connor. I can barely afford the rent and Deaglan is giving me a deal."

His hands slid up my arms to cup my head, his thumbs softly stroking my cheeks. "I do. Vault set me up nicely, although I expect they thought I'd continue to be under their control and using the money for missions, not buying a house." His eyes softened and he sighed. "Babe, I can easily support us for a while." I opened my mouth to object when he put his finger on my lip. "I'm not going to talk about you working at the bar, you know how I feel, but I'd like you to start something with your photography and if I can help with that, I want to."

Despite his persistence to get me to stop working at the bar, Connor had faith in my photography. He'd been supportive of my work when we met, too, although that was only when I'd convinced him to take us to the orphanage.

Taking photos at the Center had been like getting a piece of *me* back. I'd been thinking about doing something with my photography, but it was art and difficult to build a name.

He tilted my head up. "I fuckin' love you so damn much. You know that, right?"

I smiled. "Yeah."

"I can't give you normal with the perfect white picket fence, but I can give you the broken green picket fence."

"I'm kind of a fan of green and broken." I stood on my tiptoes and kissed him. "I love you, Connor O'Neill."

"Damn right you do."

I laughed at the familiar words and then a loud hissing and sizzle sounded behind me. "Shit, pasta's boiling over." I dove to take the pot off the stove, but Connor was there first and did it for me.

He dumped the pasta in the strainer in the sink while I added a few final spices to the sauce.

He came up behind me and kissed the back of my neck. Goose bumps popped along my skin and my chest swelled.

God, I loved when he did that. Having him pressed up against me from behind, his hands settled on my hips, inhaling his scent, the light touch of his lips on my skin. That simple gesture made all the uncertainties vanish.

Because there were uncertainties. Connor had yet to see his sister or parents, and he refused to talk to a therapist.

But he wanted to buy the house. Give us permanence.

"Babe," he whispered against my ear. "I need to jump in the shower. Two minutes."

"Okay. The garlic bread isn't ready yet." I flicked on the oven light and bent to peer through the glass.

Connor's hand caressed my ass. "Fuck. I love your ass."

A wave of heated tingles erupted. I stood straight and glanced over my shoulder at him. "I thought you liked my breasts?"

"Like those, too."

"Like?" I teased.

He chuckled. "Fishing for compliments, shutterbug?"

I smiled. "Yeah."

He swung me around so I faced him. "I love every single piece of you, Alina." He lowered his head and kissed me. It was sweet and gentle and really unlike Connor, but I discovered I loved this too. His lips roamed lazily over mine, tasting, exploring, unhurried.

But it didn't take long before he picked me up in his arms and carried me to the bathroom where he set me on my feet then with one yank ripped my shirt off.

"Connor!" I gasped.

He smirked then tugged his shirt off over his head. Next he rid me of my shorts and panties with a few quick movements before stepping out of his.

Then we were in the shower with the water streaming down on us. My back against the wall, legs around his waist while he held my ass. Our mouths melded in a fury and he groaned just before he guided his cock to me.

He slid the tip through my wetness. "Fuck, I love that."

I'd been wet from the second he walked in the door looking sexy as hell.

I closed my eyes as he slid inside of me. "Oh, God. Yes."

He tilted his hips and sank deeper. "Alina. Baby. So incredible." He kissed me again as he began to move and there was nothing gentle about it.

Raw. Rough. Real.

All control vanished as my fingers gripped his hair and he thrust into me against the wall over and over again. His deep growls vibrated against my neck as he nipped, bit, and licked while pressing his pelvis against my sex.

The sudden burst exploded and my body jerked. "Oh, God. Oh, God," I cried, thighs clamping and hands pulling at his hair as I came fast and hard.

He came right after me after two more thrusts.

Then we both stilled, our breathing ragged, lips bruised, bodies soaked and throbbing.

My eyes widened as he pulled out and I felt the remnants of him dripping down my inner thigh. "Shit, Connor. Condom."

"You're on the pill." I was now, but only since Connor moved in, so it wasn't reliable yet. "I also asked the doctor to check for everything so we didn't have to use condoms anymore." Oh. He hadn't told me that. "Those results came back this morning and I'm good. But, I told you I was never with anyone else."

"In all those years?"

He turned me so I was under the spray of the water and gently ran his hand down my inner thigh to wash me. "I spent years in a cell, Alina. Then I was on the drug and I never thought about sex. Maybe that was a side-effect. I don't know, but I do know I never had sex with anyone else."

"But why me then?"

"Tilt your head back." I did and he caressed my hair back, the water trickling over it. "I didn't know why at the time, but I got fuckin' hard as hell when you touched me." He pulled me back into him, his hand cupping my chin. "My mind may have forgotten you, Alina, but my body never did."

I choked on a sob, closed my eyes and wrapped my arms around him. I don't know why it was such a relief to hear those words. Maybe because I realized I'd done the right thing. He may have not remembered me, but parts of him had and I gave him that.

Connor's brows dropped and his body stiffened, eyes snapping to the bathroom door. "Fuck." He leapt out the shower and flung open the bathroom door. A billow of smoke clashed with the humid air.

"Garlic bread," I cried and ran after him, soaking wet and naked.

The kitchen was filled with smoke and it had begun to drift into the hallway. I grabbed a broom from the closet and ran to the fire alarm in the hallway and waved the bristles back and forth near the device.

Connor dealt with the oven and the charred garlic toast, but my attempts to keep the alarm from going off failed and a piercing blare sounded. "Damn it," I shouted as I waved the broom back and forth faster. The alarm paused then started again.

Connor came up behind me to take the broom when the front door opened. Both of us froze, our hands holding the broom in the air.

Deaglan's eyes widened and he froze, too. His gaze flicked to my breasts before he spun around. "Shit. Sorry." Then laughter emerged. He was laughing so hard he bent over clutching his stomach. "If you guys saw yourselves...." He burst out laughing again.

"Babe." Connor shoved me behind him, protecting my nakedness with his body even though Deaglan wasn't facing us.

Deaglan shook his head as he opened the screen door. "Leave you to... whatever you're doing. But try not to burn down the house. Killian's a real asshole when shit pisses him off and the house burning down would piss him off."

The screen door squeaked and bounced on the hinges as it shut behind him, the sound of his chuckle fading.

Connor dropped the broom on the floor and turned toward me. I bit my lip to keep from smiling because I was uncertain how Connor was going to take that little scene.

The second I saw his brilliant blue eyes sparking with humor, it was like being transported back to when we met. There was lightness in him, a freedom to his caged emotions and it was beautiful.

I smiled and reached up to stroke the side of his face. "We're going to be okay, aren't we?"

"Yeah. Not perfect. Not the same. But yeah."

"I don't want perfect or the same. I just want us and whoever we are now," I replied.

"Me too, baby."

Then we dried off, dressed and reheated the pasta before going out to the cabana to eat where Grandma Kane used to have her afternoon tea.

CHAPTER TWENTY-SEVEN

Question 14: Bungee jump or rock climb?

"SO, CONNOR'S STAYING with you?" London asked as she sat across from me.

We were at Georgie's coffee shop having lattes, two days after the garlic bread incident.

When I woke this morning, I was sick again and I knew it was no longer because of stress. And maybe there was the inkling that it had nothing to do with worry and lack of sleep in the beginning, but I hadn't wanted to face the possibility.

I found Connor pacing in the living room, his hand raking through his hair. The room was a mess, shelf ripped off the wall, statues broken, drapes torn from the rod. He'd lost it.

When he saw me, he walked over, briefly squeezed my hand and said, "Demons and vampires are fighting, baby. I need to take a ride."

That was his signal to me now and in a way, it made it easier because he was trying to make light of it.

He had been gone ten minutes before I called London and asked her if she could meet for coffee. She sounded surprised, because I never called her. But she readily offered to pick me up.

I'd texted Connor to let him know, just in case he came back before I did.

I wrapped my hands around the oversized yellow mug. "Yeah. The headaches are still bad and he doesn't sleep, at least not for long, but he's learning to control the anger. Read the signs before he gets out of control."

London nodded. "That's good news. The drug was potent and from what I gathered from my father's research, it affected dopamine being released in the brain. A way to stop him from feeling pleasure." My hands tightened on the mug and my stomach dropped at the mere thought of the years Connor didn't feel pleasure. It made sense now why he said he never had sex except for with me that once. "I heard the blood work came back normal."

I nodded. "Yeah."

"I wish I could do more to help, but I think it's just going to take time. It would help if he talked to someone about what he's been through."

I shook my head, that wasn't possible. I uncrossed my legs and crossed them again. "He won't and I can't blame him. He's afraid he'll lose it if he talks about what happened and then they'll lock him up and drug him to keep him calm."

"He's right," London agreed.

There was no winning here for Connor. But he was doing better, and in time, maybe he'd get back to a kind of normal.

We went on to talk about the Center and her classes then she told me Kai had been gone for a couple days to meet up with Ernie and Tyler to deal with some associates of Vault. "Kai is making certain anyone involved with Vault knows about its new direction and that he is in control." She paused. "But a few aren't so pleased." And probably why Kai had gone to deal with them. "So are you going to tell me what's wrong?" I met her eyes and she half smiled. "This wasn't just a coffee date, you've been fidgeting ever since you sat down."

I hadn't realized. The flutter in my belly increased as I thought about why I was here. "I need to see a doctor." I swallowed, my hand instinctively going to my belly. "I think I'm pregnant."

"Oh my God. That's great news," London said.

I wasn't so sure about that. "We've always used protection though."

She huffed. "Yeah, I thought I had the ultimate protection."

"You're pregnant?" I blurted a little too loud and the two men at a nearby table glanced over.

"Three months. And I'm telling Kai when he gets back tonight."

"He doesn't know yet?" I found that hard to believe, that man was hyperaware of everything to do with London.

She shook her head. "No. But it wouldn't even cross his mind as he'd had a vasectomy at an early age. It didn't cross mine either. I had the doctor do three blood tests before I believed him. When I told him why, he said there is a chance that the procedure wasn't done properly or there is a chance the snipped parts grew back together. Anyway, I've been hinting for a while."

"Oh, my God, the pets?"

She laughed. "Yeah. My period was late a week, so I did a urine test and it was positive. I was skeptical until I had blood tests done though."

"Are you nervous?"

"About being pregnant or telling Kai?"

"Telling Kai. That he may think you cheated on him."

She burst out laughing. "Kai's far too arrogant to think that. We're solid and he knows I'd never do that. Don't get me wrong, he'll be shocked and maybe even lose his cool, but he'll get over it."

"But what if he doesn't want a baby?" Connor said he didn't want kids.

She shrugged with a mischievous smile playing at her mouth. "He thinks he doesn't want anything except us, but a baby is part of us." She pushed her coffee mug aside. "You're worried about how Connor will react if you are?"

I inhaled a shaky breath. "Yes. He told me he doesn't want kids. He doesn't even want to be around them."

"Because he doesn't trust himself."

I nodded as I shifted uneasily in my seat. "I think he'll leave, London. Any progress he's made... he won't even sleep in the same room as me because he's afraid he might wake and hurt me. There's no way he'll stay with me if there's a baby." I tucked my hair behind my ears as I lowered my eyes to stare at the remnants of coffee in the bottom of my mug. "He's getting better and I even heard him talking to Deck the other day on the phone about seeing Georgie. But to put this on him now... I can't lose him again, London." Tears filled my eyes as I looked up at London.

She remained silent for a few seconds before reaching across the table and taking my hands in hers. "Okay, let's find out if you're pregnant first. We'll go to a walk-in clinic and keep this between us for now." She hesitated. "And if you are, you can decide what to do then. But no matter what your decision is, I'm behind you, Alina."

A few tears spilled down my cheeks and I slipped my hands from hers to use the napkin and wipe them away. That was when the bell above the door dinged and I glanced up to see Connor walk in. He stopped, eyes scanning the room.

There was an obvious quiet of voices as gazes turned to him. He had that effect, like he owned the room. It was also that he appeared kind of scary with the intensity that oozed from him.

His eyes landed on me and he strode toward the table.

"God, the way he looks at you is really hot," London murmured.

"That man loves you something fierce."

Connor stopped at the table. "London." His eyes briefly flicked to her before they were back on me then his hand cupped the back of my neck. He bent and kissed me. It was gentle and made my pulse race and my toes curl. He pulled back. "Do you want more coffee?"

It took me a second because I was surprised for two reasons he didn't want me to leave with him and it was his sister's coffee shop. She could very well walk in at any moment, and there were numerous people around.

"Ah, yeah, sure."

He asked London and she told him what she'd like then he went up to the counter. I noticed Rylie's cheeks heat up and her eyes grow wide, looking rather flustered as Connor gave his order.

London leaned forward, her voice lowering. "We can go to the clinic before your shift. You're working tonight?"

It was Saturday and Avalanche's busiest night. "Yeah."

"Okay, I'll pop by and take you. See if he'll drop you off a little early."

Connor came back with three coffees and set them on the table then pulled up a chair and sat beside me, his thigh brushing mine. He lifted my coffee and sipped before sliding it toward me. I loved that he still did that.

Connor slid the other coffee to London and said, "Sorry I shot you." I'd just taken a sip of my coffee and choked on it. "You suffered at the hands of Vault because of me. I'm sorry."

London half smiled. "Thank you, but we both know it wasn't you who did that, but the drug. A drug my father formulated. So, we'll just call it even."

"Done," he replied. He pushed his legs out and crossed his ankles and I melted because he was completely calm, although there was a slight tension between his eyes.

If I were pregnant, would he leave? He was improving and handled being with Danny well enough. He was in a different place than he was when he'd been adamant about not having kids. But if I mentioned it, there was the risk of him leaving.

God, I didn't want to keep this from him.

I pressed my hand to my stomach at what could be growing inside me. It wasn't just a baby. It was hope and possibility. Connor had loved kids more than anything. Could he get that back if we had our own?

"Are you still not feeling well?" Connor asked, frowning. He nodded to my hand resting on my belly.

London's eyes widened and she quickly grabbed her coffee and stood, her chair scraping on the hardwood floors. "Listen, I have to go. Kai said he'll be back today and with my crazy school schedule, Saturday and Sunday are the only days we have to spend together. Thanks for the coffee, Connor." She put her phone in her purse.

I mouthed "thank you" while Connor's attention was on her. She smiled. "See you later."

"You sure you're okay?" Connor asked. He sat up, leaned into me, his hand reaching for mine on the table.

His eyes shifted to my throat and there was no chance he didn't see my pulse because it was throbbing erratically. "Yeah."

"You weren't sick this morning?"

I didn't want to lie so I skirted around the question. "I'm fine." I forced a smile and leaned in and kissed him. "Was your ride good?"

"Yeah." He nodded then gestured to the shop. "So, this place is my sister's?"

Connor and I sat for a half hour with customers coming and going, chatting quietly with our coffees. There was a constant alertness about him, and I noticed the way he positioned his chair was so he protected me from the door and kept his visual clear.

But he was in his sister's coffee shop.

And the demons were losing.

CHAPTER TWENTY-EIGHT

London

THE DOOR SLID closed on its tracks and I locked it, before dropping my purse on a glass oblong table and walking into the warehouse. Our place was over three thousand square feet, open concept except for the two washrooms and three bedrooms, one of which Kai used as an office. The walls were brick and the ducts and pipes were exposed in the fifteen-foot ceilings.

The raw, natural feel of the place was what I love the most and the floor-to-ceiling windows on the east side allowed for mornings lying in bed with Kai's arms around me and watching the sunrise.

Walking across the hardwood floors, I made my way to the bedroom. Kai's keys had been on the glass table so I knew he was back early and I was excited to see him. But then I was always excited to see him.

PERFECT RAGE

Kai was my other half. My always. And sometimes it scared me how much I loved him because it consumed me. He consumed me.

Standing in the doorway of our bedroom, I watched Kai as he hung up his suit jacket in the walk-in closet.

Every muscle rippled as he moved and I squeezed my thighs together. I'd never get tired of watching Kai. There was so much beauty in him and it wasn't just because of his hard contoured body; it was how he moved.

Smooth and agile, combined with a fierce confidence. I'd never known anyone to be so confident with who he was other than Kai.

"I love you watching me, braveheart." He slowly turned, eyes blazing with desire. "It's a total turn-on, but I've been away for two days without the touch of your lips on mine and I'd rather them on me than across the room."

"Did business go okay?" I was about to break some rather shocking news and if 'business' was a success then this would be much easier... on him.

His eyes narrowed and his back stiffened. Shit, how did he know something was up? God, he was so in tune to me. The only way I'd been able to hold this off for so long was because it was almost impossible for me to get pregnant.

Almost.

"What's wrong?" he asked carefully.

As he strode across the bedroom toward me, he pulled his leather belt from the loops of his pants. I smiled thinking of that night in my loft when we first met and I thought he was going to spank me with his belt.

"How do you know something's wrong?"

He tossed the belt on the bed then stopped in front of me. With his knuckles, he caressed the side of my face and I tilted my head, leaning into his touch. "You'd never ask me that first. You'd ask if I was okay." Shit, true. "I'll ask you again, what's wrong?"

There was no way to ease him into this and Kai liked straight forward, so I bit the bullet. "I'm three months' pregnant."

He jerked, eyes widening, hand dropping from my face and mouth gaping.

Yep, total shock. I let him process the words and everything that came with them, which was a hell of a lot, and waited patiently for him to say something.

And it was a while because he slammed his mouth shut then walked back to the closet and finished undressing out of his suit, and then slowly pulled on a pair of jeans and a T-shirt.

I moved into the bedroom and sat on the end of the bed, my eyes never leaving him. This was Kai losing his cool silently. He was freaked and didn't trust himself to say or do anything until he pulled it together.

He walked out of the closet, briefly glanced at me and said, "A doctor confirmed this?"

"Yes."

He nodded then walked out of the bedroom. Hmmm, I wasn't sure what to do, so I went with instinct and followed him. The fridge opened and closed as he took out a bottle of water and cracked the seal before chugging it back.

I stood twenty feet away. Shit, did he think I cheated? I'd been really confident that he'd never consider that a possibility, but suddenly I wasn't so sure.

I wrung my hands together and stared at the floor as my mind panicked with all kinds of stupid things like if he'd leave me.

Suddenly he was in front of me, his hands cupping either side of my head and tilting it so I met his intense gaze.

"I see what's going through your head. Don't even go there. I'm not thinking it. I know it has to be mine." A wave of relief settled over me. "That's why you were sick." It wasn't a question. He'd been quiet because he was calculating and trying to figure it all out. "Why you asked me about getting a pet?"

I nodded.

His eyes narrowed. "You knew back then?"

"Not for sure. The test at the store said yes, but the possibility was so unlikely that I didn't believe it until the doctor did a few tests and explained to me that there is a possibility, rare but it happens."

What I wanted to hear was what he thought about having a child. We'd never considered it, and Kai had made it clear he wasn't into sharing me even with a pet.

His thumbs stroked back and forth on my temples as he took his time responding.

"The doctor says you're okay?"

"Yeah. Me and the baby."

He flinched at that and let me go before striding away. "Fuck," he muttered, his hand raking through his hair.

My heart shot off and worry invaded. Maybe he wouldn't adjust to something like this. I protectively placed my hand on my stomach where the result of our love grew.

Kai stopped at the window, staring outside, his body tense and the air heavy between us.

Shit. Shit. Shit.

Was he pissed? Sometimes it was really annoying trying to read Kai.

"What about school?" he finally asked. "It's important to you."

"I can finish my year." It would be cutting it close, but I'd be able to do my finals in April just before the baby was born.

When he turned to face me, his brows were low and eyes dark. "Is this something you want, London?"

I didn't hesitate. "Yes. I want our baby, Kai. I've never thought about it before, but now it's all I think about. But I want you to be happy, too, and I have no idea what you're thinking right now and it's driving me crazy. So can you please put me out of my misery and tell me so I can react and deal with it?"

He came toward me, the corners of his mouth twitching. He put one finger under my chin. "You want to know how I feel?"

"Yes."

He dipped his head and gently kissed me then he whispered, "You're my always." He kissed me again and his hand trailed down my chest to rest on my belly. "But, babe," — I held my breath— "this is *our* always. And a fuckin' miracle."

I squealed and leapt into his arms. He chuckled, his hands going under my ass and picking me up while I curved my legs around his waist, my arms his neck. "You're really good with this?"

"I didn't know how I'd feel about it because I don't waste my time thinking about what-ifs, babe." He carried me to the bedroom. "But, yeah, I'm good with it. More than good. I can't say I'm not going to be overprotective of you and a strict-as-hell father, especially if we have a girl."

I smiled as he laid me on the bed, him following, knees pressed into the mattress on either side of me. I weaved my fingers into his hair, drawing him closer. "Since when haven't you been overprotective?"

He smirked. "True, but now I have an excuse for it."

I laughed, but his mouth taking mine quickly smothered it. And then Kai did what he always did. He proved to me he was mine and I was his *always*.

CHAPTER TWENTY-NINE

Question 15: Favorite flower?

Connor

I CROUCHED BESIDE MY bike making adjustments, not bothering to look up when footsteps approached.

"Gate. What are you doing here?" I continued to crank on the wrench tightening the bolt.

Out of my peripheral, I saw his black leather boots, dusty from the graveled driveway. He stood on the opposite side of my bike.

"I came to see you. And no, Deck didn't ask me to."

I remained silent.

"He never stopped searching for you," Vic said. "He was bringing you home no matter what."

Deck. I expected nothing less from him because he'd do that for every single member of his team. And if our places were reversed, I'd have done the same. It was just how we worked, so despite him being a pain in my ass, I got why he was a pain in my ass.

Up until a few weeks ago, my mind hadn't worked that way. I didn't give a shit about Deck or anyone else except Alina. That had changed as the foggy blurred lines in my messed-up head cleared.

The rage lingered like a match constantly struck, but not always catching fire. I worried about Alina's safety, but I did everything I could short of leaving her in order to prevent anything from happening.

Fuck, I hated being unable to sleep with her in my arms. That was the hardest, climbing out of her bed while she slept and going to the other room. Most mornings I woke long before her and slipped back into her bed. That was if I'd had a good night. If I hadn't, I ran along the beach or rode my bike for a couple hours to get rid of the haunting images. The other night, I woke and pulled my gun on a ghost. The fuckin' ghost of Moreno.

"Did you see me at the track that day?" Vic asked.

I tossed the wrench in my leather saddlebag attached to the side of my bike. "Yeah."

"Did you hear what I yelled?"

I finally looked at him. "'Riot, you son-of-a-bitch, get your ass out here and stop being a pussy?' Is that what you're talking about?" I'd heard and seen him as I waited up in a pine tree while the rain pounded down on me.

I knew Vic was pissed as all hell because Vic Gate had always complained when it rained on missions. He hated it. No one knew about his past and he was one cruel, fucked-up asshole who never smiled and hated getting wet. I was confident there were a hell of a lot of skeletons in that guy's closet, but that door remained locked down tight. Probably how it should stay.

He ran his hand over the handlebars and after a minute of him not saying anything, I stood, flicking the dirty rag onto the seat of the bike.

PERFECT RAGE

"Sometimes it helps to do what you're good at," he said.

"You mean killing people?" I replied. Because when I was on the drug, I excelled at that.

"I was going to say hiding, but whatever." Asshole, but I felt the corners of my mouth curve up. "If killing is your thing now, there are a lot of shit men to get rid of in this world. Not saying now or in a few months, but when you're ready, there's a place for you. Get your head on straight first though. Don't need you shooting me in the ass."

I snorted.

A yellow cab pulled up in front of the house and Alina got out. What the hell? It was only ten. I yanked my cell from my back pocket to see if I'd missed a text from her, but there were none. What was she doing off work early on a Saturday night? And why wouldn't she call me to pick her up?

"She's one hell of a woman," Vic said, his eyes on Alina as she slammed the cab door and headed for the front path. "And for the record, even though your head was screwed up, leaving her in the sewer was a dick move."

Before I could throw a punch, he was gone.

I watched Alina push open the picket gate and walk along the stone path.

Something was wrong.

Her shoulders slumped slightly, her steps stiff, and the natural sway to her hips was gone. But the biggest giveaway was her eyes. They remained on the path instead of straying to the wildflowers in the garden. Every time I'd seen her walk along that path, she admired the wildflowers with a smile playing at the corners of her mouth.

Not tonight.

I picked up my rag, wiped my hands and tossed it back on the bike before striding toward her. "Babe?" She stopped, her head snapping in my direction, eyes wide with fear. What the ever living fuck?

Anger scratched at the wall of control as I immediately thought of some asshole hurting her at work. Fuck, I wished she'd give that job up.

I slowed my steps and took a deep breath to calm the roar. "You okay?" I hopped the low picket fence and weaved through the garden.

"Ah, yeah. Fine."

Oh, fuck no. She wasn't okay, her voice quaked and her eyes avoided mine. Why was she lying to me?

I stopped in front of her and put my hands on her shoulders then slid them down her arms to her hands. "Talk to me." Her head tilted so I couldn't see her eyes. "Alina, look at me."

"Connor, I'm tired and want to go to bed."

Shit. Running. I excelled at it, but Alina was the opposite. She didn't run from shit and she was running from whatever was bothering her. The scratching turned to pounding which pissed me off more because I wanted to be the one who was calm for her this time. She needed me to be.

"Was it me showing up at the coffee shop today?"

She shook her head.

"Something happen at work?"

"No." She pulled her hands from mine and pushed by me. "Can I just get some space, damn it?"

Every muscle in my body tensed. "Alina." I attempted to keep my tone soft, but it came out as a subtle growl.

She kept going, walked up the steps onto the porch, and disappeared inside the house. I stood frozen, my heart thumping, and my control on the cusp of detonation. My coping mechanism was to leave until I calmed again, but I didn't want to leave her like this.

I could do this. I had to try. I wouldn't leave her.

Walking into the kitchen, I took my time washing my hands, closed my eyes and listened to the water gently flow from the tap.

Only when the pounding eased did I shut off the water.

I found her in the bedroom already in her white silk pajamas. Her work clothes were scattered on the floor, something she never did. If she didn't put them away, she laid them on the chair by the window. She ignored me and went into the bathroom and shut the door.

The water turned on.

I picked her clothes off the floor and laid them over the lounge chair then took out my cell and gun, and placed them on the nightstand before pulling the covers back.

Calm. I had to keep my shit together. I was worried if she told me something I didn't like, I'd lose it. Fuck, I hated this. I hated the constant threat that my head would explode or that I'd see shit that wasn't there.

The taps turned off and the door opened. She looked at me. The strands of hair around her face were wet and her skin dewy and pink. Her lips lightly pressed together, not tight, but firm as if to stop them from trembling.

I decided my best approach was to say as little as possible. "Come to bed."

She hesitated then walked across the room, brushed by me and climbed under the covers. "Do you want me to stay until you fall asleep?"

Her eyes met mine and it killed me to see the pain in them and I could do nothing about it. But her words were enough to calm the disquiet in me. "I want you to stay no matter what."

Tears filled her eyes and I opened my mouth to ask her again what was wrong, but clamped it shut. She'd tell me when she was ready. Patience. I had to find my patience again. That steady control that I'd lacked ever since coming off the drug.

"Okay, shutterbug." I yanked off my shirt and slid onto the bed. I leaned against the headboard then reached to bring her into me, but she was already snuggling close. Fuck, I loved that.

I softly stroked her hair, her cheek resting on my chest, her palm next to it. The wetness of her tears on my skin nearly broke my control.

My heart thumped wildly and I grated my teeth as the anger threatened to rise. The mere idea that anyone hurt her was like the match sparking and the flame igniting into an inferno.

Instead of feeding on that, I concentrated on the feel of her in my arms. The soft strands of hair between my fingers; her heated breath on my skin.

Slowly, the fire went out and Alina fell asleep in my arms where she was always meant to be.

CHAPTER THIRTY

Question 16: What have you done that's illegal?

Alina

MY EYES FLEW open as I woke with my heart pounding and my breath locked in my throat.

Oh, God, I was pregnant.

Yesterday replayed in high-speed through my head. London meeting me at Avalanche. Going to the walk-in clinic. The doctor taking blood but he wouldn't get the result for a couple days, so he did a urine test, too.

Then…

The doctor saying with a huge grin, "Congratulations. It looks like you're pregnant. We'll confirm it with the blood work just to be sure."

My hand went to my stomach. This should be a celebration yet I was calmly freaking out. Internally freaking. Externally calm.

"Alina?"

I stiffened, realizing that Connor was in bed, his lean length pressed into me from behind.

Oh, God, what was I going to do? Did I tell him and risk him leaving? If he left, it would destroy him. Destroy us. But how could I keep something like this from him. But worse was the thought of losing something so precious.

He'd known something was wrong last night. I'd never be able to keep this from him and he trusted me.

But could I trust him to stay? Did I have a choice?

He tugged me closer, so my back was pressed into his chest. He softly kissed my shoulder then trailed them up my neck. "I love you," he said in a low graveled morning voice.

The sun beamed in through the window leaving bright sun streaks across the bedspread. I closed my eyes, attempting to hold back the tears. "Did you stay with me last night?" He never stayed the night with me.

He squeezed me. "I couldn't sleep," he murmured against my neck.

"Because of me." It wasn't a question.

"I was thinking, baby."

I turned over onto my back and reached up to stroke his cheek with my fingertips. "I wished you'd sleep more. And that you'd fall asleep with me like you used to."

"Me too, shutterbug."

My hand dropped. Yeah, and that was what worried me because I knew where this led. Where telling him the truth led.

God, he'd be a great dad. I pictured him, cradling our baby in his arms. Giving him or her their first toy. Reading together. Playing football or giving piggyback rides in the backyard. Taking our ten-year-old dirt bike riding, with me being worried as hell that he was taking our ten-year-old dirt bike riding.

Connor's eyes followed the heated path of his hand between my breasts, across my ribs to my waist where he lifted the silk material. He slid his hand beneath then laid his palm flat on my belly.

My breath hitched and our eyes locked.

"You know?"

He closed his eyes a second and inhaled a deep breath. "Yeah."

"When?"

"About an hour ago." He caressed slow circles on my stomach with the tips of his fingers. "It clicked. You being sick then starving. Meeting London yesterday. Leaving work early last night. Then seeing the conflict in your eyes. But what did it was how you slept with your hand on your belly. Protective. Nurturing."

My heart slammed into my ribcage as a million thoughts went through my head at the same time. But what forged ahead was the fact that Connor had figured it out and yet he was still here.

He was still here. He hadn't left me.

Would he stay? Hope filled me. "You didn't leave."

He must have seen the hope in my eyes because his hand left my stomach and he cupped my chin as he said, "I swore to you I'd never leave again without telling you."

His words drained the life out of me. Oh, God. No.

"Fuck, baby. I love you more than anything. But, we both know I can't stay. It's too dangerous."

I choked back the sob, my throat so tight my breath was ragged and I felt as if I couldn't get enough air. "Then talk to someone, Connor. Doctors can help you."

He stroked my cheek, his thumb wiping away the tears. "It's not so simple."

"Nothing about us is simple. You told me that." My voice rose as the panic heightened. "We can do this. You can. I know you'd never hurt a child." I was full-out crying as reality set in. And maybe that was why I'd been so upset because I knew deep down I'd never terminate the pregnancy. "Connor, please. I can't do this alone. Don't make me do this without you. Please. I'm begging you, don't make me."

Tears streamed down my face as I sobbed and he pulled me into his arms, cradling my head against his chest as he stroked my hair. I felt his lips on the top of my head with his heated breath.

It was a long time before I managed to calm myself to a somewhat civil sobbing. I hated myself for breaking apart, but that was what this was. Being torn into raw bleeding pieces.

He gently pulled me from his chest, his hands cupping either side of my head as he met my eyes. "Fuck, I hate hearing you cry. It reminds me of…." He stopped then. "I fuckin' hate it."

I knew what he was going to say, the videos Moreno had forced him to watch while imprisoned. "Then stay."

He sighed, shaking his head. "That's exactly why I can't."

"You're better," I choked out. "The baby won't be born for months. You'll be fine. You're handling the rage."

He dipped his head and softly kissed me, the tender surface of my lips clinging briefly to his when he pulled away. "Until something sets me off. Alina, I sleep in another room because I see shit that isn't there. Four nights ago I woke up and thought Moreno stood across the room from me. I had my gun on him in seconds, but you know as well as I, he wasn't there and I had my gun on a ghost." His thumbs stroked back and forth on my cheeks. "I love you more than anything, Alina. I'd love our child more than anything. But for once since I've been back, I have to do what's best for you and not me."

I shook my head and his hands slipped to my shoulders. "No. No. It's not better." I shoved him aside and scrambled from the bed.

"Alina," he called.

I stood, anger whirling through every part of my body. He slowly moved off the bed and I backed away, shaking my head. "You don't get to be all fucking calm right now, Connor. You want to leave me and your child then show me why," I shouted. "Be an asshole and show me, damn it. Make me hate you." I pushed. "Be the man who fucked me in Colombia. Be him. And maybe I'll understand why you need to leave. Fucking show me, Connor."

His temples throbbed and his hands curled into fists as he approached me.

I was the one who lost it, but I couldn't stop the words as they poured out of me. "You know what? I think you enjoy watching me cry like Moreno did." He flinched and the color drained from his face, but he kept coming for me.

I backed up until I hit the wall.

Raising my chin, I met his piercing eyes. I had to prove to him that he'd never hurt me but suddenly I wasn't so sure, because mentioning Moreno had taken him to another level. I protectively placed my hand on my abdomen. He noticed the movement and his eyes darted down then back up again.

And then the anger blazing in his gaze shattered into complete devastation as his eyes became glassy and wet.

My breath hitched as Connor fell to his knees in front of me, arms wrapping around my hips and his forehead resting on my belly. "I'm sorry. Fuck, I'm so sorry. But I can't stay."

Oh, God. I tipped into him, my arms around his head to cradle him to me.

I didn't know if his words had been to his unborn child or me.

It didn't matter.

Nothing did except him in my arms for what was probably the last time.

We stayed like that for a long time.

Both of us searching for what we'd never found—simple.

A love with no pain.

A love that brings us together not tears us apart.

A love uncomplicated.

But like he said, we didn't get simple. We didn't get the white picket fence. We didn't get the happily ever after.

And I didn't get to keep Connor.

He peeled out of my arms and stood, his hand snaking to the back of my neck. My knees weakened and my body quivered as our gazes locked.

"I need help, baby. I know that, but I can't. Being drugged again… locked up. I'd lose my mind and never come back from that. I wouldn't survive it and I'd lose you anyway. This way, I leave remembering you. That's all I have left, Alina." He put his finger on my lips when I went to tell him that maybe it wouldn't come to that. That the doctors wouldn't drug him, but the truth was if he lost it, they'd have no choice. "I'd risk everything for you and our child, and that's why I have to go." His fingers tightened on my neck. "To be a good father and the man you deserve, I need to be healthy, Alina. But I can't try to get healthy without losing my mind."

I closed my eyes unable to look at him anymore. Because I understood why and I hated that I did. He'd rather be permanently lost without me than lose his mind and forget me. "I left *me* with you a long time ago. I survived Moreno because I did." He flinched and his brows drew together. "Wherever you go, the pieces of me are in you, Connor. They'll never leave."

"Fuck, shutterbug. I love you so damn much." He tugged me into him and kissed me.

It was a kiss of desperation to never forget. To accept our complicated love that bound us together yet kept us apart.

And it was a kiss to say goodbye.

CHAPTER THIRTY-ONE

Question 17: Do you want kids? And, if so, how many?

Connor

THE BELL DINGED as I opened the door to the coffee shop and strode in. My heart sat in my throat, shredded and bleeding. Sanity was fragile; the mere slip of the fingers on the edge of the cliff and a person would be lost to the churning waters below.

That was where I was, hanging off the side of the cliff, fighting to hold on until after I spoke to my sister.

Her memories of me were already fucked.

I was her crazed brother she'd witnessed coming off a drug, chained to a basement wall, raging and wild, blood dripping from his wrists.

I was the brother who'd held a gun on his best friend, her fiancé.

And I was the brother who was leaving behind the woman he loved who carried his child.

That was the brother who was going to ride away and stay lost. But I wouldn't be the raging brother who left without explaining why.

My entire body was so tense I felt as if I were on a goddamn rack with every muscle stretched past its limits. It had been that way since the damn green gate banged closed behind me and I left Alina.

I shook so badly, it took me several tries to get my bike started. When it roared to life, I rode to my sister's coffee shop where Alina and London had met the day before. But the girl behind the counter said Georgie wasn't there, but at the other location.

So here I was, still shaking and facing the sister I'd been too fucked up to talk to. Still was, but I had to do this. I'd never be the brother she'd once idolized, and I'd live with that, but I wouldn't be the brother who left without saying goodbye. I promised Alina that and I'd do it for Georgie, too.

Georgie stood behind the counter, two pink streaks of hair hanging down either side of her face and the rest pulled into a messy knot. She chatted with a customer, her voice carrying across the room with light cheerfulness.

It was quiet being early Sunday morning and only two other people sat by the window clicking on their laptops. There was another girl behind the counter with her back turned to me as she worked a large machine that grinded and groaned then hissed.

When the girl was done, she turned with the mug in her hand and froze when her eyes landed on me. After a second, she walked over to Georgie and whispered something.

Georgie lifted her head.

Her hand flew to her mouth as she gasped, eyes wide with shock.

Neither of us moved as we stared at one another.

There were so many emotions sparking that I was unable to react.

PERFECT RAGE

My stomach churned and my pulse raced as every single memory of her pushed to the forefront of my mind.

Fuck, I'd missed her so damn much. Every single day I sat in Moreno's cell, I thought about her. Worried about her. Wondered if she was okay. Prayed she was okay.

And then the drug erased her, too.

I walked across the polished hardwood floors, the thud of my motorcycle boots like tribal drums. The customer she'd been helping took his coffee and moved away and I stopped in front of Georgie.

She held the edge of the counter as her chest rose and fell erratically, tears pooling in her eyes.

"I should've come sooner." My words came out ragged and hoarse and I cleared my throat.

She reached across the space between us and touched my arm. "You're here now. That's all that matters, Connor."

Ah, fuck. My head dropped and I briefly closed my eyes as my sister's voice seeped into me. It was the same, but different. More mature and self-assured.

I was wrong. I fuckin' cared.

"Can we, ah, maybe, go for a walk or something?" Shit, I was nervous of my sister. But it sucked toppling off that pedestal and facing her disappointment in me.

"I'd love that," she said. A tear spilled down her cheek and she hastily wiped it away with the back of her hand. She tentatively smiled. "Give me a sec."

She rushed into the back, but before the door swung closed she glanced over her shoulder at me as if to check that I hadn't disappeared or to be sure I was real.

As I waited for her, I fidgeted, shifting my weight and peering out the window. The heaviness in my chest made breathing difficult and my head was one big fucked-up mess of emotions, but the rage wasn't there. It was smothered by the pain of leaving Alina.

Georgie came around the counter and approached me. I stiffened, uncertain what to do, whether to hug her or kiss her cheek or nothing.

She made it easy for me though as if sensing my uncertainty and softly brushed her fingers across my arm then headed for the door. I inhaled a long drawn in breath and followed, grabbing the door for her before instinctively protecting her with my body and positioning myself on the street side of the sidewalk.

It was something I'd always done, that protective part of me needing to make certain I was the one closest to the passing cars.

"There's a park a couple blocks over," Georgie offered and I nodded.

Now that I was here with her, I had no idea what I'd say to her.

We walked in silence, but it wasn't exactly awkward. It was cathartic and with each step, the tension in my muscles released.

"You look different," I said as we walked. "A good different. I like the hair."

"Thanks. My hair colors drive Deck crazy because he never knows what he's coming home to, but I think secretly he likes it."

My step faltered. It wasn't so much that Georgie was with Deck. It was the mention of them having a home. Of what I would never have.

She rested her hand on my forearm. "Sorry. I don't know yet what you're comfortable talking about."

"I'm okay with you and Deck, Georgie-girl." Her breath hitched and I hadn't even realized what I'd said until after I said it.

"I haven't heard you call me that since I was sixteen," she murmured, her hand falling away and her head tilting in the opposite direction.

"Sorry, I won't call you that if you don't want me to. It just came out."

She stopped and faced me. There were tears in her eyes and her lower lip quivered as she spoke. "No. No. It's okay. It just surprised me. And I don't want you to be sorry for anything." She hesitated then added, "I have a feeling we don't have enough time to be sorry for things that aren't our fault. Do we?"

Fuck. I sighed, nodding. "How did you know?"

She pointed to a paved narrow path that weaved through the park. "Let's go over there."

We crossed the street and she was a little ahead of me and I noticed that she had a bit of a seductive sway to her step. She looked really good and I wondered if that had to do with Deck.

"It's all over your face," she said. Her hair swept across her face when the breeze picked up and with one finger, she tucked the strands behind her ear. "You used to get the same look before you went on tour. A worried sadness with your brows low, not a lot but a bit, and your lips firmly pressed together with glassiness in your eyes. But today, it's more than that. Haunting. Final, I guess."

I dragged my hand through my hair. "I worried about you every single day I was a prisoner." Her body stiffened and her eyes darted from mine. "You were okay, right? Deck protected you?"

"Yeah." She nodded a little too quick for my liking and I suspected there was something she wasn't telling me, but pushing to find out what wouldn't do either of us any good. "Deck protected me. I wasn't easy on him though." She laughed and the sound was exactly as I remembered it. "But Deck likes a challenge."

I plucked a maple leap off a low branch. "He likes winning."

Georgie nudged me with her shoulder. "You did, too. You just accepted the challenge laughing. He was always the serious one. Well, he still is but not as much as Vic. I bet Tyler gets a kick out of trying to make that guy smile."

I snorted. I sensed what she was doing, trying to bring lightness to this.

We walked in silence for a few minutes then I asked her about her coffee shops and afterward she chatted about her friends, Emily and Kat.

I listened. There was nothing of me I cared to talk about and hearing about her life was why I was here. It gave me some semblance of peace to hear that she was okay and would be okay after I was gone. When she mentioned Mom and Dad, my tentative hold collapsed.

"Never tell them. It won't do them any good to find out I'm alive. They don't need to lose their son twice."

"But they aren't losing you, Connor."

"Yeah, they are, Georgie. I'm already gone. Too far gone and there's no hope finding my way back."

"So, you just leave and we're all supposed to pretend you're dead?" Pretty much, but I stayed quiet. "Do you know what Deck has done to try to bring you home?"

"Yeah," I whispered more to myself than her.

Then she asked, "And Alina? You love her, right?"

It took a second for me to speak because just mentioning her name raged a war inside me. "What I feel for her is limitless. There is no end to the love I have for her."

She frowned. "Then why are you leaving, Connor? Why?"

The familiar tapping in my head began and soon it would be out-of-control banging. "She's pregnant."

She gasped and her eyes widened. "Holy shit. Wow. That's great—" She abruptly stopped. "And you're leaving? Connor, you're leaving the woman you love alone and pregnant?"

Turning, I headed back to the coffee shop. She remained where she was and then jogged after me.

"Connor? You can't do this." She grabbed my arm and tugged me to a stop. "Damn it, Connor." Her voice rose, "My brother fights until the end. He never gives up. He fights until he gets it right, even if it kills him."

"I'm fighting. Fuck, I've never fought so goddamn hard in my life. I'm fighting to stop myself from going back to her, so I can do what will keep her and my child safe. I won't have a kid growing up with a father they fear. Or be made fun of at school because their dad sees shit that isn't there. Or a dad who can't keep his cool. Or a dad who stalks his or her own fuckin' mother because he doesn't want to forget her. And what about when he wants friends to come over? Or when Alina gets tired of putting up with my bullshit? What then? What happens then, damn it?"

"Then we get you help now."

"I fuckin' can't, Georgie," I shouted. "I'll lose my mind and I can't lose the memory of her, too. It's all I have left."

She grabbed my arm and forced me to stop from crossing the road. "Connor, you're my big brother and I love you no matter what. I mean that. No. Matter. What. And I want more than anything for you to stay, but you're a stubborn son-of-a-bitch and I know once your mind is set, it's set in cement. But you're lying to yourself if you think you're fighting. And if your head is too messed up to know that, then you need to listen to me.

"You're running and losing. I know you've changed, and suffered more than I can ever comprehend, but there are parts of a person that are permanent. They don't change. And you, Connor, you fight and take risks. It's who you are.

"Risk losing, Connor. Risk losing everything. Because if it's limitless like you say, then isn't it worth the risk?"

Heat raged in my body as her words rallied in my head. Words I didn't know what to do with. Risk. Risk losing my mind and forgetting her? Risk losing myself to the rage if I'm locked up again?

I stared at the ground as I dragged my hand over my face. My body trembled and my head pounded. Control slipped and it wasn't so much the rage, it was the collapse of a man as tears welled in my eyes. I clamped my jaw desperate to stop the pain and be strong like I was supposed to be.

Be the protector.

Jesus Christ, I had to get the fuck away before I lost it in front of her. "I have to go."

"I know." But her hand was still on my arm and neither of us moved.

Fuck it. I hooked my elbow around her neck and tugged her into me. She landed against my chest then her arms enfolded me in a crushing hug. She sobbed into my shirt while I closed my eyes and embraced my sister for the first time in over a decade.

It was as if someone jammed a piece of me back in place as I held her. It was soiled and ripped, but the piece was my little sister.

When we broke apart, I reached in my back pocket and pulled out a slip of paper and passed it to her. "The code is for a locker at Union Station. Number twenty-eight. Take Deck with you. There's a duffel bag with some money. Buy the house from Deaglan and put it in her name. The rest of the money, put it in an account for her and the baby. It's Vault's money, but they owe me eleven years of my life, so make sure she takes it."

She shook her head, stepping back without taking the paper. "Connor. No."

I grabbed her wrist then shoved the paper in her palm and closed her fingers. "I need it done, Georgie-girl. I'm asking you to do this for Alina and my kid." I let her go. "Tell Deck he brought everyone home. Love you, sis."

Then I left my past behind.

CHAPTER THIRTY-TWO

Question 18: Someone who would help bury a body?

Three weeks later

Alina

WHEN I WALKED into VUR, Vault's Unyielding Riot, every molecule zipped through my body like missiles.
 I was angry.
 I woke up this morning angry and I figured out why on the cab ride here. The denial I'd been living in for three weeks had shifted to anger. I was furious at Connor for leaving. I was furious that he hadn't come back yet. And I was furious that Deck was doing nothing about it.
 The day Connor grabbed his things and his motorcycle roared to life, I'd said goodbye. But it was never really goodbye. Because the

truth was I always thought Connor would be back. That leaving was temporary. Goodbye had never existed between us.

But as day after day passed and I mechanically went through the movements of living, I began to crack. The denial faltered.

And this morning the truth slammed into me like a meteor and I couldn't accept it. I wouldn't.

I'd called Georgie and found out that Deck was at his office. Hanging up on her, I called a cab.

And here I was walking into the office.

"Can I help you, miss?"

My eyes barely registered the secretary sitting behind the desk as I moved past her.

"Miss. You can't go down there." The wheels of her chair rolled on the wood floor and then her heels clicked as she chased after me. I hurried down the hall, glancing at the gold plaques on the doors as I went.

"Please. Miss," she called, a few steps behind me.

I stopped at the last door at the end of the hall where the plaque read Deck Ryan.

The secretary grasped my arm. "Miss. He's in a meeting. You can't—"

I shoved open the door and walked in.

My eyes landed on Kai first, who sat on a leather couch, one leg bent and crossed over the other, his arm stretched along the back of it appearing relaxed and casual as usual, but that was more than likely complete bullshit.

When my gaze shifted to Deck, there was nothing casual about him as he sat in a high-backed, black leather chair behind a mahogany desk, his intense scowl revealing his displeasure. I wasn't sure if it was because of my rude interruption or from whatever he and Kai were discussing before I burst in.

The secretary stepped past me. "Mr. Ryan, I'm so sorry. She bolted by me and I couldn't stop her."

"It's fine, Carol. Thank you," Deck said while his eyes remained on me.

The secretary backed out the door and it clicked closed.

"Alina. How can I help you?" Deck asked, his tone gentle and the scowl gone. "Is everything okay?"

"Is everything okay? No, damn it. Everything isn't okay," I blurted. "I haven't heard from him. Nothing in weeks. I don't know if he's alive or dead. I don't know if he's watching me. I don't know where the hell he is and it's killing me." My body felt as if it were going to explode under the pressure, like an overfilled balloon. Was this what Connor felt like? All this bottled-up anger ready to pop at any moment.

Deck dropped the pen he held onto his desk and pushed his chair back. "Alina, you need to calm down before you—"

"Don't tell me to calm down!" I shouted. "I want you to tell me why you're not looking for him."

Deck's eyes flicked to Kai who shrugged before coming back to me. "There's no reason to look for him."

A cold wave of dread plowed into me. No reason? No. No. I didn't want to hear that there was no reason. What did he mean no reason?

Deck stood and came around his desk and leaned against it with his arms crossed, looking completely intimidating and yet he could be the Hulk and I'd still face off against him right now.

"Does that mean you know where he is?"

"No," Deck answered calmly.

"No?" The word was like a sledgehammer coming down on my head. "No? No, you can't find him?"

He inhaled a deep breath. "No, Alina. I mean, no, we are not looking for him. And, no, he's not watching you and, no, he isn't in town."

I had no idea what Kai was doing because my vision tunneled on Deck as I shook my head back and forth, unable to believe that he'd given up on Connor. That he wasn't searching for him. Making sure he was okay. Doing something, damn it.

"He's your best friend," I yelled as my arms dropped to my sides. "Why aren't you looking for him? That's your job. To find him and bring him home. You swore to bring him home. He told me you always bring your men home. Connor's not home yet."

"Alina." Deck's tone was soft and gentle, but his eyes were dark and narrowed. "He was home. He chose to leave. We did everything we could without forcing him."

The tightness in my chest intensified. "Just bring him back. I don't care how you do it."

He sighed, his eyes briefly closing before they opened again and there was pain swimming in the depths. "Oh, baby, you don't want that for him. And I won't ever do it to him."

I shook my head back and forth as denial slowly crushed with every word out of his mouth.

All I had left was this unbearable heated anger. I'd never felt so much anger in my life and it was like an overpowering reactive energy inside me that I had no control over.

"You won't?" Conflicting emotions pounded and I struggled to hold onto some kind of sanity and not lose my shit on the one person who could help me.

He pushed off the desk and approached me. "I know you don't want to hear this, but you need to. For your sake and that of the child you carry." Deck stood in front of me. He was tall like Connor, so I had to tilt my head in order to look at his face "He's not coming back. He can't. Not as the man he is."

My chest tightened. "No. No, he has to. He's just lost, but we can find him."

Deck's eyes went to my neck and he frowned. "What happened?"

I touched the cut on the underside of my jaw. "Nothing. I cut myself."

"I can see that. How did it happen?" he asked, his tone abrupt.

"I went to the house."

"What house?"

"The boarded up one where Connor used to stay sometimes. I took the plywood off the window so I could get in and when it gave, the corner of it hit my neck."

"Why the fuck would you go there?"

Some of the anger dispersed because Deck was looking really scary with throbbing temples and narrowed eyes. "I went to check if Connor was still watching me."

Deck ran his hand over the top of his head. "Jesus, you can't do shit like that. That house is condemned for a fuckin' reason."

"Deck," Kai said. "Shut it down before she gets hurt."

My gaze darted to Kai. "Shut what down?"

"You. This. The thinking that Connor is here or coming back," Kai replied.

I jerked. "I'm not a machine. I'm not a goddamn machine like you Kai. My emotions can't just be shut down whenever I feel like it. How the hell do you think London would feel right now if you left her?"

Some of that casual persona faded as Kai stiffened; his piercing green eyes steady on me. "That would never happen."

A typical Kai response, which only pissed me off more. Before I could tell him off, Deck moved closer, his hand cupping my chin and tilting my head so he could get a better look at the spot where the board had jammed into me, knocking me onto my ass and landing on top of me.

"Don't do that again," Deck ordered.

"Then help me find him and I won't have to."

I hadn't realized tears streamed down my cheeks until Deck wiped them with the pad of his thumb. "Connor understands the choice he's made, Alina. There is nothing more I can do. I won't force him into a facility. That has never been an option. You need to let him go."

Jagged pain hit my chest and I staggered back into the door as the reality slowly descended that this time Connor wasn't coming back.

For weeks I'd had hope that he just needed time to figure things out.

"No. No. I can't. He's coming back. I know he is. He wouldn't just leave me."

Deck's gaze shifted to Kai who now stood and was only a few feet away.

"What?" Panic rose as I looked from Deck to Kai. "Damn it, what?"

Kai spoke, "Tell her."

"Yeah," Deck muttered. Then he reached for my hand. "Sit down."

I jerked away. "What?" My eyes shot to Kai and my fear intensified because he longer appeared casual. "What's wrong?" *Oh, God, please let Connor be okay.*

"He left provisions for you and the baby," Deck said.

I gripped the door handle, wondering if it would be better if I just ran out the door before he told me anything more. If I didn't hear it, then it wasn't true, right? My hope would still be there and I could stand on the porch at night and believe Connor was out there watching me.

"He left money," Deck continued. "A large sum with instructions to buy Kite and Deaglan's house and set up a bank account for you with the rest of it. I hadn't told you yet because I was waiting on the paperwork for the house."

Connor left me money? He bought the house? My head spun as I tried to grasp the meaning of this, but really there was nothing to grasp except what I didn't want to accept.

"No. It's not true." My hand tightened on the doorknob as the fear of losing Connor for good attempted to get through the cracks of my denial and anger.

Deck walked to his desk and shuffled papers around.

"I don't want his fucking money. Do you hear me?" I yelled. "I don't want it. I want him. Just him." It was a stupid idea coming here. They'd given up on Connor, but I wasn't. I'd find him myself. "Fuck you both."

I yanked open the door and stormed out, but I only made it three steps before an arm snagged my waist and picked me up off my feet.

I saw the secretary glance at us. Her eyes wide with shock and then she quickly put her head down and went back to whatever she was doing.

"Let me go, damn it." I struggled to escape Kai's grip, but my hand shoving at his forearm had no effect. He carried me back into the office, slammed the door then plopped me onto my feet in front of the couch.

"Sit," he ordered.

I met his scowl, breathing rapid and pulse racing. I opened my mouth to tell him to go fuck himself when his brows lifted as if daring me.

I sat.

Deck and Kai stood in front of me, impenetrable boulders, but both of their expressions softened once I sat. It was like a heavy blanket settled over me and smothered the burning fire of anger and my shoulders sagged with defeat.

"I'll send London to stay with you tonight," Kai said and then turned and left the office.

"Alina," Deck said softly as he crouched in front of me.

Tears welled as I met his eyes because he didn't have to say anything.

The truth had slipped through the cracks.

I choked on a sob, hating that I fell apart, but unable to stop myself. "I'm sorry," I murmured. "God, I'm so sorry. It's selfish of me to take my anger out on you. You've done so much to help him and you must be hurting, too, and Georgie. God, I can't imagine what she's feeling."

Deck laid his hand over mine that were wrung in my lap. "I wish I could lie and tell you I think he's coming back, but I can't."

I nodded.

"It's not easy to give up on someone you love. But that's not what this is, Alina. This is being able to accept his choice. I don't know if it's the right or wrong one and I won't judge him for it. I didn't go through what he did."

"It hurts so much," I said in a quivering voice. "I can't breathe. I can't breathe without him." I raised my head and said the words that had been eating away at me for weeks. "I blame the baby for him leaving. And then I hate myself for blaming an unborn child who's innocent of all this."

"I know it's hard to believe right now, but one day the hurt will be bearable and you'll take a breath and it won't hurt so much. But I won't lie, Alina. It never goes away, you just learn how to live with it."

"Oh, God, I need him to be okay. He's alone Deck. He doesn't have anyone." I threw my arms around his neck and sobbed into his shirt. He held me close and he slowly stroked my hair as I cried.

My acceptance had busted through the denial and the last of the anger drowned in the pain of what was the truth. "He's not coming back," I muffled into his shirt.

Deck didn't say anything. He merely held me and it was oddly strengthening that it was Deck who held me. Connor's best friend who never gave up on him and now we both had to finally let him go.

CHAPTER THIRTY-THREE

Question 19: What is the best sound in the world?

Three months later

Alina

"THANKS FOR DRIVING me, Georgie," I said as we walked into my house.

The final paperwork had been signed last month and I owned the quaint, former Grandma Kane house. It didn't feel like mine though, because it would always be Connor's.

I hadn't the heart to pack away all of Grandma Kane's knick-knacks, although Deaglan had called and told me to box them up and put them in the basement apartment and he'd have his cousin Killian deal with them.

One day I'd get around to it, but mostly, I focused on just living and accepting that I was doing this alone.

Although, I wasn't really alone. Georgie came to every doctor's appointment with me and her excitement for the baby was contagious.

"Let's put it on your fridge." Georgie bounced into the kitchen and I followed smiling. "All mothers-to-be put the first sonogram on the fridge. London did, but Kai took it off and it disappeared. Kai wouldn't tell her what happened to it and she was so pissed." Georgie grabbed a magnet off the side of the fridge. "She told me yesterday it suddenly reappeared framed and hanging on the wall in their bedroom."

An ache tore through my chest and I blanched. God, that is so something Connor would've done.

Georgie put her hand on my arm. "I'm sorry. Shit. I didn't mean to upset you."

I half smiled. "It's fine. Really. I want to hear that stuff and I have to get used to it."

"You shouldn't have to," she replied quietly. "My brother would do anything to be here for you if he could, you know."

I didn't say anything and dumped my purse on the kitchen table and took the sonogram from my pocket. As I peered at the white lines and specks on the black background, joy and nervousness swept through me. The idea of being responsible for the life inside me was at times overwhelming.

But there was more than just me now. I had Georgie and Deck, London and Kai, and last month, we'd told Connor and Georgie's parents everything. Well, everything except Georgie's involvement with Vault.

It was a tragic evening with a lot of tears shed, shock, disbelief and sadness. And, yes, there was anger, too, but mostly they were grateful for the miracle that their son was alive and I was having his baby.

Karen treated me like a daughter and called me every day and I was always included in any family gatherings, although it wasn't easy being around them without it hurting and thinking about Connor.

"Here." I passed her the picture and she placed it on the fridge. The magnet clicked as it magnetized holding it in place. She stepped back to stand beside me.

"Are you going to tell me now if it's a boy or a girl?"

She'd pestered me the entire way home from the doctor's office. "Nope." I was keeping it a secret from everyone. I don't know why, but I felt as if that was something for only me and Connor to know.

She scrunched her nose. "Hard ass."

I laughed. "When are you and Deck going to have kids?"

She shrugged. "When it happens."

My brows lifted. "Are you trying?"

"Oh, we try all the time. I hope it won't be too long before one of those little suckers gets through. Deck's getting older and soon won't be able to keep up with a kid." I laughed because Deck wasn't old and I suspected he'd be able to keep up with a kid when he was eighty. She leaned in and kissed my cheek. "I have to go. Rylie wants the afternoon off and I'm filling in. Are you coming to brunch on Sunday? It should be really fun considering Kai is coming for the first time. The last time he was at our penthouse, he and Deck ended up in the plunge pool and Tyler threatened to throw Kai over the balcony."

None of that surprised me. What did was that he and Deck hadn't killed one another yet. "I'll come by for a bit, but I have a shoot booked for the afternoon in Hyde Park." I still worked at Avalanche, but only two nights a week as I was busy with freelance photography. Georgie's friend, Kat, who had an art gallery, offered to have a showing of my work, so I was trying to get enough photographs together for that.

"Okay. Cool," Georgie said, waving over her shoulder as she walked out of the kitchen.

The front door opened and then the screen door squeaked and banged closed behind her.

I stood listening to the hum of the fridge while I stared at the sonogram. The tightness in my chest ached and tears welled as I thought of Connor. Wishing he were here to share this with me. Hoping... no, praying he was okay, but knowing he probably wasn't.

The emptiness never eased, that hole inside me would exist forever because he took that part of me with him.

I leaned against the countertop, closed my eyes and two tears escaped as I caressed my belly where our little girl slept. "He'd love you so much if he were here. I won't let you grow up without knowing him, my sweet girl." I kept a journal like the one Connor once had when we met. On the first few pages, I wrote our nineteen questions and Connor's answers. Then I began writing everything I knew about him, but I wasn't done yet.

In the evenings when I wasn't working, I sat in the cabana and wrote so that one day when the time was right, I'd be able to share Connor with our daughter. It was important to me that she knew what an incredible man he was. And hopefully she'd understand why he left us. I never wanted her to be angry with him for leaving.

"Are we having a girl, shutterbug?"

I gasped, my eyes flying open at the sound of his voice. "Connor?" I grabbed the edge of the counter as my knees weakened.

Oh, God. Connor. "You're here," I murmured, afraid to go near him and find out I was the one with the hallucinations. That the bubble would pop and he'd no longer stand five feet away.

"Yeah." He shifted his weight as if he was uncomfortable and his hands rubbed the sides of his jeans a couple times. He nodded to the fridge with the sonogram. "Is that her?"

I nodded, biting my lower lip as I tried to keep the tears at bay.

He walked over to the fridge and stared at it for what seemed like forever, but was probably only ten seconds.

He turned. "And you. Are you okay?"

I inhaled a quivering breath. "Umm, well, yeah, but not really. I'm freaking out right now, Connor."

PERFECT RAGE

"Yeah. Sorry." Then he asked hesitantly, "Are you good with me being here?"

I held the counter so tightly that I heard the laminated wood moan under the pressure. "I really don't know what to say right now."

He sighed, nodding, eyes shifting to the floor. "Yeah. Fuck. I get that."

God, he looked so different. I mean he was the same, but something was missing. He also made no move to come toward me, which I found very unlike Connor.

Then it hit me. There was no anger lingering. No tension in his body, and the blue in his eyes was calm and steady. "Oh, my God, you got help."

He raised his head to meet my eyes. "Yes."

Holy shit. "But... I don't understand."

"Would it be cool if I explained after I kiss you?"

A wave of warmth blanketed me and my belly dropped. Connor was here and he wanted to kiss me.

I was unable to speak, so I just nodded.

The corners of his mouth lifted and that right there was enough to spill the tears pooled in my eyes. It took him four strides to reach me and then his hands cradled my head. But he didn't kiss me right away. Instead he closed his eyes and leaned his forehead against mine.

"Alina," he whispered. "Fuck, I dreamed about this day. The moment when I'd touch you again." His warm breath was minty and fresh as it wafted over my face. "I need to savor every second of this moment, baby." He spoke in a ragged low voice as if he had difficulty with the words.

My body quivered and trembled and I didn't know how long he wanted to savor this moment, but I wasn't as patient as I stood on my tiptoes. "Can we savor later? I really need you to kiss me right now." I needed a hell of a lot more than a kiss as my sex clenched with the thought of Connor in my arms again.

"Fuck, I missed you." He leaned closer so his lips brushed my ear and whispered, "Three, three, two, six. Three months. Three weeks. Two days and six hours I was apart from you. But I never forgot you, Alina. Not for one second."

And that was the last of any control as Connor's mouth took mine.

It was a plea being answered.

A desperate need being fed.

A craving being satisfied.

My fingers curled into his shirt as his groan vibrated against my lips and fireworks shot through my body.

His hand moved down to the small of my back and he tugged me closer while his other hand shifted to the back of my neck, bunching my hair in his grip.

No words were needed. The kiss said it all.

It was our complicated love becoming simple.

Our broken picket fence mending.

And it was Connor coming home.

He drew back and both of us inhaled ragged breaths, chests rising and falling. "God, I never thought I'd get this chance," he said. "I left thinking I wouldn't." He stroked up and down my back. "So many times I thought I'd go crazy missing you. But that's what kept me sane, knowing if I risked losing my mind, I'd get back to you." He quirked a half grin. "Sound fucked?"

I reached up and touched his cheek with the pads of my fingers. "No. It sounds exactly like the man you've always been. Risking everything. Taking a chance with your life for what you believe in."

"I think it was more selfish than that. More like for what I wanted. You." He sighed, a slight furrow of his brows. "I have a long way to go, baby. The demons aren't defeated, but my head isn't pounding anymore."

My heart burst with so much love for this man. He got help. He risked losing. He fought the demons.

"Will you be able to sleep with me?"

His hands ran down my arms and he linked his fingers with mine. "Yeah. I can sleep with you. But right now, I'm going to fuck you, if that's okay."

Tantalizing warmth cascaded over me. "Yeah, that's okay."

Connor

I lay in bed with Alina dozing in my arms after hours of tasting, touching and sinking inside her again and again.

Hearing her breath hitch before she came, her body tightening around me... fuck, it was like finally coming home.

My hand rested on her stomach, the bulge of our baby growing inside her. There was an overwhelming feeling of joy, excitement, and relief all at the same time.

A little girl. Shit, the thought terrified me and at the same time, the most incredible joy filled me. The protectiveness was there for my baby and Alina, but it was different than before. Not obsessive. This was a healthy protectiveness... like in our beginning.

My arms tightened around her.

Jesus, I never thought I'd get here. When I walked into the facility and admitted myself, I was pretty certain I'd never walk out.

But when I got on my bike after talking to Georgie, there'd been no question what I needed to do, because she was right. I had to fight harder. I had to risk losing everything if I wanted a chance at limitless.

When the doctor pushed me to talk about the memories. The nightmares. The pain. I'd never felt such rage and just like I thought would happen, I lost it and they were forced to sedate me.

I'd been terrified I'd forget Alina. That I'd forget everything. That I'd wake up not knowing who I was. Become the machine I was before.

But each day I woke, I remembered and it got easier.

Alina stretched and rolled onto her back then her eyes flickered open. She smiled, reaching to caress my lower lip. "You're still here."

A sharp pain hit my chest because I put that worry there. "I'm not leaving, Alina. I swear. I won't ever leave you again." I inhaled a long drawn in breath, my heart thumping and nerves tingling.

I'd been hanging onto this question for eleven years. Sure, I didn't know it at the time, but I did now and I wasn't letting another day go by without asking her. "Question twenty. I never asked you question twenty."

Her brows arched. "Umm, okay. But it better be good, you've had eleven years to think about it."

Lightness filtered into me and I laughed.

Alina's breath hitched and her eyes widened. "I'm changing my answer," she blurted.

"Babe, I haven't asked you the question yet."

She shook her head. "No, to question nineteen."

"Fuck, babe. That's the one question we answered the same."

"It's been eleven years. My answer can change."

"Fine. But then you have to answer my question twenty. So, what's your *revised* answer to question nineteen?"

"I'm not revising, I'm adding to it."

I chuckled. "Okay."

"Your laughter. Hearing you laugh is the best sound in the world and I never want to be without it again. But more importantly, I never want you to be without it again."

I froze, my eyes locking with hers. "Ah, fuck." I hovered over her, lowered and kissed her. It was raw and hard and it took everything not to slip my cock inside her again. But I had something more important to do right now.

When I pulled back, her cheeks were flushed and lips swollen from my kiss.

"Okay, go," she said eagerly. "I'm dying to hear what you've come up with for question twenty. And remember, you have to answer it, too."

I smirked. "Of course, shutterbug." I held her chin because I wanted to make sure I saw her eyes when I asked her. "Will you marry me, Alina Diaz?"

She gasped, her lips parting and her body tensing beneath me. "That's your question twenty?"

"Damn right it is."

She hesitated, scrunching her nose as if thinking about it. But I saw the answer in her eyes, the spark of happiness blazing.

I moved fast, grabbed her around the waist and flipped her so she straddled me. I grasped her wrist and placed her palm on my left side below my ribs. "Look at the tattoo."

She frowned, her eyes shifting to the tattoo. I waited for her to see the numbers 11528 hidden within the complex web of lines.

Then she did and her gaze darted to me. "My numbers?"

I nodded.

"But you had this tattoo before. I saw it the first night after you came to Avalanche."

"I did. I had the tattoo done when I was on the drug, Alina. I didn't know what the hell the numbers meant at the time, I didn't care either. But I did it after I fucked you in Colombia. The numbers kept repeating in my head so I tattooed them into the design."

"You never forgot."

My hands resting on her hips squeezed. "Guess I always had a piece of you with me. Now, are you going to answer question twenty?"

"This may take some time. I don't want to rush my answer," she teased while wiggling her sweet ass on my cock.

I groaned. "Answer me so I can fuck you again as my soon-to-be wife."

She bit her lip then slowly smiled. "Yes, Connor O'Neill. My answer is yes."

EPILOGUE

Three years later

Alina

"KAI!" LONDON YELLED. "You suck."

I burst out laughing, lowering my camera. "Oh, my God. I can't believe you just said that."

Kai's eyes darted to his wife from across the barnyard and he scowled. Definitely not happy. Probably more because he was pissed that he was the worst player on his team and Kai liked to be the best at everything.

London sat crossed-legged on the grass beside me. "He needs incentive." She nodded to her daughter, Hope, who played with the barn cats along with Danny and a bunch of other kids from the Treasured Children's Center. "And she needs to see her father kick ass."

"I don't think she's paying attention to her father," Georgie said, leaning forward to look past me to peer at London. "And Hope thinks her father is unbeatable. A fallacy I'm certain Kai put in her sweet little head."

London laughed, her eyes on her daughter with long brown ringlets and sharp green eyes identical to Kai's. If he ever had doubts about Hope being his, that was erased the second she was born. But I suspected Kai never had doubts.

"Cats are far more interesting and since her father gives her everything she wants, I'm thinking it won't be long before we have one of those living in our house," London said.

I was sure, too, because little girls had a special way with their fathers, meaning they knew how to get pretty much anything their hearts desired. And from what I'd seen, Kai denied Hope nothing.

"Oh, my God." Georgie leapt to her feet and bounced up and down. "Go. Go. Go. Deck."

Deck had the ball and was making his way to the goal. But right on his ass was Connor and he had that determined, cocky smirk on his face.

My chest swelled as I watched him chase after Deck, muscles flexed, hair rustled, and his skin glistening with sweat. But it was his cocky smirk that made my body tingle and my heart skip a beat.

Connor was home. I was home.

We were home.

It took us eleven years to get here, but we made it because our love was limitless. Connor loved to call it that and he'd had a local artist design a beautiful wooden plaque that said, 'limitless love'. He hung it on the cabana in the backyard where we were married a month after he asked me question twenty.

There was nothing that would break us anymore, even the mangy, underweight *orange* cat that showed up at our door last year.

And Connor's reaction when he saw the orange furball lapping at the bowl of milk I set out on the porch for it was simply, "Don't get attached."

So I did what any woman would do, I showed Skye the cat and

she proceeded to squeal with delight then went running to her dad and asked if she could keep the cute orange cat out on the porch.

Simon was now a lazy, frumpy cat who loved strutting in front of Connor and purring as he rubbed himself against his leg.

But even though Simon had an odd attachment to Connor, he was our little girl Skye's cat. He slept with her and never complained when she carried him around like a rag doll.

"Pregnancy hormones are insane and I need to get laid tonight." Georgie collapsed beside me. "It will be an all-nighter if Deck wins."

London snorted. I snickered.

Connor stole the ball from Deck and headed in the opposite direction. He kicked it to Deaglan who was, without a doubt, the best player. He and Tyler had got into an intense argument before the game. Deaglan was insistent the sport was called football, not soccer, and Tyler egged him on by calling it soccer whenever he could.

Deaglan had been back for a few weeks doing a job for Deck, although I didn't know what that job was. Connor rarely discussed VUR business, but I did know Connor did most of the investigative work rather than going on missions.

"My brother hates losing to Deck. They have a constant, fierce competition. Deck told me in JTF2 training it was a never-ending battle to be the best of the best."

I glanced at London then back to Georgie. "And why we put them on opposite teams," I said.

Georgie's brows lifted. "Oh, my God. You rigged the teams?"

London nodded. "Yep. Why do you think Alina and I insisted on picking the names out of the ball cap and not letting the guys?"

"Damn, I love you girls." Georgie laughed, falling back on the grass.

The teams were Connor, Kai, Deaglan, and Ernie against Deck, Tyler, Vic, and Tristan and the score was three-three. Every single one of them was competitive and neither team planned on losing, which made the game super intense because one team was losing. The game didn't end until one did. Josh was the only one missing because he was on his honeymoon with a girl he'd met five weeks ago in Las Vegas.

"Your parents rock, Georgie. Frank slipped me a burger and your mom hid me from the kids seeing while I scarfed it down. I'm always so damn hungry." Chess eased down on the grass beside Georgie, her hand on her swollen stomach as she leaned back on her elbows. "Never be eight months pregnant in the middle of summer. My feet are so swollen I don't even recognize them anymore."

"Can you even see your feet past that enormous belly?" Georgie asked.

"I have two in here remember. Just wait. Seven more months and you won't be making jokes. You'll be bitching and complaining, too," Chess said, nodding at Georgie's currently flat stomach. "I can't wait to see you waddle."

Georgie threw a clump of grass at Chess and the green blades scattered on her overextended belly. "This chick won't waddle. She'll strut."

"Like a rooster?" Chess said, brows lifting.

I laughed. Georgie huffed, but smiled.

"Go, baby," London yelled at Kai as he kicked the ball toward goal, but Tristan was on him.

The two businessmen, who rarely wore anything but expensive suits, were playing a game of football together in a barnyard at a barbecue. This had become a yearly event where we all got together at the Treasured Children's Center, a place that linked us all in some way. It was the only time I saw Tristan in shorts, but they were classy khaki shorts. Kai wore black cargo pants like the rest of the guys.

"This isn't hockey, asshole," Tristan said as Kai body-checked him so hard he staggered and landed on his ass. Kai grinned as he kicked the ball into the air for the goal, thinking he had it.

But Tyler swept in and head-butted the ball out of the air at the last second.

"Jesus, I hate you guys." Kai bent over, head hanging, hands on his thighs as he caught his breath. Connor came up beside him, slapped him on the shoulder and said something then they were back in the game.

It was nice to see Kai and Connor get along, but then Connor didn't know about Georgie's involvement with Vault. When Connor had been gone for those several months, Georgie had told me about the cutting, Tanner, and the assignments for Vault.

When Connor came back, everyone decided it wasn't something Connor should ever hear about. It wouldn't do him any good to know what happened to his sister and it was one part of the story their parents didn't know either.

"Mommy," Skye said, nestled between my legs, her head on my thigh. "Can I go play with Hope and the cats?"

I stroked her wavy blonde locks away from her face. She was the spitting image of Connor with her blue eyes and magnetic smile. "Yeah, sweetie." She slipped from my arms and I watched her run across the yard and immediately pick up the orange cat who'd been dumped on the property a few months ago.

Skye was daddy's little girl and I couldn't be happier about it. The best sound was the two of them laughing together and they did it often. It was Connor who put her to bed most nights and read her a story while Simon purred like a jet engine at the foot of the bed. I'd often stand in the doorway and watch them, my heart bursting at every moment we were blessed with.

Connor would look over at me and grin with a wink, without even a pause in his words as he read. But then, he probably knew the stories by heart because he never forgot anything.

Vic had the ball and used his massive body to block Connor from getting near it. "You're last name should be brick not fuckin' gate," Connor said, with laughter ringing.

Connor didn't chase him, Deaglan did. The head-to-toe tatted guy was agile and quick with his feet and obviously grew up playing the sport. And he was probably the only one who could get the ball from Vic.

Connor stopped to catch his breath, his hand running through his ragged hair, and I saw his eyes land on Skye. Everything in his body relaxed and his eyes shone with love. Then his gaze found me and he smirked and mouthed, "Love you baby."

I smiled and blew him a kiss.

Then my eyes caught the flash of white barreling onto the makeshift football field.

"Rocket. No," I shouted. But it was too late. Rocket plowed into Connor from behind and knocked him off his feet.

"Oh, shit." Chess tried to get up, but struggled with her stomach being so big. "Help here." Georgie jumped to her feet, grasped her hand and pulled her up.

We all stood as Rocket, on his three legs, raced across the yard heading straight for Kai who currently had the ball and was all alone. And he was all alone because the guys had stopped playing.

But no one warned Kai. Not even London who watched with her hand over her mouth, stifling the laughter.

Rocket bleated.

Everyone saw it transpire before it happened. Kai turned to look over his shoulder at the same time that Rocket lowered his head and butted him in the ass, knocking him over backward onto the ground.

"Damn!" Georgie exclaimed. "He got his ass handed to him."

London, Chess, and I burst out laughing, not even bothering to hide it from Kai who had to have heard us.

But Rocket wasn't done yet. He picked up the ball beside Kai with his teeth, shook his head back and forth like a dog with its favorite toy and then released it. The ball flung through the air and all eyes followed its path as it landed, bounced once, then soared right into the goal.

"No!" Tyler shouted. "That doesn't count."

"Fuck yeah!" Connor yelled and fist-bumped with Ernie and Deaglan. Kai joined them and they slapped one another on the back. There were words, but I couldn't hear what they were saying, and it didn't matter, they were smiling.

"That's bullshit," Tyler said. "I'm calling goat interference."

The guys ignored him as they headed for the yellow cooler sitting on the picnic table. Deaglan led the way with Connor and they had their heads together talking.

Deaglan was currently staying in the basement apartment while he was here, and for some reason, he and Connor hit it off. Deaglan often had dinner with us unless he was otherwise 'occupied', as the girls leaving in the morning was also an 'often' occurrence.

"Uh-oh," I muttered.

All three girls looked at me, and Chess said, "What?"

I nodded to Connor and Deaglan who were bent over, blocking the cooler. Connor glanced over his shoulder and then said something to Deaglan who pushed the lid off the plastic container.

"They better not go for Kai," London said.

"No," Georgie said and all of us said at the same time, "Tyler."

Connor and Deaglan picked up the cooler and ran for Tyler, the water and ice sloshing out the top.

'Shit!' was all Tyler managed before the contents of the ice-cold water dumped on his head. He stood shocked for a second, water dripping off him, ice at his feet. The kids playing near the barn screamed and laughed at Tyler, as did the guys, well, except Vic, but there was a lip twitch.

"Come and get it," Frank called. He held a spatula in his hand and flipped burgers on the grill where smoke wafted into the air.

He insisted on manning the barbecue every year, but when the guys weren't in the game, Deck and Connor helped, and that was incredibly special to watch because it was like brothers hanging with their dad.

Connor jogged over to the barn and picked up Skye. He carried her like a sack of potatoes over his shoulder with her laughing and squealing, her little legs kicking him in the chest. I smiled as I made my way over to the barbecue with the rest of the girls.

"Who can we set Deaglan up with? That cupcake needs a girl. When he calls you pet in that delicious accent..." Georgie sighed.

"He has plenty of girls," I said, laughing. "A rotating door of girls."

"Exactly my point." Georgie squished her lips together as if thinking about who she knew would halt that rotating door. "A girl who won't take his shit, but she has to be sweet, too."

I eyed Deaglan who squirted ketchup on his burger bun. Then my attention turned to Vic who stood beside him and nodded to something Deaglan said. "What about Vic?"

The girls burst out laughing.

"I don't think either guy goes that way," London said, laughing.

"Oh, my God, I didn't mean for each other." I slapped her on the arm. "I meant Vic needs a girl, too. Actually, I've never seen him with any girl."

"That's because he scares them all away," Georgie said. "I swear he has dead bodies in his closet."

"Babe." Connor strode over to me with Skye beside him, carrying her paper plate with a burger sliced into quarters. There were no condiments on it because Skye liked everything plain. Connor's hand snaked around my back and jerked me against him. "Fuck, I'd love to sink inside of you right now," he growled in my ear, keeping his voice low so Skye couldn't hear.

"Daddy?" Skye said, looking up. "Can I go eat with Danny and Hope?"

"Sure, baby," Connor replied, his hand stroking the top of her head. She smiled and ran off, the burger precariously close to falling off her plate.

"You realize Deck's mood is going to suck now that you kicked his butt," Georgie said as she continued by us.

He chuckled. "When does his mood not suck?"

"When I'm on my knees," she replied over her shoulder and winked, while walking off with London and Chess to their men and the barbecue.

I rolled my eyes and Connor threw back his head and laughed. If melting with love were possible, I'd be a puddle at Connor's feet.

I stood on my tiptoes and placed my arms around his neck. His T-shirt was wet, a mixture of sweat and water from the cooler that had partially spilled on him. "I love how you are with our daughter."

He smiled then tilted his head and his mouth claimed mine. It was slow, sensual, and completely possessive. And I loved every second of it as I sagged against him.

When he drew back, his eyes twinkled. "So, when were you planning on telling me you're pregnant?"

My eyes widened. Shit, how did he know? I had found out three days ago, but I'd wanted to surprise him with the news tomorrow after I had the confirmed blood test results from the doctor. I should've known he'd suspect. Connor watched me like a hawk. His overprotectiveness hadn't changed and I was okay with that because I liked his protectiveness, especially if it involved ogling me.

I bit my lip while smiling. "How about right now?"

"I'm right? You're pregnant?" he asked.

"Yes."

"Fuck yeah!" he yelled. His hands came under my butt and he picked me up in his arms. I wrapped my legs around his waist as he swung me around. "We're having another baby."

I weaved my fingers in his hair at the back of his neck. "Yeah."

He shouted, "My girl is pregnant."

There were cheers and shouts of congratulations and then there was Tyler's, "Is it yours?"

I heard a smack and then Tyler's, "What?"

Connor grinned and my chest swelled with so much love for this man.

He tilted his head, so his mouth was next to my ear, then whispered, "Limitless, shutterbug."

The End

19 Questions

Alina's answers.

1) Vampire or Werewolf? *Werewolf.*
2) What was your favorite thing to do as a teenager? *Dance on the rooftop of our house.*
3) One word to describe you that starts with a "p"? *Polite.*
4) Favorite color? *Powder blue.*
5) How do you take your coffee? *One milk.*
6) What kind of pet or pets have you had? *None. Never had a pet, but I'd maybe like a cat.*
7) Would you ever polar bear dip? *No way in hell.*
8) One superpower you'd want to have. *Invisibility.*
9) Swim or laze on the beach? *Swim.*
10) What would you give up for your family? *Everything and anything.*
11) Favorite flavor ice cream? *Butterscotch.*
12) What type of bird would you want to be? *Bald eagle. They are fierce and mate for life.*
13) Potato chips or chocolate? *Chips.*
14) Bungee jump or rock climb? *Bungee jump.*
15) Favorite flower? *Wildflowers.*
16) What have you done that's illegal? *Drove a car before I had my license.*
17) Do you want kids? And, if so, how many? *Yes, but not sure how many.*
18) Someone who would help bury a body? *Why would I ever bury a body? My brother, Juan.*
19) What is the best sound in the world? *Children laughing. Connor's laughter.*
20) Will you marry me? *YES.*

Connor's answers.

1) Vampire or Werewolf? *Vampire.*
2) What was your favorite thing to do as a teenager? *Dirt biking.*
3) One word to describe you that starts with a "p"? *Protective.*
4) Favorite color? *Blue, and I hate orange with a passion.*
5) How do you take your coffee? *Black.*
6) What kind of pet or pets have you had? *My sister had all the pets.*
7) Would you ever polar bear dip? *I have. Naked.*
8) One superpower you'd want to have? *Invincibility.*
9) Swim or laze on the beach? *Swim.*
10) What would you give up for your family? *Everything.*
11) Favorite flavor ice cream? *Cookies and cream.*
12) What type of bird would you want to be? *Great grey owl. Their prey never hear them coming. Silent and deadly.*
13) Potato chips or chocolate? *Chips.*
14) Bungee jump or rock climb? *Done both, but prefer bungee jumping.*
15) Favorite flower? *Fuck if I know. Something blue.*
16) What have you done that's illegal? *Broke into my sister's school and stole the hamster.*
17) Do you want kids? *Yes. Three or four.*
18) Someone who would help bury a body? *Deck.*
19) What is the best sound in the world? *Children laughing.*
20) Will you marry me? *YES.*

"ROCKET"

The goat, Rocket, is based on the true story of Montague, a beautiful Alpine goat with a difficult beginning that ended up living on my horse farm.

Like Rocket, Montague refused to stay out in the field with the horses and consistently jumped fences or opened latches in order to hang out with the dog near the house.

But one day Montague jumped the gate and his front leg got caught between the top rails. His leg was wedged in so badly, we had to remove the rails off first in order to free him.

Luckily, Montague didn't lose his leg, but he broke it and had to wear a cast for six weeks. As soon as it was off, he was back to jumping fences.

Montague ended up more like a dog than a goat and freely roamed the property. He slept on the front porch most of the time and if anyone drove up the driveway, he bleated, the dog barked, and they both ran to check out who was arriving. And, yes, like Rocket, he jumped on hoods of cars and dared you to kick him off.

Oh, and Montague's favorite treat was potato chips.

I hope you enjoyed *Perfect Rage*. Thank you so much for reading the Unyielding series. If you have a moment, please leave a review on the platform where you purchased the book. I'd love to know if there is a character you'd like to read more about! Your comments and reviews are appreciated and extremely helpful.

Cheers,

Nash xo

There's often a song that resonates when writing a book.
For *Perfect Rage* it's an incredible song by the Canadian rock band Marianas Trench.

"Ever After"

Thank you, Marianas Trench!

ACKNOWLEDGEMENTS

There are many people involved in bringing a book to life and I'm so grateful for every one who helped me in their own individual way.

A special thank you to retired U.S. Marine, Tom Churchill, who graciously took the time to answer my numerous questions regarding the military. I took some liberties with the story even though he told me 'that officially would never happen' to which I told him, 'but it has to'. Any discrepancies with regard to the military are my fault alone.

Susan, thank you for putting up with my random unedited scene emails. Your input was much needed, as you know, and I appreciate all you do for me.

Midian, beta reader extraordinaire. You know how this goes, because you're there for me with every single book I write. You're a true gem and my constant motivation to always have a 'likeable' heroine.

Yaya, my secret weapon. You always give it to me straight and I love that. Thank you for sticking with me and continuing to be my secret weapon, a friend, and a great supporter.

Jill, your comments and suggestions rock! Thank you for joining the team.

Debra at The Book Enthusiast Promotions, you're amazing. I think I've told you that before, but everyone needs to know it. Releasing a new book is overwhelming and there is so much to think about and do. But I never have to worry about anything when I hand over the reins of my book release to you. Everything is so organized and I love how you keep me updated, letting me know what's going on so I can easily navigate what I need to do.

Louisa this cover… it's brilliant! It portrays Connor and the story perfectly. I don't know how you do it. Thank you!

Thank you to Stacey for her final touches that make this book look so damn beautiful and to Elaine for catching the pesky little mistakes! Love you both.

I'm in awe and honored to have so many wonderful people support me. The bloggers who consistently pimp my books, the fans who motivate me to push past the roadblocks that pop up during the writing of a book and those who I've met online and consider friends.
Thank you from the bottom of my heart.

A few I'd like to mention: Jenny and Gitte, Totally Booked, Lana, Dirty Girl Romance, Lisa, The Rock Stars of Romance, Sarah, Sarit, Liz, Miki, Pnina, Lital, Lin, Sally, Aliana, Loyda, and all the Shh… girls on Goodreads, Snow, my music sister, the Unyielding Tear Asunder Babes, and so many more!!!

Thank you to my agent, Mark Gottlieb, and Trident Media Group, for all your support and hard work.

Hot Tree Editing, Becky and Donna, thank you for all your suggestions and comments. Your hard work is shown through the numerous redlines, lol. As always, you do a fantastic job!

The Romantic Editor, Kristin, I made it! Our many Skype conversations, emails and endless PMs and we're finally here. I wouldn't have made it to the acknowledgements without you!

I have the best family EVER! Thank you for understanding when I disappear into my 'writing cave', even when on vacation. I love you!

Books by Nashoda Rose

Tear Asunder Series
With You (free)
Torn from You
Overwhelmed by You
Shattered by You
Kept from You (Kite's Story) 2016

Unyielding Series
Perfect Chaos
Perfect Ruin
Perfect Rage

Scars of the Wraith Series
Stygian Book #1
Tyrant Book #2
Credo Book #3 (TBA)
Take (standalone Scars of the Wraiths)

www.nashodarose.com

ABOUT THE AUTHOR

Nashoda Rose is a New York Times and USA Today bestselling author who lives in Toronto with her assortment of pets. She writes contemporary romance with a splash of darkness, or maybe it's a tidal wave.

When she isn't writing, she can be found sitting in a field reading with her dogs at her side while her horses graze nearby. She loves interacting with her readers and chatting about her addiction—books.

Where to find Nashoda

Newsletter: http://nashodarose.us7.list-manage1.com/subscribe?u=1e800ef9a8a22144c14399928&id=b12d168284

Facebook: https://www.facebook.com/Nashoda-Rose-564276203633318/

Goodreads: https://www.goodreads.com/author/show/7246093.Nashoda_Rose

Instagram: https://www.instagram.com/nashodarose/

Twitter: https://twitter.com/nashodarose

Website:www.nashodarose.com

CPSIA information can be obtained
at www.ICGtesting.com
Printed in the USA
BVOW08s1916061116
467063BV00032B/164/P